CUSTER'S GATLING GUNS

WHAT IF HE HAD TAKEN HIS MACHINE GUNS TO THE LITTLE BIG HORN?

A historically accurate novel with startling possibilities that the most avid 7th Cavalry enthusiast will find well worth reading. The plausibility of events defies fiction.

BY

DONALD F. MYERS

CCB Publishing
British Columbia, Canada

Custer's Gatling Guns: What If He Had Taken His Machine Guns to the Little Big Horn?

Copyright ©2008 by Donald F. Myers
ISBN-13   978-1-926585-01-7
First Edition

Library and Archives Canada Cataloguing in Publication

Myers, Donald F., 1934-
Custer's Gatling Guns: what if he had taken his machine guns to the Little Big Horn? / written by Donald F. Myers.
ISBN 978-1-926585-01-7
1. Little Bighorn, Battle of the, Mont., 1876--Fiction. 2. Custer, George Armstrong, 1839-1876--Fiction. 3. Gatling guns--Fiction.
I. Title.
PS3613.Y46C88 2008   813'.6   C2008-905764-3

All photographs were obtained by the author from commercial sources.

Publisher: CCB Publishing
              British Columbia, Canada
              www.ccbpublishing.com

Dedication

*To my good friend, brother, and fellow Marine
Master Gunnery Sergeant Peter deConinck
U. S. Marine Corps Retired.*

*How often we fought the Little Big Horn Battle
in the quaint haunts of Court Street, Jacksonville, NC.*

Other Works by the Author

Tell It To The Marines
A historical collection of poems and songs

Never Kiss An Angel
A young Marine's first year of service in the 1950's

Marines Remember World War II
Concise history with emphasis on Pacific Island Campaigns coupled with
personal experience stories of men who fought in the war

101 Sea Stories
A collection of humorous, unusual and sometimes bittersweet experiences as
told by Marines, Sailors and others

Your War, My War: A Marine in Vietnam
A personal autobiographic account of a Marine during the Vietnam War

Lieutenant Colonel George Armstrong Custer
(In dress uniform three months prior to the Little Big Horn battle.)

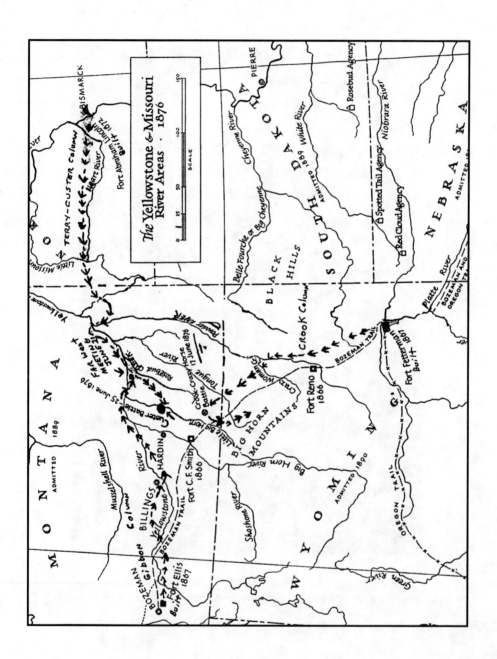

The Yellowstone & Missouri River Areas · 1876

SCALE

Acknowledgment

A special thank you to Major Edward E. Dixon, USMC Retired of San Diego, California for his advice and assistance in the writing of this book.

Also, heartfelt praise for my school chum from Kindergarten through high school, and lifelong friend, Shirley Henson-Corbett whose help on this book was valuable to the nth degree.

From the Author

This is a novel in the truest sense with a full range of author's privilege, license and imagination. Yet, serious students of the forty-day march to Valhalla of George Armstrong Custer and his 7th Cavalry will find historically accurate truths in this book as they campaigned against the Sioux and Cheyenne during the spring of 1876. It should be noted that there has never been a book written that tells of the day-by-day march of the 7th Cavalry as they made their way to the Little Big Horn. This alone makes this a writing of historical significance. I have sincerely attempted to show campaign cavalry life as near as possible as it really was without taking away the entertainment value of a fictional story or to destroy the Custer legend. Many conversations, the language, personal letters, orders and countless events actually took place and are woven into the storyline.

I am not a politically correct type of person, which those superior to me in the U. S. Marine Corps, Veterans Administration and Indiana Guard Reserve will tell you after having dealt with me for better than 40 years. Having said that, let me warn you that my book in no way intends to reflect discredit upon the American Indian. The truth of my beliefs holds that they were right and we "White Men" were wrong, then and now. I greatly admire the one time life they led and certainly understand why so many people in general have a fascination for their history. This fascination is no doubt why Dances With Wolves won an Academy Award. Two of my veteran pals, both Vietnam vets, Marine tanker and full-blooded Sioux, the late Al Tookolo and Choctaw Indian, U. S. Army combat wounded infantry warrior Ray Hudson, both gave me their blessing after reading the manuscript of Custer's Gatling Guns, saying I was honest and fair for a fictional book. Any mistakes found in telling my story are mine alone and in no way reflect on the extensive research accomplished in writing this work. I will mention that during my research I found that not all purported histories of the Custer campaign coincide on such things as time, date, place and specifics of events. What I did was use information most number of writers of my research agreed with.

I truly hope that you, the reader, will enjoy reading this book as much as I did in writing it. The following reading was invaluable to me in writing this book and I encourage any reader to give attention in pursuing these fine books if they have not already done so:

Archeology History and Custer's Last Battle by Richard Allan Fox, Jr. *University of Oklahoma Press*; Custer's Luck by Edgar I. Stewart *University of Oklahoma Press*; Custer's 7ᵗʰ Cavalry by E. Lisle Reedstrom *Sterling Publishing Co., Inc.*; The Custer Story by Marguerite Merington *Barnes & Noble Books*; A Good Year To Die by Charles M. Robinson III *Random House*; Troopers With Custer by E. A. Brainstool *Stackpole Books*; Custer by Jeffery D. Wert *Simon & Schuster*; The Book Of The American West by collective authorship R. F. Adams, B. A, Botkin, N. N. Dodge, R. Easton, W. Gard, O. Lewis, D. Morgan, D. Russell, O. O. Winther *Julian Messner, Inc*; The West by Geoffrey C. Ward *Little Brown & Company*; Bluecoats – The U. S. Army In The West 1848-1897 by John P. Langellier *Stackpole Books*; Deeds of Valor Volume 2 by W. F. Beyer and O. F. Keydel *The Perrien-Keydel Company*; The Gatling Gun by Joseph Bert *Paladin Press*; American Medals and Decorations by Evans Kerrigan *Mallard Press*; Heraldry & Regalia of War by Bernard Fitzsimons *Beckman House*.

Donald F. Myers
Indianapolis, Indiana
June 25, 2008

Foreword

Seldom, if ever, does a novel merit a foreword. A foreword is normally preserved for those scholarly tomes of great importance to help convince the book reader they are about to partake upon a grand literary experience. As far as I'm concerned those values fit Donald F. Myers' Custer's Gatling Guns, a fictional word picture leading up to the Little Big Horn battle of June 1975, to a tee. Since Myers and I are acquainted I took it upon myself as a history buff to offer a few words in behalf of his excellent tale because of the simple reason, the book deserves it.

It did not take me long as I read this manuscript before I realized I was dealing with an old machine gunner that knew his stuff. I don't want to give anything away so I'll hedge by saying the practical problems Myers had to deal with concerning the weighty cumbersome Gatling gun is more than plausible and could have been done in 1875 had someone with forethought had the ingenuity to try it then. Everything he writes could have happened just the way he describes it including the fascinating conclusion and Epilogue.

I became so engrossed reading this book that I began to think of it as not being fiction but rather an accurate portrayal of daily life on the campaign trail and the rigors of fighting the Indian Wars. I could almost smell it, feel it and hear it, that's how good it is. I'll tell you an important item concerning this book; I had a hard time putting it down once I started reading it and I bet you will share a similar experience. Oh—by the way, I was right: For the first five-years of his military career Myers was in fact a machine gunner, the old water cooled heavy .30 caliber. He remembered the nomenclature of his weapon well and used that knowledge effectively when dealing with the burdensome Gatling gun. It's a great yarn and I know you will enjoy it as much as I did. Have a good read.

Dr. Thomas M. Joyce, AD
Charter Member Military History Section, Indiana Historical Society; Founder and Past President, Fort Benjamin Harrison Historical Society, Former Assistant Officer in Charge Indiana National Guard Museum and History Section, Major, Indiana Guard Reserve retired; Attorney at Law, Chicago, Illinois.

Prologue

The Confederate patrol was a ragged, dirty group of thirty ill-equipped men. Most were without shoes and only the accouterments of war: canteens, long rifles, canvas haversacks and pistol belts, lent credence that they belonged to some type of a military organization. Besides their slovenly appearance about the only other thing they shared in common, that could be considered as a part of a uniform, was the brown floppy hats they all wore. Several of the bearded, mustached men also had red bandannas around their filthy scrawny necks but if this was meant to be a unit identification of some sort is not known. The only man among the group that wore a recognizable military uniform was a rail-thin six-footer with a scraggly blond goatee. He was clad in a butternut gray waistcoat with short tail that covered a gray vest and also what at one time had been a white shirt that sported a black cloth string tie. A wide leather belt was circled around a deep maroon-colored sash at his waist. The belt held a long, leather-flapped pistol holster that was positioned just to the left of the soldier's groin and a scabbard and sword hung loosely from the right waist. The remainder of his uniform consisted of torn, gray pants tucked into high black boots that had seen better days. He too, wore a brownish gray felt hat that shaded his pale blue eyes. Centered at the front of his hat was a large brass emblem with the letters *CSA* embossed upon it. He also wore the collar insignia of a lieutenant of infantry.

The sweat soaked Confederate infantry patrol slithered out of the wood cropping they had been in and cautiously approached a tall reed-infested section abutting a ten-foot wide stream. The only sounds heard, other than their own shallow breathing, was a gentle wind whispering through the tall Virginia pines, a buzzing of insects and an occasional call of a blue jay seeking its mate.

An equally tall, thin man with a thick salt and pepper full beard that touched his chest crouched next to his lieutenant in the traditional southern style of hunkering down on bent knees with his buttocks nearly touching the ground. His faded and torn brown shirt showed three reverted pale blue-gray stripes with a diamond on top that adorned both upper sleeves. At first he didn't say a word when he hunkered down, just stared straight ahead through the reeds to the far side of the stream as if willing his dark brown piercing eyes to penetrate the dark forest looming to his front. He took a blade of marsh grass with a dirty leathery gnarled hand and chewed on it for several seconds while contemplating what his officer must be thinking. Finally he spoke in a slow, measured drawl while at the same time fingering his beard. "Ah doan know lu-ten'ant--shor seems a mite to easy fer them blue bellies not to have pickets ore' thar." The younger man took off his floppy hat and swished away a hoard of water gnats that had been buzzing around his face. "Y'all probably rite Seth but ware else we got to go? Gen'l Lee says we got to find a place fer the army ta get outta this mess we're in an' this is the best spot we've found. Old Grant's got us circled an' it appears to me this heah place is the only chance wean'ens got to bust out."

The first sergeant was again quiet for a long moment as he nodded his head at what his young officer had spoke. With a low sigh he pointed the chewed blade of grass across the stream. "Yew say that silly ass Custer got his cavalry ore thar some place?"

"That's what ah was told at Lee's headquarters."

The sergeant turned his head and looked to his rear as if looking for reassurance that somewhere less than three miles behind him his admired and beloved general was making the final decision at Appomattox Court House on how to break through the Yankee lines so the Army of Northern Virginia could escape south to fight another day. His stomach growled from hunger, having not eaten since yesterday, and that was only a handful of cracked corn boiled in water that made for a poor soup. His breakfast that morning, April 8, 1865, consisted of what the soldiers of the Confederacy called squirrel coffee, made from boiling acorns and pine cones. He was also tired beyond endurance and he knew the other twenty-eight men, all survivors of a once proud company mustered in Princess Anne County, Virginia was in even worse shape than he. Dropping the blade of grass on the damp bank of the gentle moving clear water stream, he said, "Whal the way ah see it--is that place ore yonder is no place fer cavalry an the only way we're gonna find out if they's got skirmishers ore thar is go ahead an' make a cross'n. If'n we do it all at once the blue bellies mite think we're an advance fer a full attack and high tail it. Once we get across y'all can send a runner back to regiment an' get 'em up heah to widen th' breach."

"An' if the Yankee's stand an' fight?" The lieutenant asked soberly.

"Ain't much we can do aboot it one way nor the otheh if'n they was to do that, is thar? It's happened befoe an' we're still heah a'kick'en"

The lieutenant nodded his head at his sergeant's sage logic.

The other members of the patrol were told of the hasty battle plan and when their lieutenant stood up and waved his .45 caliber army colt pistol over his head and yelled out, "Let's get 'em boys!" They too stood up and with their bayoneted Enfield and Springfield rifle muskets held at the ready begun yelling the famous Rebel Yell as they surged into the knee deep water of the stream.

On the other side of the stream Second Lieutenant Samuel Higgins of the Indiana 5th artillery calmed his men who manned two strange looking weapons that made up the Battery. "Steady boys...you've got a good field of fire so let them get in the middle of the stream and listen for my order to fire."

"What about our infantry?" A youthful looking corporal wearing eye-glasses wanted to know.

Without turning his head from the yelling rabble approximately fifty yards to his front, the short statured Union officer in his dark blue kepi cap with red markings said tersely, "They know not to open up until they hear our action." The officer paused for a moment,

Then glancing at his ammunition handlers standing on either side of the two weapons, said, "You two just make sure to get the reloads in jack rabbit quick when the gunners call for them."

The two privates both had chalky-white expressions as they held long steel clips of .58 caliber cartridges in their hands ready for insertion in the breach slot on top of the multi-barreled guns. One nodded his head in understanding while the other offered a squeaky, "Yessir."

The rebel soldiers were now strung out in a scraggly line sixty feet across and had passed the halfway mark of crossing the stream. In a loud tone of voice Lieutenant Higgins hollered, "FIRE AT WILL.... INDEPENDENT FIRING!"

Gunners on both guns commenced to turn a brass handled steel crank placed on the right side of the weapons that caused the six barrels to rotate with each crank. As each barrel came to the breach mechanism the spring-loaded firing pin automatically fired a bullet toward the charging rebels. The gunners kept a slow steady turn of the firing crank as they had learned that turning the crank too fast would cause cartridge jams and this they did not want with the screaming rebels trying to get out of the water to get to them. But the gunners had nothing to fear as they systematically spit out death from their Gatling guns at the rate of over five hundred bullets per minute. A steady stream of bullets ripped into the charging Confederates with an ungodly force of accuracy, not so much because of good aim but rather from the sheer volume of the heavy-leaded, pointed bullets being fired. Excited orders from the gunners to reload came out in shouted commands due more from the adrenaline rush from their first combat with their lethal weapons than fear. The loaders worked smoothly as they had been trained to do in dry runs for the past two months under the guidance of North Carolina born Dr. Richard Jordan Gatling. There was hardly a pause from them replacing the empty clips with freshly loaded ones.

In the stream it was a total massacre. The .58 caliber bullets created horrible wounds, taking off hands, arms and even heads. In less than three minutes all thirty Confederate soldiers lay in a mangled heap in the stream that now ran pink from their blood and gore that seeped or poured from their wrecked bodies.

Ordering a cease-fire and ignoring the cheers that erupted Lieutenant Higgins raised his field binoculars to his eyes and surveyed the pine cropping above the stream to see if any more rebels were lurking about. Seeing no signs of activity he swept his binoculars over the scene of carnage below him, noting how effective his battery had been in destroying the onslaught of the enemy. He shook his head almost sadly as he viewed the results of the tremendous firepower this modern marvel of weaponry had caused. A factory foreman by trade in a buggy works in his hometown of Indianapolis, he had become accustomed to the carnage of battle since heeding Governor Morton's call for volunteers in '63. But never had he ever seen anything like the awesome destruction these Gatling guns had produced in such a short time. Muttering more to himself than being conscious of speaking out loud, he said, "If we'd had these at Fredericksburg the rebs wouldn't have won that one."

His battery first sergeant that was standing next to him, thinking the lieutenant may have said something to him said, "Sir?"

Somewhat startled by the obvious questioning tone of his sergeant's voice, Lieutenant Higgins quickly composed himself and provided an answer, "Take a few men down to the stream sergeant and check to see if anyone is still alive. If so, and they can be helped, then we will take them as prisoners."

The sergeant offered a reasonably decent field salute, which the officer returned, then barked out orders for four men from the battery to follow him down to the stream.

After five minutes it was determined that all the rebs were dead except for a bearded sergeant that was soon to die from loss of blood because of his mangled right leg that was hanging to his torn thigh by a thin thread of sinew and muscle in addition to an ugly stomach wound. The Confederate first sergeant had almost made it to the opposite bank of the stream when he'd got cut down. Looking up at the grim-faced Yankee sergeant who was kneeling next to him trying to be solicitous by asking if there was anything he could do for him he shook his head. The Confederate knew death was near, yet the full bearded NCO looked up at his counterpart and whispered painfully a question that had puzzled him when the first shots ripped into his men. "What y'all fellows got up thar a full battalion of carbines? Caught us good y'all did."

Shaking his head slowly the blue uniformed sergeant looked down upon his enemy and answered the man's question honestly in his nasal twang, "No....it's something new we've got called a Gatling gun. We got two of them up there and that's what we used on ya."

Choking on the blood bubbling up in his mouth the rebel said in a low voice that could barely be heard, "Gatling guns y'all say? Can't rite'ly say ah eveh herd of 'em befoe. More like guns from hell Yank." The man coughed once, his eyes glazed over and with a short spasmodic jerk he was dead.

* * * * *

Commander-in-chief of the Confederate army Robert E. Lee looked up sharply from the table where he had been viewing a map with General Longstreet. He had been distracted from a long rattling of distant musketry. Glancing at his aide-de-camp he murmured, "Wunder what on earth that could be?"

"The direction is from our southwestern line General." His aide-de-camp Charles Marshall said.

"Hmmm. I do believe you are rite Charlie." He turned to General Longsteet. "Pete isn't that the area ah asked to be looked oveh fur a retrograde movement."

"Yes suh it is." the tall bearded general replied.

"Well ah reckon we best find out what the Yankees are up to." Looking toward his aide again General Lee said, "Take care of it fur me Charlie will yew please."

"Certainly suh," The aide-de-camp walked out of the large white tent and summoned an orderly who was lounging on the steps below the broad wooden front porch of a red brick farmhouse that belonged to a Mr. McLean.

Elizabeth Bacon "Libbie" Custer

Chapter 1

Fort Abraham Lincoln, Dakota Territory
4:00 p.m., Tuesday, May 16, 1876

Elizabeth Custer, better known to most everybody as Libbie, leaned her arms on the white, painted porch railing of the wrap-around veranda of the quarters where she and her husband lived. Her pretty oval-shaped face was screwed up in concentration with her heavy, black eyebrows knitted and slight pug nose flaring somewhat over full lips. She had light gray-blue eyes that were focused intently on her husband and one of his subordinates. The two men were engaged in an animated conversation at the edge of the large parade field in front of the big two story house with its four fireplaces that she called home. The general, whom she formally called her husband because of his Civil War brevetted rank of Major General, was gesturing wildly with his hands to emphasize something he was saying to the younger officer who stood at rigid attention. Although Libbie couldn't make out any of the words being spoken by her tall, dark, blond-haired husband who had recently sheared his golden curly locks to a much shorter style; she knew from his gesturing and rapid bobbing movement of his full walrus mustache that he was giving the boy a good dressing down. This observation saddened Libbie since the lean six-foot lieutenant who also had dark, blonde, short-cropped hair parted down the middle of his head, not quite covering his prominent ears, was one of her pets. She thought the young man, with the close-set blue eyes with a perpetual squint that gave them a slightly crossed appearance, was really rather handsome other than the slight flaw of his intent gaze. She knew from conversations with the youngster that his thin-haired, blonde handlebar mustache with a scraggly patch of a small goatee barely covering the wide dimple over his square chin was an attempt on his part to look older than his twenty-four years.

Libbie also knew that the unmarried young man had graduated from West Point at the top of his class of 1871 and for the past five years had dedicated his military life to the advancement in what he considered to be the weapon of the future, the Gatling gun. She mused that the boys dedication to the gun was not helping his career any because the hierarchy of the army continued to be skeptical concerning its military value. Her husband, the general, also shared this view. Just the same Libbie had a fond place in her heart for the well-mannered young man. With her instinctive talent at

1

matchmaking she was trying to find a suitable young lady in which she would be pleased to introduce the lieutenant. "My, my," she muttered under her breath, "Autie is for sure upset with the lad about something."

* * * * *

On the fringe of the large expanse of parade field that was surrounded by officer's quarters, troop barracks, headquarters building and other white-washed, wooden structures, the 7th U. S. Cavalry at Fort Lincoln used, Lieutenant William Hale Low, (Commander of the Gatling gun platoon presently on detached duty from the 20th Infantry) was fast losing his composure from the tongue-lashing he was receiving from the lieutenant colonel brevet major general. With his temper rising he knew if he disagreed with General Custer one more time that the aquiline nosed, deep sapphire blue-eyed legend who was known as a disciplinarian could very well draw up charges for court-martial against him for insubordination. Yet he knew he was going to try one last time to convince the man to allow his platoon of three Gatling guns to accompany the Dakota column so his unit could participate in the biggest campaign and expedition against hostile Indian's ever mounted.

In a somewhat nasal voice the narrow-jawed officer interrupted his superior in a rather sharp tone. "General Custer sir, you have told me in a highly intelligent manner why you oppose authorizing my battery to go with you and your refusal on the grounds I would impede your march is understood. But general sir, you have said on many occasions in the mess and around countless campfires, that you are always willing to listen to your junior officers. Sir, you are not giving me that opportunity to fairly hear my case. I have answers for most of your concerns if you will only allow me to state them."

The young whippersnapper interrupting his dialogue had at first greatly upset the flinty-eyed, lean, well-proportioned, strong-featured cavalry commander. He was about to snap out at the boy again then changed his mind. The lad was correct----he did foster a reputation of having a willingness of listening to his subordinates and of course the boy was right on the mark about the intelligent explanation he had been offering. Trying to soften the command gruffness of his voice Lieutenant Colonel vis-à-vis Major General George Armstrong Custer spoke. "Humph.... I see. Very well Lieutenant Low, never let it be said that I didn't let a young officer have his say on something as important as a desire to do his duty by going to the field

2

of battle. You may go ahead but let me forewarn you it is doubtful that you will sway my decision. Once I come to a conclusion a herd of buffalo cannot change my direction."

Though Lieutenant Low held Custer in awe, as most young officers felt for the legendary Indian fighter and hero of the hard fought recent war of the rebellion, he still had the education, training and military presence to offer a sound argument. Without hesitation he began talking, "Sir, as I stated previous I most certainly understand your concern of not wanting to be hampered by what is for the most part considered a very cumbersome weapons battery. But you sir, more than any other officer in this command, and I would dare say more likely the entire western army, have a better first hand vision of what the Gatling gun is capable of doing as I understand sir you have seen the Gatling in action. I...."

Custer broke into what the officer was saying, "Yes, that part is very true. I was at Appomattox Court House and the day before Lee's surrender where I observed two of your guns annihilate an entire company of rebel infantry at Millers Creek. Very destructive weapon, very destructive indeed---------but that was a defensive situation and my belief is that is where the Gatling gun belongs."

Quickly reclaiming the initiative when Custer paused, Lieutenant Low immediately interjected: "Yes sir, I can see how you would feel that way with the old models but our newer eighteen-seventy one models are much more reliable and fire at the rate of well over seven hundred and fifty shots a minute. Just think what that would mean if the Indian's were to attack the seventh in masses."

Custer snorted, his long nose flaring at the nostrils as he did so. "My dear boy, that is such a grand idea if we were in fortified positions but I sir happen to be commanding a cavalry regiment who's duty is to charge headlong into the enemy and do battle. Pray tell me sir, how would you propose to go charging along with me with your rejected cavalry horses pulling your thousand pound gun in addition to its ammunition caisson?"

Lieutenant Low was prepared for this question and offered an immediate answer. "General Custer sir, I do not propose that my battery would be able to keep up with your regiment during a charge, but I have solved the problem of keeping up with cavalry units while they are on a normal days march. And while you are attacking an enemy position my battery would be unlimbering their guns so they would be used to support your action and thwart any enemy countermeasures."

The young officer's remark intrigued Custer and with hooded eyes he said, "And how would you go about doing that mister?"

This time there was a moment of hesitation before Lieutenant Low answered. Collecting his thoughts he said, "Sir, for the past six months I have been experimenting with my guns with the intention of writing a report to the Bureau of Ordinance. What I have accomplished is the ability of breaking the Gatling's down into five main components and devising a unlocking and locking system of levers and pins where the guns can be reassembled in less than ten minutes. Matter of fact one of my gun crews can do it in seven minutes. With this new design I can haul a gun on six mules or horses which I prefer, with special yokes and a sling that I've made."

"A sling?" Custer's bushy eyebrows rose.

"Yes sir. The heaviest part of the weapon is the breach-barrel system. What I did was have three sections of canvas sewn together with a cover of leather. After I devised a way to attach this strong sling between two mules, or horses I found that the animals have no trouble transporting the breach-barrel."

Custer became more interested in what the young officer was saying since he was an inventive sort himself. "And I suppose the yokes you came up with are for the wheels and carriage?"

"That's correct sir. One wheel per animal; another for the axle, gun seat and trail with one more used to carry the heavy cradle the breach-barrel sits upon,"

"And you say you can reassemble your contraption in less than ten minutes?"

"Yes sir--------I can offer a demonstration if you would like."

"I'm afraid we don't have time for that lieutenant, but what you've told me has sparked my imagination. What about your caissons? I would think that large ammunition boxes and spare parts boxes would be difficult to put on a mule's back."

Offering a thin smile for the first time since he had accosted the general while he walked across the parade field toward his living quarters Billy Low said, "Your remark is most astute sir and of course correct. However, if I were to be authorized I could put together my own ammunition pack train the same as your regiment uses."

Now it was Custer's turn to offer a small smile, which lit up his handsome face. His sapphire blue eyes twinkled. "Of course-----I should have thought of that on my own with the many campaigns I have been on." He paused for a moment, his grin instantly replaced by a brooding straight-lipped frown. After several seconds he said, "Let me re-think your request

Lieutenant Low. I shall call for you before Trumpeter Martini plays retreat."

The young officer who was already standing at attention stiffened his body to an even tighter brace and offered the general a precise salute with a crisp, "Yes sir, thank you sir."

Custer casually touched his eyebrow with his fingertips, replying, "You may carry on mister." And he waited for the youngster to do an about face and march stiffly away back across the parade field before turning toward his quarters again where he saw his dear Libbie was waiting for him on the porch.

The general briefly stroked his narrow cleft chin for a moment as he entered the small yard of his quarters through the opened white, picket-fenced gate. He mounted the steps to the big porch, his thoughts reflecting for a second that he would again be leaving his precious darling, as the morning would find him riding out to find the Sioux. Then his eyes crinkled and his thin lips spread wide in a grin, baring solid white teeth under his huge drooping mustache. "Ah dear buttercup, your Bo is home at last from the rigors of last minute planning for his greatest campaign."

A slight gust of prairie wind kissed the tight, soft, brown curls that graced Elizabeth's forehead causing them to flutter teasingly which made her smiling face come completely alive as she gazed fondly at her adored husband. "Oh Autie it is so good that you were able to come home early but dear man your sister Margaret and I have not finished preparing this evenings meal."

"Ah, that's right, we are to dine with Maggie and Jimmy this evening." Custer was referring to his brother-in-law Lieutenant James Calhoun who commanded L Troop of the 7th Cavalry and had married his only sister. "Please do not fret your pretty head my dear. I missed being with my sunbeam and excused myself from General Terry's headquarters for an hour or so to spend some time with my wonderful wife. Brothers Tom and Boss along with nephew Autie Reed are looking forward to a last home-cooked meal as much as I am and...."

As Custer continued his light prattling Libby's broad smile turned sour hearing her husband use of the words 'a last home-cooked meal.' For the past several days Libbie had been harboring a deep dread about the forthcoming campaign and had developed a premonitory fear regarding her husband's well being and safety. Her mind soared as she dwelled upon the almost biblical prophecy of a Last Supper. In many ways she thought of her strong willed, golden haired husband of being God like. And it was not lost on her that the 'meant-to-be-festive' gathering this evening would indeed

5

have her husband surrounded by his most devoted disciples. Tall and handsome Tom Custer, the brother who had been awarded two Medals' of Honor during the late war between the states. Her equally handsome brother-in-law James Calhoun wedded to Bo's only sister Margaret Emma. The general's youngest brother, 25-year-old Boston "Boss" Custer who looked so much like the general when he was younger. And there was young Harry Armstrong Reed who was nicknamed "Autie" after his famous uncle. There would be others too. Adjutant William Cook, Commander of Troop "F" Lieutenant Alger on E. Smith, Captain George Yates, and Captain Myles Keogh. Libby's mind flashed that at least the Judas of her husbands officers, who was certainly not considered a disciple of her husband, would not be among them tonight; the vile Captain Frederick Benteen, whom she detested. And Bo's second in command, the simpering Major Marcus Reno had sent his regrets that pressing duties on the eve of the expedition would prevent his attendance, Even though Libbie could barely stand being in the company of Major Reno and dealt with him socially for Bo's sake as was expected of a generals wife, she still took his declining her written invitation as another ominous omen.

Noting his wife's far-away, fixed stare, George Custer paused his conversing to ask a question. "Dear lady, is something troubling you?"

Libbie instantly directed her thoughts back to her handsome cavalier and with a wan smile said, "No Autie nothing is wrong but I was thinking about the heated talk you were having with that darling Lieutenant Low. He is such a nice boy. I just cannot imagine you feeling vexed with him. What did he do or say to annoy you so?"

"Ah, so that is it. Don't you worry your pretty little head my dear. I know how much you like Billy Low and I have no anger toward the lad. He is terribly distressed that I have ordered his battery to remain here at Fort Lincoln for the protection of the lovely ladies of this post that is understandable, as I do believe he has the heart of a warrior. And as a warrior it is natural for him to want to be a part of the action we are surely to encounter. Actually my dear, I too am fond of the boy, and though I admire his zeal and grit I just cannot see how he can expect to be a part of this campaign from a tactical and even a logistical standpoint even though he has made favorable strides in the ability of transporting his guns."

Biting her upper lip for a second Libbie Custer then addressed her husband. "Bo dearest, I have heard you expound many, many times the need to modernize the army's equipment which has changed little since the rebellion. I was amazed and terrified at the demonstration you let me watch with you last summer when you entertained Secretary of War Balkan by showing him the firepower of the Gatling gun battery. He was so impressed at the time if you remember, and even though you did not like the man, you will also remember he promised future development in weaponry at the Bureau of Ordinance. I too was greatly impressed with what I viewed. And I feel the Gatling's would greatly enhance any military expedition, especially if there was trouble." The short-statured woman paused for a moment chewing her upper lip before going on. She knew her husband loved her but she was determined to see how deep his affection really was toward her as she seldom, if ever, interjected her personal fears or feelings regarding his military decisions. What was on her mind however, was too important to ignore with the constant premonition of forthcoming disaster plaguing her soul. In a soft tone of voice barely above a whisper, her eyes brimming with tears, Libbie Custer said. "Autie, I want you to take that battery of Gatling guns with you."

Chapter 2

Fort Abraham Lincoln, Dakota Territory
5:45 a.m., Wednesday, May 17, 1876

Lieutenant William Hale Low was an extremely happy young officer. Shortly after reveille had blown on this cold, raw morning the bugler had sounded the "General" which was the call to strike tents and break camp. Even with a heavy river mist hanging over the encampment Billy "Becky" Low was in an effervescent mood.

He had been up since 4:00 a.m. making sure everything and everybody in his battery of three guns was ready to commence today's march. His elation of being told his battery could accompany the expedition had put him in such a good frame of mind that it had rubbed off on his second of command Lieutenant James Patrick Kunzite. The combined enthusiasm which caused both officers to act friendly toward their subordinates had an effect on the 32 troopers that made up the Gatling gun platoon, who went about their work in typical profane grumbling yet efficient manner.

For the third time since late last night Lieutenant Kunzite wanted to hear how his friend had boldly stood up to Custer and convinced the strong-willed commander of the 7th Cavalry to change his mind. "Come on now Becky, don't be that way. What did the general say to you last night?"

"I already told you Jimmy that I did not talk with General Custer last night. After our short exchange at the parade field where he allowed me to voice my views about how we have improved the ability of moving the Gatling's I left him with his promise that he would notify me of a final decision prior to taps, well actually he said retreat which is before taps. As it were, an orderly summoned me around eight-thirty that I was to report to the general's quarters post haste. You cannot imagine how excited I was making my way to his quarters where I found a large gathering of senior officers and several ladies enjoying the late evening as guest of the general and his charming wife Mrs. Custer. I was actually shaking from anticipation not having the slightest glimmer what news I was going to hear. I stood alone on the porch while the orderly entered the house and in about a minute Captain Custer came to the open door. He was most cordial once he came out on the porch, smiling and even shaking my hand. I suppose he saw how nervous I was and after telling me the general had requested that he talk with me, he chatted with me for a minute or so as to put me at my ease. He even offered

8

me a cigar, which I declined, for as you know I do not use tobacco. The captain did however light up one for himself and he asked me to walk with him, making the comment it was such a beautiful evening. As we strolled around the porch he informed me the general had had a change of heart and would allow our detachment to accompany him to at least to the headwaters of where the Yellowstone and Tongue Rivers meet." The young lieutenant paused for a long moment in reflection, taking off his new Kepi forage cap to swish away a hoard of fly's pestering him. He glanced at his friend and fellow officer from his deep blue eyes that waited for him to continue his story. Emitting a low sigh he went on. "I wasn't about to question Captain Custer on why his brother was only considering our participation as far as the Yellowstone and Tongue but then when the captain informed me it would not be necessary to break down our guns with what he termed 'my sling contraption' it took all of my will power to keep my mouth shut. Luckily I did mute my first inclination of wanting to ask why because he did add a quick comment like it was an afterthought on his part, 'unless ordered to do so.' I found Tom Custer to be a true gentleman and unlike his older brother whom I almost fear, he is possessed with a most amiable, friendly disposition. We parted, with him again shaking my hand with a broad smile on his face, more so I suspect because of my profuse thanking him and the general for the change in orders. I practically ran to your tent to tell you the good news. Now this is absolutely the last time I will relate this experience to you."

Shaking his head with a look of admiration on his clean-shaven face Lieutenant Kunzite said, "You are most certainly amazing Becky. I would have never had the courage to challenge an order like you did, and to the general himself. I dare say if we can get as far as the Yellowstone your presumptuousness will see us through the entire campaign."

Placing his forage cap back on his head Billy Low snorted at the meant-to-be flattery of his junior officer, then said, "First we must make sure we make it as far as the Yellowstone and Tongue with our reject mounts pulling our equipment over what is going to be terrible terrain. You see to the men and insure we are ready as I want to study the map some more regarding the planned route of march."

* * * * *

The insistent brassy, shrill, screech of a bugle could be heard to the far reaches of Fort Abraham Lincoln as a trumpeter blew for the fifth time the rapid mournful wail of a coded Warrior's melody designated to be Assembly. Trumpeter John Martini could barely speak but a few words of English, Italian being his native tongue; but the dark, mustached, square-jawed musician knew perfectly the melodic language of the twenty-three bugle calls the United States Army required to communicate its orders and will to a scattered multitude. Standing near the middle of the vast expanse that made up Fort Lincoln's parade field. Trumpeter Martini had commenced his wailing duty by first aiming his horn toward the long, white painted headquarters building and adjacent officers quarters for those single officers or those officers that also lived their because their dependents were not with them.   Trumpeter Martini possessed the common sense to know that the traditional bellow to alert the officers first with his ordered message was quite unnecessary as all of them were already standing on the fringes of the parade ground, at least most of them were. But traditions are not easily done away with in the army, especially in the 7th U. S. Cavalry commanded by Lieutenant Colonel brevet Major General George Armstrong Custer. After completing the obligatory summons for the officers, Martini then made facing movements until he had covered the four points of the compass, pausing at each point to blow the assembly call, which was supposed to insure that all personnel heard the order. When done with his fifth rendition, the short statured, dark complexioned solider smartly brought down his bugle from his puckered lips and with a flourish, tucked it under his right arm and marched stiffly off the parade field to his horse that was tethered at the headquarters' hitching rail. Martini, like the other 746 enlisted men of the regiment, had been prepared for hours waiting for the order to begin the expedition. His summoning bugle call which told his comrades they were about ready to start out on the great adventure was more than likely welcomed by most of them since boredom was beginning to take hold from waiting so long having been up shortly past the hazy dawn.

A goodly lot of the rank and file leading their mounts to the parade field in compliance with Trumpeter Martini's call to assemble was rather a low order, uneducated and profane type of soldier. This was typical of the army of the west during these modern days of the 1870's where a graft-ridden, booming, false economy nevertheless found plentiful jobs in the east and mid-west which made recruitment in the army difficult. For the most part the enlisted men that made up the body of troops for the 7th Cavalry were drifters, small town scum, jobless emigrants or youngsters looking for adventure. As a whole, they were all running away from something, including one trooper who was a deserter from the United States Marine

Corps. There were some however, especially among the noncommissioned officers and older men that were of good character and quality. It was these cavalrymen that constituted the backbone cadre that fashioned the regiment into an effective military organization. Their job was not made easier by the fact that the 7th Cavalry was grossly undermanned. The paper strength for the twelve companies averaged sixty men per company, but absences of various reasons showed the actual "on duty" rosters considerable lower as the regiment prepared to leave.

When it came to being under strength, things were not in much better shape among the officer ranks either. This was the year of the great Centennial Exposition in Philadelphia and several officers of the regiment were detailed to temporary duty there. Others were on recruiting duty, detached service of various kinds or on leave. Fortunately for Custer, one of the officers on recruiting duty was Colonel Samuel D. Sturgis, who not only outranked him but also was technically the Seventh's commanding officer. Colonel Sturgis had no great fondness for Custer, and even though his son Jack, a newly appointed West Point second lieutenant had joined the regiment, the colonel was happy to be away on detached service. Besides Colonel Sturgis, also missing today's muster were two majors, four captains and seven lieutenants. This necessitated some shifting of officers among the various companies that did not help the troop morale any in having to deal with an unknown and untested leader on the eve of battle.

The morale factor of the regiment had an odd bent anyway. As it were, the officers differed considerably in their evaluation of their commanding officer and so did the enlisted men. While some officers and troopers within the ranks admired the general without reservation with the simple reasoning that he was a fighter and not afraid of anything: others were not so charitable. Many thought Custer a tyrant, with little if any regard for his troopers under him; that he was too hard on men and horses while on the trail and changed his orders so much that it became confusing prior to, and during, the heat of battle. If Custer was not popular with some of his officers, or the idol of all his troopers, there was at least one thing they all agreed upon after having once followed him into battle. Custer would never order a man to do anything that he was not willing to do himself, nor would he send a soldier anyplace in battle where he was unwilling to go. The mans intrepid personal gallantry and his admiration for brave deeds performed by others, made serving in the 7th Cavalry worth the ordeal of serving under him and greatly manifested the overall pride within the ranks that was held by most.

* * * * *

Upon hearing the sound of his trumpeter blowing assembly the last thing on Custer's mind was the morale of his command or whether or not those he led held him in high esteem. George Custer, nicknamed "Jack" by his close associates because of his propensity of stenciling his initials "GAC" on all his military gear, was preoccupied at the moment with his darling wife's most recent and last minute demand. "My sweetest rosebud I know I have always called you my dear little Camp Crow for your willingness to follow me around everywhere I go but to allow you and my sister Margaret to accompany the column today is just placing an extra burden of heartache upon my already tormented soul knowing I shant be sharing my pillow with you in the days to come. I wanted last night's sweet exchange to be a sustaining memory for me until I can once again couple you in my arms on our warm bed of love. But now you ask me to suffer another night where it will be impossible to show my tender feelings to you and will again have to say a wrenching farewell."

Although Libbie had been married to her gallivanting swain for more than twelve years a deep blush rose to her already apple-colored cheeks and she could feel the heat surge on her pretty face hearing her husband talk of their lovemaking the past night. Just the same she wasn't going to let his lovely words deter her determination. "Autie you may just as well save your flowery discourse for I have firmly set my mind that I shall ride a ways with you."

Custer knew he was fighting a losing battle when he saw she had dressed this morning in her quaint little riding habit of a tight form-fitting shell jacket with a row of brass buttons in front along with a petticoat long flowing gray dress and high-top, laced boots. On her head was her favorite riding hat, a black felt pillbox with a long white eagle's feather affixed. He emitted a long sigh to cover the sting he'd felt when she had brushed off his gallant remembrance of their last night's passion by saying his words were flowery. At the same time he could not help but to feel flattered by the depth of his beloved mate's devotion to him, wanting to be at his side as long as she could. Still her outburst rankled his sensibilities, as he was not accustomed to, nor usually tolerated ultimatums of any kind, regardless of who gave them.

"Dear woman, did I not bow to your request yesterday afternoon and last evening tell brother Tom to inform young Low his Gatling's may accompany the expedition? I dare say you did not think my words of being flowery then when I took you in my arms to allay your fears and promised you my compliance of your desire." Having gotten his biting rebuttal in, George Custer paused for a moment, then his silted blue eyes softened, as did his tone of voice when he acquiesced to his wife's latest compulsion. "Very well buttercup, you may ride with your boy to the first nights encampment."

After Libbie kissed his cheek on tiptoes and bustled away to gather her carpetbag pack that was made special by harness makers to fit on her husbands horse Dandy, George quietly contemplated in his mind that the first days march was going to be much less than the thirty miles he had intended on pushing his column this day. His quick mind determined he would send back Libbie and Margaret with the paymaster and security detail after a shortened march since he didn't want the love of his life, or his sister, exposed to the danger that lay beyond the Little Heart River.

Brigadier General Alfred H. Terry

Chapter 3

Fort Abraham Lincoln, Dakota Territory
7:10 a.m., Wednesday, May 17, 1876

A group of young boys, with a scattering of girls, beat on tin pan drums while a couple of the children carried flags made of ragged bits of cloth they had tied onto sticks. The dozen or so pre-teen youngsters marched along stiffly like they thought soldiers should march with their chins jutting out and solemn, fierce-looking expressions blanketing their round white faces. They made their way along the edge of the parade field following the lead elements of the 7th Cavalry that cut across the wide parade field heading toward the front gate of Fort Lincoln.

There was an air of confidence, pomp, and regalia as the mounted cavalrymen made the wide circle around the parade ground, and to a man they stiffened somewhat in their saddles with prideful bearing when the 7th Cavalry band began playing their war song Garry Owen.

General Custer stood next to his wife Libbie and sister Margaret, in front of the Fort's Headquarters Building along with Brigadier General Alfred H. Terry and his staff, as platoon after platoon of the 7th U. S. Cavalry passed in review before their commanding officer and expedition commander. The long, black-bearded general with his drooping mustache had ordered the parade, at the suggestion of his lieutenant colonel. Custer felt a pass in review was warranted so civilians, Army dependents and possible Indian spies, could view the regiment in all its splendor and fighting strength. The noble-looking, angular faced brigadier turned his head and with a soulful gaze from his brown eyes spoke to Custer. "Pities there are so few spectators to view your formidable regiment Jack. But it must give you a great sense of pride knowing they have the obvious ability to cope with any hostiles they might encounter."

Custer fingered the cleft in his chin with thumb and forefinger before replying. "I believe sir that most of the families said their goodbyes before assembly sounded but if you will notice there are faces peering from most all the windows and there is still a goodly number of officer and non-commissioned officer families present."

Squinting his sad looking eyes to better see at a distance General Terry said, "Yes, I do believe you are correct."

Libbie Custer spoke up in her soft style of speech. "Autie dearest I don't see the Gatling guns at the rear of the column."

Custer, who was dressed in his usual field attire of buckskin, removed his gold tasseled, blue-black campaign hat and using the wide brimmed head gear as a pointer, answered his wife's concern. "I sent them ahead my dear to form up with the rest of the expedition that is down in the valley on the plateau at Cannon Ball Creek."

He received a beaming smile from his mate who turned back to watch the remainder of her husband's regiment pay him the respects due him.

* * * * *

The band of the 7th Cavalry stopped playing Garry Owen when General Custer ordered a brief halt of the formation just as the first platoon reached the front gate. Custer allowed his married officers and enlisted men to dismount so they could bid a final goodbye to their families who had been following along next to the horses. Custer chatted with Brigadier General Terry for a few minutes while the married personnel with families took a last leave-taking. Outside the huge log gate Airfare Indian scouts who had led the parade were still beating their skin-covered drums and wailing their melancholy chanting songs about warriors leaving for battle. The eerie noise was a haunting sacrilege on an otherwise sedate sitting.

"Oh why do they have to repeat over and over that prolonged piercing cry?" Libbie said to her sister-in-law in a distressed manner.

Before Margaret Calhoun could venture an opinion her brother George answered the question in a serious tone: "What you are hearing is actually a religious anthem, They are calling upon those braves who died valorous deaths in battles with their enemies to impart their spirits from the great hunting ground for a short while to show them the path of courage. Its really quite moving when you understand what it is. I suppose you could say it is their way to bolster their resolve much the same as I have chosen Garry Owen as the sevenths war song." But Custer did not like to see his wife upset and he took his large, gold, pocket watch from its fob pocket on the front of his fringed jacket and opened the dial cover. Noting that it was a few minutes past 7:00 o'clock he turned to his orderly trumpeter and gave an order. "Martin----blow To Horse."

Trumpeter John Martini was accustomed to his dual last names which was caused by a lazy recruiter and with a heavily accented "Yes suh!" he brought the mouth piece of his horn to his lips and blasted the half dozen sharp blasts that told those dismounted to get on their horses. Company trumpeters also took up the call and for a few seconds the white man's screeching horns drowned out the wailings of their red faced brethren,

As the formation started moving again the band once more began to play. The stirring melody well known to all American soldiers floated wistfully across the parade ground as the band gave forth with the tune, "The Girl I Left Behind." The regiment moved slowly but smartly towards the west.

Custer took his leave from General Terry and with his wife galloped off to take their place at the head of the long column.

* * * * *

The camp on the plateau overlooking the narrow sluggish Cannon Ball Creek had been established during George Custer's absence when he had been detained in Chicago on insubordination charges levied no less than by President Ulysses Grant. (Grant was highly upset with Custer for implicating his brother, Orville Grant in the Indian Bureau corruption scandals. When Custer left the Clymer committee in Washington, D.C. without permission, Grant not only had him arrested but also relieved Custer from command. It had taken the personal intervention of General's Terry and Philip H. Sheridan to convince Grant to allow Custer to rejoin his regiment.) Located roughly four miles west from Fort Lincoln the campsite was the primary staging area for the large amount of men, horses, mules and equipment that made up the Dakota Column. Awaiting Custer and the other 27 officers and 747 men of the 7th Cavalry were two companies of the 17th Infantry, and one company of the 6th Infantry, at strength of eight officers and 135 enlisted. In addition to Department Commander and overall leader of the expedition General Terry and his staff, there were 45 enlisted Airfare Indian Scouts better known as "Rees" Scouts. The wagon train consisted of 114 six-mule teams, 37 two-horse teams, and 70 other wagon type vehicles, including ambulances and a field blacksmith shop. A total of 179 civilian drivers had been hired and there were 85 pack mules. There were also several additional horses and many mules being used that were not accounted on the official inventory roster of the expedition. These extra animals belonged to Lieutenant's Low and Kunzite, or at least they had control of them if not ownership. When General Custer, through his brother Tom Custer, had given the authorization for the two officer, 32 men Gatling gun platoon of three guns to accompany the expedition, nothing official had been said about how to go about acquiring the additional animals needed to assist young Low's transport theory. Billy Low had taken it upon himself to

17

procure the required mounts. Finding 12 extra horses to supplement the four horses per gun and caisson already authorized had not been that big a problem. However, Lieutenant Low had not dared ask questions on how rapidly the extra horses had come about after telling his men the short time span there was to solve the dilemma. On the other hand, finding a dozen or so mules within a matter of hours had posed a major problem. The slightly cross-eyed officer found he had an enormous talent at sheer audacity, when at his wits end, he approached the civilian seller of mules for the expedition demanding to know why his contingent of mules had not been delivered. The totally confused and rattled mule handler tore through his manifest papers like a mad man and naturally could not find the requisition order the very disturbed looking lieutenant was talking about. When Lieutenant Low suggested they should take the matter up with General Custer the mule man pooh-poohed that thought immediately and miraculously came up with a document of authorization that Billy Low signed a receipt for which gave him 15 young, strong and very nasty mules.

He had arranged with the pack train master to let his 15 mules tag along with the regular pack mules with no one the wiser except the Gatling gun platoon. Attaching two extra horses per gun carriage and caisson would not attract any undo attention.

As the long line of men and horses of the 7th Cavalry ascended down into the broad valley on their way to the long flat plateau, the early morning mist mirrored by a raising sun created an illusion that they were riding in the sky. The mirage deepened as the mist slowly began to lift, letting the sun rays create a beautiful colored rainbow.

General Custer, his spirits buoyed by the most rare of all plains phenomena, took it to be a sign of good luck. "Look my dear buttercup, God has seen fit to let us start the campaign by riding on the clouds of his heaven with the arched gates of that wonderful paradise shimmering in the distance. Oh what a good sign my dearest."

Libbie Custer offered her husband a wan smile but held her tongue for her thoughts were far from being that the spectral she was seeing was a miracle brought forth from God. A cold chill ran down her spine with a renewed premonition of disaster, which flooded her soul. She considered the mirage as an evil omen and the fiery colored rainbow as the summoning gates of hell. Libbie was glad when the ascending sun burned away the wispy mist, ending the illusion.

The approach of the 7th Cavalry was greeted with more wailing chants. This time the foreboding wail came from the teepee section of the camp that was the quarters of the Indian families that had followed their men. The families of the Rees scouts set up a wailing, mournful dirge that was the custom of the primitive Indians who were very fatalistic when sending their braves off to war.

Someone among the troopers called out a disparaging remark that the 7th Cavalry would see to it that the squaws of the Sioux tribes would soon be chanting their death songs also. While some troopers guffawed at this crude, dark humor, another one yelled back, "Jus make sure it ain't yer scalp they're a' wailing 'bout Johnnie!"

Captain Tom Custer, having heard the short exchange, waved his hat at the passing cavalrymen, shouting loudly, "I wouldn't fret none about them taking any of our scalps lads...a single company of you fellows can lick the whole Sioux nation!"

The morale boosting remark made by the younger brother of George Custer has its expected effect as troopers up and down the line began cheering loudly.

Chapter 4

Heart River, Dakota Territory
8:00 a.m., Thursday, May 18, 1876

An early morning 5:00 a.m. reveille had been for naught. Any expectation of leaving the Heart River area on a timely base to start the day's march was dashed because of Custer's lollygagging. The campsite had been made early yesterday after a short march of only fourteen miles over easy terrain of rolling prairie. The troopers were surprised when General Custer had called a halt at 1:30 p.m. after having made such good progress and several hours of sunlight remaining. They were not aware their commander had no intention of taking his beloved wife and sister any further than the river and gladly went about the business of setting up an overnight camp. After pitching their two-man pup tents many of the soldiers did a little exploring and it wasn't long before it was discovered they had made camp next to a large enclave of rattlesnakes. This news did not sit well with Libbie Custer or her sister-in-law Margaret, and a number of troopers found themselves assigned to a twenty-four hour picket duty as "rattlesnake watchers." During the night there had been more excitement when a tremendous prairie fire threatened the campsite and over a thousand men were kept busy for several hours fighting the fire to keep it from spreading through the camp. By the time the men had the chance to rest after their exhaustive labor it was past 3:00 a.m. and when the trumpets and bugles sent out their piercing wails before dawn it was not met with enthusiasm. While grumbling troopers went slowly about the task of breaking camp Custer's engineering officer discovered another problem the 7th Cavalry was faced with. The day before the officer had made a brief inspection of the river that had to be crossed and found it to be about thirty yards wide, and only three feet deep with a fairly firm bottom and slow moving current. But what the engineer had not thought about at the time was the sheer abruptness of the banks on both sides and when he moved his horse down to the water this morning it came to him that the crumbling, slippery banks would have to be dug out and corduroyed to get the wagon train across. Custer was not pleased at all when this report was conveyed to him and he ordered that two troops be assigned pioneer fatigue duty to do the necessary work. The hard labor was made extra difficult for the men who were still soft from the long winter months of having been confined to garrison which resulted in a long three hour delay.

At least the delay gave the paymaster more than enough time to pay the troops their back pay owed them. As each man received his money, that ranged from $52, for four months pay for most and for a few, a little more or a little less, when each man was handed his several U. S. gold treasury bills he was also issued an admonishment. He was told to pay any outstanding personal debts, especially anything owed to the Subtler

When a green recruit asked his sergeant why the paymaster had been so strict with what amounted to a direct order concerning his pay the young trooper got some sage information from his grizzled, tobacco chewing non-commissioned officer. "Well ladies I'll tell you. Most the fells would do that anyway as they's a mite superstitious 'bout do'en into a sure 'nough fight a'know'en they owed moony to som'body. An if'n they was to get kilt it would shorly been on their conscious as they made their way to heaven or hell. 'Sides, they sure as hell don't want no Sioux brave or his squaw to be a'gett'en thar moony except maybe for a few coins that the Injuns would use to pretty up a necklace or bracelet with. Let's jus say it's bad luck not to settle up what you owe and leave it at that ladies."

The ashen faced youngster who wished he'd kept his questions to himself, nevertheless quickly make his way to the sutler's wagon with a large canvas awning hanging by two poles that made a crude office and got into the long line of waiting soldiers.

The young recruit had also wanted to know why the paymaster hadn't paid what was owed the men back at Fort Lincoln but the answer to one question had been enough for his inquisitiveness for one day. This question had a logical answer also and had the greenhorn heard it he would have certainly understood. General Alfred Terry had ordered the men to be paid after the first days march because of his well-grounded fears learned from past campaigns. The rough and tumble city of Bismarck was too close to Fort Lincoln and had the men received their pay before starting the expedition Terry knew the fleshpots and saloons there would be too much of a temptation for the troopers. With a regiment already under-strength the last thing General Terry needed was to have it further weakened by desertions, drunken debauchery and riddled with diseased men.

At a little after 8:00 a.m. the first wagon gingerly made its way down the log covered graded ramp that had been hacked out of the river bank and the teamster urged his pair of horses on into the gently moving stream with a flick of his rawhide whip and coarse voice. In a matter of a couple of minutes he had his team pulling the ration-laden wagon up the corduroy roadway on the other side. A mounted trooper, positioned purposely above the far bank pointed his arm westward and shouted for the driver to keep moving. One by one the other wagons waiting in line made their way across the river crossing without mishap. As the last of the wagons prepared to cross the Little Heart River, the long wagon train could be seen heading west as far as the eye could see in this rolling country. The wagon train was over two miles long and it wouldn't be long before the front of it would be totally unseen from the rear elements. But this did not present a problem since the 7th Cavalry had been split into two wings by General Custer, one wing commanded by Major Reno, the other by Captain Benteen. The wings were further broke down into two battalions of three troops each, a troop being the equivalent of an infantry company. One battalion was assigned as the advanced guard, one was rear-guard and the other two marched on either flank of the wagon train. The last units consisted of an infantry company and the Gatling gun platoon that was sometimes erroneously called "battalion."

George Custer had waited with his wife Libbie and sister Margaret at the paymasters' wagon that would take the two women back to Fort Lincoln until the last wagons and the company of infantry had made it across the river.

As the three Gatling guns with caissons in tow passed the small group on the way to the cut in the river bank, Lieutenant William Low, seeing General Custer astride his horse near the paymasters wagon, gave a sharp "eyes right" along with a formal military salute. General Custer stiffened his relaxed position in his saddle and instead of his usual casual return of the military courtesy gave a rather good salute of his own, calling out loudly. "And may the good Lord be with you throughout the campaign Billy Low."

Whether this kind gesture was meant for his wife and sister would be hard to say but it did gain an affectionate smile from Libbie Custer who offered her own heartfelt comment. "My dearest Bo, you will never know how pleased you have made me by allowing that darling boy to accompany you."

Custer had a rather strange quirk of seldom showing his emotions to his wife in public when he knew eyes would be watching and did not return her smile, but did say, "I am most happy you feel that way dear lady but then have I ever denied you anything?"

Libbie continued smiling, knowing her man to be of strong, simple emotions and apt at times to take himself too seriously. "No Autie I cannot think of you having ever denying me something I truly wanted."

"I am distressed to tell you it is time for me to go now. As it is it will be a hard ride for me to catch the head of the column but I do not like being away from the front of my regiment for very long as you know. Pray take care of yourself as I will do the same and I shall see you sometime in early September, if not sooner." Custer leaned in his saddle and gave his wife a dutiful peck on her uplifted rosy cheek.

Libbie was accustomed to her general's self-centeredness, and ignored the selfish content of his parting remark that made it sound like she was holding him up, and she maintained her smile. "Goodbye dear Autie. I will have you in my thoughts and prayers each day, and be careful dashing to the head of your regiment." Then almost playfully, Libbie looked down at John Burkman, her husband's orderly who was holding the reins of her horse Dandy, and said. "Goodbye John. You'll look after the general for me, won't you?"

Orderly Burkman was a little taken back by the friendly familiarity of the woman he adored as much as he did her husband, but quickly rallied his wits to answer, "Why Misses Custer ma'am, you know I'm going to do just that like I always do. I'll take real good care of the general, even more so now that you asked me."

"Thank you John. I know he'll be in good hands," and she gave her husband a last glance with a dazzling smile before saying, "I'll take the reins now John."

George Custer stared at the back of his retreating wife and sister for a long moment as they rode away keeping pace with the rattling paymaster's wagon and the detail of mounted soldiers assigned to guard it. He emitted a long sigh; shaking his head. Looking across to John Burkman he spoke to the man in a low tone of voice. "A good soldier has two mistresses John. While he's loyal to one, the other must greatly suffer."

Nodding his head up and down Burkman said, "Yes sir, I understand what you mean sir."

Reining his horse to the right General Custer offered a grim smile. "Well my boy I hope you are up to a hard ride. We have a good five miles at a fast gallop in front of us. Are you game?"

"Sir------I'll follow you anywhere at anytime."

"Good fellow," and Custer spurred his horse toward the cut in the riverbank.

* * * * *

Leaving Fort Lincoln the day before the majority of the riding horses that were well fed, after having wintered for several months in garrison, were extremely frisky and ready to go. They had given the troopers a fit trying to keep their mounts under control during the first day's march that tired both animal and rider. The constant fight between man and beast quickly broke the horses' spirits and they now moved along dejectedly with bowed heads, feeling worn out after only one day. Even the half wild new horses the regiment obtained just prior to the onset of the expedition were weary of the mile-by-mile slogging with 250 pounds of man and equipment on their backs. Evidently General Custer didn't notice how tired his cavalrymen were or the poor temperament of their mounts, but General Terry did. Terry had the reputation of looking out for his men and at 1:00 p.m. he sent his orderly to fetch Custer,

"Jack, the men had a bad time of it last night fighting the fire after a first days ride then having to dig that crossing this morning. You know how it is after they've laid around garrison for a while--a little soft and what not---takes a little time to build up their stamina. I think it best if we break 'em in easy as we've got a lot of miles to cover and I want alert men, ready to fight when we find the Sioux. So I want you and Charlie Reynolds to ride on ahead a piece and find a suitable campsite for us to make an early stop----say around...oh I suppose around two o'clock."

"But general sir that will only make it about a ten mile march for the day. Surely we can do better than ten miles over easy ground." Custer pleaded.

"No Jack I don't want to push 'em too much the first couple of days. There's going to be a lot of work to do before we reach the Yellowstone and I want to rest 'em while we can. You go ahead and do as I have requested and tell the head drover of the cattle herd to butcher a sufficient quantity of steers, that I want the men to all have steaks in their bellies tonight."

There was one thing about George Armstrong Custer. When he was given a direct order he cheerfully obeyed it. And a request from a superior was a direct order. "Very good General Terry, I'll see to it right away." and after a perfunctory salute galloped off to find his chief scout "Lonesome" Charley Reynolds.

"Lonesome" Charlie Reynolds

Chapter 5

Branch of the Sweet Briar River, Dakota Territory
3:00 a.m., Friday, May 19, 1876

It was the habit of General George Custer to always select the overnight campsite and under normal circumstances when he was in full command it fell to his decision not only where his regiment would halt for the night but also when. Actually it was pretty unusual for the department commander, General Terry to override any decision his golden-haired subordinate made since he knew Custer had a vast amount more experience fighting Indians than he, plus the fact Custer had traveled the approximate line of march before.

The manner each night's camp was set up was predetermined in regards to general characteristics. First, and foremost, a river or stream was the primary concern when locating a campsite. In extremely poor terrain Custer would still try and get near the closest water point as possible. The formation of the camp was always set up in the form of a rectangle with the longest sides occupied by the cavalry wings and the infantry headquarters at one end nearest the water source. An infantry company would man the other end of the rectangle, and the wagon train would be staged in the middle of this long box. The first priority after calling a halt for the day was to see that the animals were watered, then taken to graze outside the enclosure under the watchful eye of troopers assigned to stable guard detail.

Another item that was practiced each evening was the calling of the roll by the various first sergeants sometime shortly after sunset. This was done to insure no one had strayed and was unaccounted for plus to make sure the men had all their equipment near at hand. During this time all the horses and mules were taken inside the perimeter enclosure and tethered to picket lines. The first sergeants assigned troopers from their units to report to the provost marshal to be a part of the night's main guard who was responsible for the security of the camp. Also, an early warning system was used in the form of Indian scouts being posted on hills a distance from the camp where they kept watch throughout the night in shifts.

Since Custer didn't have a choice but to stop early yesterday because of General Terry's "request," it did not deter him from exercising what he felt to be his right of command when he ordered reveille sounded at 3:00 a.m. For most of the troopers it had came as no surprise as one veteran cavalryman groused after the early morning trumpet call had rudely awakened him, "You can bet when Old Georgie Boy does som'thin nice like stop'en early and fed'en us steaks that we're do'en to pay fer it the next day!"

After a hasty breakfast of fire-grilled bacon, Johnnycakes and strong coffee, civilians and soldiers were ready for the days march. By 5:00 a.m. all the fire pits had been covered over with the clods of sod they had been dug from and the advance element of the regiment started out from camp. The lead party of cavalrymen traveled about three-fourths of a mile when they were halted by a long ravine with high, rushing water boiling through it.

I Troop of the 1st Battalion of Major Marcus A. Reno's Right Wing had the advance detail that morning and the troop commander, Lieutenant James E. Porter sent a messenger back to the command group directly in his trace requesting that General Custer ride forward and for the column to stand easy.

Within a few minutes Custer and a party of three scouts was at Lieutenant Porter's side staring at turbulent water cascading through the deep ravine.

"Well gentlemen, I dare say we shant be able to bridge this and we certainly cannot ford it," General Custer said in a disgusted tone of voice. He took off his light gray, low-crowned, broad-rimmed hat he always wore in the field, his gold-fringed dress hat having been stowed away in his field trunk, and slapped it sharply against his fringed buckskin trousers. "Blast it all--------you would think that we could travel a mile, just one day---without having to face an insurmountable obstacle!"

Lieutenant Porter lifted his heavy black eyebrows that almost matched the thickness of his mustache, and trying to brighten his commanders outlook, said, "General Custer sir, I could send a few riders further to the north around that bend there to see if the river flattens out any and maybe find a suitable fording place or a location where we can use pontoons."

The young lieutenant's attempt to placate Custer's ruffled feathers back-fired on him and he paid for it by his commander's wrath being directed toward him: "Mister---you should have thought of that before leading us into this stalemate! Why is it that I must personally oversee the simplest of chores? I have scouts...and I have trackers that say they know the land and I have commissioned officers sent to me from West Point that are supposed to be intelligent but drat it all, I still have to do the thinking for everybody!"

As Custer paused from his tirade for a moment the two white scouts and one of the six Crow scouts attached to the seventh, inched their mounts away from the general and the red faced lieutenant, less the general focus his wraith on them as well.

But Custer's anger faded as quickly as his outburst, which was another personality trait of his character that those who knew him well was aware of, and he spoke in a calm voice that still carried an authoritative tone. "No, there is nothing else to do but to return to our old campsite and find a place to go around the ravine at a shallow ford." Turning in his saddle to see where "Lonesome" Charlie Reynolds had got off to he saw his old friend a few paces in back of him. "Charlie ride on back and advise General Terry we've got to find a fording place and inform him that I'm going on ahead to do it myself."

The slim, rangy, bearded scout spit out a large brown squirt of tobacco juice before bringing his left fingertip to the brim of his sweat stained wide brimmed brown hat. "I'll do'er Jack. You go ahead and take George and Curly along with you and one of 'em can ride back when you fine a ford. Reynolds was referring to civilian scout George B. Henderson who was a reliable man, having lived in Tullock's Creek region for several years, and to Curly Head the 18-year-old Crow buck that Custer had taken a liking to. Handsome Charlie Reynolds, whose right hand was all but incapacitated by a serious inflammation of the finger joints called "felon", spurred his horse and with his left hand reined her around and headed back down the now useless trail he had blazed.

* * * * *

General Custer found a suitable ford within half an hour but before the last of the long wagon train was able to get across the shallow fast moving water the front of the column once again ran into problems. This time Custer had no one to blame but himself since he had stayed ahead with the scouting unit. Roughly a mile from the stream crossing Custer and the scouts came across a prairie dog village directly in the line of march. It was a good 500 yards wide and the land area on either side was found to be too soft for the safe passage of the heavily laden wagons. So Custer called another halt and ordered the wagons, cavalry and infantry to close up. Then he had the troop that was assigned pioneering work to bring up their two spring wagons carrying axes, pickaxes, shovels and wood planking for the construction of small bridges. He set them to work with shovel and pickax to knock down the largest prairie dog castles and fill in the burrows so a narrow passage could be made. It was back breaking labor not made easier by the incessant squeaking chattering of thousands of frightened and irate rodents.

Just the same good progress was made after cautiously passing through the prairie dog village. Charlie Reynolds even managed to bag a large antelope with a well-placed shot that elated Custer who remarked the scouts and senior officers would have a tasty supper that night. Then the noonday sun was suddenly blacked out by rolling thunderclouds and within a matter of minutes a violent thunderstorm struck: pelting men and beast with large balls of hail. The storm raged for several hours on into the afternoon, making headway extremely difficult and slow.

Bad weather or not, the continuous downpour did not stop messenger scouts who rode from Fort Lincoln with mail and news. The mail would have to wait until the evening but the news, which was not good, was given immediately. General Terry and Custer learned from the dispatch rider that a large party of men had been massacred in the Black Hills by Sitting Bull's braves. As upsetting as this information was the two senior officers at least shared a common thought.

General Terry held a short conference with his troop commander: "It just doesn't do any good trying to convince those gold seekers to stay out of the Black Hills Jack."

"It was the same thing back in seventy-four general. Did my best then to tell Washington not to open up the territory but once the gold fever took hold it was Katie-bar-the-door. No stopping them then and there's no stopping them now." Custer paused for a second before going on. "Begging your pardon general, but the way I ponder on it is we had a treaty with the Indians and we broke it and you cannot blame the Indian's for that. Far as I'm a' thinking though we shouldn't have tried to deal with the savages in the first place. Shouldn't be making promises we don't mean to keep. Yet we gave them reservations and they won't abide to stay on them. White man's going to settle this land and no Indian is going to stop that. It's always sorry to hear about white men getting killed like that----Indians can be more brutal than any rebel soldier I ever came across and the good Lord knows what fierce fighters they were. The way I look at the news about this most recent massacre is the Indians made a big mistake. While I'm sorry to hear about all those men getting killed we at least know now that we're heading in the right direction, make no mistake about it."

In a sober tone of voice, doe-eyed General Terry nodded his head and spoke. "Well Jack, that was quite an informative bit of dialogue you gave me there, and while I may view some of the things you had to say in somewhat of a different manner, I concur with you all the way that we now know a large war party is roaming the Black Hills and appear to be heading north. It may very well turn out that those thirty men who died at the hands of the Sioux did not die needlessly, for I too am convinced we are heading in the right direction------and I make no mistake about it!"

* * * * *

At 5:00 p.m. the main artery of the Sweet Briar River was reached by leading elements of the 7th Cavalry. Although the rain had stopped, the cavalrymen stared in dismay at the newest obstacle facing them.

Custer looked at Charlie Reynolds then looked back at the raging torrent that was at least a full fifty feet wide. "That's over ten feet deep if it's an inch Charlie. Ain't no way we're going to be able to bridge that."

"I suspect you're rite a' saying that." The tall, thin man glanced to his right and then to the left. "And I don't think we're gonna have any luck if'n we was to head north. Seems to me you best start think'en 'bout take'n a southern trek tomorrow."

Custer reflected for a moment what his scout had told him before answering in an unhappy tone of voice. "If I keep heading south I'm going to end up down in the Wyoming territory along the Oregon Trail."

The remark tickled the scout's funny bone. "Lonesome" Charlie Reynolds gave a rare chuckle and with an even rarer smile, said, "Oh, I wouldn't go so far as to say that George, maybe jus down to the Big Cheyenne," he laughed. Then instantly composing himself to his usual stern faced demeanor, he rubbed his sore right hand with his left one, then said, "What I'll do in the morning is take a couple of the boys with me, say real early, and I'll scout down a few miles and find us a place to get around this thing."

"I'd be most grateful if you would do that for me Charlie."

Switching his chaw to his other jaw Reynolds let fly with a dark brown squirt of juice. "Taint no problem."

"Well, I thank you just the same old friend." Sometimes, Custer was polite to a fault, especially to men that seemed to admire him.

It was after nightfall when the last wagon teams entered the rectangle-boxed perimeter. The column had progressed almost 14 miles since the less than auspicious start at 5:00 a.m.

Chapter 6

Sweet Briar River, Dakota Territory
8:00 a.m., Saturday, May 20, 1876

"Lonesome" Charlie Reynolds was well known as a man who kept his word. An hour before daybreak he and a fellow scout, Isaiah Dorman, a Negro who had worked with the Buffalo Soldiers, an all black cavalry regiment led by white officers, was several miles south of the camp. The two were accompanied by Curly who was asked to come along because of the young Crow's excellent night vision. He safely led them along the riverbank in the early morning darkness as they sought a reasonable fording area.

Reveille sounded at 5:00 a.m. and soldiers busily went about their morning chores preparing themselves for another day on the trail.

General Terry and Custer breakfasted together in the general's large white tent he used for his headquarters and living quarters.

"This antelope gravy is quite tasty Jack." General Terry offered as he reached for another flour biscuit and after splitting it ladled a healthy spoon full of dark gravy from the still steaming tureen centered on a camp table.

"Hmmm, yes sir, very much so," Custer answered after wiping his mouth with a white linen napkin, then pointing to his china coffee cup for the white jacketed mess orderly to refill that hovered over the two senior officers.

Just because a military expedition was fielded in the mostly uncharted wilds of the Dakota Territory it did not mean that gentleman officers would forsake all the amenities of a civilized society. General Terry's personal baggage wagon carried among other items of comfort a large chest of china and silverware with necessary bowls and platters that could set a table for 12. White linen tablecloths and napkins were also included as was an orderly who upon proper occasion, such as this morning's formal mess, would wear a white twill jacket. The orderly would be used as a messenger during times needed but for all intent and purpose, was essentially a manservant as befitted the exalted position of a brigadier general of the United States Army. Custer's orderly John Burkman, who comrades called a "striker", was employed part-time in the same capacity. Naturally the average soldier didn't enjoy this style of living and their lot lived a much cruder existence; which in all fairness they were accustomed to and most wouldn't have known how to act if invited to eat at a fine laid out, table-clothed table.

"I understand yesterdays dispatch riders brought with them one of your horses. Is that the animal your dear wife Libbie rode back on to Fort Lincoln?" General Terry asked in polite conversation.

"Yes general. It was my mount Dandy that Libbie used and the paymaster was kind enough to send her back to me as Dandy is one of my favorites although I prefer riding Vic if battle is imminent."

"Well both are fine animals but then you always did have a good eye for excellent horseflesh."

"Thank you sir."

"Jack----let me ask you something. What made you change your mind about bringing the Gatling gun battalion along? You were dead set against that proposed plan during our pre-expedition planning at Fort Lincoln."

Custer looked up from his breakfast plate rather sharply to look at the general's face to see if there was any hidden meaning behind the unexpected question. Seeing nothing on the general's face other than an inquisitive expression it still took him a long moment to answer. "Lieutenant Low has labored quite extensively on his own initiative to develop an unlocking and locking mechanism which enables him to tear down then reassemble his guns within a reasonable amount of time. When the Gatling's are in the broke-down phase he claims the heaviest components can be readily hauled in this sort of a cradle sling he invented that can be placed between two mules, although I believe he said he preferred horses now that I think about it. Whatever it was makes no difference, mules or horses, he is convinced his guns can now keep up with me on a scouting patrol."

"Have you seen this ah...cradle sling as you called it in operation?" General Terry asked in mild interest.

"No sir but I did however view his scheme that gives him the ability to disassemble the guns and then enables him to put them back together as good as new. Quite extraordinary really----I was..........."

The general always enthused when hearing about new developments in weaponry, interrupted Custer with a thoughtful question. "Yes, yes----I would think that is extraordinary, but tell me now, how did he manage to tear the weapon down without damaging its design stability? I've seen Gatling's operate and the recoil almost shakes them apart as it is."

"I thought the same thing and questioned young Low on the very point you've brought up. That is when he showed me what he'd done at our first nights camp when Libbie wanted to pay her respects to the young man whom she's got in her sights on to find a girl for."

General Terry chuckled at the well-known game officers ladies played at matchmaking. "Go on," he urged

"Yes sir. Well what he's done is to bolt a heavy rod device to the bottom of the breach barrel portion of the gun and then on the cradle it rests on he's bored out a hole that the rod fits into snugly. He has two lever pins that hold the rod in the hole, keeping in mind it was originally put together as a solid single unit using several bolts. Now on the three clamps that hold the cradle to the axle frame he has similarly used three heavy pins that can be quickly unscrewed by strong hands as they too are levered. The levered pins are ingenious and he even utilizes them on the wheel hubs through the axles and can take the wheels off and back on quicker than a jack rabbit."

With a thoughtful expression General Terry murmured, "Sounds as if the lad should have a letter of commendation placed in his personnel file. I may just do that." In a stronger tone of voice the general went on, "I would certainly think the Bureau of Ordinance would be most interested to see a report of the results of a field test of what Lieutenant Low has come up with. You haven't actually seen the weapon fire with this new lever system you described holding it together have you Jack?"

"No sir, but Low did inform me he has fired his Gatling's after making the modifications and insured me the guns were no worse for wear after having done so and fired without problems."

"I see. And I suppose he has repaired all three of his Gatling's with these new fangled levers?"

"That is my understanding general."

"Humph! Well why then are they preceding with us the same as the artillery cannons with caissons in tow? It would seem to me that this would be a good time to find out if young Low's theory of mobility is poppycock or not."

Fingering his long mustache Custer paused a long moment before answering the pointed question. "I greatly admire Low's desire to want to be in the thick of things during this expedition that will surely find us in battle against the savages. On the other hand I have yet to find it in my thinking to place full confidence on the ability of the Gatling gun platoon to withstand the complete rigors of an offensive nature. I do think the Gatling is a marvelous weapon in defense but keeping up with my regiment during an attack? I think not. But I also feel that Low is trying to prove himself as an officer and soldier and for that, if for no other reason, I have endorsed his enthusiasm by allowing him to be a part of our campaign."

"That is most commendable of you Jack and answers my curiosity on the matter. You never can tell, we may find use for Low's services before this campaign is concluded."

A bustle of activity on the other side of the tent flap that separated the office portion of General Terry's tent from his living quarters where he took his meals distracted both officers from their conversation. One of Terry's aides, a major, opened the flap and stuck his head inside. "General Terry sir. The chief scout is outside and wants to talk to Colonel Custer."

Noting Custer bristle with a frown when the aide did not identify him by his preferred brevet rank, General Terry let a thin smile crease his triangular face when he said, "By all means, send him in."

Charlie Reynolds bent through the tent flap and entered. "Sorry 'bout busting in on your breakfast but figured you gen'ral's would want to hear I found a spot 'bout two miles down stream we can cross at."

* * * * *

The good news "Lonesome" Charlie Reynolds had brought was not acted upon immediately. Due to the hard going of the day before the command was sluggish in getting everything in order for a move and did not break camp until after 8:00 a.m.

After fording Sweetbriar River the long caravan of wagons still found it rough going as yesterdays rainstorm found the route of march extremely soggy. Wagon after wagon got mired in the swamp like mud, especially those bringing up the rear of the column that had to follow in the rutted trace of those preceding them. Cussing troopers had to help the teamsters pry out their stuck vehicles from the thick goo that sometimes caused wheels to come off from using leveraging poles which made matters even worse. Although lower areas near rivers and streams were avoided as much as humanly possible the spring rains had left all the ground soft and soggy that sometimes sank a wagon up to its hubs.

The only amusing thing that occurred to lift the troopers spirits was when a team of horses pulling an artillery piece stampeded and took off across the prairie as if the devils from hell was chasing them, leaving a strewn path of gear and equipment for half a mile before finally breaking off from the cannon and caisson which flipped over. Of course the artillerymen from the 20th Regiment did not find the incident amusing since they had to give chase to their wayward horses before catching them better than a mile from the rest of the column.

Then it began to rain again which effectively put a damper on most everyone's morale.

General Custer virtually threw up his hands in defeat when he learned a bridge was going to have to be built to get the wagons across the Little Muddy River that was less than ten miles from this morning's campsite. So a halt was called at a little before noon and bone-tired construction pioneers worked until nightfall building the bridge under a drizzling rain that stung their faces, being driven by a strong westerly wind.

Chapter 7

Little Muddy River, Dakota Territory
6:30 a.m., Sunday, May 21, 1876

Aroused from their bedrolls at dawn, weary construction pioneers worked diligently to finish building the bridge under the watchful eye of Captain Thomas French, who commanded the provisional 4th Battalion that was part of the Left Wing led by Captain Frederick W. Benteen. Two of Captain French's troops: "H" and "K" had been detailed to General Terry for pioneering work as was the custom when on the march, leaving Custer with ten troops for scouting and wagon train security.

Bridge building in the wilds was at best done very crudely with no expectation of a lasting structure. For one thing sturdy timber was at a premium and good, strong wood was scarce in the area the expedition was traveling. Depending on the size of the river or stream that had to be crossed had a lot to do with the stability of the bridge once built. Usually, the shorter the bridge the stronger it was. The longer bridges were for the most part rickety affairs that groaned and swayed on the verge of collapse under the laden wagons that inched their way across them. Many times after the wagons had traversed a water obstacle those troopers assigned to pioneer duty would then stay behind to dismantle the structure or at least, if not in its entirety, to salvage the pine board planking.

General Terry and Custer were informed at 6:30 the bridge was completed and the two senior officers ordered the waiting teamsters to commence the day's march.

General Terry advised his lieutenant colonel that he would ride always this morning at the front of the column with him that an amiable Custer gracefully accepted.

Riding side by side offered the regular commissioned general who preferred his Army blue uniform to his subordinates' buckskins, the chance to chat some more.

"The weather looks threatening again Jack," the general observed looking up at the heavy dark clouds overhead that were emitting a thin mist.

Custer followed his leaders gaze to the gloomy sky then said, "Those are rain clouds sure enough but the way they're rolling northward I think the worse of it will pass us by."

"I hope you are right as it appears this old trail we're following is solid footing for the wagons and we should make good progress."

Both officers fell silent for a few minutes until Terry's saddle squeaked from his moving on it while he turned around to see who was near the two of them. Noting that the nearest riders to him and Custer was out of ear shot, including his ever present trumpeter, General Terry voiced a concern to his cavalry leader that had been bothering him. "You know Jack---when I aided you in composing your letter to Grant that went through Phil Sheridan, I endorsed the request you made which asked to be permitted to join this expedition with a final remark that your services would be very valuable to me. I don't know if that influenced Sam's decision to change his mind or not but I do know that Sheridan's comments on your request were not at all favorable and I think Bill Sherman had most to do with convincing the President to allow you this chance to prove yourself. As you know when Sam Grant withdrew his objections he told General Sherman to make sure you understood to be prudent and not to do anything to bring the slightest discredit upon our profession." General Terry paused for a moment and glanced at his long-time acquaintance with his sad doe-like eyes.

George Custer returned the glance quickly without comment as he waited for the point to be made from this distressing talk he was being forced to listen to that sounded ominous.

"I want you to know I have the fullest confidence in your ability Jack and intend to give you the utmost latitude with any written or oral order I may give you in carrying out the mission of this campaign. However, it has come to my attention that there is a malicious bit of gossip circulating that I want you to be aware of, so it gets nipped in the bud right here and now. Someone has spread a rumor that when you left St. Paul to rejoin your regiment you reportedly told another person that you intended to act independently as you saw fit once the command was underway and would avoid following orders from me. Now I know that has to be balderdash coming from an irresponsible source somewhere but I did want to confront you with this to see if you have any thoughts why such a tale was being spread?"

Custer's ruddy features caused by sunlight playing havoc with his sensitive skin that embarrassingly brought out a large sprinkle of freckles blanched a chalky white upon hearing Terry's ending remarks. Just a few seconds previous George had been elated when Al Terry had prefaced his bombshell by talking about the confidence he had in him and the latitude of command he intended to give. Now Custer felt sick in the stomach because somehow a loose remark made earlier in the month had come home to roost at his doorstep. St Paul? It had to be that Captain Willie Ludlow of the Engineer Corps who was on transfer orders from Terry's staff I accidentally bumped into on the way to the hotel in St. Paul after getting the telegram to return to my regiment. What was it I said to him? I remember how excited I was when I told Ludlow I was rejoining my command. Ah yes---I did blurt out my intention I would cut loose and swing away from Terry once in the field. Ludlow must have passed this remark on. Good Lord! I've got to squash this right now! "That's the most astonishing actuation I've ever heard General!" Custer said loudly. "The only person I recall having greeted in St. Paul, other than yourself, was Captain William Ludlow, late of your staff who was on his way to Fort Riley. We conversed warmly for a time and you can imagine how excited I felt regarding the news you had given me about being allowed to proceed to Fort Lincoln to resume my duties as commander of my beloved regiment. It could very well be that in my exuberance I may have said some things that may have caused a misunderstanding and Ludlow took the wrong way." Custer paused for a couple of seconds to glance over to his commander, the prior ashen hue of his face now replaced with a growing redness. In a lower tone of voice he continued talking. "That would be the only foundation I can think of where such prattling has surfaced. Good Lord Alfred----I owe you my career. I would never contemplate such a disobedience and let me assure you of my total loyalty and subordination."

General Terry remained silent for a full minute while his horse clopped along at a slow, steady pace with Custer's Dandy doing the same at the geldings' side. Then with a short grunt as if he'd reached a conclusion, General Terry spoke softly, yet with a steely edge. "We go back a long way George and I appreciate how troubling it must be to be reverted from a brevet major general of volunteers to a lieutenant colonel in the regular service. The odd thing that you would not know about for I've never made it a point until now to bring it up, is that I have never thought of you as a lieutenant colonel. It does not embarrass me or rankle me the slightest as it does some ranking officers when you are addressed as general. My reasoning on this is quite simple: I know you think of yourself as a general and I suppose it could be said that I've accepted that and have learned to live with it. You sometimes get into mischief and let yourself get caught up in personalities, but none of your indiscretions have ever tainted your fighting spirit. There is no reason why we cannot continue to work together and as I stated earlier I will give you the fullest rein possible as conditions and circumstances allow. And I trust the loyalty you expressed you have for me will be met with a degree of sound judgment when I do give you an order. We will talk no more regarding whatever it was you may or may not have said to have initiated the scandalous whispering of treachery that came to my ears but just remember Jack----I am depending on you and expect that subordination you spoke of."

Custer's face was totally red now which his floppy hat could not hide. He looked like a schoolboy holding his breath and about ready to burst. His conscience bothered him greatly for having got caught, yet he also felt a measure of well-being after digesting everything his commander had said. In a sincere and contrite tone of voice, he said: "General Terry sir, I will not let you down, and thank you sir for all you have said and for the trust you have placed in me."

The two senior officers continued on in silence for some time until a gunshot from behind them caused them to abruptly turn in their saddles completely alert. They saw outriders on the left flank galloping toward a lone pony a hundred yards away that was prancing but being held by its reins by a trooper laying on the ground.

General Terry motioned for one of his enlisted orderlies to come to him.

When the private spurred his mount to the general's left side, General Terry gave him a terse order: "See what that's about."

In just a few minutes the orderly was back. "Sir, a trooper accidentally shot himself in the heel with his pistol."

Shaking his head in a negative gesture General Terry issued a totally unnecessary order since the trooper in question was already being taken care of. "See that the dunderhead is treated and placed in one of the ambulances. Dang if I'll hold up the march for one mans stupidity!"

Custer was even less sympathetic. "A forty-five caliber Colt most likely took his heel clean off. He'll be about as useless as tits on a bull for the entire campaign. What we should do is court-martial him!"

"Now, now Jack. You know as well as I do that some of these lads have never fired a weapon of any kind before joining up. He's probably one of those new recruits you got back at Fort Lincoln that we didn't have time to properly train on the firing range."

Terry's blond headed warrior glanced down for a moment at two of his four staghounds he'd brought with him for hunting that were snarling at one another. He edged Dandy over to them giving a sharp yell at the dogs. "Scat you curs---stop it right now!" Dandy's long ears went up from the bluff noise of Custer's shout and shied toward the dogs in a dancing prance. "Whoa there Dandy, didn't mean to spook you," Custer soothed, reining his pony back around to the side of the general. His yell, coupled with Dandy's antics effectively broke up the dog fight and he finally got around to answering his commanders remark; who had viewed the small distraction with mild amusement: "Perhaps what you say is true. As you know I received sixty raw recruits only a month before starting out on the campaign and none of them boasted prior military experience nor were most of them adept horsemen and as you pointed out none was overly familiar with firearms. Another hundred or so that came to the regiment when I was in Washington are ill trained too which I place solely on the shoulders of Major Reno for this neglect although he much protested my observations on this. Reno's logic is he had little choice to see to training during the time I was gone when considering the practical demands of post life during winter months and what he calls his lack of close supervision due to many of the companies being quartered elsewhere other than Fort Lincoln. The thought of delegation seems to escape the Major but it is true I am burdened with many greenhorns not proficient to the military lifestyle of the cavalry. I often say that ignorance is the huge enemy of our profession, especially at the basic training level. It leaves little doubt in my mind that the young trooper who just shot himself in the foot is an example of that philosophy. But of course you are correct; I shouldn't talk of court martial for the youngster because he lacks proper skills and his painful lesson may serve as a lesson to others that firearms are not something to play with."

General Terry nodded his head as if in agreement, then said, "You have such interesting viewpoints Jack but in this instant I do believe you hit the nail into the horseshoe when you say the wounded trooper will make others ponder on the danger of not handling weapons properly if that was the case."

* * * * *

The long column endured the typical delays of stops and movement as it snaked its way through the Dakota high butte area the expedition was now traversing. First timers traveling this rolling land with the many tall rock formations dotting the countryside were awestruck when viewing the distant towers. They were further flabbergasted when older veterans called out the names of the high pinnacles: Wolf's Den, Rattlesnake Den, Cherry Ridge, The Maiden's Breast. These exotic sounding titles were written in many diaries and letters home by young troopers that night who marveled at the true adventure they were a part of. Another shot rang out in mid-afternoon that echoed off the tall buttes; only this time it was a legitimate firing of a Colt pistol by a trooper who was ordered to dispatch a diseased mule. Custer noting the time was approaching 4:00 p.m. and seeing how weary his troops assigned to pioneer bridge building were, called a halt and ordered camp set up for the night. The lengthy cortege had covered the distance of 13 1/2 miles for the day: a good day's march.

Chapter 8

Glenullen Pass near a branch of the Heart River, Dakota Territory
3:00 a.m., Monday, May 22, 1876

Lieutenant William Hale Low could hardly believe his ears when the blaring of a trumpet disturbed his sleep. The big-eared officer at first thought the camp was being attacked by Indian's as he struggled into his uniform inside the fairly large white tent he and fellow officer Lieutenant Kunzite shared. From the other side of the dark tent the squinty eyed young man could hear his companion grunting, no doubt struggling with his own clothing, when it finally came to him the bugle call was screeching reveille.

"Good Lord Pat that's reveille call. What time is it, I feel I've just went to sleep?"

The distinct scraping, rasping sound of a sulfur match being struck was instantly followed by a yellowish-orange flare of firelight that illuminated the shadowy figure of James Kunzite who touched the tiny flame to a candle stub on a box next to his cot. Groping on the bedside box Kunzite came up with his large gold pocket watch. Peering at the timepiece with his narrowed, not fully awake eyes, he coughed, then spoke in a raspy voice. "My watch must be faulty its showing a little past three." As he put the watch up to his ear the scuffling noises of a camp coming to life could be distinguished outside the thick canvas.

"I don't think there's anything wrong with your watch Pat." Becky Low murmured reaching for his boots.

* * * * *

Custer, having felt a degree of compassion yesterday for his weary pioneer troopers, had let them sleep in. But this morning to offset this compassionate moment of emotion that he considered a weakness anyway, he ordered an early reveille. But as usual, his willingness to set an example was above reproach and he was already up, shaved and dressed before Trumpeter Martini blew his first note. While his command went about the ritual of coming alive for the day Custer fussed around in his large tent getting his personal tools of war ready. He checked his two Forehand and Wadsworth English-made, self-cocking, white-handled .32-caliber pistols and satisfied himself they were oiled and clean. Wiping the inside of his tooled leather holsters with a dry, old, oil rag he inserted his pistols inside the holsters then wiped the canvas cartridge belt clean of yesterdays dust before sitting it aside on his field cot. Remembering having used his hunting knife for cutting an apple this morning he looked around the tent to see where he had put it. Finding the long blade stuck in the middle of the camp table he lifted it out and after wiping it off placed it in the beaded, fringed scabbard on the cartridge belt. The last item of weaponry he picked up to inspect was his fondest possession; a Remington sporting rifle, octagon barreled, and calibrated for firing the 50-70 center-fire cartridge. Custer had lovingly cleaned and oiled the rifle last night and he just wanted to make sure that no rust had spotted it in the crisp, damp air. Satisfied the beautifully gleaming firearm was still immaculate he took it to the tent flap where his saddle was sitting and placed the rifle snugly into the Spencer carbine scabbard he used. Placing the broad-brimmed, low-crowned, light gray hat on his head he fingered the brim to a good fit then parted the flap of canvas separating his living quarters from his command post office, walking out into the cluttered area where his orderly John Burkman lived. In a bluff tone of voice General Custer said rather loudly, "Confound it John, isn't my coffee ready yet?"

Burkman was accustomed to his idol's meant to be humorous play acting which almost took place every morning and with a smile, answered, "I got it right out here on the fire like I always do general."

Returning his "strikers" smile with a thin one of his own Custer held out a heavy white clay-fired mug while the orderly poured it full with strong bean crushed coffee which produced a delicious aroma from a wafting spiral of steam. Holding the mug in both hands to put some heat on his stiff fingers the general said, "John, I want you to pack up post haste as I want an early start today and don't intend to dawdle here all morning. Tell Trumpeter Martin I said to help you and as soon as you complete your task saddle up Vic for me as he will be my mount for the day."

"Yes sir general, but what about your breakfast?"

"Oh, I've already had an apple and I'll cabbage a piece of bacon and a biscuit at General Terry's mess where I'm heading now."

* * * * *

Even with the early wake up call and General Custer flitting around all over the camp in his energetic way urging speed so they could be on their way, it was still after 6:00 a.m. before the first wagons with adjoining cavalrymen started out across the wide expanse of flat ground that was considered a pass between the buttes. The distant tall buttes called Young Maiden's Breast acted as visual guiding post and teamsters pointed their wagons in that direction over much drier and harder roads.

The nearer the expedition got to the fringes of the Bad Lands the more the terrain changed. By early afternoon large patches of alkali was seen and before long the civilian drivers, mounted soldiers and infantrymen were passing large balls of sage that rolled down from the cactus-covered hills on either flank. The rocky hills offered many strange formations for recruits to stare at and most of the hills were deep scarred with ravines that constricted scouting to a minimum. These hazards however did not stop Rees Scouts from bagging twelve antelope. Charlie Reynolds also killed three antelope that he would sell to officers. This was a usual practice and while game was plentiful the scouts normally had the better opportunity of bagging a goodly share. The Ree's would no doubt earn a little extra money this evening selling the meat to soldiers, which added a little variety to monotonous army rations. Custer encouraged his men to hunt when time and circumstances permitted for the simple reason he felt it would help improve troopers' marksmanship. If they in turn ate their kills, fine: if not, that was their business as Custer wasn't concerned about his troops eating habits other than preaching they should eat wild fruit occasionally to stave off scurvy.

General Custer was up front with his trumpeter at his side that he demanded to be within hailing distance at all times. When he came across his old track of his 1874 campaign leading from the Black Hills the 35 year old man whooped and hollered and rode Vic around in circles like some kid at a circus. All his life Custer had resisted maturity and his antics just further proved his retention of a youthful exuberance for life. Guiding Vic along the trace for a while as he renewed old memories he finally brought the big horse back to the present trail and stood by it telling every officer that passed by the significance of the old rutted north-south trail they were crossing. As General Terry approached, Custer was about ready to go into his enthralling spiel when a tremendous wrenching sound was heard coming directly behind the general. One of the heavily laden wagons had accidentally got its left front wheel caught in a sink hole turning it over, spilling all its contents and seriously injuring the driver who got caught under the wagon when it fell on top of him. The rear of the column was held up for better than 45 minutes while the assistant surgeon, Doctor George Lord with his hospital orderly, corporal John Callahan, did what they could do for the injured driver who had suffered internal injuries as well as broken bones. They got the teamster into an ambulance and after troopers straightened the wagon and put on a new wheel, they reloaded the vehicle and got a spare driver to take it over.

Traveling as part of a military expedition on the uncertain terrain in this part of the Dakota Territory would get more hazardous with each passing mile. It was a wonder the wagons held together as well as they did considering the constant jolting and abuse they were subject to. It was a tribute to the pride of American craftsmanship that wagon makers put into their labor of producing strong, sturdy vehicles that for the most part stood up under extreme abuse. But none of this fazed Custer since he thrived on hardship, and thought everyone else should do the same.

It was almost 6:00 p.m. when the last of the long line of wagons creaked and groaned their way into the nights bivouac area that had been selected by General Custer in a grove of Box Elders next to a branch of the Knife River called Thin-faced Woman Creek.

Young Lieutenant Low spent the remaining couple of hours of daylight giving his Gatling guns a meticulous inspection. He had his men disassemble one of the guns and looked closely for signs of wear and tear on the parts he had created. Noting nothing amiss he ordered the gun team to lubricate all the levers, pins and holes with thick gun grease and reassemble it. While the men grumbled at the invented work they still had to agree they had a couple of good officers in command of them, especially Lieutenant Low who almost treated them as equals.

Custer treated himself to an antelope steak, brought to him through the courtesy of Charlie Reynolds. He prepared for bed in a good mood, most pleased with the almost 16 miles his regiment had traveled today.

**Gatling Gun and Crew. There are no known pictures of Lt. Low.
(It is possible this photo is taken of his battery at Fort Lincoln.)**

Chapter 9

Having marched from Thin-face Woman Creek,
to Young Men's Buttes, Dakota Territory
9:00 a.m., Tuesday, May 23, 1876

Usually nothing fazed the grizzled veterans of the 7th Cavalry as they had been on too many campaigns chasing the winds and seen too much and done too much to be overly impressed about most anything. This sentiment was more than true when it came to the whims of their officers. When a halt was called a little before nine o'clock, after having only been on the trail for about four hours, those old troopers that chewed tobacco just shook their heads and let loose a stream of brown juice to stamp their opinions that you should never be surprised at anything that goes on in the army. At the same time veteran campaigners knew full well that unless they were in close pursuit of renegade savages or tracking a fresh trail, that most cavalry marches were purposely done in fairly easy stages. But even with that knowledge the average trooper thought the day's march of eight miles was idiotic. As one leathery-faced, raw-boned sergeant put it: "The gen'eal, as I recall was sure 'nough eager ta gitty-up-go on this fame an' glory jaunt of his but I a' reckon he must' of forgot all about that little pep talk he gave us, 'bout how hard he was a'going to push us. Taint much chance him being president of this here U S of A the way he's dawdle'en along."

The old-line sergeant was referring to Custer's well-known desire to run for the nation's highest office; and made no bones about it, how a successful punitive campaign against the Sioux could very well propel him into the White House.

The population back east considered this part of the nation as being a part of what was quaintly called *The Great American Desert.* While it is true that the Bad Lands are barren to a certain degree the land did boast many small oasis where clear water and firewood was found. This is exactly what the men of the expedition were enjoying now; a fairly large refuge near the headwaters of a Knife River tributary that offered good grass for grazing, plentiful wood and sweet water. The reason passed down to the soldiers for such an early stop was that Custer wanted to take advantage of the pleasant surroundings before facing the terrain rigors that would be met within the next couple of days. It was also said that Custer was intending on pushing everyone hard the next day and expected a march of 20 miles and this early halt would give horses and mules a good rest with abundant water and rich grass for them to enjoy.

If it came to any of the trooper's minds there was no mention that the stop was also meant for them to rest up it was kept to their own thoughts. If Custer worried more about the condition of four legged animals more than he did his two legged warriors; the troopers ignored that possibility by taking full advantage on what was for the most part a full day off: Being a soldier on the march was rough duty with many hardships but in many respects there was sufficient relief to make it sometimes feel like a Sunday picnic outing and that's what the men made of it this day. A baseball game was organized and fire pits dug to accommodate game that various hunting parties would surely bring back. Two of Custer's Staghounds broke loose from their tether and with loud barking went in pursuit of an antelope that led the dogs a merry chase much to the amusement to everyone watching. Although it was cool and clear with southerly winds many troopers still romped in the cold water of the stream, making the most of a good thing. One of the soldiers' favorite pastimes was indulged and a dozen or so card games of one variety or the other were being diligently played. All the card games were of course played for money. With nothing else but a few sutler items to spend their greenbacks on, which continued to rankle many troopers, quite a few of the men squandered their back pay gambling. They blamed Custer for their field pay, thinking he had made sure they didn't get the chance to blow their money the way they would have like to have done in Bismarck. Just the same there were the few enterprising ones who managed to stow a few bottles of cheap hooch either for personal use or to make a few extra dollars selling the raw whisky to thirsty troopers. Among those who felt the need to bring along hard spirits was the senior major of the 7th, Major Marcus A. Reno, who sat morosely alone in the tent he shared with Captain Benteen drinking quietly from an unlabeled white bottle that held a reddish-amber liquid.

The length and duration of a days march was always at the discretion of the commander. And when it came to Custer, the how far and how long mostly depended upon the mood he was in. Unknown to those he commanded, the primary reason George Custer made the decision to halt after an eight mile march, had much more to do with command responsibility than mood swings or the condition of the horses and mules. For he had stumbled upon the first evidence of the elusive enemy he was seeking.

* * * * *

Earlier in the morning, Custer, along with Charlie Reynolds and a couple of Rees scouts, had forged ahead of the column on a hunting party expedition. It was near 8:00 a.m. when the four men found themselves about five miles in front of the wagon train, up in a stunted tree area alongside a narrow gully near a tall butte.

Charlie Reynolds had already bagged an antelope which was draped across his saddle horn, field-gutted but not skinned. Hearing the clatter of hooves Reynolds spun around in his saddle and quickly pointed toward a small dry arroyo. "Jack! Elk do'en lickety-split to your left!"

Custer instantly gave chase, spurring Dandy to a fast gallop down the center of the narrow gully. After a hundred yards the steely-eyed brevet general saw that his quarry had led itself into a trap. The arroyo dead-ended with shale like walls four feet high creating a box coral. Seeing what it had done the big deer scrambled frantically at the rocky side of the enclosure in a desperate effort to scale the wall. Custer unsheathed his Remington 50-70 and taking deliberate aim squeezed the trigger putting one bullet in the back of the Elk's head just below its ears from a distance of fifty yards. Although Dandy was a good cavalry pony the horse still whinnied sharply, tossing its head with upright ears, doing a little two step dance with its forelegs. "Whoa there Dandy, steady old boy."

The Elk had tumbled over backwards from the instant killing shot and now laid still in a death posed heap where it had fallen at the rear of the box. Nudging Dandy forward, Custer whispered to his animal as he gently patted its main. "Let's go see what we've bagged."

As he slowly rode toward his kill Custer suddenly became alert at seeing a whiff of smoke emitting from between two jagged pillars of rock to his right. Quickly dismounting, with rifle at the ready, the well-built cavalry officer cautiously approached the large fissure prepared for any eventuality. With his back almost touching the shale wall he peeked around one pillar into the eight-foot wide windbreak nature had carved out of the rock. In the center of the erosion hewed gap was a small campfire blazing merrily away. Custer was noting other evidence of human activity and what were obviously signs of a hasty departure when he heard the distinct clop, clop sound of approaching horses. He recognized the noise as being shoed horses from the minute scraping ring of iron on rock but just the same he was very careful when stepping out of the crevice to expose himself. Catching sight of "Lonesome" Charlie Reynolds, followed close by the two Indian scouts he gave the three men a silent wave with his rifle over his head then pointed the barrel of the weapon toward the upper level of the arroyo in a jabbing motion.

Chief scout Reynolds instantly recognized the generals' gesture as a signal that something or somebody was above them and he quickly dismounted. The two Rees scouts did the same. They tied their ponies to tuffs of scrub brush then walked slow in the direction of Custer keeping their eyes peeled on the ledge a few feet above their heads.

When Reynolds got to within a hundred or so feet from Custer he placed two fingers behind his head over his right ear in an upraised vee in a pretense of twin feathers. Custer understood the question and nodded his head up and down two times in an exaggerated manner. Reynolds two Indian companions understood the pantomime taking place between the white men and performed a few hand gestures of their own among themselves for communication. One of the Rees scouts turned around and headed back to the tethered horses and once there stood guard. The other Indian slung his carbine and with quick dexterity scaled the side of the rock wall. Once on top he remained in a crouched position for better than a minute slowly moving his head in a sweeping arc away from the direction of the arroyo.

In the meantime Charlie Reynolds had crept next to his friend. In a whisper barely deciphered he talked in Custer's ear. "How many?"

In an equally low tone of voice Custer answered. "At least two, maybe more. I must have caught them by surprise because they left behind two different kind of medicine bags in the recess there."

Charlie Reynolds was about to ask another question when the Rees scout on top of the ledge above them forty feet away hollered out. "Yellow Hair--- look to the ridge!"

Custer and Reynolds looked to the direction of the scouts pointed rifle and finally located two half-naked figures scaling a cliff 500 yards distance that went up to a small mesa.

In a normal tone of voice "Lonesome" Charlie spoke: "They look Cheyenne to me."

"I don't know Charlie, could be Sioux." Custer mused.

"Whal, whatever they are they're long gone and skedaddled. Taint do'en to be any chance a' catching 'em." Charlie let fly with a good squirt then moseyed into the gap to examine the Indian campsite with Custer close on his heels.

"They must have left their ponies up in the bluffs," Custer ventured. "It would be hard for me to believe they were afoot."

"Whal, I suspect you're probably rite a'think'en that. Could be a'hunt'en party or even scouts. Never can tell. But one thing fer sure, they's warriors. These here charm bags are only carried by braves gett'en ready to do battle."

White Swan interrupted the two, the scout that had went to make sure the horses would not be stolen, that he now brought with him. "Yellow Hair get fine buck but antlers break when fall on rocks."

Hairy Moccasin, the other Indian scout who had spotted the fleeing hostiles, began gutting the huge wapiti Custer had brought down while the general scribbled a note with pencil to General Terry on his field order book he always carried. The finished note read: *"Came upon two hostiles. Recommend halt. Best not to tell men at this time but form several scouting parties as hunting excursions. Will return post haste with ten pt bull Elk I bagged. YOS-----Custer."*

* * * * *

When General Terry read the note handed him by White Swan he had to suppress a small smile forming. He handed the note to his Acting Assistant Adjutant General, Captain Edward W. Smith of the 18th Infantry. "It's just like Custer to end an order to his superior by abbreviating Your Obedient Servant with YOS and at the same time brag about a big game kill after seeing the enemy. However, I agree with his analysis so take care of the details Ed."

* * * * *

Lieutenant Becky Low fidgeted nervously as he waited for General Custer to notice his presents. He had been summoned by an orderly to report to the great man for reasons he had not a clue. Now he had cooled his heels for over twenty minutes while the general held a pow-wow with a gathering of the Indian scouts. The six foot, lean officer noticed how well General Custer got along with his scouts and seemed perfectly at home with them. There was much animated arm movement and laughter taking place and it was a revelation to Low looking at all the grin creased faces on the Indians who normally wore such stoic; grim expressions that made them appear so fearsome.

Another five minutes passed and Lieutenant Low was amusing himself by pushing small stones in a pile with his heavy infantry shoes when a loud voice startled him. "Ah yes--Lieutenant Low!" Custer boomed. "Doing a little engineer work there for the ants are you?"

Low's face reddened, but he overcame his embarrassment of having got caught playing like a child and snapped to attention, and offering a crisp military salute. "Lieutenant Low reporting to General Custer as ordered sir!"

Custer, who was uncovered, brushed his forehead with the pair of gloves he was carrying and said, "Stand easy young man. I was having a conference with my primary Indian scouts and trust you didn't have to wait too long..."

Low didn't know if he should answer or not, but quickly decided to say, "No sir, no problem at all sir."

With a bemused expression at the interruption, Custer went on. "That's mighty nice of you to say that Lieutenant but the reason I called for you is General Terry is interested in seeing your Gatling's fire since your... ah...modifications. He is a little concerned you went ahead with your experimental alterations on your own without the blessing of higher authority and I believe he wants assurance that the weapons are not damaged from doing the work they were originally designed for."

"Am I in trouble sir?" Low wanted to know.

"No lad I wouldn't say that, unless of course your guns fall apart or fail to function during a firing test." Custer paused, taking out his pocket watch, then snapping the dial cover shut, said, "It's a little past four, can you have your battery ready within the next half hour?"

"Yes sir." Lieutenant Low paused momentarily. "General Custer sir, where would General Terry like for the firing test to take place?"

Custer scanned the countryside to his immediate front for several seconds, then pointing toward a line of jagged buttes about a thousand yards distance, said, "See that large cluster of tall cactus with all those scrub trees lined around them about half way back from that parapet of buttes?"

"Yes sir I do."

"Go get your guns and unlimber them right here and you can fire towards the cactus and trees."

* * * * *

The rumbling noise of the three Gatling guns with their caissons in tow tearing through the camp aroused the curiosity of the entire expedition, especially when the word filtered through the camp that the guns were going to put on a firing exposition. As Lieutenant's Low and Kunzite watched their 32 men efficiently set up the battery for firing they were joined by an audience of over 1,000 other men.

Custer, and all his officers, stood with General Terry and his staff on a small hill that looked down on the busy Gatling crew. Where the large group of officers situated themselves offered a clear view of the flat expanse of land in the direction of the buttes. They amicably chatted with one another: a few offering an occasional pointed arm toward the cactus grove surrounded by a dozen stunted scrub trees. All of the senior officers had binoculars hanging from their necks or spyglasses held in hands. A goodly lot of junior officers also carried similar viewing devices to get a closer look at the forthcoming show.

The entire thing had taken on the aspect of a carnival atmosphere and troopers pushed and shoved their comrades to get a better vantage point to view the action. Most had never seen Gatling guns in action before and there was a certain excitement in the air as men laughed and joked in anticipation of the coming event.

The infantry troopers turned battery men were so well drilled in getting their weapons into position and set up that they were ready to go in less than ten minutes. They all knew this wouldn't be the case if they would have had to assemble the Gatlings from being broke down, but with an excellent moral of men who take extreme pride in who they are and what they were capable of doing, they knew it would have only been a few minutes longer had the guns been broken down into the five components. The ten men per gun stood at a relaxed form of attention awaiting the order to fire the guns.

The gunner sat on a small steel seat placed on the guns trails that he straddled. The firing crank was within easy reach and he aimed the weapon over an iron sight. A loader stood by near the tall left wheel of the Gatling with a fully loaded clip of .50 caliber cartridges ready to insert in the bullet feeding hopper or clip insert as it was better known on the newer 1871 models. Next to the loader was a ready man with an additional full clip of ammunition that he would hand the loader and also retrieve empty clips. Behind the ready man were two ammunition carriers whose job was to insure full clips were available and to pass back empty ones. The Caisson Sergeant filled new clips with bullets from open ammunition boxes and would call upon one of the ammo carriers or the horse handler if need be to assist him. The position of horse handler was just as it implied, to take care of the horses, with the additional duty of driving the limber team while on the march. At the right wheel of the gun was the spotter. His job, which usually called for a senior NCO, was to spot targets for the gunner, traverse the weapon when necessary and was the ranking man on the gun. Behind him was the waterman/oilier that had the responsibility to keeping the six barrels of the Gatling cooled down if they became overly hot from firing and to lubricate the gun as required, even when in action. His assistant was called the water boy. The water boys job was simple: make sure buckets of water were ready for the oilier to use which meant sometimes a dashing run to the nearest stream, pond, spring or river.

Most of the jobs on the guns were interchangeable but seldom changed unless there were causalities, discharges or promotion. In addition to the gun crews the battery had a first sergeant and an orderly/runner.

Lieutenant Pat Kunzite nudged his commander. "They're ready Becky, better tell the general's."

Nodding his head Lieutenant Low stroked his blond mustache a couple of times then walked stiffly, yet purposefully to the small mound where the officers were gathered. With a precise salute, he said: "General Terry and General Custer sirs. My battery is prepared to fire."

General Terry, wearing a long-coated, blue uniform that stood out in contrast to Custer's buckskins, issued the order. "You may commence the exercise Mister Low."

Terry returned the lieutenants salute and while the young officer was returning to his battery he turned to Custer. "What do you think Jack. If they don't break down, do you think they'll be able to reach that scrub area you selected as a target area?"

"From what I've read that's been issued by the Bureau of Ordinance and seen in several Army- Navy Journals, the Gatlings are supposed to be effective at better than three hundred yards and with its blow back muzzle velocity can reach a thousand yards over flat terrain. I estimate that grove of cactus at around three hundred yards. If they stand up without malfunctions the guns should not have problems reaching that area."

"Well I reckon we'll soon know won't we?" Terry replied, turning back to the front, ending the short exchange.

"Gun Sergeants, attention to orders," Lieutenant Low shouted "On my command guns one, two and three will fire independently at pre-selected targets. Ready-------COMMENCE FIRE!"

No sooner did the three non-commissioned officers repeat the same order individually to their gunners in a loud tone of voice than the gunners began turning their firing cranks.

The instantaneous eruption of extremely loud chattering gunfire had a startling effect upon the on looking troopers. Even the veterans who had seen their share of combat were taken aback from the sheer volume of flaming lead that streaked from the three six barreled guns. The stuttering, spitting weapons that put out a continuous hail of gunfire shocked most of the troopers sensibilities and defied their logic of how wars were supposed to be fought. Much the same could be said for the astounded cluster of officers standing transfixed on the small knoll watching the extraordinary destruction of plant life taking place three hundred yards from their place of observation.

While the Gatling gun teams worked with a precision of excellence down range from their position, they had created an awesome scene of terrible obliteration. Before the dust got so bad from the bullets kicking up the earth and smoke from the brush fire the hot shells had started, officers and men viewed the entire destruction of the grove of cactus, stunted trees and small bushes.

No one had told Lieutenant Low how many clips to fire so he had taken it upon himself to expand 500 rounds per gun. While he was pleased at the chance to allow his men some live fire practice he was conscious of how precious his consignment of .50 caliber ammunition was and he decided to be conservative. He had also ordered his gunners to fire at a slow rate of speed but even at that the show was over in just over two minutes. It made no difference, for he had impressed the Department Commander to no end and certainly proved his point beyond a doubt what his weapons were capable of doing.

When the on looking troopers and civilians finally came to realize the demonstration was over, for several seconds there prevailed a deathly silence. Then suddenly, as if on cue, the whole crowd broke out in wild cheering, whistling, and clapping of hands.

General Terry walked down from his mound, with his staff, Custer, and other officers following, and congratulated Lieutenant Low. "That was most impressive son and your battery does not look any worse for wear. Tell your men for me that they did an excellent job and that I'm proud of every one of them. And to you sir, I salute you." And the general gave the stunned young lieutenant the military courtesy of greeting, which Low quickly returned.

General Custer was likewise profuse in his praise. "Outstanding presentation Billy Low. By all means add my similar sentiment as General Terry's to your men and to your second in command." Custer paused for a moment, then his face lit up with a broad smile, "You could surely show those savage Indian's a thing or two about the power of modern technical might if the opportunity ever presented itself."

* * * * *

Unbeknownst to General George Armstrong Custer, the opportunity of seeing the Gatling guns at work had already presented itself.

At dusk a band of eight Uncpapas-Sioux, which included the two braves Custer had caused to run for their lives, made their way from the line of buttes that overlooked the valley where the cactus had stood, and headed toward the Coteau mesa which was three miles away from the hated white soldiers' camp.

Chapter 10

Heading West from Young Men's Buttes, Dakota Territory
12:30 p.m., Wednesday, May 24, 1876

Billy "Bucky" Low and Jimmy "Pat" Kenzie both were beaming all morning as they led their three horse-drawn Gatling guns on the excellent trail the expedition was following. Compliment after compliment had been given the two officers during the early morning travel about what a grand display of firepower they had shown at yesterday's demonstration. The complimentary praise had started shortly after the day's march commenced with Captain Tom Custer, the general's younger brother.

Captain Custer had made it a point to ride back to where the Gatling's were lumbering along just prior to joining his brother for a day of hunting up in the northern butte area. Doffing his gray, wide-brimmed, high-crowned hat, the friendly officer accosted his two fellow officers with a wide grin. "My hat is off to you two gentlemen for your extraordinary performance at yesterday's exhibition. I do believe you proved to one and all that witnessed your feat that the Gatling's surely have a place in the armies of the future, and perhaps even now. What a brilliant display of firepower!"

Tom Custer swept his hat downward like a chevalier of old with a slight bow. His handsome features glowing in the early morning sunlight that emphasized the scaring on his neck and face where a rebel soldier had shot him at Sailor's Creek during the Civil War.

The gesture readily astounded the two younger officers. Both junior officers held the captain in the highest esteem. The fact that he had earned two Medals' of Honor in the War of the Rebellion, something his brother had not accomplished with even one, was awe inspiring to say the least. His down-to-earth manner and friendliness made him even more respected in their eyes than the general. Lieutenant Low was near stunned at the words given from a man he held in such high regard and as usual his face began to flush from hearing the heady praise. "Captain Custer sir, your kind words are most appreciated and I want to thank you again for your interest in my battery and the support you showed back at Fort Lincoln."

With his blue eyes glinting, his narrow jawed smile continuing to grace his face under the well-trimmed mustache, Tom Custer, said. "The pleasure of your company that evening prior to our departure was most gratifying as well as enlightening. Tell me Low, are you still convinced you can keep up with a cavalry patrol?"

"Oh yes sir!" Bucky Low answered at once in an enthusiastic tone. "There is no doubt in my mind we would not be a hindrance on such a venture."

Custer then looked directly at Low's second in command. "And you, Lieutenant Kenzie. Do you to share your commander's views?"

"I most certainly do sir." Pat Kenzie said in a squeaky dry voice that embarrassed him and he cleared his throat before going on. "Humph...humph. And I also share Buc... Lieutenant Low's opinion that it shan't be very long before we see a much lighter version of our machine gun, even one that can be transported by men, not horses."

"What an interesting term...machine gun." Tom Custer interjected as he trotted his horse at an easy gait next to the two mounted officers. "And, an even more interesting theory." Looking back at Low, he remarked, "So you envision this----machine gun as Kenzie called it, to be so portable in the future that soldiers will be able to carry it by them selves?" The question was asked with a bemused raised eyebrow.

"Yes sir I do. There is an American born engineer and inventor now living in England by the name of Maxim that has already made great strides in reducing the weight of weapons such as our Gatling and some of the journals I've been reading tells of one of his plans of a single barreled weapon with a water reservoir around it to keep the barrel cool during firing. Maxim states he believes his new system will allow this machine gun, as he has termed it, to fire well over one-thousand bullets per minute without any sort of problem.

"Low, you are truly dedicated to your weapon and for that I congratulate you. I'm most sure Armstrong will take this bit of news with the attention it deserves but if what you say is true it will change the face of warfare. I cannot foresee any glory or honor with a weapon you call a machine gun that will scythe soldiers down as if mowed by a grim reaper in a wheat field." Tom Custer replaced his hat on his short, cropped-haired head that he parted in the middle. He touched the hat's brim in a casual salute then reined his horse around and with a final word rode away, "Keep faith Bucky Low, I may ask for your help one day!"

That had been the start of a continuing stream of soldiers and civilians, from private to the chief of scouts, coming up to the two officers to voice their platitudes on what they felt was an amazing and dramatic performance.

* * * * *

With two of the Custer's off gallivanting for big game, General Terry ordered Major Reno, the next ranking officer in the 7th Cavalry, to take command of the regiment and try not to delay the column. Reno, who was a good enough officer when higher authority supervised him, took General Terry's admonishment to heart and ordered all troop commanders to have their men not stop for a noon meal. This was not that unusual of a demand on soldiers as they were accustomed to eating in the saddle or afoot; and a noon meal was not considered that important anyway, although soldiers did dearly love their hot coffee. So troopers and teamsters ate hardtack biscuits (some dating back to the Civil War), or dried meat southern border Indian's called Charqui, but the more popular Pemmican was eaten also; a dried venison and wild berry concoction pounded into cakes with fat. A few enjoyed pickled eggs while others subsisted on cornmeal cakes.

The cool, clear, dry weather made marching easy and excellent progress was made. The cavalry with its attached infantry had passed the survey line of the Northern Pacific Railroad earlier that morning where they had ran into a prospector by the name of Dickinson. General Terry conversed with the man who appeared to be in his thirties, and the general was very curious on how the prospector had managed to keep his scalp. Dickinson's answer was typical of the attitude of adventurous white men seeking fame and fortune at a location he had absolutely no business being at: "Them injun's mind thar business, an' I mind mine. Ain't got no quarrel with 'em an' don't give 'em any reason fer 'em to have one with me." Very seldom did the red man share the same sentiment. They had been lied to and abused by the white man for so long that trust was long past and the only thing that remained was a deep hatred for the intruders that dared invade their sanctuary. After giving the prospector a small quantity of dry rations, floor, coffee, salt and sugar, the column left him standing near the small stream where they'd found him which was a tiny branch of the Green River.

Just before General Terry called a halt at 3:00 p.m., after a good day's march of 19 miles, two dispatch riders from the steamer Far West caught up with the regiment carrying military communications and mail. The mail however, would have to wait until a decent camp was set up.

The location Terry had selected could not have been better. As a matter of fact the site was the best-to-date that the troopers and civilians had experienced, with a goodly amount of wood available, plenty of excellent grazing grass and the South Big Heart River for cold sweet water. For better protection a medium sized hill was chosen for the campsite and troopers were ordered to throw up earthen breastworks as a defensive measure.

Yesterday's first contact with hostile Indian's was not lost on General Terry and his decision to be overly prepared than not was carried out by soldiers striped to the waist welding pickax and shovel. Naturally, this labor was thought to be totally unnecessary by the cavalrymen who went about their work with the normal cussing and bitching that soldiers from the days of Christ have done when it comes to real work. The infantrymen, on the other hand worked more quickly and efficiently with their digging, and with less grumbling, since scooping out little warrens and piling dirt for parapets was something this arm of the army was more accustomed to doing.

While the soldier dug holes and made earthen walls, the regimental Sergeant Major supervised three enlisted men from the Quartermasters Corps in the issuance of rations. Company and Troop First Sergeants came to the wagons transporting rations and along with their fatigue detail of two or three privates waited their turn for their unit's food.

It was going to be bean night and it wasn't long before roaring camp fires doted the hill with covered cast iron cauldrons boiling away on steel spit rods. Designated cooks fussed around their pots adding their own little extras to spice up the beans and salted fat back such as with wild onions. Extra buckets of water from the river stood ready to be added when the beans boiled down, for woe be it to the man doing the cooking if he were to scorch or burn the evenings meal. The more imaginative or talented cook would bake up a batch of Indian corn cakes in large cast iron skillets or on flat rocks. Those troopers whose mess cook had less culinary aptitudes would have to get by with soaking hardtack in their beans if they desired some type of bread with their meal.

After the breastworks were dug all troops not assigned to some other fatigue duty were allowed to bathe in the icy cold water of the South Big Heart River at the bottom of the hill. Most took advantage of this opportunity to get the days trail dust and sweaty labor grime off their bodies and soon a section of the river looked like a kids swimming hole with naked men splashing in the cold water. The more sportsmen of the regiment were soon seen upstream from the bathers with handmade fishing poles angling for the abundant fish swimming the river; their catches to be made a part of their grub for the night.

General Custer and brother Tom came loping slowly into camp in the late afternoon their horses moving slowly because of the huge elk George bagged. Tom Custer had draped across his saddle horn a ninety pound Bobcat he had shot at a range of 200 yards which was good marksmanship in any mans army.

George Custer liked having his kinfolk near him and though Captain Tom Custer was on the rolls as a troop commander he was in all actuality an unofficial member of his brothers staff. The older Custer ordered that Tom, Boston "Bos" and "Autie" Reed tent near him and these two brothers and nephew naturally got into the habit of spending some time each evening with the "general. More often than not Custer's brother-in-law Lieutenant James Calhoun would be a part of the family gathering. But not tonight. After a shared supper of elk steaks the four men enjoyed one another's company after it got dark. The large command tent was warm from the nights chill with two large kerosene oil lantern lamps burning that hung on tent poles. The lamps reflectors cast a bright yellowish-white light and a spiral of black smoke curled upward from both lanterns caused by their wicks being raised high to offer better illumination. Since George was the only one among the four that received mail today he shared his letter from Libbie by reading it aloud: *"My own darling swan: I dreamed of you as I knew I would. Your safety is ever in my mind as it should be. My thoughts, my dreams, my prayers, are all for you. But tell Tom, Bos and Autie Reed that they are not forgotten and I know you look out for their welfare, as you should do your own. The servants are doing very well........we are raising chickens. We have forty-three. So many cats about the garrison keep the rats away. The weather is very hot, but the nights are cool. The lights about hills and valleys are exquisite. The river now is too high for sandbars to be seen. About a hundred men with John Stevenson in command have gone to the Black Hills. Nearly twenty-five teams have passed by. Carter has returned and is chief trumpeter. He really sounds the calls beautifully. But his long-drawn notes make me heartsick. I do not wish to be reminded of the Cavalry. God bless and keep my darling. Ever you're own Libbie. P.S. Dearest Bo--- please extend my kind wishes to young Billy Low. I am ever so grateful you took him with you."*

There was a long moment of silence after George Custer finished reading the letter from his wife, then Tom Custer spoke up. "Truly a sweet letter from a truly remarkable lady."

General Custer looked sharply at his brother to see if there was any hidden meaning coupled with this short statement. George well remembered the rumors that came to him the summer of 1867 that brother Tom was paying just a little too much attention to Libbie, which resulted in an unauthorized cross country dash to Fort Riley to deal with his family. This fit of jealousy caused him the embarrassment of a court-martial, which dragged on until the winter before it was cleared up.

The Custer's nephew, Harry Armstrong "Autie" Reed caused the irksome memory to be erased from his beloved uncle's mind, whom he was named after, by saying, "Who is this Billy Low, dear Aunt Libbie speaks of?"

Boston "Bos" Custer, serving as a civilian forager for his brother, answered Autie Reed's question with a dazzling smile on his handsome face. "He's the officer in charge of the Gatling gun battalion. Your Aunt Libbie talked your uncle into allowing these pop guns to tag along with us."

George got red in the face at his brothers remark as Autie Reed offered a puzzled "Oh!" Then went on to say, "I was most amazed at seeing the guns fire yesterday. They are really something to watch and I'm not ashamed to admit they rather terrified me."

The teenager's off-hand remark was met with a quick second or so of silence but he had effectively broken the ice of a tense moment when his three uncles gushed forth a spate of laughter. "What's so funny?" the youngster pouted.

"My dear boy," his Uncle George said, "They are intended to be terrifying, but not for our side, rather for the enemy in which they are fired on."

Before the young man could further explain his comment, Tom Custer interjected with a question of his own, directed to his older brother. "What about the Gatling's general----are you going to keep them with us past the Yellowstone?"

The other two brothers and Custer's nephew stared at the general while he took a long interval of contemplation to form an answer. "I want the three of you to know that what I say in no way reflects any indecision or weakness on my part but by all that's mighty from the grace of our dear Lord---------I have just not made up my mind yet!"

BOSTON CUSTER, BROTHER

Sickly, 25-year-old Boston joined the expedition, partly for the benefit of outdoor life, as a civilian forage master.

CAPTAIN THOMAS CUSTER, BROTHER

Twice a Medal of Honor winner in the Civil War, Tom led Troop C at Little Bighorn and fell near his brother.

HENRY ARMSTRONG REED, NEPHEW

George Custer's favorite nephew, 18-year-old civilian Autie rode with the 7th Cavalry as his ill-fated uncle's guest.

LIEUTENANT JAMES CALHOUN, BROTHER-IN-LAW

Calhoun led the 7th's L Troop to its destruction. He died on a rise several hundred yards from Custer's final position.

Chapter 11

Charismatic and forceful principal chief of the Ogallala's Sioux Crazy Horse sat cross-legged next to Sitting Bull, chief medicine man and recognized leader of the Uncapapas Sioux. The two red men were seated at the place of honor among a surrounding of lesser chief's in a large circle that made up the governing council for the huge gathering of tribes. Dully-reflected flickering fingers of firelight danced teasingly off a myriad of teepees boarding the circle from a roaring log fire crackling in the center of the oval. The fire created eerie moving shadows that reached back many yards to brush the silent faces of young and old women peering out of the flaps of their homes, staring forlornly towards the bright light with its orange cone of sparks reaching to the heavens. All of the Sioux and Cheyenne's squaws and maidens knew something very important was taking place because rarely did a council meet this late at night. The females also knew they would have to wait without making any noise until their men came to them to explain what had taken place.

Flanked on either side of Crazy Horse and Sitting Bull, whose Indian name actually translated to Buffalo Bull Sitting Down, was several other important chiefs. Old Bear, Chief of an impoverished band of Sioux, Lame Deer, Chief of the Minneconjou Sioux, Dirty Moccasins, the warrior chief of the Cheyenne's, Two Moons, a Sioux Humkpapa Chief, Low Dog; Ogallala Sioux Chief, Charcoal Bear; Chief medicine man of the northern Cheyenne's and the great warrior Hunkpapa Sioux chieftain Rain-in-the-face,

Completing the circle of seated Indians were more than seventy of the various tribes most respected warrior leaders and standing behind all those that sat cross-legged around the fire was a throng five rows deep of other warriors and young bucks.

The hastily formed council had been called less than an hour before after four exhausted riders had limped into the village camp on their worn out ponies. These warriors had ridden hard for over 150 miles, traversing extremely difficult terrain, to bring news of what they had seen. They had completed this feat of travel in just less than 48 hours.

Leader of the scout warriors was a dark round-faced Hunkpapa Sioux who had magnificent deep-set hooded eyes Crow King. Shortly after the sturdy built Crow King had given his chief, Rain-in-the-face a quick version of what his scouting band had discovered Rain-in-the-face raised the cry in demand of a council gathering so all could hear what his man had to say.

Now Crow King, with his wide, thick lips moving slowly, stood between the roaring fire and the group of sitting chief's, telling his story, with all the Indian's listening intently.

"..........and besides the soldiers that walk were many pony soldiers that I would say is as large as a small herd of buffalo. There are great many wagons with a large number of horses and mules. I viewed many low class scum of the white man, mostly Arikara but also dirty Absaroka Crow filth that help the white man find his way. Big Nose and Flying Hawk were almost caught in a narrow gully below a formation of tall buttes where the rest of our party was located observing the distant dust cloud which we later found to be the many soldiers traveling towards the falling sun. Two white men and two Corn Indians hunting game came upon Big Nose and Flying Hawk and they had to flee for their lives." Crow King paused for a moment in his less than eloquent sequential description as if he wanted to make sure everyone was listening to him. In a strange gesture he lifted both his large hands behind the single feather in his long blue-black hair at the back of his head and poised as such spoke again in his deep voice. "The white man that flushed my warriors as if they were nesting quail had the short golden locks of the yellow haired white warrior the Crow call Morning Star that we know as the Creeping Panther."

A rumbling mummer was heard from the ranks of Indians.

Sitting Bull, his hatchet hewed face framed by two long ornately festooned braids, which came to his lap, wanted to make sure he understood what the Hunkpapa had said. "Are you telling this council Crow King that the white man you saw is Custer?"

"Yes, mighty wise and great one, it was Yellow Hair-----Custer, the Creeping Panther...but I have more to tell which you have interfered with my doing so."

"There was no disrespect intended Crow King when I asked you this question. My old ears fail me some time and I sought assurance regarding what it was you had said. Please brave warrior continue on with what you have to tell us."

Nodding his head in a civil manner to the old medicine man, Crow King lowered his hands and continued talking. "Instead of running away as I'm sure the white men thought we would do, I decided to trail them back to their camp. One of the Corn Indians had went ahead to warn the soldiers of having seen us which gave me the direction of their camp and using the back side of the long string of bluffs to hide our movement the eight of us found the soldiers in their camp before the sun went down over the mountains. At first I was amazed, as I'm sure the other warriors were also, that all of the soldiers were formed in a giant arc in a half-circle around these three wagon wheel guns that go boom the white men use to hurl large balls of iron. We were looking right down on these wagon guns from high on a ridge but when they shot all at the same time they were not boom guns at all." Crow King again paused while he sought words to describe the awe-inspiring spectacle he had witnessed. "They started firing very rapidly," he said shooting out both his hands in a back and forth jabbing movement in front of his body. "And it was like watching all the arrows in a quiver being launched at one time, though the barbs of steel were not arrows but bullets like we fire from our rifles. These thunder machines threw bolts of lighting faster than a hundred braves can launch their war spears and only did so for a short time. But in the time it takes to wade a small stream the thunder machines ruined a cactus grove, ripping it down to its roots, leaving not one standing and causing them to burn with a bright blue light that was frightful to watch. I say to all that we must avoid Custer and his thunder sticks, for they are evil medicine that will cause us much harm if we were to come into contact with them."

There ensued a full minute of silence while chiefs and warriors thought over what Crow King had told them.

Finally, Rain-in-the-face stood, then went to stand next to his brave. Scanning the onlookers with his expressive eyes, he spoke. "We all know what a great warrior Crow King is. He has eaten the hearts of many of his enemy and has no fear of the white man or the detested Corn Indians and those tribal allies who fight with them against us. I have never known of him to brag falsely or to exaggerate his exploits. Therefore, I say unto you at this council that what he has told us this night is the truth of what his eyes have seen as well of what have been witnessed by seven other of my warriors. We must take steps to heed his warning and stay away from this thunder stick the white eyes have brought to slay us."

Lame Deer spoke from the ground. "It was with feelings of dread that my large band of Minneconjou made this pilgrimage to the camp of the great Sitting Bull. My belief was that our assembling with our brothers would create such strength in numbers that the white man soldiers would be afraid to attack us. Is this not so, even with this terrible thunder stick you speak of?"

Rain-in-the-face thought over the question for a long moment before answering. "The famous and respected Lame Deer is right in what he says that the combined strength of our many camps will put fear into the black hearts of our enemies. But even the bravest of warriors cannot fight a devil that spits out death like a swarm of locust crawling a grazing field."

Numerically, the Uncpapas Sioux had the greatest number of warriors than all the other tribes. They were also considered the most fiercest fighters in battle and the most belligerent in their feeling towards the white man. The great spiritual leader of this band Sitting Bull was well known by the white man as well as the red man in so far as his values were concerned in maintaining the civilization of his people and their traditional way of life. The simple way he went about doing this for his followers was to keep away from the white man. He had refused all help offered by Indian agencies and had never broken a treaty with the white eyes due to the fundamental reason he had never signed one. Therefore, when he stood to talk, every ear strained to hear what this wise man would have to say. "We now know we have soldiers coming at us from the east and they have this terrible thunder stick that Crow King speaks of. There is also a large hoard of soldiers that have been reported marching from the south. If they too have these thunder sticks I know not. My heart tells me that sooner or later we will have to fight these soldiers and I believe it will be a battle for our very existence. Of our right to be able to walk this land, to hunt and to live so we can give honor to the great spirits that look over all of us as our forefathers have done before us But as it is, I agree with what Rain-in-the-face and Crow King have said that we must do. We will go north past the Yellowstone to try and avoid these soldiers and their thunder sticks and I say that we should do this right away."

There was no argument from the others about Sitting Bull backing the proposal of retreat away from the hated blue-shirts. As the council meeting broke up and warriors walked quickly to their tepees to tell their women to start packing for tomorrows move, Crazy Horse had a last word with Sitting Bull. "You were right when you spoke of what your heart was telling you. It will not be long that we will find ourselves fighting the white man again."

Sitting Bull paused from moving away from the fire. He looked deeply into Crazy Horses dark, piercing eyes as he spoke. "Yes young warrior chief, I fear that is correct. And much blood will stain the earth of both white men and red men. It is good Crow King left scouts behind to keep watch on Custer's movements. This may give us the opportunity to choose the time and place of the great battle the two of us know will surely happen as it is written on the winds by the spirits."

* * * * *

General George Custer became distracted from the letter he was writing his dear Libbie when the first mournful notes of Taps sounded. The drooping walrus-mustached cavalryman sat up straight on his campstool and stared blankly towards the direction from which the slow dirge like wail was coming from. With the ink pen frozen stiffly between his fingers his mind went back in time a dozen years ago and for a moment he reflected on the great battles he'd participated in that had brought him so much glory and adoration. The first time he had heard, what was then, a new bugle call telling soldiers it was time for them to be in bed had been at the Rappahannock the winter of 1863, and he remembered how apt he thought the sad melody was to put men to sleep. When the last long note faded Custer continued to stare off at nothing, still lost in his own thoughts, until a pesky mosquito annoyed him with its incessant buzzing and he dispatched the insect with one of his gloves when it dared to land on his pen hand. With a grunt he looked down at the letter he had been writing and picked up the heavy paper and began reading what he had written: *"My Darling--I know you will forgive your Bo for this being such a short note. Please do not be anxious about me. You would be most surprised how I heed your warnings to be careful and to take care of myself. This I do cheerfully with full knowledge my little buttercup is awaiting my return with a beating heart of all her love she can muster. Oh how empty my bed seems as I yearn for my sweetest of dreams. I have my hands full trying to be the best regimental commander I can possibly be plus assuming much of the responsibility of directing the entire column at the beseeching of Genl. Terry. As I scribble this note so it will go out in the morrows mail to Ft Lincoln, a part of my mind is on the preparations I must make before this lonely night is over to make sure my scouts leave before daybreak to blaze the advance for the van. The command camped tonight next to a feeder stream of the southern tributary of the Heart River. I have marked my map Duck Creek, the name my men have given the little stream because of a flock of migrating Mallard's taking refuge upstream from where we bivouac. The pioneers were forced to build another bridge today but luckily it was accomplished with our portable pontoons and we did not experience an undo delay. Completed 19 miles today and it shan't be long that we will be marching through the Little Missouri Bad Lands. I had to order two mules killed because they were diseased and the only other item of interest is we are plagued with tens of thousands of locusts that is raising thunderation with our grazing. Oh, before I forget--Your Bo arranged for young Lt. L. to demonstrate the utility of his btry two nights ago. He did a good job. I learned his close friends call him Bucky. I will have to remember that. I...*" The letter stopped and Custer pondered on what he had about been ready to write but whatever it had been the thought escaped him. It also obviously escaped his attention that his burden of command had nothing to do with General Terry's "beseeching" or was it he that arranged for Low's demonstration. He fiddled with his nib pen for a few seconds before dipping the instrument back into the ink well. *"Thought about you dearest and how lonely it must be for you when the trumpeter played Taps a couple of minutes ago..........."*

Sitting Bull
(Note: There is no known picture of Crazy Horse)

Chapter 12

In The Hilly Butte Area 35 Miles East of the Little Missouri River,
Montana Territory
3:00 p.m., Friday, May 26, 1876

Fast-As-The-Pony-Rides and his companion Still Water gazed down into
the valley below them at the activity that was going on. The two scouts who
had remained to shadow the 7th Cavalry were laying belly flat on top of a
huge rock that had fallen onto the ledge of the tall butte they were occupying
when the earth had trembled hundreds of years before. Their ponies were at
the reverse base of the butte being attended by their two comrades who had
also stayed behind when Crow King had decided to find Chief Rain-in-the-
Face to tell their leader of their discovery.

Fast-As-The-Pony-Rides muttered his thoughts in his harsh guttural tone
of voice. "It looks as if the white eyes are making a camp. Can this be true?
They have only traveled but for a short time."

Still Water grunted before making a reply. "When it comes to the way of
white men I am surprised at nothing they do." Still Water shifted his bronze,
muscular body a little and gazed upwards towards the bright sun. "It is only
a little past the full sun overhead in the sky but I agree with you, they are
making camp."

"Our squaws, children and lame old men walk further in half the time,"
Fast-As-The-Pony-Rides snorted.

"Perhaps the locust scared them," chuckled Still Water.

Fast-As-The-Pony-Rides joined his friend in a low chuckle.

Custer's troopers were not scared of the millions of tiny locusts that
covered the grass but the young grasshoppers certainly had been annoying
since the start of the morning's march, which commenced at 6:00 a.m. It had
been unavoidable for horse or man to take a single step without stepping on
dozens of the pesky insects.

Enjoying having amused his companion, Still Water offered another
observation. "And did you notice when they traveled through the heavy
cactus that Yellow Hair made some of his soldiers put their pack of dogs into
those wagons with the crosses of red painted on the white canvas. I could
hardly believe my eyes the blue shirt devils worry about walking their dogs
through cactus and ride them on wagons. And I've heard they do not eat
their dogs, can you imagine that?"

"I did not see any of them gather the locusts for food, so yes I can believe they don't eat their dogs, although Sitting Bull has told stories of them eating their ponies and mules."

"Ugh! I would have to be starving before I would eat a mule." The thought of eating must have made Still Water think of his own stomach and he reached into a little pouch that hung from his waist and took out a hunk of a greasy looking substance that had a rank odor about it. Gnawing on the blob he reached the bag over to the other Indian. "Would you like to have a little deer fat?"

Getting a whiff of the half-spoiled meat, Fast-As-The-Pony-Rides declined his friend's offer.

"Look, they are digging ditches to fight from," Fast-As-The-Pony-Rides said with a laugh.

"I wonder who they think are going to attack them?"

"I would be willing to get a few coup tonight as the soldiers lie in their little white teepees but we promised Crow King to keep out of sight and not let the soldiers see us."

Still Water grunted. "Yes, it would be easy to sneak upon the blue shirt solders camp but it is best to heed Crow King and keep our eyes on them. In two suns from now we will send back either Black Face or Bright Sun to tell Rain-in-the-Face of Yellow Hair's progress."

"That is a good thought Still Water, but what will we do when there is no one remaining to send?"

"When I send you old and faithful friend you will tell Rain-in-the-Face to let you return with more scout braves and we will do it all over again."

"Ah...you have always been the wise one, even when we were children together. Yes that will work nicely, but just remember to stay hidden as I do not want to come back to find your scalp hanging from one of their wagons."

Still Water snorted again, the wide mouth on his flat face a narrow slit of disdain. "No white squaw has give birth to a blue shirt yet that can take this scalp." And he patted his round head with its long main of black hair that had a single eagle's feather embedded in it.

Fast-As-The-Pony-Rides was silent for a long moment in quiet reflection, thinking about what his boyhood friend had said while staring down on the enemy camp. Then turning his head back to his comrade he spoke in a husky tone of voice. "It is the way I feel too Still Water; no white man will take my scalp, nor will they ever take me as a prisoner like they did Rain-in-the-Face."

"Yes I remember----before the snows of last winter. It was Yellow

Hair's brother that rides beside him as a soldier that tricked Rain-in-the-Face at a trading post, then tied his hands and took him to the white man fort they named after their great chief. Rain-in-the-Face spoke at a powwow of his experience. He said the white soldiers treated him better than the Ree Corn Indians or the Crow. But still he was placed in a small log box and held there for four full moons until breaking away from the box with two white men of all things."

"I did not know that. About the white men I mean. They helped him escape?"

Nodding his head Still Water answered, "Yes two white men that are not soldiers who were also prisoners in the log box. They worked together with Rain-in-the-Face and dug under the logs to flee from the soldiers. As I said, the ways of the white man are very strange and nothing they do or say surprises me. Rain-in-the-Face owed his life to the two white men and he gave them his protection in return when they traveled with him to the Black Hills to hide. He even showed them streams where the yellow metal could be found before leaving them. But that was little more than showing his gratitude and he hates the white man more than he ever did and has vowed he will one day eat the heart of Yellow Hair's brother."

The two Indians remained silent for several minutes as they kept their eyes on the camp below them. The weather was hot and dry, this being the first day the two scouts had experienced any real heat during the day since monitoring the soldiers for the past five days. But they considered the beating rays of the sun a luxury; warming winter aching bones that had grown stiff from inactivity.

Fast-As-The-Pony-Rides stirred a little, his buckskins making a soft scraping noise on the flat rock surface. "What is it they are doing now?"

Still Water understood why Fast-As-The-Pony-Rides had asked the question. The soldiers had been waving their hands around their faces for the past ten minutes and many of them slapped at their heads with the straw hats they wore. Other soldiers who were bare back looked as if they were having fits, scratching at their bodies. While Still Water gazed at the soldiers' antics he noted four different groups of them feeding grass and cactus to roaring fires which were blazing upwind from the camp. Huge billows of smudgy white smoke began drifting slowly towards the camp, and it came to Still Water what the blue shirts were doing.

With a short laugh, Still Water, said. "It is the bug that bites which can make you sick with fever that is plaguing them. They must be swarmed with the little black things. See how they are causing their fires to smolder so they make much smoke? They are trying to drive away the biting insects."

"Ah I see. I do believe you are correct Still Water. We are fortunate to be so high that the mosquitoes do not annoy us."

All of a sudden, the two Indians heard a rattling, clicking sound behind them. Both looked quickly to their rear and saw that a very big rattlesnake was now sharing the flat rock. Fast-As-The-Pony-Rides spoke softly: "A great warrior friend has decided to join us to also enjoy the sun."

The Indians voice, even though uttered in a low tone, caused the rattler to open its wide jaws and flick its long split veed tongue between two large hanging fangs and let loose with another series of clacking rattles from its coiled tail. Picking up a loose stone Still Water said, "Perhaps he was agreeing with you that it is nice up here without the fever bugs bothering us." And he heaved the stone with accurate aim that hit the snake's head with a resounding blow, killing it instantly. Crawling back to fetch the rattlesnake he cut off the reptile's head with his hunting knife he kept in a goat-hide sheathe, then slit its stomach from neck to tail. After gutting the six-foot long snake and peeling its outer skin, Still Water laid the white remains on the flat rock to sun dry and bake. Returning to Fast-As-The-Pony-Rides, who had been watching his preparations with the snake, Still Water said. "We will eat good tonight."

Before Fast-As-The-Pony-Rides could make a reply a cawing sound came from the downward side of the tall butte. Twice more the odd, bird like tone was given causing Still Water to smile. "Bright Sun and Black Face wants to watch the soldiers for awhile. I will leave half of our warrior friend for them and you and I will rest in the shadow of the bluff and tend the ponies."

"You will take the snakes rattles with you won't you Still Water?"

"Oh yes. They are fine rattles and surely a good omen sent by the great spirits from one warrior to another. I will fashion a leg bracelet to wear into battle. This is good medicine and will bring me much luck."

"As good of a fighter as you are Still Water you don't require luck."

Smiling at his friend, Still Water said, "That is kind of you to say, but we will need much luck if we have to face those thunder sticks we saw the blue shirts fire three suns ago. I will share my luck with you old friend." And he broke off half the horny joints and handed them to Fast-As-The-Pony-Rides.

Chapter 13

Stream Head of Davis Creek, Dakota Territory
6:30 p.m., Saturday, May 27, 1876

Private William E. Morris, of Troop M commanded by Captain Thomas Fench, swatted a mosquito with his General Ulysses Grant hat as he sat cross-legged on the ground trying to enjoy an after supper smoke with his beat up old pipe. Fanning his face with the low crowned Navy straw hat, which was permitted to be worn in the field, Billy Morris noted that his head cover was on the verge of falling completely apart. He idly picked at a jutting piece of woven straw coming out from under the sweat stained blue-black ribbon going around the bottom crown, which was a mistake. Without meaning to do so he pulled a long sliver of dirty yellow straw out of the hat, causing the crown to sag on one side. "Dag burn it all! I might as well taken a fifty cent piece and tossed it out on the trail. Now I've got to get to the sutlers wagon and buy me a new one sure 'nough."

His buddy, and fellow Company M trooper, Private William C. Slaper, of Cincinnati, Ohio, had not been paying attention to what Morris was doing and said. "What'cha say Billy?"

"Oh it's my dag burn hat. I fiddled with it and now it's fallen apart."

Billy Slaper smiled at his friend that made his big ears on his square head stick out even more. The young man's high cheek bones made his deep set blue eyes appear to sink back under his broad forehead when he smiled. "Not much to spend your money on out here anyway Billy since the gen'ral got us paid in the field. I got nigh on forty-five dollars stashed an' suspect you got 'bout the same since we both had four months pay a' coming to us."

Morris grunted, taking his pipe from his mouth and emitting a thin stream of bluish-white smoke as he spoke. "Them card sharkies got a goodly amount of my back pay this past week."

"Ya can't say I didn't warn you to stay away from those three-card-monte games."

The only reply Slaper got was another grunt from his buddy who began sucking nosily on his pipe.

The two Billy's had become quick pals not quite a year ago when both had traveled to Jefferson Barracks, St. Louis, Missouri on the same train to commence their six weeks recruit training, after both having enlisted in Cincinnati. Not only did they share the same first names, they also had other things in common, such as both being twenty-one years old and being raised in small farm villages. Billy Slaper was born in Sharonville, Ohio, a small burg thirty-five miles north of Cincinnati, to where his family eventually moved. In early September 1875, Slaper was without a job and out of prospects of getting one. The twenty year old observed a sign **Men Wanted** in front the downtown Cincinnati U. S. Army Recruiting Station and reluctantly climbed the long flight of stairs to the second floor office, about half hoping he would be rejected. Out of ten applicants that day only two were accepted as being physically and mentally qualified to take the oath to serve Uncle Sam for the grand sum of $13. per month. He was one of them and Billy Morris was the other one. Much the same, Billy Morris was born and raised on a small farm outside of Connersville, Indiana, a small farming community fifty miles to the east of Cincinnati. Slightly older by two months than his buddy Morris wanted to escape the dreary life-style he was living and ventured to the large city on the Ohio River to seek fame and fortune. Instead, he found worse poverty than he'd left behind on the Indiana farm and three months later, half starved, he too raised his right hand and swore allegiance to defend the United States and to obey those officers and non-commissioned officers over him. The wiry, round faced lad who was trying to grow a mustache without much success, had deep blue eyes like his buddy Billy Slaper, whom he was very fond of. Usually where you saw one of the two young men, you saw the other. Their sergeant, First Sergeant Timothy O'Hara, a robust, squinty eyed, tobacco chewing Irishman with twenty years of service, had got to calling the boys "Billy One" and "Billy Two," instead of using their last names like he did with the rest of the privates under him. The nick-names caught on and everyone, including Captain French, used the Billy one or two names. While both of the young men were equally thin, Private Morris, being the older by a couple of month, was also several inches taller, being around six feet, where Private Slaper stood at five feet, eight inches. Therefore, he was known as Billy One.

Billy One knocked the burnt ashes from his pipe out on the ground using the heel of his hand and while doing so glanced across to his buddy who was staring off in space, chewing on a long stem of reed weed. "What'cha trying to do, get some vegetable taste a'gnaw'en on that piece of grass?"

Billy Slaper chuckled without saying anything.

"I'm so sick and tired of beef and bacon that I could scream! Boy, what I'd give for a lovely plate filled up with new grown carrots, and some corn-on-the-cob an...and some fresh snap beans," he trailed off with a dreamy look on his round face.

"We has some beans the other night," observed Billy Two.

"Humph! Taint the same, that's for dang sure."

"Well that boiled beef we had this evening was tolerable."

"Boiled beef, braised beef, fried beef, roast beef, it's all the same...beef, beef, beef, day end and day out. "Cept of course the constant ration of bacon they ration us for breakfast. Don't reckon the Army every heard of some good old fashioned griddle cakes out in the field, with some hot maple syrupy and thick butter to put of 'em. Hmmm, hmm. Now that's good eat'en."

"I still say those beef chunks Aspinwall fixed up this evening was right tasty. Some of the other company cooks just let it boil then serve it up, but old Aspinwall thickened his up with flour which made a fine gravy."

"Yeah, well like you said it was tolerable but I miss my vegetables."

The two remained quiet for a minute or so until Billy Slaper spoke up. "We did a right smart bit of marching today. Heard Captain French telling that Lieutenant Low who commands them Gatling guns that we did nigh on eighteen miles. After that rain shower we had last night I thought maybe it'd slow us down but it shore didn't."

Picking up the new theme of conversation, Morris offered his observation. "I don't suspect old Custer was too happy 'bout the twelve miles we done yesterday but with those darn locust and a'hav'en to go through that cactus forest, it shore 'nough slowed us down. Dang heat yesterday and today both was a hot kettle which I heer is sort of rare in June in this part of the country. But maybe it'll cool down some tomorrow. Tis a shame the water's starting to show alkali but I suppose that can't be helped now we're in the middle of the Bad Lands. Well, not exactly the middle but far enough in to make a difference anyway. We're just darned lucky that we've got a good supply of new growing grass 'round us to take care of the ponies and cattle."

"You're right there Billy," Private Slaper said in agreement, "But I think we'd done even better today if'n them nutty scouting parties they sent out wouldn't have ran all over the countryside trying to locate General Stanley's old trail. Jus a good thing we got old Lonesome Charlie Reynolds along that's been this way before and for the most part remembers the right way to take us."

"You said something 'while ago 'bout that Lieutenant Low. What did you think 'bout that demonstration he put on the other afternoon? That was really som'thing to see sure 'nough."

Billy Slaper's face took on a solemn look as he was quiet for several seconds before answering. "I told you 'bout my father gett'en killed the first year of the war, an' so did my uncle, my mother's brother, an' a cousin plus my mother's brother-in-law. When I saw those Gatlings chewing up that sage brush and cactus, the first thing I thought about was my father and other relatives that got kilt. To this day I don't know how it was for them and I often wondered how my father died as no one ever wrote us about it other than a letter from some company adjutant saying he'd got kilt during a skirmish near Warwick Court House, Virginia. Didn't say if he got shot or blowed to smithereens or how it happened, just that Pa was dead. But if they died even coming close to the way those bullets tore up everything in sight, then I don't want to see men die that way."

"But Billy Two," Morris almost yelled in an aspirated tone of breath. "Those guns are going to be used against savage Injun's and that's not the same as when your daddy got kilt."

"What you say may be so, but just the same I'm not tak'en no big hanker'en on what we're sitt'en out to do."

"You ain't scared are ya?" Billy Morris exclaimed.

"I don't reckon I'm no more scare't than the next fellow an' I'll sure 'nough do my job when the time comes, but that don't mean I have to like it!" Slaper answered with conviction.

Offering his friend a toothy smile, Morris said. "You had me worried there for a second, I thought maybe you'd done gone an' got a yellow streak but I guess I can see it your way that you don't have to like it just as long as we get the job done. Now for me, I'm a'rar'en to go and I'm go'en ta get me an Injun scalp just as sure as you're sitting there and you just wait an' see if'n I don't make a purse outta it like some of the old veterans got."

"Well you ain't going to see me a'watch'en you make no purse you can bet on that. You just best make sure no Indian uses your pretty curly hair for his purse mak'en." Billy Slaper voiced.

Before Private Morris could make a retort, First Sergeant O'Hara came bustling up interrupting the two with his gruff voice. "Billy One lad--- you've got picket duty tonight so's you better get crack'en and prepare yerself. You'll be wanting to make sure yer carbine is clean and ready and take yer fifty rounds with you."

Getting to his feet Billy Morris spoke in a disgusted tone of voice. "I swear I just had picket three nights ago and pony watch the night before that. Are there only ten of us that gets put on your dang blasted guard roster?"

"Now lad, you watch yer tongue and don't get sassy with me or I'll have to bonk you one and that I promise you, you don't want to happen. When you get yerself ready report to Corporal Benton and he'll assign yer sector." The professional old soldier said in a menacing tone of voice.

No sooner had First Sergeant O'Hara admonished Private Morris, than the sound of musical instruments being tuned and warmed up came from the center of the encampment.

"What's the band doing," Billy Slaper asked to no one in particular

With a broad Irish grin First Sergeant O'Hara said. "They're go'en to serenade you in a minute or so Billy Two at the request of his honor the general himself bless his soul. Georgie Custer likes fine music as does meself and I'm sure we'll be a'hear'en some grand Irish tunes." As the NCO turned to leave, he looked over his shoulder at Private Morris. "See Billy One, I arranged it all for you so you'd have some grand ole band music to lullaby you while yer a'do'en yer sentinel duty a'protect'en all of us." With a horse laugh the crusty old sergeant ambled away.

"Hey that's great," Billy Slaper said to his buddy who was walking away to fetch his rifle. "I really enjoyed hearing them play a few tunes on the march today. But a full concert will make it seem like the fourth of July."

"Yeah--but if you hear any fireworks it'll be me shooting at a bunch of Injun's up in the hills that came down to watch the show." Billy One muttered resignedly.

* * * * *

Private William E. Morris, M Troop, 4th Battalion, Reno's Left Wing, would never know how close he came in making a correct estimate regarding the true facts of the situation.

Nestled in a large crack that split one of the hundreds of tall rock formations that dotted this part of the Bad Lands, and not more than 600 yards from the Davis Creek encampment, sat four stone faced Sioux with icy fixed stares looking down upon their hated enemy who were milling around like so many scattered ants.

* * * * *

The 15 member 7th Cavalry Band, supplemented by a mixed dozen buglers and trumpeter volunteers from the various troops, was nearer at being a drum and bugle corps than an outright band. However, even with all the brass horn instruments in attendance the assemblage managed to sound like a good military band.

With a booming clang of cymbals, coupled with the low, rattling rumble of snare drums, the 7th Cavalry Band commenced its evening concert with a stirring, brassy rendition of Francis Scott Key's Star Spangled Banner which was becoming recognized around the world as the National Anthem of the United States of America. Following a custom that was fast taking hold across the nation, officers and enlisted men as well as the large gathering of civilians, stood with their hats doffed once the patriotic song was identified. When the last note of the anthem faded a big cheer went up from the enlisted ranks with many soldiers tossing their hats up in the air. They hardly had time to settle down when the band struck up The Battle Hymn of The Republic which was just as popular, if not more so, than the Star Spangled Banner. Some men even sang along with the bands playing and as before, when it ended another roar of "hurrahs" was heard. Then the band settled down and began playing old time favorites and popular songs that most the soldiers dearly loved. The Blue Danube floated beautifully across the nearby Bad Lands as did The Mocking Bird and Artist's Life. More lively tunes were played too: When Johnny Comes Marching Home, Darling Clementine and Johnny Cracked Corn were well received with much foot stomping, hand clapping and singing along. Then the band subdued the crowd with a sentimental favorite After The Battle Mother, quickly followed by Danny Boy and I'll Take You Home Again Kathleen, then paused for a short break after playing the popular The Girl I Left Behind.

Up in the rock formation area Fast-As-The-Pony-Rides listened incredulously at the far reaching melodies that echoed off the walls of his hiding place.

Bright Face broke the almost trance like state of his fellow partisan when he spoke in an awed tone of voice. "Blue shirts have most strange war songs. I barely hear their tom-toms but the screeching of their horns very loud and very unusual."

Still Water also had something to say. "Strange yes but I find a soothing rhythm to a few of their chants that have a sad sound about them. They are like a warrior's death song that is sung by our women."

"What about the fast paced ones though," Black Face asked. "I feel my pulse quicken and it is upsetting to my ears yet it must be war songs as Bright Sun spoke of. I have never heard such music before."

Fast-As-The-Pony-Rides grunted. "It makes no difference my brothers. Before too many Moons our children will be playing with the White eyes music makers like they are toys that we have carved from hollow reeds."

The watching Hunkpapa's resumed their silent observation without anything else being said.

The band played until shortly after 8:00 p.m. The sweet strains of Swanee River and the lively tune Camp Town Races were among the last four songs rendered. But what got everyone's attention was the next to the last song which General Terry himself had personally requested. When the first notes of Dixie lifted into the air, at first there was a stunned silence, then the southern boys and the old rebel soldiers now serving in the blue Army started cheering. Before long cheers were taken up by the remainder of the regiment who hooted and howled the rebel yell as loud and enthusiastically as their former enemy

General Terry turned in his camp chair to Custer who was sitting to his right and the mild mannered general officer said. "If old Abe Lincoln can request that song after hearing of Lee's surrender, there's nary a reason I cannot do the same."

George Custer leaned over a little toward his commander to make a remark of his own. "It's always been one of my favorites. Marvelous war song with bully spirit to motivate men's morale. See how well the men like it."

Private Billy Morris begrudgingly admitted to himself it was the best night he had ever stood picket duty. His post was on the outer fringe of the western perimeter near the creek and he'd found himself tapping his foot inside the freshly dug trench line he was in. Billy had also sang along with a few of the songs the band played and when he fiddled around with his tobacco pouch to fill his pipe he heard other nearby sentries doing the same. And when the band ended its performance with a long rendition of Garry Owen, the regiments' personal battle song, a chill of pride went up his back and he unconsciously stiffened his body to a posture of attention.

Chapter 14

The Twisting Davis Creek, Dakota Territory
4:45 a.m., Sunday, May 28, 1876

General Terry's Staff Chaplain, an Episcopal prelate and Army Major, Cyrus Billingham, was somewhat disgruntled he would not be allowed to hold services that morning.

The general, a Methodist by birth, the same as Custer, held no qualms against Episcopalians, other than finding their ritual of intoned prayers, chanting and processions rather boring; but he treated his chaplain with the utmost respect. He even called his chaplain Bishop that seemed to please the short, squat, dour-faced major who wore small octagon eyeglasses. When Chaplain Billingham heard the unit was to move at dawn he rushed to Terry's tent a little before 4:30 a.m. requesting permission for Terry's Bugler to sound Church Call at 5:00 a.m. The normally kind-hearted, easy going, general officer was tersely abrupt. "Bishop, I am conducting a military expedition and only acquiesced to your participation on the campaign because of your incessant nagging to be allowed to come along. I advised you from the onset I would not condone the slightest interference and thought you understood my rational for such a decision. No---you may not hold services this morning but I will see to it that you may do so this evening."

So the good chaplain waddled back to the tent he shared with Doctor H. R. Porter, one of the three civilian surgeon's accompanying the regiment. Major Billingham's feelings had been hurt from the general's snap dismissal but of more concern which bothered him worse was the general's last words which carried a warning ultimatum. While scurrying around stowing his gear for the days march General Terry's final admonishment still rang in his large oversized ears: "And when you conduct your services this evening I expect you to strictly follow the Manual for Religious Ceremonies and adhere totally to the nondenominational theology therein. If you practice this order a few times you may find you will be blessed with a larger congregation."

General Terry had touched upon a sensitive subject within the Army's fledgling Chaplaincy Corps that had mushroomed into prominence during the Civil War. The difficulties of clergymen not to stress the ideologies of their particular sects religious beliefs and tenets was almost an insurmountable obstacle when dealing with a military that loosely demanded a generic approach to the holy prostration for their personnel.. At the same time, military chaplain's had their work cut out for them. The majority of their "flock" was a profane, vulgar, whisky guzzling, tobacco using, gambling, and harlot carousing lot with little education or sensibilities. While most professed a strong belief and fear of the Almighty, their actions lacked the piety of devoutness that their words suggested. This was especially true among the large enlisted group of Irish Catholics that made up a goodly percentage of the 7th Cavalry and who were the most robust sinners of all the many ethnic assortment represented. When it came to the drinking of hard spirits and drunkenness, they were without peer. The Catholic soldiers were also the most vocal when it came to praising God, motherhood and the soldierly qualities of General George Armstrong Custer. They also comprised the nucleus of the non-commissioned officer leadership of the entire U. S. Army and no one, including the Chaplain Corps, would ever offer a disparaging remark about their fighting spirit and ability to face battle in a cheerful, professional manner.

A large percentage of the Officer Corps, who were ordained gentlemen by the sweeping hand of Congress, were only about one step above the continence level of those they led. It was near legendary that convivial drinking was expected in the various garrisons that dotted the country. How else would a young officer get to know his commander on a social basis if he didn't partake of the camaraderie offered in the form of an open bottle in the closed officer's messes, field headquarters tents or constant soirees held to thwart garrison boredom? Of course there were some that had the moral strength to be abstainers, both in the enlisted ranks as well as the Officer's Corps.

General George Custer fit that mold of character and he would not touch an intoxicant to his lips. That is not to say he didn't try his hand at drinking but he had learned at an early age that he was constitutionally unable to hold his liquor. This had came about when he was home at Monroe, Michigan on convalesce sick furlough during 1861, after his promotion to captain, having been cited for bravery at Bull Run. Custer met with several of his old school chums in a back room of a store in sort of an impromptu reunion. Applejack flowed freely and Custer soon found himself stupefied. He was barley able to stagger home and once there passed out. When Custer awoke from his stupor he found his step-sister Ann kneeling next to his bed praying fervently her brother would be "delivered from the evil clutches of Demon Rum." No doubt seeing his sister's fervent behavior had an influence but more so was his own mind that wouldn't tolerate the idea of losing control of his mental and physical faculties. He never again touched intoxicants. Yet, Custer was never overly prudish in his abstention, other than occasionally counseling his brother Tom, who drank his fair share, about the evils of alcohol. Others, including his brother officers, consumed hard drink around him all the time which he accepted as being a part of a soldier's life, although more than likely feeling himself superior by being above their weaknesses. And he would never presume to chastise the enlisted men for their habits because of the simple reason he considered them his pawns on his path to continued glory. Unless of course they crossed that line that called for punitive discipline, but that in itself was a broad line. He did however hold a special admiration for his brawling Irish boys, for he knew they loved him and because of their fighting ability, he was right fond of them too.

The column crossed Davis Creek for the first time at 5:45 a.m.

Lieutenant Low's Gatling guns were having a bad time of it. The route of march was now almost due south and following the tortuous course along the creek put a strain on the ability of the heavy weapons to keep up.

"Why don't you request from the general to allow us to break down the guns?" Pat Kenzie asked his commander.

Bucky Low had just ordered his three gun team sergeants to skirt a heavy growth of cottonwoods and willows to enable them to work their way around the trees by taking them out of the line of march. Glancing over to his second in command as their horses gingerly snaked around large rocks hidden by sage brush near the high walled banks of Davis Creek, he said. "This so-called Sully's trail is making it slow for everybody. How far have we traveled? Maybe six or seven miles and we've had to cross and re-cross the creek five times already."

"Yeah the thing has got more turns and bends than a corkscrew, that's for sure; but that's the reason you should ask General Custer to let us break our weapons down and haul them on the mules and horses. It's the perfect time to show him what you've came up with and he's bound to be impressed if he sees we can keep up better than the wagons."

"That's the point right there Pat. Its not just us, it's the wagons that's making it slow going. No, I want to wait until a large scouting patrol is sent out, then I'll ask if we can send a gun along."

"Well, suite yourself, but I think you're missing a grand opportunity." Pat Kenzie said tersely.

Not taking offense at his friend's curt remark, Bucky Low smiled and said. "Yeah, I'm sure I would impress the general if I delayed the march even more by asking for time to dismantle my gun carriages."

Lieutenant Kenzie didn't have a ready answer for Low's remark and could only offer a grunt in reply.

* * * * *

Feverish working Pioneers were not only forced to blaze the trail by hacking down countless numbers of small willow trees that inhibited the direct route of march since wagons couldn't navigate around them, they had also constructed four bridges. The expedition was supposedly following the same trek mapped out by Brigadier General Alfred Sully when he led four thousand cavalrymen through this section of the Bad Lands during July 1864. General Sully's non-decisive Battle of Kildeer Mountain against the Sioux was well documented of having traveled the now named Davis Creek, but either his map makers confused the topography or the ensuing twelve years created some major changes in terrain features. There was no mention of the heavy wooded area next to the creek, which at one time was obviously a raging river because of the millions of various size rocks lying above the steep bank that had been part of the river. These rocks were imbedded in a sandy gravel that made it ill-conditioned for iron-shoe-hoofed animals to traverse. Nor did Custer's Pioneer's find any evidence of old bridge construction or marked fording places. They may as well have been the first white men to have ever traveled this section of the Bad Lands.

By the time the tenth bridge had been built in the late afternoon both Terry and Custer had had enough for one day and though they realized little forward progress had been made, a little less than eight miles, the two officers mutually agreed to call a halt. Scouts were ordered out to find a little high ground to get the command away from the enormous clouds of mosquitoes that had been swarming the troops and animals all day.

Since there are no real mountains in this part of the Dakota Territory it wasn't that easy to find an elevation that could accommodate over a thousand men, plus rolling stock and animals. Finally, after forty-five minutes of searching, scouts found a location almost 900 yards from the creek. This meant guard pickets for water details coming down to the creek even though everyone was told beforehand to fill all canteens and buckets before heading towards the little rise the scouts had found.

More smoky fires were built from the abundance of sagebrush and cottonwood limbs to ward off the mosquitoes and other biting insects and the normal activity of camp life occupied everyone.

At around 7:00 p.m. the sound of a bugle blaring Church Call was heard which other buglers and trumpeters soon took up.

Cherubic faced, white, curly-haired Captain Fred Benteen took his pipe from between his medium thick lips and with his slightly budging blue eyes twinkling, said to his tent mate Major Reno. "Well old bean, are you going to join his honor at church services this evening?"

The squared-jawed handsome officer furrowed his dark brows and glanced at his fellow officer with a savage look from his close set blue eyes. "Sure, same as you Buster Brown," and he reached for the silver flask on the makeshift stand next to his cot

Chapter 15

Following Davis Creek South, Dakota Territory
12:00 Noon, Monday, May 29, 1876

Private Michael O'Laughlin leaned on his shovel down at the bottom of a high perpendicular bank where he had been digging out the earth from a hole his bunk mate had hacked out with a pick axe. The broad shouldered, well built cavalryman was a member of I Troop under Lieutenant James E. Porter, whose company had drawn pioneer work for this days march. The hole O'Laughlin had been working on was for a log piling to help support the fifty foot cantilever bridge being built. Now he was looking at his mate Private Francis O'Leary with one green eye closed and a mischievous grin on his red, freckled face. "Is me ears a'deceiving me Frankie me boy, or was that truly Mess Call that just sounded?"

Private O'Leary returned his big bunk mates smile with a wide one of his own and the lean redhead replied. "Yer ears are hearing good Big Mike, let's go fix up some grub."

As the two soldiers were in the process of climbing out of the deep trough they had been doing a balancing act in their first sergeant; First Sergeant Timothy O'Keefe met them as they stuck their heads over the creek bank. His arms akimbo as he looked down upon the two upturned faces he spoke in a sarcastic tone of voice. "And pray tell jus whar do you two lads think yer a'gon'en?"

"But First Sergeant," blurted Private O'Laughlin, "We'en's heard the trumpet blow'en Mess Call and...."

First Sergeant O'Keefe uttered a harsh laugh. "That wasn't a trumpet lad that was a bugle a'telling those infantry boys you fellows are so slow a'gett'en this wee trickle of water spanned that they'll have the time to brew 'em up a cuppa coffee. Now get yer lazy arses back down there and get that piling laid."

A dozen or so other I Company troopers who had been idly standing around watching the show began guffawing, which was a huge mistake. With a baleful glare First Sergeant O'Keefe shook his fist at the group of soldiers. "And that goes for you lads too. I don't see none of you doing anything, so you, you and you," pointing a finger at the three closest bare shirted men, "get down there with 'em and I want to see that hole done in about ten minutes with the piling standing tall."

"What about our chow?" One of the newly appointed volunteers wanted to know.

"Don't be a'worrying yerselfs 'bout yer bellies. I'll see to it that Carmichael brews you up some real nice coffee to soften yer ration biscuits I'll fetch for you." With a loud tone the first sergeant bellowed. "Now all of you get yer arses back to work. You can be cutting timber or getting those planks ready for laying. I don't want to come back a'seeing none of you a'horsing around and may the Saints preserve you if'n I do. Corporal Smith! Where you at lad?"

A dark featured, medium height, wiry soldier wearing the two reverted yellow chevrons of a corporal ambled out of the grove of cottonwood trees above the creek and waived his hand. "I was doing a nature call first sergeant, what can I do for you?"

First Sergeant O'Keefe gave his junior NCO, whom he'd known for twenty years, a baleful stare, his green-gray eyes budging. "You can damn well do a better job of supervising your detail Tommy Smith or I'll have yer stripes again me lad!" Without expecting an answer the senior NCO turned on his heels and strode purposefully back down the trail from which he'd came.

Swatting at a swarm of mosquitoes as he climbed back down into the muck to the hole he'd pick-axed out, Private O'Leary grumbled loud enough for everyone to hear him. "Sweet Mother Mary and Joseph! One of these days O'Keefe will push me too far and we'll see what happens then, and that's the God's truth by heaven!"

With a smirk on his ugly pockmarked face Corporal Smith answered the bold threat. "That'll be the day lad. I've seen Timothy O'Keefe take on five Johnny Rebs all by himself, he did, and killed every one of 'em. So I'd be watch'en me tongue if I were you. Okay boys everyone be a'work'en hard now and I don't want to see any more Tom-foolery."

Back along the trail where all the stalled wagons were waiting in a long line. Lieutenant James Porter, astride his horse, spotted his first sergeant talking with Private Carmichael. The bug-eyed officer with thick black arched eyebrows and close clipped mustache nudged his mount and went over to his two men. "First Sergeant O'Keefe. Did you take care of that bit of stupidity the infantry caused by blowing Mess Call?"

The irascible non-commissioned officer had saluted his officer once already today and figured that was enough for one day and answered his commander's question without even coming to attention. "Yes sor I done jus that. Tol the lads the picnic wasn't for them but I would get 'em a cuppa coffee and some hardtack to carry 'em over. That's what I'm doing with Carmichael here a'gett'en him started at brewing up some coffee for our boys."

Accustomed to his senior sergeant's salty ways, Lieutenant Porter nodded his head, then brushing an insect off his sunken chin, asked: "And about the bridge. Are they coming along?"

"Yes sor, I'd say they should be a'put'en planks across in the next ten minutes. It's a cantilever and they just about had the last anchor support in when I left 'em a few minutes ago. Being supported on one end makes it a lot easier and we'll use ropes tied to trees to steady the roadbed beams. I'd give it a good half-hour sor."

"This will make the thirteenth bridge since yesterday. Just hope it's not an unlucky one."

The highly superstitious first sergeant quickly crossed himself while saying, "Saints preserve us Sor, that shorly won't happen."

"For all of our sakes I hope you are right first sergeant. General Custer has got his dander up with all of the delays the past two days and I assure you I don't want to be the cause of any further standstills. Charlie Reynolds is scouting ahead and let us both pray that he finds a couple of fords for our next crossings."

"Praise be yes to that sor!"

* * * * *

Whether or not any actual praying took place is not known. But Lonesome Charlie Reynolds did in fact find several fording locations downstream that greatly enhanced the rate of march. Except for one major situation.

* * * * *

One ford was seventy feet in width with a sandy gravel bottom. The middle of the fast moving water was at a depth of about four feet.

General Terry, his staff and baggage train had crossed Davis Creek without mishap with the last high-sided ambulance making its way just ahead of the following Gatling gun platoon.

Lieutenant's Low and Kenzie watched as their first limber and gun carriage eased down the crumbling soft clay embankment through a gap pioneers had dug out to form a steep ramp.

"Seems to be handling it pretty well." Pat Kenzie observed

"I don't know. It looks to me there's a terrible strain on the limber. See how it's twisting with the weight of the Gatling's carriage dragging behind? Maybe I should have split them up like I've done before. Had I known about this ford ahead of time I could have even had rafts made to get the guns across."

Pat Kenzie took his commander's last remark as a rebuke since it was his responsibility to check out the lay of the land the battery would be traveling over. "When General Terry's orderly informed me Charlie Reynolds had found a ford I did look it over. When I viewed it the pioneers were digging out the cut and I didn't think it looked treacherous at all," he trailed off lamely.

Slapping at a pesky fly that had flew up to his face from a warm pile of horse droppings, Lieutenant Low said. "I suppose I was thinking out loud because it's too late to do anything about it now anyway."

With the first caisson and gun carriage now in the water and the driver urging his six horses to go further into the swift current, the second Gatling gun limber commenced its downward movement on the slick clay ramp. The corporal teamster was having trouble controlling his six horses that didn't seem to like the idea of walking down the mushy incline. Just as the lead team reached the waters edge, the big reddish brown bay harnessed to the gee side whiffletree reared its head with a loud snorting whinny shaking her head up and down. The weight of the heavy Gatling gun at the same time was pushing down on the limber and when the bay reared up her front feet the bay in the left traces lurched mightily in its mate's direction, nipping at the other horse's mane. The other four horses began a prancing stomp wanting to escape being tied to the doubletree and before the corporal driver could fully react a wrenching groaning noise quickly finalized with a tremendous loud snapping sound as the limber broke free from the gun carriage. With the restraining weight of the Gatling gun no longer hindering the teams pulling ability, and as if on cue, the six horses lunged into the creek and made good headway with the two wheeled limber until reaching deep water where they started thrashing around again which caused the wheeled ammunition and parts chest to tip over. Meanwhile, the gun carriage with attached Gatling gun was sliding side ways down the ramp and with a resounding crash turned over into the creek near the shoreline.

On the far side of the creek General Custer on top of Dandy saw the entire episode. So did 1st Battalion commander, Captain Myles Keogh who was riding his favorite mount Comanche.

Custer had been conferring with Captain Keogh about personal matters concerning Keogh's Wing commander Major Reno when the accident occurred. Visibly upset, Custer road into the stream shouting back to Captain Keogh. "This is the problem I've been saying all along about those damn Gatling's!"

Custer, who rarely cursed, considering profanity a weakness and outward sign of a lack of education, high stepped Dandy at a trot through the water until reaching a depth that slowed his horse to a slow walk. He reached the corporal who was untangling himself from under the limber while the now calm team stood motionless in the middle of the creek up to their bellies. "Are you okay son?"

Spitting water but seeing whom it was the corporal attempted to come to attention and salute but Custer waved him off. "Don't worry about that corporal, I asked if you are injured?"

"N...Nosir," the corporal stuttered.

Satisfied with the man's answer Custer spurred Dandy to move forward without saying anything more. By the time he reached the other side of the creek, Lieutenant's Low and Kenzie was knee deep in the water along with a dozen of their men looking over their upturned weapon. Still irate, Custer lit into Billy Low right away. "That has got to be one of the most disgraceful exhibitions of crossing a ford I ever had the displeasure of witnessing Mister Low. I suggest you stop looking at your damn so-called machine gun as you described to my brother and find some pole levers to get the beast back on its wheels!"

Lieutenant Low's face got instantly red as he assumed the best position of attention he could muster under the circumstances and bringing his right hand swiftly to the edge of his forage cap with its large brass letter G pinned in the middle, said, "Yessir, I'll see to it right away sir!"

Without returning the lieutenant's salute, Custer grunted and reined Dandy around to head back to the other side. Turning a little in his saddle as Dandy slowed in deeper water, Custer yelled back towards the milling group of battery men. "And you wonder why I didn't want to take your damn pop guns along on this expedition!"

Lieutenant Low was very distressed when he turned nervously to Lieutenant Kenzie. "Mister Kenzie, personally supervise a work detail to get the Gatling righted and hitched back to the limber." He took a halting step towards his turned-over caisson out in the middle of the creek then abruptly changed his mind. "And don't be concerned about any damage as we'll closely inspect the gun at this evenings bivouac. And if necessary jury-rig the vehicle to hold it together if its seriously damaged, we'll do any repair tonight also. It's extremely important we do not hold up the march any more than...ah...than we already have." He ended in a low voice.

Snapping to attention and offering his friend a rare salute, Lieutenant Kenzie formally said, "Yessir, don't fret about it sir, it will be done!"

Lieutenant Low sort of waved his gloves at Kenzie as a return for the salute, and walked back to the remaining caisson to check on the doubletree fittings that connected to the gun carriage beam.

In the middle of the creek General Custer passed the corporal, who with the help of some on looking cavalrymen had got his limber upright, and was now guiding his team back to retrieve his gun carriage. The corporal gave a salute, saying, "General Custer sir, I thank you for asking about my welfare awhile ago sir."

His anger ebbing somewhat, Custer returned this salute with a formal one of his own. "That's okay son, just wanted to make sure you did not require medical assistance."

With his buckskins soaking up the water like a sponge George Custer was wet clear up past his waist and the heavy pants was starting to chaff his sensitive skin which in return rekindled his irritably. Climbing Dandy up the natural grade on this side of the creek he saw a commotion going on about forty feet up the trail. There was a trooper lying on the ground with a group of seven or eight other troopers standing around him. It appeared another trooper was bent over the prostrate soldier. Trotting Dandy towards the group he noted Captain Myles Keogh astride his horse Comanche looking down on whatever was going on over the heads of the ring of troopers. Stopping Dandy next to Comanche he made a loud inquiry to no one in particular: "What in the blazes happened now?"

The narrow faced Keogh, who resembled Lieutenant Low a little except his mustache and chin whiskers was dark brown, but did have a cross eyed look about him, replied to his general's question. "Rattler bit him sir."

Custer then noticed the rattlesnake bitten trooper's trouser leg had been ripped open and he had a tourniquet tied high on his upper leg. "They already cut him?"

"Yes sir. The fellow that got to him first sliced an X and that's what he's doing now sucking the blood out."

"Who is he" Custer asked.

"A trooper by the name of Myers sir." Keogh answered immediately.

"Which Myers? We've got two you know. One's a bugler in Reno's wing and he's got a cousin serving under Benteen."

"I...I don't know sir," Keogh stammered. "You there by the tree," he pointed a finger at a private kneeling down next to the bitten trooper. "Which Myers is it?"

Looking up at the captain with a worried expression, the private who had been consoling his buddy said in a loud voice. "Donald F. sir."

"Sir it's Dona....."

"Yes, yes--Lord man I'm not deaf and heard him as good as you did! Well, let's get a stretcher team up here and get him to an ambulance. Not much chance he's going to be riding a saddle anytime soon."

Feeling the sting of the general's short temper Captain Keogh was quick to say, "Already taken care of general. I sent a runner for the surgeon and his orderly as soon as I saw what happened."

Custer slapped his gloves against his damp leg, which was already drying. "Tarnation! What's going to occur next? Every dag-blasted man has been warned this is rattlesnake country: you would think they would be a little more careful with such a hazard around." He paused for a moment, and then almost muttering, said, "Well at least there haven't been any signs of Indians around to torment us."

* * * * *

General Custer, or his scouts, just weren't looking in the right places.

* * * * *

Not more than 75 yards from where the snake bitten trooper was being administered to, was located a grass and leaf-covered sage brush warren nestled between a cottonwood and willow tree, which held a pair of watchful Sioux.

"Stupid yellow stripe got no better sense that let kissing warrior snake with fork tongue bite him and poison his soul." Fast-As-The-Pony-Rides whispered.

Still Water whispered a reply: "And then his companion stab him with hunting knife to try and kill poison, and then sucks on the wound. Never have I seen such a thing!"

"I have heard of this having been done before by the Shoshone people' but it is so much easier to place the plant of magic healing on the bite which draws the poison from the soul."

Still Water snorted. "Then the Shoshones are as stupid as the white man to practice such bad medicine. And I find it amusing that it takes so many of the blue shirts to tend to their comrade. They mill around like old women wringing their hands after a great battle."

"I must remember to carry a basket full of our hissing cousins the next time we fight the white soldiers. They would scatter like sage brush in the wind."

Still Water snickered at his lifelong friend's humor.

Chapter 16

On the East Bank of the Little Missouri River, Dakota Territory
9:00 a.m., Tuesday, May 30, 1876

When the men of the lead troop of cavalry found out they were going to set up camp on a grassy plain near the east bank of the Little Missouri River after trail marching for only four hours, a loud cheer went up.

General Alfred Terry, who with his staff was riding out of the huge grassy cul-de-sac created by three surrounding high hills, heard the loud hurrahs. Turning to his aide-de-camp, he asked, "What on earth are the men cheering about?"

The tall, dark-haired lieutenant hesitated just for a moment, and then replied. "General sir, I believe they're cheering you because of you having selected such a grand campsite." With a minute pause the clean-shaven officer then quickly added. "And of course they are more than likely pleased of such an early morning halt."

Smiling in satisfaction at the thought Custer's men held affection for him, the doe-eyed general said. "I would dare say their burst of exuberance has a lot more to do with setting up camp for the day at nine o'clock rather than your suggestion of the location I picked."

The general's good-humored smile was infectious and his engineering officer offered a remark, also smiling. "I don't know sir. You selected an excellent site. Plenty of room without overcrowding, abundant wood and forage, a natural fortification and just a short walk through that cottonwood grove for good water."

General Terry kept his smile when he said. "Very kind of you to say so captain. I'll have to brag to Colonel Custer how well I have done and hopefully he will be as pleased as you and the men seem to be."

"Oh, I feel sure that General Custer will be more than pleased sir."

With a short laugh General Terry said, "My remark was intended as a clumsy attempt at satirical wit captain. I really don't give a hoot if Colonel Custer approves of the location I have chosen or not."

"My apologies sir I didn't mean to...."

General Terry held up his hand and interrupted his engineer officer. "No need at apology. I realize my attempts at humor fall flat most of the time. However, if you will excuse me I need to confer with my Adjutant General for a moment." Terry ignored the red faced officer's "Yessir," and turning to his assistant Adjutant General, Captain Edward Smith, said. "Ed, tell the commands as soon as they have their tentage up and so forth that the men may have free run at fishing but I don't want any hunting as it could attract any Indian scouts that may be about and I'm still trying to maintain an element of surprise in so far as our movements are concerned."

Captain Smith replied with a "Yes sir!" along with a salute, then rode back into the cul-de-sac past the long line of wagons that were going into the area, to find the 7th cavalry's Adjutant Cooke.

General Custer, along with Lonesome Charlie Reynolds and a Ree scout, had departed the old campsite a little before 5:00 a.m. to conduct a long scouting expedition for signs of Indian's. His absence is what sparked General Terry's desire to exercise his command prerogative.

Charlie Reynolds stared down into the small valley from the bluff where he and General Custer stood beside their mounts on. "We can mosey on down thar general but from the looks of things I don't reckon we's a'going to find anything worth look'en for. Far as I tell there taint been a sign one of any hostiles since we started out this morning."

With his eyes roving the valley floor Custer said. "It does appear we've had a brisk twenty mile ride for nothing Charlie."

"Mite closer to twenty-five miles the way I figure it," Charlie gave a terse answer followed by a squirt from his chaw.

The Ree scout was looking at the overhead bright orb and noted the moving clouds that were beginning to show blue-black bottoms. "It time we go back. No place for two white men to be after dark." Or a friendly Indian scout, which he failed to mention. Glancing again at the growing thunder boomers, he added. "Heap rain coming." As if to add emphases to his observation, the afternoon sky became brighter for half a second with a two pronged silvery purplish-blue streak of lighting.

"He's right general. We best be high-tailing it back north and find your regiment. It's gonna rain a good one and that be a fact."

The three men mounted their horses and reined them back towards the directions from which they had came.

* * * * *

The same streak of lighting that had ever so briefly told of the coming storm was also seen by the hundreds of men lining the east bank of the Little Missouri that had fishing poles in the water.

Billy One and Billy Two were among the hoard of anglers.

"You got another one!" Billy One yelled out. "Be careful of your pole and make sure you got him hooked good. Don't let 'em get away like that one 'while ago."

"I know, I know," Billy Two panted as he jerked his long willow branch fishing pole he'd made from the branch of a sapling. His timed jerk of the pole effectively set the barbed hook he'd bought from the sutler back in Fort Lincoln and a large river bass leaped out of the water.

"Lookie that thing jump!" Billy One squealed. "Billy me boy I think you got yourself a three, four pound striped bass."

"He's sure making a fight out of it, I'll tell ya that!"

Several other soldiers that lined the river bank near the two Billy's watched the action with interest as Private Slaper struggled with his catch. One of them, a short, wiry, bantam-rooster older man, shouted over a piece of encouraging advice. "Better get holt of yer line boy and start pull'en him in by hand."

Seeing the logic of the old timer's instructive suggestion, Billy Slaper handed over his pole to Billy Morris, saying, "Here, take hold this and I'll drag him in but make sure you don't let go." As soon as his friend had a grip on the eight foot long sapling branch Slaper got his hands around the heavy string he was using for line and began pulling the fish to him hand-over-hand. The happy private soon had the bass at his feet where he was standing a foot out in the water and he held it up with a large grin. "Ain't that a beaut?" He exclaimed joyously."

"Sure 'nough is." Billy One agreed. "I tell ya we got a rite smart mess of 'em and I'm getting hon'gray. How 'bout we hustle back to our tent an' fix 'em up."

"You're always hungry Billy. But I suppose you're right. Let's pack it up and do it."

"Hey diddly doo, it's gonna be good eat'en tonight! Better'an beef and bacon, beef and bacon. You know what I always say. And you know what? We got enough here that we can have some for breakfast too."

* * * * *

General Custer and his two companions got back to camp a little past 6:00 p.m. after having to ride a lot further than they thought they would have to; thinking they'd meet up with the outfit much closer to the bluff area they had been in. Custer was a little dismayed of the short distance the column had traveled but begrudgingly conceded that General Terry had chosen an excellent campsite, regardless of the lack of distance covered. The first item of business upon riding into the cul-de-sac past the parapets that had been erected for defense at the open end, was to report to General Terry.

Sitting on a camp chair outside the front of his large white tent, General Terry looked up at his 7th Cavalry commander with his sad, drooping eyes. "So, no sign of hostiles whatsoever huh? Well it could be they're just hiding from us real good. I don't know, I've got this feeling they're out there right now looking at us, but then, it's just a feeling. You've had a hard day of it Jack and I appreciate you taking the time to come directly to me but you go ahead now and get yourself cleaned up and get some food in you."

The general's last words were punctuated by a long rumbling boom of distant thunder cumulated by a spectacular display of lighting.

George Custer raised his eyes to the darkening sky, then said. "Well general, if there's Indian's out there close, they're sure in for a bad night."

* * * * *

General Custer fancied himself as almost having supernatural powers of the mind which he called his "Custer's Luck." Most of this "Luck" came from his uncanny ability during the Civil War of guessing about a given situation that bordered on an invitation of disaster then pulling his chestnuts out of the fire without getting badly burnt. But his offhand remarks since the beginning of the present campaign were becoming that of a clairvoyant.

* * * * *

High on one of the tall hills that looked down into the cul-de-sac where the soldiers camped sat Fast-As-The-Pony-Rides; trying bravely to ignore the cold that ravaged his body caused by the continuing downpour of heavy rain that was storming.

Fast-As-The-Pony-Rides and his boyhood friend Still Water had had a long discussion that morning on which one should leave to find the camp of their leader Rain-in-the-Face. At first Still Water had taken it for granted it would be he that would stay behind to monitor the white soldiers' movements, but Fast-As-The-Pony-Rides had a different thought on the matter. After much talk Fast-As-The-Pony-Rides finally convinced Still Water that he should be the one to report to Rain-in-the-Face, using the logic that Still Water had a better way of expressing himself. Still Water rode off to find their warrior chief to tell him how slow the blue shirts were moving and where the blue shirts were at. Fast-As-The-Pony-Rides told Still Water to inform Crazy Horse and Sitting Bull that if the tribe counsel desired to avoid the soldiers then go north as fast as they could since the soldiers were heading directly west again.

The deluge of rain hitting Fast-As-The-Pony-Rides without letup was accompanied by a steady boom of thunder and glaring colored flashes of lighting that lit up the night. Placing the few leaf-covered branches he was able to find close over his head, Fast-As-The-Pony-Rides mumbled aloud a quiet remark using the Indian name for the Little Missouri. "Maybe the rain will make Thick Timber River flood its banks and rush in on the white devils and drown them all." His spirit stimulated by the thought, Fast-As-The-Pony-Rides grunted in satisfaction and felt better awaiting the morning sun.

Chapter 17

On The West Side of the Little Missouri River, Dakota Territory
10:00 a.m., Wednesday, May 31, 1876

The day had started early for four troops of the 7th Cavalry that had been ordered by General Custer, as ordered by General Terry, to scout the surrounding countryside for any recent sign of Indians. It wasn't a case where Terry disbelieved his cavalry commander's report of yesterday, but rather a reasoning that 125 men could better canvas the area than two scouts and a senior officer. Therefore, Troops C, D, F, and M, guided by Lieutenant Varnum and twelve civilian and Indian scouts, found themselves up in the hills as the sun came up.

General Terry had explained to his staff and senior officers, before leaving Fort Lincoln, his hunch that the command may very well find the hostiles around the Little Missouri River area. The long faced, narrow-nosed general expressed this view with a personal belief that with plenty of water, wood and pasture grass, the heavily timbered valleys would be ideal for the Indians to winter. It was because of this that he ordered the extra effort to be made in hopes to prove his theory correct.

After breaking camp around 8:00 A.M., the remaining cavalry and infantry units, along with the long wagon and pack mule train, got started on the days march. Initially, there was a fear that last nights storm would hinder their progress, especially the forthcoming river crossing. This concern was manifested by a heavy overcast sky of dark clouds and distant rumbling thunder that made it appear the command was in for more rain. Despite the original outlook an hour after breaking camp the cloud cover began to lift and while the air was very cool, marching conditions were pleasant. The main body of the expedition traveled south for a few miles before crossing the river without mishap at a good ford which was found near the rock and clay tower called Sentinel Butte. It was here that General Terry found out his cavalry commander was missing.

General Terry, looking up from a folding camp table he'd been using as a desk, raised one eyebrow and rather loudly said, "What do you mean you cannot find him?"

The question was directed to Captain Smith, the general's acting Assistant Adjutant General. "General sir, I conversed with both Major Reno and Captain Benteen, and both say they have not seen General Custer all morning. After finally locating Adjutant Cooke, he hesitantly informed me of his impression, as he put it, that General Custer accompanied one of the troops that left earlier this morning on scouting patrol."

"By whose authority?" The general's voice rose an octave.

"Begging the generals pardon sir, but if you didn't authorize his leave of absence to join the patrol parties. then I will have to assume General Custer took it upon himself, sir."

"I see. Yes of course Ed, I shouldn't have asked you the question in the first place." General Terry paused, tapping his wood and metal tipped quill pen on his order book he'd been writing in. After several seconds he spoke again. "When the good general decides to rejoin us, please pay him my compliments that I would like to see him."

"Yessir, general sir!" After offering a salute, Captain Smith took one step back from the impromptu field desk, did an about face and went to see about his other duties.

General Terry remained seated, staring off in space for a long moment before shaking his head back and forth a couple of times in a resigned manner, then bent his head back to the order he had been penning.

The general was catching up on some administrative paper work that needed his attention and while the wagon train made the slow, laborious crossing of the Little Missouri River, he was sitting in the lee of his baggage wagon writing, after having been the first to cross. Custer's sometimes lack of respect was becoming more annoying all the time and Terry was most irritated with his chief subordinate at this latest episode. The general chastised himself for his inability to be more forceful with Custer but at the same time was reminded of his own lack of field experience against the Indians that made him rely so much on the man. General Terry rummaged around in his personal foot locker until he found his diary. Flipping through the pages until finding his last entry dated 5/31 - 8 AM, he dipped his pen in the ink well and with his neat longhand began writing under the Broke Camp entry: *"10 AM: In addition to Custer playing Wagon Master the last few days he has now taken it upon himself to play Commander of Scouts by leaving the expedition on his own volition without my authorization."* Blowing lightly on the entry to dry the ink, General Terry felt much better, having vented his irritation on paper.

* * * * *

At about the same time General Terry was jotting down his frustrations

101

regarding his errant second in command several members of that early morning's scouting patrol were goofing off under a rock overhang up in the bluff area northwest of Sentinel Butte. Four of the cavalrymen were from M Troop and the fifth soldier was a member of H Troop. Lieutenant Varnum had split his four companies into smaller sections he designated as squads and sent them out in a fan to conduct a thorough reconnaissance. With not enough non-commissioned officers to lead all of the squads many of them were straw bossed by senior privates and like all good privates most took to thinking about their comfort more than about the sudden bestowal of leadership responsibility thrust upon them. This was the case with senior private John G. McCullough who made the command decision to rest for a spell under the huge rock overhang from a small bluff overlooking a vast rolling valley below his small group.

A young M Troop private who was a natural born worrywart type, asked First Class Private McCullough a question for about the third time. "You sure we should be procrastinating like this Mac? Shouldn't we be checking out that valley for hostiles?"

A 12 year veteran of the cavalry who sported a drooping mustache that curled below his chin when not waxed, Mac McCullough let out a horse laugh. "What was that you said Calvin? Procasterating? Now jus what in the blue hell does that supposed to mean city boy? Is that got som'ten to do with cutting the balls off a horse?" McCullough turned to his other two men with a smirk on his face while twirling a right finger in a circular motion at his temple.

"No, no," the short, blond haired youth protested. "I mean aren't we neglecting our duty, you know like shirker'ing."

"What I'd tell ya just awhile ago boy? Didn't I say we're up here observ'en. There taint nothing down in that there valley that we can't see a'moving from up here. An' as far as shirker'ing our duty, let me tell ya this rite now buster so ya can heer it real good and don't forget it. I'm in charge of this here detail and what I say goes. An' if'en I say we're doing a little reconnoitering eyeball'en, then by God that's what we're a'do'en. Now put that in your pipe and smoke it and I don't wanna hear tell of you going around blabbing anything different when we get back to camp. You got that soldier?"

The menacing tone of voice had the desired effect Private McCullough wanted it to have and Private Calvin Switzer meekly said, "I wasn't trying to start no trouble with you Mac and I know how to keep my mouth shut."

"Well that's good to hear Calvin, 'cause you shore ain't been do'en a very good job of it the past fifteen minutes or so. An' then trying to pull your east coast, big city, education on me with all your high-for-flutt'en words." Turning to one of the other privates, McCullough asked. "What was that he said to me Luther----Procas'apatating?"

"Yeah Mac, someth'en like that."

Turning back to face the now, red-faced young private, McCullough went on. "Well here's a couple of words you can look up in your dictionary boy. Getcha self down there in that little crack that looks like a trench so's you can offer som enfilade fire in case a echelon of Indjun's tries to envelope us. And while you're do'en that keep your eyes on the horses Calvin boy. Now do you think you've got enough duty to do to make you keep your mind of all that neglect'en and shirk'en?"

Without answering Private Switzer picked up his carbine in a sulking manner and butt slid down to the crevice senior Private McCullough had pointed to.

McCullough turned back to doing the important job he had been performing, carving his first two initials, last name and company letter on the hard sandstone service of the rock overhang the other three privates were using for shade.

Private Walter C. Williams, the lone representative from H Troop, unsheathed his hunting knife, making the remark as he crawled out from the overhang: "I think I'll carve my name next to McCullough's. Maybe a hundred years from now some folks will pass by and see it."

Private Fritz Neeley said, "Mite as well and go ahead, I've already done mine before Mac started do'en his."

As Private Williams stood next to Private McCullough on the long ledge overlooking the valley, starting his carving effort, the other M trooper, Private Luther Higgins, called out. "Hey Williams---how'n the hell you end up out here with us anyway? You're the only fellow from H Troop I seen on this here scout'en patrol today."

"Oh...taint no good reason I can tell ya that," Williams responded while working on the letter W. "Captain Benteen has let Lieutenant Gibson run the company while he's commanding the Left Wing and Captain French has been the acting Fourth Battalion CO. Anyway, Gibson had Officer of the Day the other night and caught me napping on picket, and told me he was going to teach me a good lesson. His intention is to send me out on every patrol that's not civilian or Indian scouts alone, so I'll eventually run into some hostiles. He told me once I've seen what real sonofabitches the savages can be I won't be going to sleep on my post anymore."

103

McCullough offered a reply to what the H Trooper had said: "Gibson is a prissy ass, snotty-nosed bastard, but I tell ya what Williams, he did ya a rite smart favor. Back during the late war if'n ya got caught sleep'en on picket by an officer it was always a court-martial an' more likely than not you ended up get'ten shot. You was considered lucky if'n a first soldier or three-striper caught ya 'cause they'd just beat the living tar outta ya where ya couldn't walk for a week and let it go at that."

From under the rock, Private Luther Higgins let out a loud chuckle. "That sounds like the voice of experience talk'en if'n you ask me."

Not fazed at hearing the truth of what his drinking buddy had just said, McCullough smiled, then said, "I'll tell ya this much Devil," using Luther's nickname which was obvious why he was called "Devil." "Once ya get the special treatment from one of those zebra arms you get to think'en it would'of been smarter to have got shot. One thing about it though, you ain't never go'en to fall 'sleep on post again. Old Williams here got off easy I say. More so since they ain't any Injun's within a hundred miles from here."

* * * * *

Fast-As-The-Pony-Rides laying flat on top of the large rock that stuck out from the bluff the two soldiers were carving their names on would have disagreed with senior Private McCullough, had he been able to understand their language.

* * * * *

General Terry's prior order not to fire weapons unless engaging in battle with hostile Indians was issued for the sake of reducing sharp noise reports in an effort to maintain a measure of stealth. Evidently no one in the command took into consideration at this juncture that the blaring of trumpets echoing off the walls of bluffs and buttes created a loud, resounding blast which could be heard for miles, which of course was the intent of using trumpet and bugle calls in the first place.

At around 1:00 p.m. the main column of wagons, cavalry and infantry continued their punishing trek over the rolling, broken terrain; encountering one large hill after another that had to be crossed.

Suddenly the tinny screech of trumpets blowing Recall was heard.

Up in the butte area the many small squads hearing the order to reassemble were guided by the same blaring tone ever five minutes or so to hone them in where their command post was located.

When senior Private John G. McCullough heard the initial Recall message blowing he quickly became a very professional soldier. "Okay fellows, get your gear stowed and lets get saddled up."

Climbing down the bluff to reach their horses, McCullough came upon Private Switzer who had diligently performed the senior private's "Keep him busy" order, given a few hours before. "C'mon Calvin, it's time for us to get back now."

Getting stiffly to his feet Switzer answered, "As you say--- sir!"

Grinning, Private McCullough put an arm around the young trooper's shoulders, saying: "Aw now Calvin, don't be that way now. I thought we'ens were buddies. You know you don't have ta call me sir. Hell man! I'm jus a private in the rear ranks jus like you are. Tell ya what! When we get back to camp I'm a'gonna tell Captain French what a fine job you did out here today and maybe he'll even pass it on to Captain Benteen. Now how does that sound to ya? We're still buddies right?"

The good humored bantering from the long time private seemed to mollify Switzer and he offered a thin smile in return, saying: "Yeah----I reckon so Mac; but you shouldn't embarrass me in front of the fellows like you did just because I finished high school. You really mean it about going to say something to Captain French? I mean I did do what you told me to do didn't I?"

"You stuck with it all the way boy and you're darn shooting I'll say something to the captain." With his arm still around the young private's shoulder, McCullough paused for a quick moment before resuming talking. "An' I know Calvin old buddy you ain't go'en to be tell'en no one how we'ens set up this....ah...our observation post because I'm a'gonna be do'en all the talk'en, rite?"

"Why sure Mac, you're the senior private in charge of the detail."

Taking his arm from around the boys shoulder, senior Private McCullough patted him on the back a couple of times. "That's my boy; that's my buddy sure a'toot'en." Then turning to Private Walter Williams, McCullough said. "An' the same goes for you too Williams rite? Especially since I'm gonna tell young Lieutenant Gibson what a bang up job you did for me today. Jus mite cause him to ease up a bit on ya, don't ya reckon?"

"That's mighty kind of you McCullough, I'll shor appreciate it. Like you said, we gotta stick together as we're about as far down in the rear ranks as we can get." The errant private replied with a small smile.

Offering a sly wink the senior private said. "Thought you mite see it that way. Okay boys, lets get a'crack'en...them beans and beef are a'waiting!"

On top of a small hill several miles away from senior Private McCullough's detail General Custer was conversing with Lieutenant Varnum. The two officers were flanked on either side by four company guidons planted in the ground for the merging troops to see from a distance.

"That about the last of them Charlie?" Custer was referring to the two groups of men that just rode into the small valley from different directions to where the four companies were reassembling.

Scrutinizing the large force of mounted men in loose company formations twenty yards below in the small valley from where he and the general sat on their horses, Lieutenant Charles Varrnum answered. "General sir, I do not believe so: with your permission sir I'll ask for a report sir."

"By all means do so Charlie, I'm just a tag along. This is your command...so use whatever command judgment you deem necessary."

Lieutenant Charles A. Varnum was in charge of the Indian scouts and was not accustomed to having the responsibility of four companies of cavalry. The narrowed eyed, aquiline-nosed officer nervously fingered his short bushy mustache for a second, then responded. "Yes sir, thank you sir." The lieutenant paused for a couple of seconds, then after clearing his throat, he bellowed out in a loud voice. "Troop Commanders-----REPORT!"

Although there was not an instantaneous answer to his order, within a matter of seconds, the F Troop commander yelled back an answer. "Sir! F Troop--All present or accounted for Sir!"

Lieutenant Varnum returned his junior lieutenant's salute and another company made its report. "Sir, D Troop all accounted for Sir!"

The company commander of C Troop was next. "Sir, two squads not accounted for sir!"

After a long moment of hesitation while Lieutenant Hodgson, temporarily commanding M Troop, conferred with his company first sergeant, the lieutenant finally made his report. "Sir--all accounted for--except for one squad, sir!"

After accepting Hodgson's salute, Lieutenant Varnum turned in his saddle a little and started to speak. Before he could say anything Custer held up one hand. "I heard them Charlie. Well, considering some of them probably reconnoitered better than twenty miles out, getting back jack rabbit quick is a trifle difficult. I'm sure they'll be along shortly."

"Yes sir, I agree sir."

Putting his hand up to his mouth to cover a yawn, the general then said. "Plenty of daylight even with the clouds building up again. Have your trumpeter's find higher ground and take one of the guidon's with them and sound off every three minutes: that should do the trick and we don't want to take any chances leaving any of the boys out here."

"Excellent idea sir, and of course you are absolutely correct about not leaving untrained scouts out here alone."

Always flattered when a subordinate recognized his genius, Custer chuckled, then jovially remarked. "Well your Ree's are excellent scouts lieutenant, as they should be since they know this land better than most white men, but you take some of those old campaigner corporal's and privates that's been around for twelve, fifteen, maybe twenty years, and I believe they could show some of the best trained scouts a thing or two."

"You will not get a disagreement from me on that point sir. Our veteran campaigners are surely the backbone of the regiment sir." Lieutenant Varnum gushed.

"Humph---Yes, I suppose they are at that lieutenant....with proper guidance and leadership example from the Corps of Officers of course."

"Oh yes sir, absolutely correct sir, that's exactly what I should have emphasized. Thank you for pointing that out sir."

"No thanks required Charlie." Custer felt smug that he'd set the young lieutenant straight on just who it was that keep the 7th Cavalry running smoothly like a well-oiled piece of machinery. Feeling a sudden chill in the air General Custer's hearing picked up the snapping flutter of the four swallow tailed pennants whipping in the wind.. Glancing at the two silk guidons to his left that were small versions of the American flag except for the 35 stars being in a circle, he noted they were standing straight out, being driven by a northwestern wind. "Charlie, I think you better get those trumpeters moving double-quick-time as I do believe we're in for a pretty bad storm coming our way from the way the winds picking up. Have them take my command staff pennant for the stragglers of see."

* * * * *

The coldness in the air and increase in wind velocity of a gathering storm, wasn't the only one brewing as George Armstrong Custer was to find out.

* * * * *

General Terry had called a halt to set up camp at 2:00 p.m., after a 13

107

mile march. Even though good mileage was accomplished in a relative short eight hour period, the men and animals were worn down to the last of their effective endurance. This was the fifteenth day of the campaign and the expedition had traveled almost 200 miles since leaving Fort Lincoln. It was more than likely many more miles than that, considering all the ups and downs and around obstacles, with all the twist and turns they had taken. The 22 miles of the past three days had been treacherous and this day, even with the 13 miles, had proven to have been so zigzagging up and down the high, steep buttes that the pioneers couldn't lift another log to build one more bridge. Once again in consideration of his men and the animals, General Terry selected a grassy valley with a nearby wooded area and small stream as a campsite.

It was near 4:30 p.m. when the distant blare of a trumpet announced the return of the four companies that had left that morning on scouting patrol.

General Terry was busy inside his headquarters tent writing a long dispatch to Lieutenant General Philip H. Sheridan when a light tap on the front flap tent pole made him look up. General Custer stuck his head inside the flap and said, "Your Adjutant General said you wanted to see me general."

General Terry put down his pen and looking sternly at the face peering at him, said. "Yes Custer---I want to talk to you."

Custer knew instantly General Terry had his dander up about something because the brigadier general never addressed him by his last name only unless he was highly upset.

As if to fortify this feeling, when George Custer started to set down, since he was accustomed to being rather casual around Terry, whom he considered to be a fellow general officer, Terry stopped the curly-haired lieutenant colonel with a terse. "I have not given you permission to set down yet sir!"

Stunned, Custer reverted to his West Point days by bracing himself and saying, "Sorry general. Reporting as ordered sir!" Though his face flushed from the humiliation of Terry's stinging rebuke, he still could not make himself utter the full wording of the proper manner of reporting to a superior officer: *Lieutenant Colonel Custer reporting as ordered sir.* The thought of calling himself *Lieutenant Colonel* was repugnant to him.

Allowing Custer to remain in his brace for a few seconds, General Terry then said. "You may be seated colonel."

As Custer took his seat he all but blurted out. "Have I done something to offend the general?"

"Custer, I have been as lenient with you as an expeditionary commander could possibly be. Yet you take it upon yourself just to come and go as you please without having the common courtesy of advising, or for that matter, requesting permission from your commanding officer to make these jaunts you go on. I'm beginning to wonder if anyone around here looks to me as the commander of this expedition! Well by thunder I am the commander, and I expect in the future for you to be more prudent of that fact."

Custer was astounded, if not dumbfounded. For once in his career he was innocent of the allegations because of a true misunderstanding. "General Terry sir, may I be allowed to have a word?"

"Go ahead and have your say."

"Sir, I swear to you as a Christian officer and gentleman that I would never purposely be impertinent or contemptuous of your authority. When you told me many days back that you intended to give me the broadest latitude possible it never occurred to me that this granting of a free hand prevented simple field decisions on my part. I am truly sorry that I misunderstood this and I will make it a point to maintain a much better liaison with you in the future."

Custer was speaking the truth. When orders were clear and to the point he obeyed them to the letter. But left to his own interpretation on an ambiguous order he pretty well did as he pleased.

Custer had him and General Terry knew it. How could he argue with such glibness? "Just keep me informed as to your whereabouts in the future sir."

Then softening his tone somewhat, General Terry asked Custer to give him a full report concerning the large patrol that had been mounted that morning since it was obvious he had first hand knowledge. The two officers spent more than an hour together and Terry learned he had been mistaken and no hostiles would be found in the Bad Lands. Much to his distress, knowing it would be a much longer campaign, the expedition would have to continue west.

Latter that afternoon as General Terry was putting the finishing touches on his dispatch to General Sheridan with the news that no hostiles had been located at his present location, a rattle of gunfire erupted which sounded as if it was not that far away. Slamming down his pen, he yelled out to his aide-de-camp. "What in tarnation is that all about!"

It took 20 minutes for runners to get information and report back to headquarters.

Captain Edward W. Smith made the report to General Terry. "General sir, it appears that war correspondent Mister Mark Kellogg, along with Charlie Reynolds, are out hunting."

In an icy tone of voice Terry said tersely. "Inform General Custer to send a detail of his cavalry out to fetch the two gentlemen and when the two civilians are returned to camp, bring them to me!" He paused for a second before making a final comment. "Does anyone around here ever follow my orders?"

* * * * *

That evening, the other stormy weather broke loose and it rained heavily until shortly before midnight. Then the temperature took a sudden dive and thick, wet snow flakes began falling.

Chapter 18

Small Valley 13 Miles Southwest of the Little Missouri River,
Dakota Territory
5:45 a.m., Thursday, June 1, 1876

Half asleep, Private Billy Slaper fumbled around in the crowded confines of the small pup tent he shared with Billy Morris trying to pull his brownish-green wool blanket closer around his shivering body. The only thing he accomplished was to yank most of his bunk mates blanket off which aroused his companion.

"What in tarnation are you doing Billy?" An equally semi-asleep Private Morris grumbled while sitting up in the four foot high A framed white twilled canvas tent.

"I'm cold," muttered Billy Slaper.

When Billy One jerked upright it had created a sound he couldn't identify. Scratching his bony chest between the unbuttoned top of his Army issue brownish-gray-white undershirt he yawned and sleepily said. "You heer that?"

When his buddy didn't respond Billy Morris shook him by the shoulder and repeated his question. "Hey Billy what was that slithering, scraping noise?"

"What confounded noise you jabbering 'bout?" Billy Slaper finally answered in an irritable tone of voice, raising his head that bumped the side of the tent that caused another whispering sound like something was sliding down the side of the tent.

"That noise rite thar!" Billy One responded.

Billy Two pushed his finger at the drooping canvas, which brought on more of the sliding noise. "Well I'll be darn if that don't beat all!" Then noticing how the canvas was sagging inward he did some more poking which made more noise. "Dang if it don't look like the tents caving in. Other than that scraping sound it's as still as a tomb---what time is it anyway?"

Billy One searched around in his belongings until finding his pride and joy; a five dollar Elgin gold plated pocket watch with a long chain and fancy skull fob with red glass eyes. Squinting in the dim light at the white faced dial he said. "You ain't gonna believe this but it's almost a quarter to six."

"Oh my gosh! Did we miss reveille?" Billy Two exclaimed. "Sergeant O'Hara will have our hides!"

Both Billy's immediately started scrambling around in the small space getting their trousers on over their long white drawers and then putting on their scuffed, black leather high-top shoes.

As Billy Slaper hitched his wide red suspenders up over his shoulders a bellowing voice was heard from outside the tents front flap that convinced him his prediction of being in trouble had come true. "Oh, oh---we're in for it now."

To support his fearful concern a banging on top of the front tent pole shook the entire pup tent. "Billy lads, stick yer heads out so I'll know yer alive."

Hearing the brash voice of their first sergeant the two young troopers glanced at one another for a brief moment, then with a resigned shrug of the shoulders, Billy Morris pulled the four tied bows to untie the flap strings holding the flap together and opened the flap.

Both soldiers were startled by the full white glare that hit them as they stuck their heads out of the front flap of the pup tent like two curious moles emerging from a hole.

First Sergeant O'Hara, holding onto a long stick from a tree limb like a cane, gave out a lusty laugh. "What's the matter lads, never seen snow before?"

Now the two troopers knew what the strange sound had been. Snow sliding down the sloping side of their pup tent.

"Well bless my soul, would you look at that," Billy Morris marveled looking at a good foot of drifting snow.

Before Billy Slaper could make a reply with his own observation, First Sergeant O'Hara spoke up. "Here's the order of the day lads: we won't be doing any marching today, so fix up yer tent so it don't cave in by clearing away the snow, then tidy up yer personal gear and clean and oil yer carbines so they don't go rust'en up on ya's. You can move around if you feel like it but don't go astray'en too far as I'm not intending to form up any search parties to go alook'en fer ya. Now go find Corporal Benton and draw a ration of coffee beans, bacon and hard tack as everybody go'en to be mak'en thar own breakfast this morning. Billy lads didja understand everything I had to say?"

Billy Morris answered with a "Yes First Sergeant," while Billy Slaper replied with a quick, "Yessir!"

Smiling at the later soldiers courtesy, and though pleased at his manners, First Sergeant O'Hara still went ahead with a good humored admonishment. "Tis nice of you Billy Two lad to show me the same respect as you would

112

yer Da, but you should know better than to be a'call'en me sor, as you don't see no shoulder boards on me now, do you lad? Now the both of ya's get a'crack'en and getcha-selves som grub."

* * * * *

Billy One pounded a rawhide leather bag with a round stone to crush the coffee beans inside while Billy Two nursed a small fire in front of their pup tent. On either side of the two troopers, and all up and down the long row of tents, other soldiers were likewise doing similar tasks of preparing their morning meal.

The damp, green wood was giving Billy Slaper a fit due to it smoldering and sending up a small dense cloud of white smoke. Choking, and eyes watering from being right next to the fledging campfire while he blew gently on the small bed of orange embers to keep it alive, Slaper finally had to come up for air. "I need some drier tender to keep the fire go'en."

Having just dumped the crushed beans into a tin pot, Billy Morris said. "Get some of that prairie grass we used to sleep on last nite. It jus might work."

"Good idea," Billy Slaper said, crawling into the pup tent while Morris got a handful of snow and placed it on top of the coffee beans inside the pot.

The half dried out grass did help and a flaming fire snapped and crackled after about twenty more minutes of Billy Slaper attending to it. Billy Morris placed the quart-sized pot on a flat stone overlapping the fire then took a fairly large sized cast iron skillet that held ten thick slices of bacon and put it over three rocks centered near the middle of the leaping flames. In less than two minutes the sizzling sound of frying bacon was heard accompanied by its delicious aroma.

Sitting on his haunches, country-boy-style, Billy Morris turned the bacon over with his fork in the bubbling grease and noted that the melted snow was beginning to boil in the make-do coffee pot. He got another handful of snow and placed it in the pot, which quickly melted so he measured in some more snow until satisfied he had a full pot of water.

Billy Slapper scratched his bare head after looking around the area for a couple of minutes, then said. "Where in the sam hill did the dang Hard Tack get off too?"

"Oh---I got it soaking over here in the snow," Billy Morris said, pointing a finger at a small mound of snow the two men had brushed off their pup tent. "I figured I'd go ahead and fry it up in the drop'ens after the bacon fries up. Guess I should'a said som'then to you."

"That's okay, I like 'em that way," Billy Two offered.

Using his own cooking pot Billy Slaper stretched a stained piece of linen cloth over it while Billy Morris poured, the strong black brew of coffee from his pot onto the cloth that acted as a strainer. The boys ended up with about three-fourths a quart of coffee. Putting the used coffee beans back into the pot, Billy Morris added the remaining crushed beans he'd saved and went through the ritual of brewing up another pot. Meanwhile, Billy Slaper had dipped their two tin cups into the already finished brew and sat the steaming cups on a flat stone. "You got any sugar left Billy?"

"I think I've got a little left in my saddle bags wrapped in small piece of paper and in a tobacco tin."

The two comrades enjoyed a leisurely, if meager breakfast under an overcast sky that threatened additional snow.

"I still can't hardly believe old Pappy O'Hara let us sack in till after five." Billy Morris said while chewing on a hunk of grease laden Hard Tack.

Smiling, Billy Sapler replied. "Boy, I really thought we were in for it. Especially when he started banging on the tent with his stick. Felt good getting the extra sleep though even if I was a'freez'en my arse off."

"Yeah, tell me about it. You were sure try'en to warm up yer arse with my blanket. It's not too bad out here now though with our coats on, although I suspect we're gonna see som more snow afallen 'fore too long."

"What we gonna do with our free time?"

"Well, it looks like O'Hara done got assignments for his hundred and one little horse crap details he dreams up, so's I jus mite mosey over to Shanklin's tent and play a little cards."

"Got in mind to lose the rest of your pay do you?" Slaper said with a smile.

"Aw c'mon now. What kind of friend is that? Why don't you wish me some good luck an' if I wins I'll take you out to a big chicken dinner when we get back to Bismarck with all the fresh vegetables you can eat."

"You an' your vegetables. But since you're bound and determined to do it anyway I don't suppose there's any harm in awishing you good luck."

"That's what I like to hear. So what you gonna do with your free time?"

"I think I'm just gonna stick around here and rest up. I got a shirt I ripped down the back an' think I'll sew it up, then take a nap."

"Well feel free to use my blanket this time," Billy Morris smiled.

* * * * *

The first thing George Custer noticed when he entered the tent of his two most senior subordinates was the half-pint silver flask sitting in the middle of the makeshift camp table. Eying Major Marcus Reno, Custer nodded toward the flask, saying. "Good morning gentlemen, a good day to have a nip to take the chill off."

In his almost courtly manner, the dark-faced handsome officer sometimes affected, Major Reno said, "I would be honored to invite you to partake in a small libation General but respect your disinclination for such an indulgence sir."

Captain Frederick Benteen's bulging eyes squinted mischievously as he tried to control and impish grin.

"Humph...yes, ah thank you for your kindness. What I came by to talk to you about regards a meeting I just now concluded with General Terry. It seems that Doctor Williams has advised the general not to attempt a forced march during the current weather conditions as it could cause a rash of bad health ailments for the men, such as diarrhea and grippe. General Terry asked my advice and after thinking it over I calculated we would be most fortunate to traverse ten miles anyway, and that would be done under most hazardous conditions, and while the men might withstand the rigors of such a venture I felt certain the animals would suffer terribly. The animals are having a bad time of it as it is from exposure to the cold wind and being unable to graze except for a dwindling forage supply. And it appears we are in for another blizzard from the looks of the sky. Therefore, General Terry has made the decision that we will spend at least one more day at this campsite with the hopeful prospect of leaving the morning of the third. I want you to tell your men to take care of themselves as we cannot take the chance of filling the ambulances with invalids. It would probably be best if they spent most of their time in their tents" Custer paused to collect his thoughts, then remembering another situation he resumed talking. "Oh yes--- the Ree scouts are acting up, taking our present circumstance as another sign of bad medicine as they seem convinced with all the problems we have faced so far that it's proving their omen of pending disaster for the command. I will require your help to keep those superstitious heathens in line so develop a plan to get them separated by spreading them around your battalions on one pretext or the other." Pausing again, Custer could not think of anything else he had failed to bring to the attention of his senior troop leaders. "Are there any questions or suggestions?"

Captain Benteen spoke up. "What about wood supply? If we're in for another blizzard wouldn't it be a good thought to send some details up to the tree line now to fell a few trees? Take horses along to drag the timber back to camp and the men can chop up their own needs when required."

"Excellent suggestion Captain Benteen. The two of you arrange to have that accomplished within your battalions. Anything else?"

Major Reno did not have any fruitful ideas but he did offer a comment. "This territory has proved once again how unstable and freakish the weather can be. What we should do is let the hostiles have it, and good riddance!"

* * * * *

It was a good thing that General Terry decided to keep the command in bivouac because a freezing northwesterly wind brought with it another raging snowstorm that dumped an additional two feet on the ground. With the drifting of snow caused by the blowing wind, shivering soldiers found their pup tents turned into miniature igloos.

* * * * *

Deep in a small ravine several miles from the soldiers, Rain-in-the-Face was beginning to shake again in spite of his willpower not to feel the cold. After killing his pony he had gutted the animal and crawled inside the slimy, warm confines of its belly. Now the frozen carcass was not offering much insulation from the steady blowing wind that managed to cut through the ravine. After last nights snow storm Rain-in-the-Face had tried to make a run for it but the dropping temperature had forced him to seek shelter. He softly chanted to himself to strengthen his will to live, bringing his stiffened thin blanket to cover his head. The Indian knew if he even survived the night it was going to be a long walk back to wherever his tribe was.

Chapter 19

Valley of the Little Big Horn, Montana Territory
6:00 p.m., Friday June 2, 1876

It took Still Water the better part of four days of hard riding, covering better than 200 miles, to finally locate the smoke rising from the large village of his meandering compatriots. He had been slowed in his search by the same snow storm that now threatened the life of his childhood friend. The snow had effectively erased the normally highly visible signs of Indian tribe movement and it wasn't until this morning that he'd at last came upon the rutted trail created by hundreds of dragging travois's, which led him into the valley of the Little Big Horn. He had been amazed when entering the village. Never had Still Water ever seen such a gathering of his race that he now witnessed. When he asked for the tent of Rain-in-the-Face, the Cheyenne he talked to shrugged his shoulders and Still Water barely understood the few words his fellow Indian had spoken. Besides great numbers of Cheyenne's, Still Water saw Ogallala's, Minnie Conjouk's, Sans Arc, Brule's Uncpapas, Blackfeet, and Santee's before gratefully finding his own people, the Hunkpapa's.

The warrior scout was warmly welcomed by his tribesmen and after being fed and given water to drink he was ushered into Rain-in-the-Face's huge teepee. The Uunkpapa Sioux chieftain's usual stoic expression changed to a thick-lipped smile that lit up his oval face when Still Water entered his home. "Welcome my warrior friend. Come sit near the fire so you can feel its warmth while you tell me and the others what it is you have seen."

The "others" Rain-in-the-Face was referring to were Crazy Horse, two Cheyenne chief's; Dirty Moccasins and Lame White Man, the Brule's Chief' Iron Shell and Black Moon, another Sioux warrior chief. Crazy Horse shared the place of honor with Rain-in-the-Face on the pallet of Buffalo robes at the rear of the teepee. The other four chief's sat in a semi-circle next to Crazy Horse and Rain-in-the-Face. A brightly flaming wood fire in the center of the tent gave off sufficient heat to take away the chill and also good light to see by. A long spiral of smoke from the fire curled upward to vent through a hole at the top of the tepee.

Before sitting down on a buffalo robe near the fire facing Rain-in-the-Face and Crazy Horse, Still Water uttered a Sioux phrase that loosely translated into English as such: "Thank you for inviting me into your home oh great chief."

Waving off the courtesy with a flick of his wrist, Rain-in-the-Face said. "I know you have traveled a long way and are surely tired, but we are most anxious to hear of your experience. Please take your time and recount what you have seen. Is there anything I can get you before you start?"

Still Water answered with the equivalent of "No sir."

"Then you may commence." Rain-in-the-Face said with a nod of his head.

Still Water stuck to the facts without going into very much detail of a digressing nature. He gave the average rate and direction of the Dakota Column's march, emphasizing the number of wagons and animals that slowed down the white men. He did get a few chuckles when telling how clumsy the blue shirts were in crossing rivers and streams and also the rattlesnake incident when trooper Myers was bitten. Still Water also told the group of chief's of the approximate location of the soldiers and his thoughts concerning that if they continued on in the direction they were taking that the only way to avoid them would be to head further north. Then he paused before asking a question that had puzzled him since his return.

"Great chief, I do not mean to be impertinent, but why is Black Face and Bright Face here with you? Both greeted me when I was eating and I could not believe my eyes when I saw them. When I asked them why they were here and not heading back with more scouts to keep an eye on the blue shirts, they told me you forbid them from doing so. Why?"

Rain-in-the-Face was not offended by his warriors question but it took him a long moment to form a tactful answer so not to nettle the other chief's who helped make the decision not to send more scouts out. "When Crow King, Black Face and Bright Face returned, they too sat with a council of chief's, just as you are now doing, and told us of the soldiers and of the terrible thunder stick they are bringing with them. It is true that we want to avoid these soldiers if the Great Spirit allows it. But the soldiers seem determined to hunt us down. As I talk to you at this moment another great body of soldiers are coming toward us from the south. This we learned just a few days ago. And some of our Cheyenne brothers from the west have said that many soldiers are marching from that direction also, although we have no proof of this as yet. So you see Still Water there is much to be concerned about." Rain-in-the-Face paused for a couple of seconds, then spreading his arms wide in a gentle sweeping motion to indicate he was including the others in what he was about to say, continued talking. "We chief's meet daily, sometimes two or three times a day to discuss the events that we see happening. While it is true that our warriors are all brave, we know that the sensible thing is for us to do is flee these white men who seek to destroy us and our way of life. Our strength is in our numbers. Never before in the past have so many tribes united as one for the common cause of survival. So we must gather all of our wandering warriors that still rove the mountains, valleys and Plaines to help make us even stronger by having them with us. That is why your three brothers were told to stay in camp and why I did not allow other braves to go find you and Fast-As-The-Pony-Rides. I only hope that Fast-As-The-Pony-Rides sees the vision of what we are doing and returns soon to join us. You are a fine warrior Still Warrior and one day will have the full wisdom that comes from being a chief. It was a decision that was made after much thought by all of the chief's and it is the right decision. Now you understand why replacements were not sent to you."

Crazy Horse grunted, then remarked. "Well said Rain-in-the-Face."

The other four chief's murmured a like sentiment.

Still Water thanked his chief and said he now understood.

Chief Iron Shell voiced an opinion. "It is written on the wind that the white man ruins all that he touches. They have brought us nothing but grief with their diseases and killing of the great buffalo herds. We do not have enough game right here in this wonderful valley to sustain our people that at one time was full of elk, deer, buffalo and bear. But which way will we go? We fret this way and that as if we have no direction. Dirty Moccasin tells me we will be moving back to the creek of the Rosebud in a few days. Is it not but a full moon that we left that place to come here? Still Water is right. We must move north even if we have to cross into the land where the white man soldiers wear bright red coats."

Crazy Horse had another idea. "What you say has the voice of truth about it Iron Shell. But we must also think of our families. Do we keep running from the white eyes forever, or is there a time when we must stop and turn on the white devils and say to them---this is our land and we will fight for it?"

"You speak like the great warrior you are Crazy Horse," answered Iron Shell. "I know the difficulties of keeping our young bucks from going out right now to do battle with the blue shirts. But when you remind us to think of our families then I must say to you that the empty lodges of fallen warriors which will be mourned by our women is a heavy price to pay to seek the revenge you talk about."

"Revenge?" Crazy Horse eyes narrowed. "No my brave friend, while it may be true that I have much to seek revenge for, even the death of my wife and child because of the white man's disease, it is not revenge I am looking for. It is the pride of wanting to live like a man?"

There was almost a full minute of silence as all within the tent contemplated what they individually considered as living like a man. Finally Lame-White-Man broke the spell. "I have to agree with Crazy Horse that we must live like men, but I must add there comes a time when a warrior must have the pride to also die like a man."

Chapter 20

At the Dakota, Montana Territorial Line
2:30 p.m., Saturday, June 3, 1876

First Sergeant Gustavus Frederick Steiner; on detail from the 20th Infantry as the Top Soldier for the platoon of Gatling guns attached to the 7th Cavalry, sat astride a borrowed horse as he watched the last of his three guns cross over into the Montana Territory. The senior non-commissioned officer, who had joined the Army at age 16 in 1850, looked at his men one by one as they passed by from his wide set, steely-blue, piercing eyes that seemed unblinking in their gaze. "Gus", as the few soldiers knew him, considered his contemporaries, was a compact, pigeon-chested man of about five feet, eight inches in height, weighing about 165 pounds. His short, cropped, blond hair had a silvery cast about it because of the grayness slipping in and he appeared to be almost bald because he kept it cut to a stubble on his square-shaped head. His equally square face was smooth skinned which belied his 42 years, 26 of those years in the infantry.

When the last caisson went by, its gun sergeant, a fellow soldier of German heritage, Sergeant Adolph Gottlieb, who was sitting next to the driver on the limber, waved his hand and said. "Solch wetter! Schnee ein augenblick hellen der nachst, ya?"

Lifting his heavily muscled long right arm and pointing a finger at the sergeant who just remarked in German: *"Such weather! Snow one minute, bright and clear the next, you agree?"* First Sergeant Steiner grumbled in a deep, loud voice, "Gottlieb, you are in the American Army now so speak English, you got that?"

The former German Army lieutenant automatically responded to the curt command with a "Jawohl mien ober..." Then catching himself, offered a rueful smile and said in precise English, "Yes, of course my first sergeant. It is a nice day, do you not agree?"

Gus Steiner's wide nostrils flared a little on his straight nose, which made his small Prussian bush mustache quiver as he did his best to surpass a big grin that was forming. "Yes Sergeant Gottlieb, it is indeed a nice day and it is good to see the sun shining. And even better, I figure we've done a good seventeen miles in roughly nine and a half hours and that's a good half-days march in any mans army."

The straight backed sergeant riding on the limber nodded his head in agreement as the caisson and gun carriage dipped down into a small valley on its westward trek. Turning slightly in his seat, Sergeant Gottlieb made a final comment. "I have heard that many tribes of Indians can sometimes make a days march of fifty miles."

With his long arms dangling at his side giving him an ape-like appearance alongside his thick, stubby legs, First Sergeant Steiner allowed a grin to crease his large, thick-lipped mouth as he hollered a response at the retreating back of the former German officer. "Yeah...but they ain't lugging along the greatest weapon that's ever been built!"

Gus Steiner was born in Germantown, Pennsylvania in 1834. His father had been an enlisted armorer for the German Army before immigrating to the United States nine years before Gistavus's birth where he became a much respected gunsmith. By the time Gus was 15 he was making his own muskets and pistols. His expertness in weaponry had gained him fast promotions in the Army and he found himself as a 27 year old sergeant in charge of the ordinance at Fort Sumter on April 14, 1861. He had heard the first shot of the Civil War fired and had participated in one of the last actions of that war on April 8, 1865, when his battery of Gatling guns destroyed a Confederate patrol. Although Gus dearly loved the Gatling gun, and was as much devoted to the weapon as Lieutenant Low, he still remembered that next to the last day before Lee's Army surrendered when his guns had killed the Rebel soldiers. His lieutenant at the time by the name of Sam Higgins from Indiana had sent him down to the stream to check to see if any of the enemy was alive. Gus had knelt next to a dying reb first sergeant that had called the Gatling's---- *Guns from Hell,* and for some reason that term had always stuck in his mind.

First Sergeant Steiner squared his infantry field cap on his bald-looking head, nudged his borrowed pony and trotted after his platoon.

* * * * *

Private William Lerock of F Company rode next to another F trooper Private Anton Dohman. Both were outrider flankers with the Right Wing and a part of their duties today was security for the 7th Cavalry command group. Both soldiers must have thought that being on the security detail entitled them to shadow the wagon train pretty close because instead of being the normally expected 100 yards out when terrain permitted, they were not more than 30 feet from a slow moving line of rolling ambulances.

Lerock catching sight of Hospital Orderly John Callahan riding next to the driver on Doctor George Lord's wagon hailed him with a greeting. "Hey Callahan you want to trade places for awhile?"

The thin, bespectacled medical technician offered a limp handed wave and thin smile. "No thank you Bill. I'm quite happy where I'm at."

Trotting his yellowish-brown sorrel a little closer to the wagon Private Lerock then said. "How's that fellow do'en that got snake bit Johnny me boy?"

The Hospital Orderly turned his head around and looked to his rear as if wanting to make sure the ambulance carrying Trooper Myers was still in the column, and seemingly satisfied that it was, turned back to the inquiring cavalryman. "He's doing just fine. Doctor Lord said he could rejoin his company in a couple of days."

"That's good to heer. Say---is it true if ya get snake bit the doc will give ya a slug of brandy?"

"I don't know where you came by that information," Orderly Callahan replied, "but no, that is not a reason for the automatic dispensing of medicinal brandy, although in Myers' case the doctor did order a couple of ounces to settle him down."

"For him or Myers?" Lerock laughed.

"I fail to find the humor in that so won't qualify it with an answer." Hospital Orderly Callahan sniffed.

Private Dohman, who had sidled over next to his fellow trooper prodded him. "Go 'head an' ask him Billy."

Somewhat miffed at his buddy's lack of finesse Bill Lerock gave him and angry look as Hospital Orderly Callahan said. "Ask me what?"

Feeling boxed in Lerock had no choice but to request what it was he had come to ask for in the first place. "Well......ah...I was awonder'en if there's any chance you mite slip me one of them bottles of brandy? Be will'en to give ya a dollar fur it."

His question caused the driver of the medical baggage wagon, another private, to glance sharply at the orderly to hear what his answer would be.

"You know better than to ask me to do that. Why we'd both be up on charges if we got caught and I don't have no mind to spend time in an Army stockade."

The driver let loose with a long stream of tobacco juice to punctuate the orderly's terse reply

Unbeknownst to any of them Regimental Sergeant Major William Sharrow had quietly rode up behind the two F Company troopers. "What in the hell are the two of you doing over here pestering Orderly Callahan about?" Without waiting or expecting an answer to his bellowed pointed question, the heavy chested, six footer said in a loud voice. "Now get your asses back out there on the flank where you belong and don't let me catch you moseying up to the wagons again ask'en for any handouts!"

The two startled troopers instantly spurred their mounts and galloped out to the grassy plain.

Sergeant Major Sharrow eyed the hospital orderly for a moment, then said. "You did the right thing orderly---don't let none of 'em pull the sheep's wool over on ya!" Spurring his big gray horse he headed towards the front of the column at a fast trot with Callahan calling out behind him: "No need to tell me that Sergeant Major as I surely know better."

The private driver lifted his butt on one side and farted loudly, then further showed his displeasure of knowing he wouldn't be getting any brandy to drink tonight by letting loose with another stream of brownish-black spittle.

Far out on the right flank Privates Lerock and Dohman licked their wounds the best they could.

"Boy that's just Jim Dandy," voiced William Lerock. "I just got off extra fatigue duty for get'en caught snitching some extra rations from the quartermaster wagon. Now old full-sleeve-stripes Sharrow has to nab me try'en to pull a fast one on Callahan. Taint no doubt I'll be walk'en extra picket from now to dooms day."

"I reckon you ain't gonna be by yourself as he seen me as well as you....." Private Dohman paused for a second having been distracted by two riders tearing across the plain to his front. "Well would you lookie thar. I wonder what that's all about?"

Lerock followed his bunkies gaze and saw the two riders riding hard, coming down the north bluff area from their right and heading toward the front of the column. One rider was a white man and the other an Indian. "I suspect theys dispatch riders coming from either Gibbon or Crook."

* * * * *

The Bismarck Tribune's special correspondent Mark Kellogg approached General Terry with some tepidity. He knew Terry had no fond thoughts whatsoever for newspaper reporters and his present situation was precarious as it was, other than the fact of being in hostile territory, for technically he wasn't supposed to be along on this expedition in the first place as ordered by General Philip Sheridan. Speaking softly he addressed the expedition commander. "By your leave General Terry sir, would it be possible for me to send out a short dispatch to go out on the steamer Far West?"

Terry was in a little better mood since his lieutenant colonel general had been striving rather diligently the past few days to keep his mind on the business at hand instead of gallivanting around the countryside enjoying himself with his brothers and nephew. "What do you consider a short dispatch Mister Kellogg?"

The correspondent showed the general a large brown envelope about half and inch thick. "I can take some of the stories out if this is too much." Kellogg said helpfully.

Eying the big envelope like it contained poison the usually affable general officer remarked. "What on earth could you possibly find so much to scribble about? Good Lord man, we haven't even been in contact with the hostiles yet."

Fidgeting a little the rather portly younger man scrapped one foot back and forth on the ground but had the sense to look the general in the eye when he replied. "It's mostly about the boys sir, what we in the newspaper business call human interest articles. The public is really interested in what you're doing out here and they cannot get enough of what I write, or so it seems," Kellogg trailed off lamely.

"I see," the general said waving away a pesky fly. "Very well Mister Kellogg---you do not have to take anything out. If the lads see their names in print I feel sure it would be good for morale. I'll write a note to General Gibbon to send your material out by either the Far West or our dispatch riders to Bismarck, whichever is heading that way first."

"Thank you sir, that is very gracious of you." Kellogg smiled for the first time as he handed his packet over.

* * * * *

The Dakota column made its best march to date by covering a total of 25 miles in 13 hours and 20 minutes. Camp was established on the banks of Beaver Creek with the first elements of the van reaching that location at 6:20 p.m. In the few remaining hours of daylight pioneers worked frantically to put another bridge across the creek when it was found that the bridge Stanley's expedition had built years ago had been mostly washed away from flooding spring water.

* * * * *

The Terry/Custer command wasn't the only human beings that made excellent marching time this day. Fast-As-The-Pony-Rides was 35 miles distant, on foot to the southwest, after having hacked himself out of the frozen carcass of his pony at 4:00 a.m.

Captain Frederick W. Benteen

Chapter 21

Bad Lands Following Beaver Creek South, Montana Territory
4:00 p.m., Sunday, June 4, 1876

A spectacular western sunrise greeted the members of the Dakota Column as they prepared for their early morning departure. The robin egg blue of the topmost portion of the sky complemented the pink and purplish grays that intermingled among the puffs of white clouds, which was caused by the bright yellowish-orange color streaking the distant horizon. The beautiful display of nature awakening the land for another day told the soldiers they were going to be in for a warm march even though they now felt the chill of morning filling the air.

But just to prove that you can never outthink what the weather is going to be like, from one minute to the next, the entire day turned out to be cool and clear.

Most of the day had been spent in bridge-building as General Terry made the decision to travel southward along Beaver Creek that turned out to be a very circuitous route of march. Even though the weather was cool, after about four miles of marching the general became faint riding his horse and Doctor Lord ordered him to ride in an ambulance, suspecting the general was suffering from fatigue and possible sunstroke.

One primary item of interest the column encountered was another huge prairie dog village which slowed down the rate of march considerably as much caution was taken to insure that horses would not step into the deep burrows. There was one other item of interest that got General Terry's attention as well as the attention of General Custer. In the early afternoon scouts came across three Indian wickiups with fresh green leaves on them. Some time was spent examining the three little huts made of sapling limbs that were bent to form a crude shelter with leaves and grass as cover. This first major sign of Indian activity greatly excited General Terry and aided his recovery of feeling ill.

* * * * *

"Please be seated gentlemen," General Terry bid his senior officers including a few of his personal staff.

When the 10 officers retook their seats after having come to attention when the general had entered the command post part of his tent from his living quarters, the sad eyed officer waited a few seconds until the shifting of chairs, clearing of throats and scraping of boots had settled down. Behind where General Terry stood was a large map of the middle, eastern portion of the Montana Territory. The map, which was secured to a table top laying on its side on top of four hardtack boxes, was an updated version of Custer's Black Hills reconnaissance of 1874, combining information of General Hancock's operations in the Indian country and General Stanley's 1872 expedition. Using a bayonet as a pointer, General Terry said. "This is where we are at right now gentlemen which some of you will recognize as General Stanley's old campsite area of four years ago. Now most of you know my original intention was to march to the mouth of Glendive Creek coming off the Yellowstone...." His bayonet moved upward to show the Glendive Creek, Yellowstone River area...."However, after reading dispatches from Major Moore, who is at Stanley's Stockade," the bayonet moved again, "which reports there are no hostiles between the Yellowstone and our location, I advised General Custer this morning that I was abandoning my previous decision of going to the Glendive." Terry paused to nod at Custer who was flanked on either side by Major Reno and Captain Benteen. Again using his bayonet to trace the course he was describing, he continued; "Therefore, we will continue our southern march along Beaver Creek, then strike west across the divide roughly here, then go directly to Fallon Creek and keep moving until reaching the mouth of the Powder River." The general paused again, this time because of the minor stir he'd created coupled with an undertone of mumbling that took place. Noting Captain Benteen shaking his head back and forth with a nasty smile, General Terry asked. "Something you disagree with Captain Benteen? Perhaps you would be kind enough to share your thoughts with us."

The smart aleck grin instantly vanished as the cherubic-faced officer began he hawing around, having being pointed out. "Ah...ah...why general sir I...I...well the fact is...er...I really don't have a comment to make at this...ah...time."

Hearing Major Reno snigger, General Terry pointed the bayonet at him. "Do you have something you want to add Major?"

Caught off guard, Custer's second in command stammered, "No....no sir."

General Custer unfolded his arms from across his buckskin shirt and gave both his junior officers a baleful glare.

Besides Reno and Benteen, the four-battalion commanders of the 7th

Cavalry had also been invited to attend the briefing and Captain George W. Yates held up a finger saying, "General Sir."

Custer snapped his head around at the unexpected audacity of one of his junior officers wanting to make a comment but General Terry very nicely said. "Yes Captain Yates, you have a question or comment?"

"Yes sir I do," the captain replied, getting to his feet in a gesture of respect. "I understand exactly your logic of making a due west crossing to the confluence of the Powder and Yellowstone, but I am wondering about re-supply sir. If I understand correctly from previous information given by General Custer I believe we were to meet up with the Far West or Josephine at Stanley's Stockade. Assuming the Yellowstone is navigable further west, will there be supplies awaiting us once we reach this new location?"

"Sensible question Captain." General Terry voiced. "Yes we will have our supplies. I have already sent instructions to Major Moore to move a boatload of supplies to the junction of the two rivers and establish a new depot at that location. The Josephine is already on her way back to Bismarck but the Yellowstone is in near flood stage so the Far West will remain on station to assist us." Spotting his aide-decamp waving a finger at him General Terry said, "Yes, what is it?" The aide whispered a few remarks in the general's ear and Terry nodded his head, and then said. "I was just reminded that I should tell you that since it now seems obvious that we are within the close proximity of finding the hostiles that orders have been sent to Colonel Gibbon to halt the eastern movement of his command and remain where he is at until he receives further instructions. Is there anything else that should be brought up?"

There issued a long moment of silence before General Terry then said. "Very well, that's all I have to say. And a good evening to you gentlemen."

Outside General Terry's tent, Custer buttonholed Captain Yates. "The next time you have the urge to ask a question of the expeditionary commander, I strongly suggest you come to me with it first. Do you understand this Captain?"

The wide-set eyed officers long, thick brown mustache twitched involuntarily from his tight lipped effort of maintaining his composure and with an almost hiss he managed to utter a low. "Yes sir, I shall do that in the future sir."

Just then Major Reno and Captain Benteen passed by on their way to their tent and Custer made another remark to Captain Yates that was intended for the other two officers. "At least you had the common decency to voice something of a pertinent nature instead of disgracing me in front of General

Terry with simpering giggles. You may carry on sir."

Captain Benteen paused in his stride and started to turn around.

Although Major Reno had no great fondness for the former Civil War brevet colonel he bunked with, he grabbed Benteen by the arm and muttered. "You best let it go Fred or he'll have your head served up for morning breakfast."

Uttering a loud grunt, the short-statured bantam rooster with a bulldog scowl, resumed his direction of walk, mumbling loud enough that he hoped his commander would hear. "I just hope I'm around when a certain prima donna falls off his horse."

"Shush--he'll hear you," cautioned Reno in a low voice.

"No horse shit----you really think so?" Benteen snorted sarcastically.

Mitch Bouyer

Chapter 22

Colonel Gibbon's Headquarters on the Yellowstone River,
Montana Territory
7:00 p.m., Monday, June 5, 1876

Lieutenant James H. Bradley, the appointed Chief of Scouts for Colonel John R. Gibbon's Montana Column, waited impatiently outside the large, white Headquarters Command Tent for his requested audience with the 50 year old full colonel. Sitting next to the lieutenant on the rude log bench was a half-Santee Sioux, name Mickel "Mitch" Boyer, who lived among the Crows, and considered the next best scout-guide in the country alongside the renowned Jim Bridger.

The 31 year old lieutenant, who had the reputation of correctly analyzing the strength and movements of Indian tribes, tossed the willow stick on the ground he'd been whittling on and said disgustingly, "You would think that the importance of what we have to report would have precedence over a late supper party the colonel's having!"

The dark faced, dark haired half-breed with svelte, delicate features who was very personable, offered a short laugh, and then said. "Do you think he's going to listen to us anyway Jim?"

Equally handsome as well as slim, the well groomed, mustached officer grunted an answer without saying a word. James Bradley, an Ohio native, had been an enlisted volunteer during the Civil War and because of his intelligence coupled with a daring spirit was commissioned a second lieutenant at the wars end. Now as a first lieutenant, he had the awesome responsibility of being the eyes and ears for the 27 officers and 409 enlisted men that made up the Montana expedition. This combined group of infantry, cavalry, one 12 pound Napoleon field piece and two Gatling guns, along with a scouting detachment, teamsters and packers, had been on the march longer than the other two converging columns, the first units having left Fort Ellis on March 23rd. Jim Bradley was good at his job and took his responsibility very seriously, which was more than could be said regarding the inaptness of his commander, Colonel Gibbon.

Mitch Boyer hinted at Gibbon's lack of good judgment when he made a remark to Lieutenant Bradley. "The way I look at it, about the only smart thing the colonel's done so far was making you in charge of the scouts. You put together some real good boys but it taint going to do no good if'n he don't act on what you bring him. You take old Tom Leforge who's in charge of the Crow scouts. Him and Barney Bravo have both lived among the Crows for years an' when those two fellows tell ya there's a whole bunch of Sioux out thar, you can best bet your last red cent that they ain't making up no tall tales."

"I thank you for the good words about my capabilities, but you don't have to convince me about the hostiles being close. This is the third time I've seen 'em with my own eyes, plus what you told me a little while ago."

"Oh--they's moving, no doubt about it. What you seen back in May was just them gathering together. What Gibbon's should have done then was to follow up his decision to move against them when they were only thirty-five miles away. That was a bunch of hogwash about him turning back just because his cavalry had trouble cross'en the river. Then, when you told him of you and Leforge seeing all them lodges and the valley full of ponies where the Rosebud parallel's the Tongue, that should have smarted him up right then and there that they ain't moving north----they's gon'en west to the Rosebud; and I'll tell ya something else: they ain't scared of us."

Lieutenant Bradley nodded his head in agreement. "What you told me about seeing upwards of a thousand warriors moving today, not more than twenty miles from here, has got to be made known to General Terry and General Crook. There is no possible way we can engage a force that size." The veteran officer paused for a long moment and bent down to pick up the willow stick he'd tossed on the ground. Fiddling with the smooth white piece of wood he stared off in space for a few seconds before talking again. "After pondering over everything that's come in to me, plus what you've reported and what I've seen for myself, I have surmised the hostiles are working their way between the Rosebud and the Little Bighorn. I suspect they will pause there for a time and as you have said, they don't seem to have a fear of us which tells me there are evidently a lot more warriors gathered together than we already know about. I've got an odd feeling that we've got a huge battle facing us. Just got to make sure that all three of the fielded expeditions work in close harmony as we've got to work together on this. If Gibbon's drags his feet about what we've learned, someone could be facing some serious difficulties."

* * * * *

But Colonel Gibbon's, who wasn't feeling very well health wise, was at the moment trying to cheer himself up by relating a bit of gossip to the gathering of his officers who were smoking cigars and partaking a fairly decent vintage brandy as an after dinner treat. "....so when General Terry informed me he was assuming direct command of the Dakota Column, I knew right away that Custer was apparently in some sort of trouble...."

* * * * *

Even though Colonel Gibbon's had extremely important military intelligence to pass on, for some unexplainable reason, he kept this valuable information to himself.

Captain Grant Marsh
Commander of the steamboat Far West

Chapter 23

Steamer Far West at Stanley's Stockade, Yellowstone River,
Montana Territory
8:45 p.m., Tuesday, June 6, 1876

Captain Grant Marsh's cabin could hardly be called spacious but it was large enough to accommodate several people for a meeting the eight feet by ten feet space offered.   The steely eyed, narrow jut-chinned steamboat captain wasn't concerned about the size of his combination office and quarters anyway as he sat on a chair next to his built-in, drop leaf, wall desk listening to Major Orlando Moore, of the Sixth U. S. Infantry, relate information he had received in dispatches.

"...and bring along commissary goods, general quartermaster supplies, medical supplies to include medicines you may have, ammunition of all calibers and forage if you can spare it." Major Moore looked up from the sheet of paper he had been reading from and said. "What General Terry has ordered is to establish a new supply depot at the Powder River so what I'll do is leave one company here at the stockade and take the remaining troops with me to the new base camp."

"That will not present a problem," the neatly trimmed mustached steamer captain said. "But what I don't understand is why not take all the supplies we have here and abandon this place entirely."

"I thought of that also and to be honest with you that particular issue wasn't made clear in what General Terry ordered. Therefore, I do not feel I have any choice but to obey the request for another supply depot while at the same time continue to follow my original orders of maintaining a presence here at Stanley's Stockade."

"Well, the way I see it, since you put it that way, is go ahead and get the vessel loaded and we'll start moving downstream before noon tomorrow. With the water as high as it is, there shouldn't be any problem getting back up the Glendive," the 58 year old skipper observed.

Major Moore smiled at the captain who wore a long blue coat, a white shirt and black bow tie. "Sir, your excellent reputation of being able to take the Far West anyplace where there's enough water to keep her bottom wet leaves me no doubt you can get back here if circumstances require."

Captain Marsh's heavy black eyebrows furrowed and his normally stern looking face creased in his version of a smile at the compliment. "Mighty kind of you to say that but if you navigated these waters as long as I have then you'd learn to sail her on a good morning's dew. She's very manageable in the high winds we get up here because she's made light with no Texas deck or large cabin space in the middle. The two high piston stroke fifteen-inch engines and two steam capstans makes her as speedy as she is strong. Probably the best river steamer the Pittsburgh yards built in seventy." The Captain paused, running a hand through his short-cropped brown hair that was speckled with gray. This was an old gesture when he realized he was babbling too much and getting back on track to the business at hand, he said, "Is there anything else in the dispatches that would be of interest to me?"

The slim, wiry built major shook his head, saying. "No sir, that's about it. General Terry wrote a note that he wants me to scrutinize the contents of some news reports a war correspondent wants sent to his paper in Bismarck to insure its fairness and accuracy, and if I come up with any interesting tidbits I'll share them with you. I do want to thank you again for allowing me and my officers the use of your cabins; certainly makes it more comfortable atmosphere than living in a tent."

Waving his big hand in a depreciating manner Captain Marsh said. "Think nothing of it Major. Just be thirty cabins going to waste if you soldiers weren't using them. You mentioned those dispatches from the war correspondent: with the Josephine heading back to Bismarck and our pending move, you intend on getting them back with one of your couriers?"

"Yes. I'll be sending out dispatches with a rider tomorrow to Fort Lincoln and if after reading them if they're not too disgraceful I'll send them along."

* * * * *

Infantry Captain Josh Weavers, hearing laughter coming from the cabin next door to his stood up from the bunk bed he'd been sitting on and went to the small slated door that led to the upper railed deck of the Far West. A moment later he had his head stuck in the door of his commanding officer. "You are certainly in a good mood tonight Orry," he remarked using Major Moore's nickname.

"C'mon in Josh----you've got to hear this." The good-looking officer invited.

Sharing his friend's humor the tall, angular captain grinned before knowing what was so funny and entered the tiny cabin.

Pointing to a camp chair near the center wall Major Moore said. "Have a seat and I'll read you this dispatch from this character Mark Kellogg who's sending it to his newspaper in Bismarck."

Once the officer was seated the major picked up a thin sheet of paper off his bunk bed which he had been using as a desk and shifting around his camp chair so he'd be facing his subordinate, said, "Listen to this: In the field with the Seventh Cavalry--General George A. Custer, dressed in a suit of buckskin, is prominent everywhere as we travel the Bad Lands. Dashingly handsome this cavalier of the cavalry flits here and flits there, to and fro in his quick eager way, taking in everything connected with his command. His caring, yet steely gazing eyes of deep blue views his surroundings with the keen, incisive manner for which he is so well known. He pauses to talk to one of his troopers who appears to be saddle worn, and shows his concern. Then another and another, he gives comfort and encouragement to. Is it any wonder why his men love this gallant warrior so? The general is full of perfect readiness for a fray with the hostile red devils, and woe to the body of scalp-lifters that comes within reach of himself and brave companions in arms. I am honored to be in the company of such a distinguished leader of men who radiates the warmth of his care and welfare for his men and holds forth an air of confidence rarely seen in these western wilds." Major Moore paused for a couple of seconds as he looked up at Captain Weavers with a smile on his face. "Is this the same Custer that I know whom deserted his command so he could ride home to be with his wife? And who left men behind after a battle that was slaughtered by the savages he didn't have time to hunt down! It's hard to swallow that Kellogg is writing about the same man that Colonel Sturgis described as a very selfish man who is insanely ambitious for glory."

Shaking his head, Captain Weavers said. "No wonder you gave such a harsh laugh a few minutes ago. How can a person write such rubbish?"

"Oh this is not all, let me read on; it gets deeper than a pile of horse shit." Major Moore waved the dispatch at his companion, then read on.

139

Chapter 24

The Custer Quarters Fort Abraham Lincoln, Dakota Territory
12:50 p.m., Wednesday, June 7, 1876

Libbie Custer uttered intelligible words aloud in her sleep as her lithe body, which was clad in a white linen nightgown, moved spasmodically in an agitated manner on the damp bed. Open, screened widows throughout the living quarters offered a pleasant June evening cross-breeze that filtered through the house and gently fluttered the long, heavy curtains in the small bedroom. But the cool air was not offering a refreshing caress on Libbie's pretty, heart shaped face as she was having a disturbing dream in her restless sleep that raised her body temperature. The woman's face had a flush look about it and thin beads of perspiration formed a crystalline mustache above her dainty mouth. She appeared almost feverish with the much heavier accumulation of perspiration above her dense finely haired eyebrows, which plastered her soft brown curly bangs to her forehead.

The dream Libbie was experiencing was in a sense a re-occurring episode, at least the general theme was similar to past dreams that flashed scenes which plagued her unconscious state. This particular imaginary vision held a picture of an open battlefield with hundreds of corpses of blue uniformed soldiers; their bodies strewn in a disorder of jumbled heaps among dead horses and ruined military equipment. The scene embraced a vista panoramic setting as if she was viewing it close overhead in a broad low sweep of the ground while moving very slowly. As the dream progressed Libbie saw in the not to far distance a view of many swallow-tailed cavalry guidons fluttering on a knoll in a shifting wind. Most of the dozen or so pennants were the more common variety the Army utilized with split in half red over white fields with single black letters sewn in the middle indicating what company the banner represented. She strained her eyes to see what companies the guidons belonged to but the letters grew blurred the closer she got to them. Then she noticed a planted staff standing alone from the others and it was very clear to her. It boasted a white starred blue field with red and white stripes much like the Grand Union Flag of the Republic. She recognized it instantly as being the personal battle flag of a major general. Already in a fearful state from viewing the ghastly piles of bodies Libbie felt a worse sense of dread as she approached nearer to the battle flags and she began voicing words of apprehension that she could not understand as the hollow sound was like a dull echoing wail as if Indians were chanting. As she hovered over the blue-starred major general's standard standing upright in the ground, her thoughts were mixed. A part of her being was telling her to flee this field of carnage while another part was forcing her down to earth to satisfy a morbid curiosity that was eating away at her soul. In a flash---- she got a close-up view of what she had been dreading of having to see all along: her beloved Bo lay among the dead piled around the flags. Her husband's eyes were tightly shut as if in a deep sleep; his brow furrowed, and the solemn expression on his handsome face looked as if he was studying a complex question that he could not come up with an answer for. Libbie bent to her husband and tried to awaken him. When he did not respond she began to shake his shoulders harder. The more she shook and called his name the more it seemed the still body was beginning to dissolve right in front of her eyes. Harder and harder she shook the fading aspiration when suddenly she stared directly into the black, hollow eyes of a grinning skull that stared back at her------and she screamed.

The thirty-four year old woman came awake with a start shouting over and over "No, no, NO!" Tears ran fully down her rosy cheeks and her warm body trembled as she jerked upright in her bed. In her emotional state it took several seconds for the tragic dream vision to fade and for her to finally realize she had experienced a terrible nightmare----again!

Swinging her legs off the bed Libbie Custer sat stiffly on its edge breathing deep gulps of air until her eyes grew accustomed to the inky darkness of her surroundings. Taking a long sulfur stick match from an ornate tin holder on the table next to her bed she struck the match on the raspy side of the container that burst into a bright flare of yellow light. Libbie lifted the glass chimney of the bedside kerosene lamp and touched the match to the exposed wick. After lowering the chimney she adjusted the little knob control for the wick that heightened the illumination in the room. She stepped into slippers and stood up and padded across the room to a heavy wood constructed washstand with a marble top and sunken ceramic washbowl. She poured the full amount of water from a large blue and white water pitcher that had the same flowered pattern as the washbowl into the bowl. After splashing water onto her face and dabbing her neck and cleavage she took a towel from the washstand hanger rack and patted herself dry. The pouring of the water coupled with the light rinsing of her face, neck and upper breast brought on an urge in her bladder and she bent down to take out a glazed blue metal night pot from under the wash stand curtain. Taking off the lid that made a tinny scrape Libbie raised her nightgown, squatted, and quickly relieved herself. She then poured the water from the washbasin into the blue pot and replacing the lid put it by the door. From a wall hook Libbie took down a light fabric morning duster and slipping it over her gown picked up the lamp, retrieved the blue bucket by its carrying handle and walked out of the bedroom and into the big western-styled frontier kitchen. Libbie deposited the waste pail by the back door for the housemaid to take care of in the morning then walking to the sink pumped herself a glass of water. Drinking half the water she poured what remained down the drain, which gurgled its way through cast iron pipes to the outside where it spilled into a stump hole. After placing the empty glass on the drain board she left the kitchen and went into the spacious front living room. Libbie lifted her lamp to better see the thirty day wind up Regulator pendulum wall clock that offered the only sound in the otherwise silent house with its comforting tick, tocking. Noting it was almost midnight she shook her head resignedly with the knowledge she'd got less than three hours of troubled sleep and now felt wide awake.

For a moment Libbie thought about reading a book but quickly discarded that idea knowing she wasn't in the mood for light reading. Just the same she walked over to the shelves where her husband kept his many books near his big roll top desk. She scanned the titles with little interest, other than the fact they were her Autie's possessions that made him seem closer to her in a way. Sitting down at the opened roll top Libbie wiped her hand across the polished surface of the dark oak desk in a melancholy gesture of reminiscence. She mused how Autie did his serious writing, such as the autobiography he was working on, at the nearby wall table so she could set across from him and watch him work and answer his questions from time to time while she knitted. Remembering this personal trait of her husband caused Libbie to conjure up the images of her most recent nightmare. Shuddering a little Libbie pondered on her dream for a couple of minutes as she tried to analyze its meaning along with similar dreams which was making her have an almost constant premonition of disaster facing her golden-haired soldier husband. She had tried many times to shake off this feeling but it always came back to haunt her.

Wanting to take her mind off this dilemma Libbie then thought about the time when the Far West had made its way to Bismarck and then navigated over to Fort Lincoln. How she and several of the other officer's wives had went down to the landing to get news about their husbands and to see if Captain Marsh and any mail for them. The steamer captain had showed a gallant side by inviting all the ladies aboard his vessel for a luncheon. But when Libbie had broached the subject of allowing her to go back with him when the Far West returned with additional supplies, Captain Marsh had refused her request on the basis he would never assume such a responsibility. He also pointed out there was no suitable accommodations on his craft for a lady to embark upon such a venture since his charted river boat was totally committed to the all male Army.

At first Libbie had been very piqued at the captain's abrupt refusal, but in reflection she realized that being a "camp follower" had its draw backs and as much as she wanted to be with her beloved "boy" she would have probably distracted him from his duties and would have been in his way. Libbie also concluded that General Terry would have looked upon her arrival with a not so fond eye. So she continued her lonely wait with hope and prayer for her husband's safety and quick return while suffering the unneeded nocturnal dreams that kept her in a disturbed and distraught state of mind.

Sitting morosely at the big oak desk, with her hands folded in her lap, Libbie went back to her other thoughts on why she was wide awake at half-past midnight with no desire or will to crawl back into the lonely bed which she had shared with her husband for the past twelve years.

Talking aloud for the first time since earlier realizing she was shouting in her sleep, Libbie voiced her real fear to the pigeon-holed desk. "I will not chance a resurgence of that awful dream the remainder of this night!"

Having issued her ultimatum she glanced at the neatly lined row of writing pens laying next to large ink well and her spirits lifted. "What I shall do is compose a nice long letter to Autie and tell him how much I miss him."

Finding her rose colored stationary in a desk drawer Libbie began to write in her neat, precise hand:

Dearest Autie,

I feel so badly I was not on board the boat, but I might have found myself without employment, which as you know, is my safety valve, and I would have been so conspicuous on the steamer, if you had gone off on a scout. I cannot but feel the greatest apprehensions for you on this dangerous scout. Oh, Autie, if you return without bad news the worst of the summer will be over.

The papers told last night of a small skirmish between General Crook's Cavalry and the Indians. They called it a fight. The Indians were very bold. They don't seem afraid of anything.

The Belknap case is again postponed. Of course that worries me. The Prosecution is going to call you as a witness. Politicians will try to make something out of you for their own selfish ends. But I hear you say, "Don't cross bridges till you come to them."

I am perfectly delighted with your "Galaxy" War article, but I wish you had not spoken for McClellan so freely. Still, I don't see how you could have consistently given your opinions on the War without giving him his just due. It finishes Mr. Chandler as a friend I fear, and for that I am sorry as he can be a very tenacious enemy...and of late has been only a passive friend. I honestly think you would be better off with some policy, with such powerful enemies. A cautious wife is a great bore, isn't she Autie?

You improve every time you write. There is nothing like this McClellan article for smoothness of style. I have this month's "Galaxy" with the Yellowstone article. How fortunate you had left it with Mr. Sheldon. I am anxious about the one you sent by the Buford mail. The mail was dropped in the Yellowstone and they must have attempted to dry it before the fire, for all our letters are scorched. Maggie's to Jim had been re-enveloped at Buford.

I think to ride as you do and write is wonderful. Nothing daunts you in your wish to improve. I wish your lines had fallen among literary friends. And yet Autie I wouldn't have you anything but a soldier.

It is the hottest day of the season, yet cold chills are running up and down my back at your description of the Yellowstone fight. I am glad you gave Tom his due. Of course you appreciate his valor as a soldier, yet you do not want to be puffing your own family. Mother will be so pleased for "Tommie." Your mention of him would satisfy the most exacting of mothers.

I cannot but commend your commendation of General Stanley.... To ignore injury and praise what is praiseworthy is the highest form of nobility. I could not do it. My soul is too small to forgive.

I know you have a gift for finding roads, but how nice of General Terry to acknowledge your skill and perseverance that way.

Maggie and Em entertained Dr X and Mr. G in the pallor last evening. I went in for manners, but was too heavy-hearted to stay. Mr. B called. He told me of Buttons' resignation because Grant treated him unfairly, but it was withheld till after the convention.

The wild flowers are a revelation; almost the first sweet-scented I have ever known. The house is full of bouquets. Em gets presents all the time.

With your bright future and the knowledge that your are a positive use to your day and generation, do you not see that your life is precious on that account, and not only because an idolizing wife could not live without you.

As always I shall go to bed a dream of my dear Bo.

Libbie.

After Libbie reread the letter she frowned. She really didn't like it but also did not like the idea of tearing it up and starting over, so she folded it and placed it in an envelope. After writing her husband's name on the front of the envelope she placed the letter in the middle of the desk to go out with the day's mail. Consoling herself, she said aloud. "He knows me better than I know myself so I'm sure he'll understand all that I wrote. Oh damn Autie! When will all this madness of war be over?"

Elizabeth Custer bit her lip and looked furtively around the room as if expecting to discover a witness to her bit of temper and unlady like conduct of speech. Then she begun to weep. Tears ran fully down her flushed cheeks. Libbie sobbed mournfully until being overcome with hiccups. She held her breath like she'd been taught to do as a little girl until the spasmodic contraction abated then staring at the pigeonholes in the desk again, she again spoke aloud in a choking voice. "Oh Autie-----why is it that we cannot have children? The dear Lord knows we've tried...oh dear Autie, a little boy or girl would be such a comfort to me....and...and...I would always have a part of you....no matter what."

Chapter 25

Branch of the Powder River, Montana Territory
7:30 p.m., Wednesday, June 7, 1876

The same day that Libby Custer went through her nightmarish experience at Fort Lincoln her husbands command had descended into the valley of the Powder River, having marched 32 miles, the longest trek the column had managed to accomplish to date. While she put away the day-to-day china she used for regular meals, after having a late supper with her sister-in-law Maggie and Emma Reed, older sister of Autie Reed, two of her husband's men were having an after dinner chat.

* * * * *

Senior Private John "Mac" McCullough was a man who usually kept his word, giving the circumstances of whatever it was that he may have promised. The reed thin, over six foot tall Texan had in fact kept his promise to fellow M Trooper Private Calvin Switzer, when he'd told Calvin he would tell Captain French what a good job the youngster had done on the May 31st scouting patrol. The long drooping mustached, pale blue-eyed Texan who had opted to fight for the Union during the recent war, had ulterior motives by his gesture of camaraderie; which wasn't unusual as this too was normal for him when he did something nice for somebody else. Now it was time for the reddish-blond haired, 30 year old private to collect some additional interest on the debt the 19-year-old high school graduate from upper New York State owed him.

"Hey Calvin ole buddy how'ya do'en this evening?" Private McCullough asked with a broad smile.

Looking up from a book he was reading in the fading light the boyish faced trooper said. "Oh...hi Mac. I'm doing okay----just got off wood detail for the officers."

"Ain't that som'thing--damn stiff shirts can't even gather their own firewood. Boy if I ever got to be an officer I'll tell ya one thing, I'd shore nough be out collect'en my own wood and water an' that's a fact."

Placing a blade of grass between the page he'd been reading to mark his spot, the toe-headed, hefty teenager shook his head. "Aw I don't mind it, especially since it was for Captain French. He's been treating me real nice

146

since you put in a good word for me. He's even called me Calvin a couple of times, do you believe that?"

"Whal, sometimes it don't pay ta get yerself to whal known by those in charge of ya.." Mac said as he hunkered down next to the young private, "..but I'd say in this case that's a pretty good sign he's tak'en a favorable shine to ya."

Somewhat pleased at this remark Switzer asked kindly. "What have you been up to Mac? I haven't seen you all day."

"I was on the detail that guarded the pioneers today. It looked bad when we started out before five this morning and I'd of bet anything it was go'en to pour down rain on us with that heavy cloud cover but all it did was drizzle a little. Spent most the day watching those boys hack out roads for the column and I'm here ta tell ya they worked their tails off. With all the rocks we had to go over I heered quite a few wagons got damaged and horses and mules were a'drop'en out left and right."

"No wonder I didn't see you then," Calvin interjected, "You spent all your day up front with General Custer while I was near the middle of the column on the security party for General Terry. You must have been up front then when Lonesome Charley got lost. Boy was General Terry ticked off about that. He said what good was it to hire scouts for path finding when General Custer ends up doing most of it anyway."

"Yeah, old Charlie Reynolds got lost sure 'nough. I thought it was funnier than hell when Custer came riding up all red-faced yell'en an' screaming tell'en Reynolds he couldn't find his way up Broadway in New York City. Old Reynolds ain't no man to mess with but he shore didn't have much to say when Custer lit into him. Course him gett'en lost yesterday by leading us astray up the wrong fork of O'Fallon Creek didn't put him in good steed with Custer any and Reynolds knew it. And today's mess is the reason we still got wagons com'en in and I'll bet ya we'll be see'en 'em com'en in after dark. They're spread out to hell an back down the trail."

"What did they do with the horses that fell out from their teams?" Calvin wanted to know.

"The ones that could still walk they jus let go but some of the mules and horses that went down and couldn't get up they shot."

"Is that right...that's awful, gee I'd hate to have to kill a horse. Did you get the word that we can't go hunting anymore and if you shoot your rifle without permission it's a court-martial offense?"

"Yeah...whal a part of that reason is because of those two Company A troopers getting thar dumb asses lost a couple of nights ago and having to

147

spend the night in the Bad Lands. But I think the main reason now, is because General Terry's convinced this time thars hostiles nearby and he don't want to tell 'em anymore that he has too 'bout whar we're at. Course---that's 'bout the fourth time old Terry's given the no shoot'en order but I suspect he means it this time. And as far as shoot'en horses, that's jus something that's gotta be done from time to time, ain't no get'en aroun' it...worse to leave 'em to suffer."

Wanting to get off the subject of killing horses and mules, Calvin made another remark. "I heard General Terry was fit to be tied when McWilliams shot himself in the leg yesterday with his revolver."

McCullough slapped his knee with his hand and let out a horselaugh. "Boy you done said a mouthful thar! McWilliams only makes about the fifth one that's done went an shot hisself. You know what Terry told Custer? He says at this rate all the Injuns have to do is ta wait us out and we'll have shot up our command all by ourselves. That makes the third trooper from H Company that's done plugged hisself and I heer tell that prissy ass Lieutenant Gibson is walk'en stiff legged from the ass chewing ole Custer gave him, which jus breaks my heart all ta pieces it does."

This last remark from Mac got a short laugh out of Calvin and the senior private thought it time to make his pitch that he come for in the first place. "Say Calvin ole buddy, I got a favor to ask from you and I'd really appreciate it if you'd help me out."

"Why sure Mac, if I can do it I sure will. What is it?"

"Whal Captain Benteen's been giv'en the order to form up a scouting patrol for tonight, ah...gonna start pretty late I guess you'd say, not go'en ta leave till past ten. Be go'en up stream till we find the mouth of the Powder River." Mac paused for a moment while he scratched the side of his face. Then, looking up at the attentive face of his young comrade, he said. "Anyway, I've been detailed to go on the patrol and I don't feel rite well and was a'wonder'en if maybe you might volunteer to take my place?"

Without hesitation Calvin Switzer answered. "Why Mac I'd be happy to stand in for you but I've got picket tonight starting at twelve midnight." Calvin also paused for a second, then snapping his finger, said. "Hey---we can ask Captain French if we can switch. That way if you get feeling poorly while standing picket you could ask the Corporal of the Guard for a supernumerary to relieve you."

It was difficult for Private McCullough to hide the disappointment that now creased his frowning face. A brief thought flashed through his mind that sometimes the best laid plans went haywire. "Naw...that's okay Calvin,

I reckon I'll jus have to tough it out."

* * * * *

About the time Libbie Custer awoke screaming from her nightmare, Private John G, McCullough was inching his way behind a mounted trooper in front of him along the mushy banks of the Powder River. McCullough was half scared out of his wits because he didn't like night marches to start with and the treacherous footing he was traveling could bring disaster to him and his horse at any moment.

Steamboat Far West

Chapter 26

Along the Powder River, Montana Territory
3:30 p.m., Thursday, June 8, 1876

Mark Kellogg took advantage of the long delay the main column was experiencing by putting the finishing touches on a dispatch he was writing for the Bismarck Tribune. The delay was due to the extremely slow movement of wagons traversing a ford that had been found as the only one suitable for the wagon train to cross. Kellogg had found some shade under a supply wagon belonging to the Gatling gun platoon that would be among the last to go across the Powder River. Using his large black leather dispatch case as a desk the reporter sat cross-legged under the wagon and wrote with his pencil in the brown leather covered dispatch book: *"The Powder River located in the eastern quarter of the Montana Territory, has got to be the filthiest stream in America or anywhere else. It is too thick to drink and too thin to plow. It is four hundred miles long, a mile wide, and an inch deep. Well known explorer Captain William Clark of the famous Lewis and Clark expedition, originally named this sludgy waterway "Red Stone River." I have no idea where the good captain came up with "Red Stone," but I can most certainly assure the readers of the Tribune that whomever renamed it the Powder River, did so with absolute accuracy. Not because of the deep yellowish color of the slow moving water but rather from the dark colored powder-like sand that is found along its banks. One of Genl Custer's scouts which I have written about previously; "Lonesome" Charlie Reynolds, kindly explained to me that the river's upper reaches, which we are headed, has deep and narrow canyons fringed with cottonwood, ash and several different type of berry bushes. "Lonesome" Charlie also informed me that these canyons and trees give excellent protection against the winds of winter, which makes it a favorite camping place of the Sioux. What lays in wait for the brave men of the Seventh Cavalry as we make our way to the mouth of the Powder River is of course unknown as of this writing. However, we do know that savage hostiles are in close proximity to our present location as this very morning scouts returned with the news that patrols sent out by Col. John Gibbon have been driven back to their encampment by the murdering devils."* Kellogg stopped writing and read over what he had written. Then he stared off in space for better than a minute as he pondered whether or not he should continue on with this story or save other information he had for another article. Deciding to continue on with a few more paragraphs the stout reporter reached for a newly sharpened pencil and after tapping the end against his large front teeth for a couple of seconds, bent his head and started writing again: *"While the heroic figure of Genl Custer leads his famous regiment on this campaign, I must remind readers that the Expedition Commander is BGenl Alfred Terry. Genl Terry is an exceptional officer in his own right and I had the honor to see him ride off this early afternoon at the head of two of the Seventh Cavalry's Companies. The two companies are Troops A and I, led by Capt's Miles Moylan and Myles Keogh respectively. Genl Terry has certainly shown his men what he is made of by scouting ahead with these two troops right into the jaws of where the hostiles are reported to be. This is a grand measure of courage that stands right beside the well-known courage Genl Custer is so well known to possess. Woe be it to the savage Indian that face these two warriors of the west."* Kellogg smiled at his embellishment. He knew that readers ate up this kind of talk and he prided himself of being among the best to offer what the readers wanted. Then he mused that it would possibly put him in better graces with General Terry if he could somehow think of a way to make sure the general got a gander at his article before sending it out. He didn't have to use soporiferous tactics when dealing with Custer as that general loved seeing his name in news dispatches. All Kellogg had to do when he wrote something grand about Custer was just take it to him and ask him to look it over for possible "editing." It worked every time and the war correspondent felt this had a lot to do with the excellent rapport he had with the man

A scuffling of feet directly in front of Mark Kellogg's impromptu shelter gained his attention. Hidden under the wagon like he was all Kellogg was able to see two pair of legs clad in robin egg blue uniform trousers with darker blue broad stripes running down the sides. The reporter's first inclination was to make his presents known but when he heard the voice of the young lieutenant that commanded the Gatling guns talking he decided to stay out of sight and eavesdrop.

"So first sergeant you say you've double checked the traces and trees on all the limbers and gun carriages?" Lieutenant William "Bucky" Low asked First Sergeant Gustavus "Gus" Steiner.

"Yes sir, that I have sir and they're as secure as we can make them. Checked each one myself, I did sir."

"That's very good. Ah..how about the extra strapping device I came up with; are they working on the limber beams and carriage couplings?"

"Sir, that was a right fancy idea you came up with there. I was able to do a little requisitioning that the lieutenant really doesn't want to know about, but managed to come up with sufficient reins and other leather tackle and the boys fashioned some right smart holding straps with them. We put extra eye rings on the double trees and beams and with triple straps going through each of them I do believe they would hold the caissons together even if the couplings did break like they did on Sergeant Gottlieb's gun when crossing Davis Creek a week or ten days ago."

Lieutenant Low had grinned when his first sergeant mentioned slyly how he'd come about procuring the needed leather strapping for this latest invention. "I'm really pleased to hear that first sergeant and you are correct that I do not want to know how you came about obtaining the necessary material to try out my experiment. Suffice to say that I do believe I've inherited the biggest bunch of bandits since Jesse James decided to start robbing banks and trains."

First Sergeant Steiner could not suppress a grin of his own after hearing his lieutenant's remark. "Well sir, it does seem at times that the Gatling gun platoon is pretty far down the supply chain."

"Speaking of supply chain, were you able to replace the ammunition we expended at the demonstration we put on a couple of weeks ago?"

Still smiling Gus Steiner said. "That was just a tad bit of a problem sir as the cavalry only uses a handful of rifles that require fifty-caliber cartridges, mostly a few Sharps and Springfield's. Anyway, it came about that I served with the seventh's ordnance sergeant back at Fort Harker in Kansas in sixty-nine. Took a little sweet talk but I got enough boxes to replenish what we used up plus a little more."

With his grin widening Lieutenant Low said jokingly. "I joshed a minute ago about having a platoon of bandits now it sounds like I'm going to have to start addressing you as First Sergeant James, as in Jesse, if you get my meaning."

"No idear at all what you're talking about sir." Gus smiled back.

Lieutenant Low paused for a few seconds as he watched a lumbering supply wagon cross the wide, muddy river with the four-horse team straining through the soft sand bottom. Pointing a finger towards the river, he said. "That really concerns me with the problems they're having getting the wagons across. The bottom is so soft its like quicksand and I can just picture all our guns getting stuck up to the hubs. General Custer got real upset the other day when we had to lower our guns down the side of that cliff by using rope and tackle; I can just imagine what he'd say if we couldn't get our caisson's across." He shifted his eyes back across the river. "And I see the general over there in the cottonwood grove and it looks to me he's keeping an eye on everything crossing."

"Well sir, it's not too late for us to raft 'em across." First Sergeant Steiner suggested.

"No---I'm afraid it is too late to consider that first sergeant. Won't be more than another forty-five minutes and it'll be our turn to make the crossing." Lieutenant Low chewed his lip for a few seconds while Mark Kellogg continued to listen in with great interest from under the wagon. An idea came to the young Gatling gun officer and he looked at his first sergeant. "Gus have you checked on our mules lately?"

This was the first time his lieutenant had ever addressed him by his nickname and First Sergeant Steiner was both amazed and pleased at the same time, for he really liked the personable officer. "Yes sir, at least not more than two days ago. I'm keeping that muleskinner supplied with tobacco and slipped him a bottle of rotgut I confiscated from one of our boys at the beginning of the march 'cause he couldn't hold his liquor. He's taking care of our animals just like they were his own."

"Mighty good, mighty good. Listen, here's what I want you to do Gus. Get a few men to round up-----oh...I'd say around a dozen mules and bring them back here. I don't remember if I saw the pack train cross over or not, but it makes no difference: if they have to chase the mules down on the other side that's fine; they can ride them back. After you pass on that order find Lieutenant Kenzie for me and give him my compliments that I want him to oversee the breakdown and packing of two of the guns, then he's to report to me."

"Yes----sir!" First Sergeant Steiner started to turn to carry out his commander's orders but he hesitated then asked a pointed question. "Begging the lieutenants pardon sir, if you're of the mind to do it sir, may I ask what you're gonna do?"

"Well I'll tell you first sergeant, I'm going to deal a hand of cards from a stacked deck and hope I don't burn my fingers doing it. We've got about forty minutes left before we have to ford the river which gives us plenty of time to break down a couple of the Gatlings and get them rigged up for patrol transport."

"Hot damn! That's sure enough is a bully idea. I don't know why I didn't think of that myself as much drilling we've done with that invention of yours. But did you say two guns sir? Why not all three? We've got the time to do them all."

"That's part of my stacked deck first sergeant and why I need the extra mules. They're going to have to help pull out the assembled Gatling that's sure to get mired down in the middle of the river."

Gus Steiner gave his officer a puzzled look until it finally came to him. "You're gonna put on an exhibition for General Custer, aren't you sir?"

With a thin smile creasing his handsome face, his small blond mustache twitching and slightly crossed eyes twinkling mischievously, Lieutenant Low said. "You're peeking at my card hand first sergeant."

After First Sergeant Steiner departed to carry out his orders, Billy Low went to the back of the supply wagon and pulled apart the canvas flaps to look inside. While he was satisfying himself that the yokes and leather slings were stored in the fully packed wagon, Mark Kellogg crawled from underneath the wagon and brushing the dirt off the back of his britches put his black leather dispatch case under his arm and begun whistling a tune as he strolled toward the rear of the wagon like he just happened to be passing by.

Alerted by an off tune but recognizable rendition of Garry Owen being whistled, Billy Low took his head from the back flaps of his supply wagon to see who it was that was murdering General Custer's favorite battle song. Spotting the war correspondent for the Bismarck Tribune approaching him the lieutenant smiled, saying, "You seem to be in an excellent mood this afternoon Mister Kellogg."

"Why hello there Bucky, how'ya doing old salt," Kellogg answered in his glad hand style he used on junior officers. "What are you up to this fine day?"

"Oh, just waiting our turn to make the crossing."

"I see, I see," Kellogg said jovially. Nodding his head to the far side of the river the reporter went on to say, "I see the general over there watching the column pass by. I reckon he'll be eying your battery before long, huh?"

"Well, if he sticks around I suppose he will at that," Billy answered in a soft tone of voice.

"Anything special going on with your Gatling guns that I should know about that would be worth reporting to the folks back east?"

"No, not that I can think of. I do want to thank you for that nice article you wrote up about my platoon after the demonstration we put on for the generals."

"Think nothing of it. I was most impressed by that exhibition and was happy to write my views. I truly believe what I wrote is factual that the evolution of the Gatling within a few years will change the future of warfare for all times. Armies of the future will have to change their tactics dramatically with lighter weight versions of the Gatling....ah what was it you termed it----machine weapons?"

"Machine guns." Lieutenant Low answered.

"Ah yes that's it, machine guns." Kellogg paused for a moment before going on. "I understand you have a theory that your present day Gatling's should be allowed to accompany cavalry scouting patrols. How do you propose to do that with all the problems you've faced already on this march? I remember how upset the general was when one of your guns held up the line of march when it turned over in that river a week or so ago and I thought he was going to have a fit when your outfit got lost during that night march a few days back. Do you think you can regain his confidence to allow your heavy guns to go with him on a scouting patrol?"

Bucky Low bristled a little from the pointed observations the reporter was making, which unbeknown to him was intended to get him riled up so he'd say something that would be of interest for Kellogg to write about. "I have developed a method where as the Gatlings can keep up with the cavalry."

With a smirky smile Mark Kellogg said. "Oh, is that right? And what method is that and why aren't you using it already since you haven't been keeping up too well so far?"

Low was really getting hot under the collar now and he answered rather tersely. "The manner I have developed to transport my weapons is intended solely for patrols and not a regular days march?"

"Is that right. Well now I find that interesting. Is General Custer aware of this marvelous method you have developed?"

"Why don't you stick around and find out!" Lieutenant Low spit out between clenched teeth.

In a very friendly manner Mark Kellogg said. "Why thank you Bucky, I'll do just that."

While Lieutenant Low was getting more perturbed by the second with the brash talking war correspondent, his men were running into some problems with a couple of ornery mules who were not happy about the heavy weight on their backs. Four mules already had a gun wheel affixed to them on A frames and two others didn't seem to mind the cradles strapped on their backs. But the two mules designated to carry the Gatlings trails and axils were loudly braying their displeasure.

First Sergeant Steiner stepped around a fresh pile of mule dung and approached Lieutenant Kenzie. "Sir, there ain't no way those two stubborn jackasses are going to take both the gun trails and the axle's."

"Drat it all!" Lieutenant Kenzie replied. "One mule carried that heavy of a load when we tested weight distribution at Fort Rice before we got orders transferring us to Fort Lincoln. What's happened?"

Looking at his young officer from hooded eyes the grizzled first sergeant felt like shaking the lad by his shoulders and saying *"what's happened is the damn mules won't carry the fucking pieces."* but instead said. "Sir, the gun seat and trail are the next heaviest part of the gun besides the barrel. I don't know what happened but I do know we're either going to have to redistribute the loads or get a couple of more mules to help out sir."

Realizing by the first sergeant's calm answer that he had got off track by asking a dumb question which wasn't going to solve the current dilemma, Lieutenant Kenzie said, "Yes, of course first sergeant." Pausing for a moment as he considered the options and knowing that time was passing he made a decision. "Try putting the axle's on the mules carrying the cradles. That will lighten the load considerably don't you think?"

"Yes sir I think it will," then offering his officer a small verbal pat on the back to keep him happy, said. "Good idea sir."

Mark Kellogg was viewing the two teams of horses standing quietly not more than twenty yards from the Gatlings supply wagon that had the weapons breach-barrel system nestled securely in the pouch like leather slings tied between the horses. "That's quite a get up you got there. Sort of an off the ground travois rig in a way. How'd you happen to dream that up?"

Looking up from his dispatch book he had been penciling in Lieutenant Low glanced at the four horses that were placidly swishing their tails to keep flies and other insects away from them. "Actually I sort of stole the concept after seeing how injured men that have to be transported when no ambulances are available. You've probably seen the fore and aft method of placing a stretcher between two horses or mules to carry a man. Matter of fact I tried that way when I first came up with the idea of breaking the guns down into various parts for carrying, but found out it wouldn't work transporting a heavy Gatling barrel because it was too easy for it to roll off the stretcher. However, that led me to the idea of using a sling between two horses which seems to work right well."

"Have you shown your method to either Custer or Terry?" Kellogg wanted to know.

Still a little miffed at all the questions the correspondent was asking, Billy Low answered tersely. "Not yet."

Before Kellogg could ask another question Lieutenant Kenzie came walking up at a hurried pace and began talking while still a few feet away.

"Bucky, I need to talk to you for a minute about the guns."

Seeing a quick way to get away from the Tribune reporter Lieutenant Low turned to Kellogg, saying. "Pardon me I've got to converse with my second in command on some military matters of a private nature."

"Sure go right ahead," Mark Kellogg replied in his jovial, glad hand manner. "I'll just mosey over to where they're lining up your animals and take a gander."

"That's fine, you do that Mister Kellogg," Billy Low said.

"Hey---you can call me Mark. After all we're almost like friends aren't we?"

"Yeah...sure...ah----Mark."

When the reporter strolled away Billy Low said to his second in command. "That guy irks me to no end. He must have asked me a hundred questions."

Pat Kenzie had a ready answer for that remark: "You gotta watch them newspaper reporter types like a hawk. You can say one thing to them and it ends up in print totally different from the way you meant it to be. If you don't believe what I'm saying ask General Custer. He's up in hot water to his neck with the President because of some things he had to say to a reporter."

"Oh I believe every word you're saying when it comes to that. I tried to be careful on what I said to him but you never know what he's going to make out of it."

"Look like he knows what you're up too." Lieutenant Kenzie said with a frown.

"Well, to tell you the truth I sort of did that on purpose, because if this small test works out like I hope it does I may end up using Kellogg to put some pressure on General Custer to let us go with him on a scout. Anyway, I've got something to say to you but you mentioned you wanted to talk with me so let's hear what you've got to say first. What do you have?"

"A couple of those mean ass mules wouldn't take the gun trails and axle's so what I did was put the axles with the mules lugging the cradles."

"How's it working out?" Lieutenant Low asked.

"So far, so good. The stubborn mules seem to be doing okay now with less weight on them but I think you may have to consider a new method of carrying the trails. Gus Steiner reminded me what heavy sonsofbitches they are and you may have to come up with a sling affair for them too."

Billy Low thought over Kenzie's remark for a few seconds before answering. "You know, I think you've come up with a good proposal there.

I'll have to mull that over for a while but I can see your point that it would probably work out better. Wonder it there's a way we can disassemble the trail more or make it lighter," he mused aloud, then catching himself got back to what he wanted to talk to his second in command about. "What I wanted to see you about is I want you to carry a message to General Custer for me," he said, nodding his head toward the grove of cottonwoods on the other side of the river. "Wait a minute and let me finish writing."

Before handing the dispatch to Lieutenant Kenzie Billy Low said. "What I want you to do after passing over my message is ask the general if you can stay with him until I reach the other side. If he has any questions you should be able to answer them for him."

"That's no problem at all," Pat Kenzie said with a smile. "What's in the message? Can I read it?"

Handing the small piece of folded paper over to his second in command Lieutenant Low said. "Yes, I want you to read it now so you won't get nosy half way across the river and drop it in the water."

Taking his commander's remark in good humored spirits, Lieutenant Kenzie took the slip of paper and opened it and began reading: *Genl Custer sir: I intend to offer a small demonstration of the ability of my guns to withstand the rigors of a cavalry scouting patrol. My second in command, Lt J. P. Kenzie will be available to answer inquiries if you so desire sir. With esteem and greatest respect, your obedient servant, W. H. Low, 1stLt 20th Infantry, Commander, Gatling Gun Platoon.* Looking up Pat Kenzie said. "Wow! You really got your neck stuck out this time don't you Bucky?"

"Let's hope not," Billy Low replied at the same time the signal came for his unit to ford the river. "There's the signal sergeant waving his flags for us to commence our crossing, so you get cracking with my message while I get us started."

"Yes sir!" Lieutenant Kenzie said with a grin and went to get his horse.

Within a couple of minutes, while Lieutenant Low was ordering his first sergeant to have Sergeant Gottlieb start his limber and gun carriage into the sluggish, brown water, Lieutenant Kenzie was splashing through the stream to its three foot middle depth.

General Custer, who was mounted on Vic, sat beside his brother Tom, orderly and message runner John Burkman, and Trumpeter John Martini in the shade of the grove of cottonwoods. Noting the infantry officer riding toward him George turned slightly in his saddle and said to his brother. "Pray tell this officer is not bringing bad news about another breakdown of the Gatlings."

Captain Tom Custer squinted his eyes a little to better focus across the wide river and remarked to his brother. "I only see one caisson of the battery, the one that's entering the water now. Where are the other guns?"

Before the elder Custer could make a reply the infantry officer had stopped his mount a few feet to his front and offering an excellent salute said. "Compliments of Lieutenant Low sir, I am delivering a communication."

Returning the officers salute General Custer muttered to his brother as he took the message from the young officer. "What did I just say?"

Captain Custer just grunted in answer to the question.

As he read the message from Lieutenant Low, General Custer's eyes opened wider from the slit eyed, frowning scan when he had started reading. After he finished it he handed the communication to his brother saying. "Looks like we're in for another exhibition that young Low is going to put on for us." Then looking directly at Lieutenant Kenzie he said. "Very well mister, you may join my party and we shall see what we shall see."

As Billy Low suspected would happen, the limber and gun carriage became mired near the middle of the soft sand and gravel bottomed river. Corporal Gerald "Jerry" Suttmiller drove the caisson. Suttmiller was the same NCO who had driven the gun across Davis Creek on May 29th, when it flipped over from the unruly horses. As the struggling horses tried to get unstuck from the sucking, glue like muck the red-faced corporal yelled out to his companion setting next to him Sergeant Adolph Gottlieb. "Oh no---not again!"

In his precise manner of talking when he wanted his English understood clearly, the former German Army officer said. "I do not think to worry Jerry for I think Ober-Lieutenant Low know this time it would hoppon."

Lieutenant Low was satisfied his Gatling gun was stuck fast in the river. Turning to his first sergeant he said in a low voice. "Okay Gus see to it the other guns get across on the mules and horses without mishap. As soon as they're on the other bank have the men reassemble them jackrabbit quick. As soon as I see you're across alright I'll send the two limbers and they shouldn't have any trouble making it without the weight of the gun carriages. Once the limbers gets to you get them hooked back to the gun carriages as fast as can be done and have them move on down the trail. Sergeant Clarke will use the extra mules to help get the mired caisson to the other bank. Probably have to unlimber it from the gun carriage but that's okay, by that time the general will have seen what I wanted him to see."

"Yessir!" First Sergeant Steiner said, giving his officer a respectful salute. "By the way lieutenant; the gun that's stuck is staying in one piece.

Those extra straps are doing the trick---good job sir."

Glancing toward the mired limber and gun carriage Lieutenant Low smiled, then said. "Thank you first sergeant, that's most kind of you. Now lets finish up this job."

Captain Tom Custer pointed a finger at the line of mules passing the mired caisson and the four horses with the sling attachments carrying the two Gatling barrels. "Well, well would you look at that! So that's where the other two Gatling's got off to. I'll be dang if Bucky Low isn't sure enough giving you a show. Going lickety-split right past that stuck gun."

"Yes it does seem that young Low is trying to make a point, doesn't it?" General Custer answered.

"Well, I'd say he's doing a good job of it," the younger Custer said with a wide grin.

A half hour later when the once mired caisson was safely ashore and moving on down the trail in trace of the other two caissons, Billy Low was listening to General Custer offering a few comments on the accomplishment the general had just viewed. "Well mister you took a chance to prove a point but allow me to congratulate you for you did it in a manner that hit home your idea of moving your weapons. Suffice to say that I am in fact impressed what I have seen and perhaps I will call upon you soon to offer another field test. What do you think Tom----think the Gatling's can be of service on a scouting patrol now?"

Tom Custer offered a broad smile to Lieutenant Low and Lieutenant Kenzie. "General sir...with these two officers riding herd on those guns I'm firmly convinced they can take them to the moon if need be."

Mark Kellogg, who had joined the cluster of soldiers, put in his two unsolicited cents. "Now that will be something to write about-----machine guns going into battle with the cavalry!"

Chapter 27

At the mouth of the Powder River on the Yellowstone River,
Montana Territory
7:30 a.m., Friday, June 9, 1876

A tremendous bright jagged fork of white-blue lighting lit up the gunmetal gray eastern horizon with a flash intensity so strong it was if God was taking a photograph of his domain. A booming roar reminiscent of the rumbling of distant artillery quickly followed the three seconds of illumination. Large droplets of wind-driven rain created a staccato tattoo against the big window of the tall, box-like Pilot House located aft of the taller twin stacks of the steamer Far West.

Fatigue showed in Brigadier General Alfred H. Terry's doleful eyes that were emphasized by dark blotchy bags under the lower eyelids. With a gentle tone of concern in his voice General Terry spoke softly to Captain Grant Marsh, the skipper of the Far West. "In your opinion Captain, do you believe the pending storm will delay our departure or create undo problems for you in moving down the Yellowstone?"

Both men were dressed in similar attire; long, dark blue, frocked coats with vest, white shirts and bow ties. The major difference in their uniform appearance was General Terry's shoulder boards with the single silver stars of his rank and Captain Marsh's visored seafaring cap with an anchor centered in the middle.

Captain Marsh did not hesitate in answering General Terry's question. "No sir I do not foresee any difficulties. I've navigated this river in much worse weather conditions including ice and snow and while a heavy downpour may limit visibility I'll have signalmen up forward on the bow roof to keep me centered in the channel."

"That is very good to hear Captain Marsh. I would have postponed my desired meeting with Colonel Gibbon if necessary but must confess after finding you late last evening I have been most anxious to continue on so I may confer with the good colonel."

"I understand the military expediency involved sir. My Chief Engineer George Foulk is a master in getting steam up and he's in the engine room at this moment supervising our firemen as they stoke the fireboxes. I am confident he will be blowing in my tube shortly telling me we're ready to go," Captain Marsh said, nodding his head toward the brass voice tube standing upright next to the boats five foot tall spiked steering wheel.

General Terry glanced at the communication device, then back to the steamboat captain. "Once we get started Captain, how long do you think it will take us to reach Colonel Gibbon's location?"

Captain Marsh used two fingers to rub his neatly trimmed bushy mustache in a pinching manner for a few seconds while he formed an answer. "If the scouts are correct that he's less that thirty miles downstream and heading this way as you've ordered we should have no trouble in reaching him under two hours. If I push the old girl I can get twenty-miles an hour out of her but my First Mate Ben Thompson gets peeved at me when I try to go that fast: tells me I'm shaking his precious gal apart," he said with a small smile.

Returning the short smile with a thin one of his own, General Terry said, "No need to get your second-in-command upset then. Whatever normal speed you deem appropriate is quite satisfactory with me. The reason I inquired about the length of time is because I was hoping to get an hour or so of rest. These old bones are getting too weary for night marches but that comes with age does it not?"

"Yes sir, it certainly does. I'm here to tell you I'm feeling my fifty-eight years with each passing day........" A knock on the pilothouse door interrupted Captain Marsh. "Yes---come in," the captain said in a loud voice.

A tall, slim in stature man, who looked to be in his late thirties, or early forties, wearing a cap similar to Captain Marsh stepped over the floor sill after opening the back door of the pilot house, and spoke in a raspy voice. "Sir, wanted you to know I just came up from the engine room and Foulk says he's ready when you are."

"Very good Dave. General I'd like you to meet our other pilot Dave Campbell. Dave this is General Terry, commander of the expedition."

The tall pilot doffed his cap then shook hands with the general. "Pleased to meet you sir. You've traveled a long way by horse."

"The pleasure is all mine in meeting you Mister Campbell and yes we've came over three hundred miles as the crow flies and while it would be a thousand mile trip for you and the Far West, you'd still make much better time."

Dave Campbell smiled, then said. "Well that's probably true general but then we wouldn't be lugging a couple-three hundred wagons with us would we."

General Terry smiled also, making a short reply. "No, I don't suppose you would."

Captain Marsh spoke up. "Dave, I'll head her out then you can come on up and take her over. Please tell the first mate to cast off the lines and we'll get underway."

"Aye sir," Campbell said offering a civilian style two-finger salute across his thick black eyebrow.

Captain Marsh then turned to General Terry. "If you'll excuse me sir, I'll be rather busy for a while."

"One last item I failed to mention Captain. I intend to get back to Custer's command tonight so this will be a round trip."

"Understood General...tis no problem."

Then offering the steamboat skipper a salute of his own which was also a brush of his hand across his forehead, General Terry offered a parting remark. "I'll be in my cabin if I'm needed."

* * * * *

Blue-coated Union officers encircled a long plank table supported by empty barrels located on the cargo deck of the steamer Far West. General Terry sat at one end of the fifteen foot make-do conference table with his staff officers sitting on either side of him, including his Adjutant General who recorded various points of the meeting. At the other end of the table was Colonel John Gibbon who was flanked by his immediate staff. Down both sides of the table were unit commanders of various ranks. General Terry had brought along Captain Myles Keogh and Captain Miles Moylan: also Captain Jason from the 6th Infantry and Major Brisbane and Captain Clifford of the 7th Infantry. A like number of Colonel Gibbon's junior officers sat across from these officers. Standing or sitting on barrels away from the long table were several scouts both Indian and white, one of them being Mitch Bouyer, the half-breed friend of Major Orlando Moore who was at Stanley's Stockade.

General Terry was sitting in his favorite position when in conference: back leaning hard against the high-back chair, right elbow on a crate next to him with his arm cocked at an angle with fingers propping the side of his face. The talk had been going on for better than forty minutes when the general made a casual observation. "Now I want to understand this very clearly what you've told me Colonel. You say you have solid evidence based upon encounters of your command with the hostiles, that there was a large encampment on the Tongue River and now they're massing on the Rosebud. Is this correct? Have I heard you right?"

Steely eyed, long-nosed, with short wavy dark hair, the ruggedly handsome former brevet major general knew his long time acquaintance was setting a trap for him, but he had nowhere to hide. "Yes sir, those are the two major contacts we've had." Colonel Gibbon replied.

General Terry remained still for a long pregnant moment as he stared narrowed-eyed at the far end of the table. Then in a voice barely above a whisper, he said. "And you did not think this information worthy of intelligence to be sent to me?"

Colonel Gibbon's full, but graying walrus mustache twitched a little and a minute tremble of his lips was hidden by his thick and equally graying chin beard as the trap door sprung open. "Sir, if the general will recall I did send scouts to you, one Indian and two white scouts, to inform you the Sioux were south of the Yellowstone and in considerable force." Pausing to turn to his adjutant Gibbon's asked the captain a question in a breaking voice. "When was that we sent those scouts out to General Terry's command?"

Flipping through his order book the young captain quickly found the needed information. "We sent them out on one June sir, should have reached the general's headquarters not later than the third of June." The adjutant paused for a second, then finding what he was looking for quickly added, "Yes three June...ah they reported back to us they spent the night of three June at the General Terry, General Custer encampment and arrived back with us on the morning of the sixth. Ah...sir, this was the same men that should have informed General Terry about the two soldiers and civilian forager that got killed by hostiles while hunting downstream from the Yellowstone."

Before Colonel Gibbon could make a reply, General Terry spoke up in a little louder tone of voice that still carried the same calm quality. "Yes, yes, I was made aware of all that but I certainly wasn't aware of the fact we seem to have a division of them not more than fifty miles from here!"

After a slight hesitation Colonel Gibbon said. "Perhaps I should have been more astute in my reporting methods general. Let me assure you sir I shall be in the future."

General Terry nodded his head as if agreeing with the colonel. He knew that any future information would be passed on to him in a timely manner. The basically kind hearted general didn't want to overly embarrass Colonel Gibbon in front of the other officers anyway. He knew he had made his point without having to be more forceful in chastising the man further. He shifted his posture to a more upright position and placing both elbows on the rude table, said. "Let us move on to my intentions. First of all I want Major Moore notified that all supplies remaining at Stanley's Stockade at the mouth

of the Glendive will be moved to the new supply area on the Powder River."
Glancing at Captain Marsh he then said, "I think it will be sufficient if I write
an order for Captain Marsh to carry to Major Moore without having to send
an emissary as I'm sure the good major is more than capable of handling
things at his end."

Captain Marsh punctuated Terry's last remark with: "That he is sir!"

"Ah...yes, thank you captain," General Terry offered a thin smile, then
continued talking. "The Josephine should be making another supply run in
the next few days and all her material and goods will also be stored at the
new supply location. I am working on a plan to get some re-supplies to
General Crook's Wyoming column as I suspect he is more than likely in dire
need of replenishments." Terry paused again while considering his next
remarks. "With what you have told me Colonel Gibbon, along with the
excellent reports made by several of your officers and scouts, I have
determined that we need to thoroughly scout the upper reaches of both the
Tongue and Powder rivers before moving any further west."

A rippling murmur of whispering voices forced General Terry to pause
yet again and he held up a hand to still the disquiet. After regaining
everyone's attention he went on. "This in no way reflects any doubt or
censure upon the Montana Column because you have done your job and
found the general location of the enemy. However, it is my desire to have
the entire region cleared before we go further west for the simple rationale to
either eliminate or chase away any small detached bands of hostiles that may
be lurking about in this area." The general offered a small smile. "And
besides we don't need any enemy reinforcements in our back yard." This
remark got the guffaws, grins and another rippling murmur he had intended
his little joke to produce. "I will order General Custer to mount the primary
long range scout but expect the Montana Column to do your part also,
keeping in mind that I continue to rely upon you to be our blocking force in
the event the hostiles decide to head north. And I also hope that scouts from
the seventh will be able to communicate with members of the Wyoming
Column who I believe should be near the Little Powder River." This is really
all I have to say. Is there anything more we should discuss or does anyone
have comments or questions?"

There ensued a shuffling of feet but otherwise silence that lasted for a
number of seconds until Colonel Gibbon broke the spell when he stood up
and said. "General Terry sir it has been an honor and pleasure having you
with us. I personally thank you for your insight and advice. Your strategy is
brilliant sir and to use your own words, "we shant leave any hostiles in our

back yard." As a small measure of my esteem I would like to offer the services of our finest scout Mitch Bouyer to assist you with the projected reconnaissance you have planned."

"Very kind of you Colonel Gibbon. Mitch Bouyer will be a most welcome addition to our Dakota Column. Gentlemen, if there is nothing else----this concludes the conference."

With a quick scuffling of chairs being scooted back all the officers present came to a stiff attention and remained braced until General Terry said. "Be at your ease gentlemen, please carry on."

* * * * *

General Terry drove himself and his escort almost to the breaking level of endurance, for after the ride back on the Far West to the head of the Powder River, he immediately ordered a forced march back down south on the Powder to find Custer and the 7th Cavalry.

Chapter 28

Along the Powder River, Montana Territory
8:00 a.m., Saturday, June 10, 1876

Lieutenant William Hale Low was very nervous and he could not keep still. To offset his nervousness he was pacing to and fro in front of the huge headquarters tent belonging to General Terry.

The number two man in charge of the Gatling gun platoon, Lieutenant James Patrick Kenzie attempted to calm his friend down. "Bucky, you're wearing a path in front of the general's tent. I tell you there's nothing to be concerned about as we haven't done anything out of line."

Lieutenant Low stopped abruptly in his tracks and fixed his gaze on his fellow officer with his slightly crossed eyes. "Lieutenant Kenzie, no doubt you haven't any feelings of worry for the simple reason you are not in the position of command. One of these days when you are faced with that responsibility then perhaps you too will find cause to be apprehensive. For your information, this is the first time I have ever had my breakfast interrupted by a general's orderly bringing compliments from the general to report to his headquarters with my second in command and first sergeant double quick. And you wonder why I pace?"

Stung by his commander's remark Pat Kenzie's face reddened somewhat and he blurted out rather loudly. "That's not fair at all for you to say that! I have as much concern for our battery as any man in this expedition! Why...."

First Sergeant Gustavus Frederick Steiner interrupted the rising voice of his superior. "Shush...Lieutenant Kenzie sir, they'll be a' hearing you inside the tent sir."

Embarrassed that an enlisted man had told him to tone down his voice Lieutenant Kenzie's first reaction was to snap out at the first sergeant, but a baleful glare from his commanding officer made him realize he had been out of line. In a contrite tone of voice Lieutenant Kenzie said. "Thank you first sergeant," then glancing at Lieutenant Low, said. "Sorry Bucky. I am as concerned as you but believe it or not I was worrying about you and what you're going through right now than thinking about why we were called."

Bucky Low was also embarrassed because of his nervous outburst. "Hey Pat I'm sorry too. There was no need for me to strike out at you like that. I know you was just trying to settle me down." Then he smiled broadly saying. "And guess what-----it worked! I don't know why I fret about things that I have no idea what the problem is, or for that matter, if there is a problem."

First Sergeant Steiner, who had one foot cocked against a wagon wheel he was leaning against with his arms crossed, gave a little grunt, then muttered. "Don't cross bridges till you come to 'em."

Still smiling Lieutenant Low asked. "What was that you said first sergeant?"

The long time senior non-commissioned officer had been around too may young officers in his career to hold a fear for them and he didn't hesitate to speak up. "It was just a saying I first heard during the war that made sense to me when it comes to fretting about things a person don't really know about. Don't try and cross a bridge until you come to it."

"Say---that isn't bad first sergeant, I'll have to remember that" Billy Low said.

Before the lieutenant could voice the saying himself, which he was about to do, a commotion of raised voices could be heard coming from inside the headquarters tent. The three Gatling gun men had heard the low buzz of voices emitting from the tent during the fifteen minutes they had been standing outside waiting without actually hearing what was being said.. But now most of the words being said could be clearly understood. It sounded like General Custer was very agitated about something.

".....By God what I have to say is that I resent not being allowed to lead the reconnaissance! I am the next senior officer of this expedition and this scout calls for a cavalry leader!"

General Terry's equally loud voice was then heard. "Your comments are noted sir. However, I will remind you sir that it is I that commands this expedition and if I wish to divide assignments and responsibilities then by heaven that is just what I shall do because it is my prerogative to do so. This is the last I want to hear of the matter and the very last I want to have a decision of mine questioned. Do you understand that lieutenant colonel?"

There ensued a good thirty seconds of deathly silence. Then, the still belligerent voice of General Custer was heard to say. "Very well General Terry, I understand your order sir."

The two officers and first sergeant standing outside the tent flap looked at one another wide eyed with odd expressions on their faces. Finally Lieutenant Kenzie broke the spell with a whispered comment. "I don't think you have to worry anymore Bucky about being in hot water of some kind. Appears to me it's someone else that's taken that position sure enough."

First Sergeant Steiner let out with a low chuckle. "I'd say General Hard

Ass has got his ass chewed right good."

With a short laugh Lieutenant Low said. "What was that you said first sergeant?"

"Oops---sorry sir, thinking out loud again: guess it's a sign of getting old. I just couldn't help but thinking how General Custer's boys call him Hard Ass behind his back and from what we just heard it looks like General Terry's doing a little hard assing of his own."

"Why first sergeant. That's downright disrespectful." The smiling Lieutenant Low said. "Hard Ass huh? I can just imagine what my boys call me."

"Probably Lay 'em low Low," Pat Kenzie replied gleefully. "Get it? low Low."

Billy Low shook his head at his second in command. "That is really dumb Pat."

"Actually sir," Gus Steiner said, "about the only thing I ever got a glimmer on was overhearing something like Gatling Sam. Where they came up with the Sam I don't know but that's all I've ever heard 'em call you behind your back."

"Gatling Sam huh? Well that's not too bad I guess," Lieutenant Low chuckled.

"How about me first sergeant---the boys have a pet nickname for me?" Lieutenant Kenzie wanted to know.

Gus hesitated for a moment, then shrugging his shoulders replied. "The only thing I ever heard was Killer Kenzie sir." What the first sergeant didn't say was the full nickname he'd overheard: "Killer Kid Kenzie."

"What? Now where in the sam hill did they come up with that? Killer Kenzie huh? I kind of like it. It sort of...."

Before Lieutenant Kenzie could finish his remark the tent flap flew open and a cluster of officers started walking out led by General Custer and his brother Tom Custer.

All the officers were talking in various forms of animated conversation. As the two Custers' pushed by without given the three Gatling gun men a second glance, the three Gatling gun soldiers overheard General Custer. "....damn thing is going to be a wild goose chase anyway but my only concern was that with Reno leading the scout about the only thing he'll accomplish is to alert the savages of how near we are......"

The next group of officers passing by had a smiling Major Reno among them along with an equally smiling Captain Benteen. Captain Benteen was saying. "Well old bean I'll say we saw some feathers get ruffled this morning, but by damn we know for sure who's running this campaign; taint that the truth?"

The last few officers trailing out of the tent included Custer's adjutant Lieutenant William Cooke, Custer's brother-in-law Lieutenant James Calhoun and another Custer devotee, young Lieutenant Jack Sturgis who had been allowed to attend the briefing to gain field experience. Adjutant Cooke was expounding in his high-pitched Canadian brogue, "Totally uncalled for, that's what I say. The man's been behind a desk for the past twelve years and he comes out here and doesn't pay a farthing's worth of attention to the vast field experience the general has. All your brother-in-law was trying to do was save Terry the embarrassment of a bad decision."

The Gatling gun platoon officers and first sergeant were astounded at hearing such remarks right on the door step of the expedition commander.

A couple of minutes went by and no other officer emerged from the cavernous tent. Lieutenant Low was about ready to knock on the center post of the once again closed tent flap when suddenly it parted and Captain Edward Smith, General Terry's Acting Assistant Adjutant General, came walking out. Seeing the three men he came to an abrupt halt and said. "Oh for heavens sakes! With all that has been going on I completely forgot the general sent for you. Come now, follow me and we'll get this over with."

The two lieutenants eyed one another as they entered the tent, the mention of "we'll get this over with," ringing in their ears.

The four men walked pass the long conference table of boards that had been set up until coming to the end of the tent where General Terry was busy writing upon his field desk. Captain Smith hesitated, holding up one hand to the other three in a gesture to stand fast, then purposely cleared his throat before saying. "General Terry sir, sorry for the interruption. Lieutenant Low of the Gatling gun battalion is here sir."

The sad-eyed general officer looked up from the work he was doing and for a moment it seemed he was a little befuddled, then his eyes lit up as if he'd remembered something and said. "Ah yes---Lieutenant Low. I..."

Bucky Low braced himself and as soon as the general noted his presence and began a formal reporting. "Sir Lieutenant Low rep....."

General Terry quickly waved a hand, saying. "No, no. No need for that Low. Ah you and your subordinates stand at ease."

When the three men relaxed their stiff postures somewhat the general said. "Lets see now, this would be Lieutenant Kenzie, you're second in command."

Feeling it was better to be safe than sorry, Pat Kenzie came back to attention and said, "Yes sir!"

General Terry nodded his head. "Yes...please stand easy mister Kenzie. And First Sergeant Gus Steiner I know. We go back a few years now don't we Gus?"

Gus Steiner likewise braced back to attention to make his reply. "Yes sir general, that we do sir." And without being told to do so, Gus relaxed his position of attention after having answered the general's question.

Seeing the somewhat stunned expression on the two lieutenant's faces as they eyed their first sergeant, General Terry allowed a small smile. "It appears Gus has not mentioned that we served together in the late war of the rebellion." With a low chuckle the general continued, "It was during the Siege of Petersburg the summer of sixty-four when General Butler purchased twelve prototype models of your gun with his own money from Doctor Gatling himself. Gus here was already well-known for his ordnance expertness and was one of the first men General Butler volunteered to organize working batteries with the Gatling's. That fall the rebels made an all out effort to breach our entrenchments but none of them got past Gus here or his Gatling. He received three wounds that day; ended up manning the gun all by himself after his crew was killed one by one, and I had the pleasure to endorse the recommendation for the Medal of Honor in his behalf......"

"Medal of Honor?" Billy Low voiced, glancing at his first sergeant and interrupting General Terry.

Taking no offense at the breach of conduct from the junior officer General Terry offered a bemused smile, then said. "You mean he never told you? Well that sounds like him, it sure does. Maybe you can get him in a good mood one of these days and he'll tell you how he put General Butler himself to work on one of the Gatling's during an attack. That right Gus?"

"Yes sir, if the general says so sir." First Sergeant Steiner said lamely.

"Well now I suppose that's enough reminiscing," the general said, getting a more serious look on his face. "Gentlemen, and first sergeant; the reason I asked to see you has to do with the ten day reconnaissance scouting patrol I ordered to be sent out this afternoon under the command of Major Reno and the six troops of his Right Wing. Lieutenant Low, Lieu...ah General Custer has informed me of your remarkable demonstration this past Thursday when I was away up on the Yellowstone. I think it time to find out just how well your weapons transportation system works under the stress of a combat employment. I've heard you have been wanting to put your theory of keeping up with a cavalry patrol to the test so here's your opportunity. I want Lieutenant Kenzie and First Sergeant Steiner, along with one of your Gatling guns with full crew, to accompany the patrol. Are you prepared to participate in this undertaking as I have outlined?"

Bucky Low was so stunned that all he could do was squeak out a stuttered "Yes sir".

Chapter 29

Night in the Montana Badlands, Montana Territory
9:00 p.m., Sunday, June 11, 1876

"Ouch! Dang it all, will you watch what you're do'en!" Private James O. Wade yelled widely. The balding ammunition handler on Sergeant Gottlieb's Gatling gun jerked his hand back from the pack mule he'd been unloading which allowed the gun cradle to crash to the ground with a resounding thud, just missing the privates foot. "Now see what you made me do! Darn near smashed my finger you did!" Wade said holding up his right hand. "And caused me to drop the cradle."

The soldier Private Wade was yelling at was another ammunition carrier, Private Harold B. "Holly" Stratton, who was standing on the other side of the mule holding onto a loose rawhide strap that had broken into. Looking across the mule's back Stratton's florid features almost glowed red in the dim moonlight as he yelled back at the other trooper. "Damnit! Do you think I let it slip on purpose? Can't see a damn thing I ado'en and besides a damn strap broke."

Somewhat mollified Private Wade started to make a conciliating rejoinder when Sergeant Adolph Gottlieb stepped lightly up to the pair and in a hissing, low voice, said. "Ach you dummiesel's! Do you not know sound discipline on a night march? Are you trying to tell the enemy where we are at? Keep your mouths shut!"

Wade and Stratton had been around the former German army officer long enough to know he sometimes reverted to his native language when cussing at them and both knew they'd just been called "dumb asses." But since neither one had a good defense to justify their previous noisy outburst the only way they could cover their guilt was to use the logic privates down through the ages have tried when wanting to vindicate stupid actions: bull shit excuses. In a hoarse whisper Private Stratton tried his luck. "Damn sergeant, we're having a time of it try'en to unload these damn pack mules in the dark. That Major Reno had no call to force march us at night like this." Then holding up the split rawhide strap: "And lookee heah, this broke right smack in two it did."

Private Wade jumped on the bandwagon from the door his buddy opened. "He's right. Who ever heard of unpacking and sitt'en up camp in the middle of the night? Can't even have a cuppa coffee with no fires allowed," then seeing no sympathy in the stern blue eyes of the tough disciplinarian, he trailed off lamely holding up his hand. "Liked to lost my dag-burn hand when that cradle fell off---I did."

Shaking his head in disgust Sergeant Gottlieb hissed at them again. "You're soldiers, you do what you are told to do without question. For your information I will say to you this one time that due to the late start of this patrol leaving the base camp yesterday is the reason we marched at night. We have many miles to cover and must do so with, with, how do you say...verstohlen...ah with concealment. This is goot because the savages would never think we do this and we surprise them, ya? And this is reason you eat cold rations with water, ya?" Having went by the code of a German officer to inform the ranks of cattle from time to time on what was taking place, Gottlieb then hissed a final warning. "You not do as I say and make more noise...by Himmel, you two will carry that cradle on the trail tomorrow and give the mule a rest!" With that, he turned on his heel to see how the other privates were doing in getting the disassembled Gatling gun off the pack mules.

Blonde headed and rather short with wide shoulders, Private William T. Krier, who was a loader and had been helping the two ammunition carriers in off loading the cradle, wheels and axle, uttered a mirthless, low chuckle. "I tell you what boys----he'd do it too. I can just see you fellows trying to lug that heavy sonofabitch tomorrow."

"Damn foreigner, sauerkraut bastard! What he do'en a sergeant in our army anyway?" Holly Stratton asked in a muffled voice.

"I'll tell you why!" A low gruff voice said as First Sergeant Gustavus Steiner appeared like a ghost from nowhere to stand next to the three privates. "Because he knows more about soldiering and about machine guns that the three of you and the rest of the gun crew put together!"

"Oh sweet mother of Jesus first sergeant------I didn't mean to......"

"Keep your damn voice down Stratton!" Gus Steiner hissed. "We're out in the middle of hostile territory in case you haven't figured it out yet. That's what Sergeant Gottlieb was trying to impress on you. Hell! We could be surrounded by Injuns right now!"

That got the three soldiers attention and they looked around them quickly to see if any savages was sneaking up on them right that moment. Then Jim Wade had a bright thought and in a whisper, said. "Yeah, but we've also got six cavalry companies with us first sergeant."

"I'm not going to stand here and have a debate with you Wade," the first soldier said in a menacing tone of voice. "I don't care if we've got a brigade of horse troops with us, you just worry about doing your job and doing it quietly without any sass or back talk and do what your gun sergeant tells you to do. You got that?"

Wade offered a contrite, "Yes first sergeant."

"Good. Now the three of you get over there and help the others get the gun trail off the pack mule. Then fix up your place to sack out for the night."

First Sergeant Steiner moved away a few steps with the three privates trailing him. Private Krier whispered a remark to his companions. "You two really handled that well, you did."

The first sergeant stopped dead in his tracks and spun around. "What was that you said Billy boy?"

The rising three quarter moon streaked Bill Krier's ashen face as he stuttered. "I...I jus said to the fellows that, that...maybe it'd be well if'n we all bunked together tonight first sergeant."

"Yeah...well see to it you don't snore and fart too loud as you'll be wanting your scalp come daylight." Gus Steiner turned and walked to the group of soldiers struggling to lift the heavy gun trail off the back of a weary mule.

The three soldiers he'd left behind bent to their task again of picking up the dropped cradle to place it on a piece of canvas for the night when a wolf howled its presence. All three looked at each other sharply.

"That be a wolf 'taint it?" Private Wade asked in a small voice.

"I shore hope so." Private Krier whispered back.

* * * * *

Major Marcus Reno was engaged in conversation with Lieutenant Pat Kenzie: "...and you say if need be you could put your gun back together at night?"

The junior officer only hesitated a moment before answering. "Yes sir that would not present a serious problem although it would take a little more time than the ten or so minutes the Gatling gun crews have been trained to do it during daylight hours. But as I stated sir, there would really be no problem in assembling the gun under conditions of darkness. Actually, there are only six main components and to be perfectly frank sir I think the men could do it blindfolded."

Scudding dark clouds moved across the moon causing eerie shadows to be cast over the face of the 7th Cavalry's second in command. The major's white teeth gleamed in the dim moonlight as he smiled while offering a comment on what Lieutenant Kenzie had just said. "That is very good to hear sir and I find that most enlightening. I must confess to you that I am not all that well acquainted with your gun, but I was most impressed by the demonstration your battery performed a while back. General Custer seems to have the view that your Gatling's should be used in a defensive posture only. Yet I understand General Terry evidently shares your commander's belief that the guns can be used offensively as well."

Lieutenant Kenzie was finding Major Reno, who had the reputation of being very dour and not getting along well with his fellow officers, to actually be an easy person to converse with. When the major summoned him to his small command post tent for a chat Pat Kenzie had at first been very tense and stiff. But, within a short time the reasonable speaking senior officer had put Pat at ease and he answered the man's questions freely without apprehension. "Yes sir, that is correct sir. As you know sir. General Terry is the one who ordered my unit to accompany your scout patrol. I feel the general has a confidence about our battery that may override any objections from...ah...from other: I mean to say what other officers may harbor."

The dark featured major, who's handsome face looked puffy in the subdued moonlight maintained a thin smile when he spoke. "I understand what you are implying lieutenant. General Custer can be most stubborn at times and I take no note of insubordination intent of a superior officer on your part by speaking the truth. And yes, I am aware of General Terry's desire concerning your guns. When the general assigned the reconnaissance mission to me he advised that he wanted to put to rest for once and all whether your guns can perform satisfactorily on a cavalry patrol or not." Major Reno hesitated a moment before going on. "In all fairness I must say that your mule train did an admirable job this afternoon and evening in keeping pace with the other six mule trains. That leather pocket affair you have manufactured to hold the guns barrel in is quiet extraordinary as is the yoke collar device you use to insure your horses stay together when moving the piece. If this ability continues I will be most happy to report a favorable finding to General Terry."

"That is very gracious of you to say that sir," Pat Kenzie responded. "Under reasonable circumstances and conditions the value of a Gatling gun engaging massed hostiles would be incredible. I am firmly convinced the contribution Gatling's can provide as an offensive weapon would astound the most skeptical of those whom do not understand or appreciate the full potential of the weapon."

"What do you consider to be favorable circumstances...how did you put it? Under reasonable conditions and circumstances. Just what are those?" Major Reno asked.

"I apologize sir for not making myself clear. What I was attempting to express sir is those conditions ideal for cavalry. In mountainous terrain I don't think the Gatling would be an effective offensive weapon, but in valleys and rolling hills it would protect your flanks, or clear your front, for a charge. And what I meant by conditions sir is the requirement of time needed on a volatile battlefield to assemble the gun."

Major Reno ran the flat on his fingers across his well-groomed mustache before saying. "Your explanation is sound and if as you say your gun can be assembled in less than fifteen minutes my experience on the battlefield environment would dictate sufficient time in most all situations." A howl of a far away wolf gained the major's attention for a few seconds, then he turned his head back to the junior officer. "If that full potential you spoke of is even near your expectations of what I witnessed at your firing exhibition--- what? Ah...three weeks ago?"

"About that sir, twenty-third of May," Lieutenant Kenzie slipped in.

"Ah yes...the twenty-third. Well, I for one would not mind at all having that kind of firepower at my disposal and I'll tell you straight out that if its within my providence I shall see to it that at least one of your guns is attached to my wing when we seek battle, whether Custer wants them or not."

"That is bully to hear sir and I know Bucky Low will be pleased as punch when I relate your remarks to him."

"Low?" Reno's brow furrowed in concentration for a few seconds. "Oh---of course! That's your commander, Lieutenant Low. Yes. Lieutenant Low. He seems like a capable young officer, which is saying something in this outfit that has more than a share of knaves and scoundrels. A word of advice Mister Kenzie; don't ever cast your lot with incompetents whose only chance to get ahead in the army are over the bleached bones they step across at both the garrison and during a campaign. A man has to learn to think for himself and to look out for himself if he intends on surviving in this day's army."

There issued a contemplative void of silence that Pat Kenzie finally decided to fill. "Yes sir---thank you sir for sharing that viewpoint with me sir," he said uneasily.

Major Reno realized his last remark had made the young officer feel ill at ease. For a moment he thought of dismissing the man and letting him to return to his gun crew. And had he not felt so lonely he would have done so. Under normal circumstances Major Reno prided himself at being a loner with an aplomb based upon his personal estimation of his worth. He suffered being almost completely ostracized by his fellow officers, except in the line of duty of course, but this seemed not to bother him. His sullen attitude and sharp critical tongue made him no friends and he withstood the company of Captain Benteen, whom he actually despised, only because they both shared an equal passion of hatred for George A. Custer. But not wanting the young man to leave just yet he had to do something after having allowed his perfidious feelings to surface. Putting on a facade of an older brothers camaraderie in an attempt to erase any poor image he may have created in the eyes of the young officer, he spoke in a jovial tone of voice. "Forgive my berating behavior lieutenant. I sometimes let my strong sense of professionalism overcome by better judgment by indulging in deep-rooted feelings of animosity I have toward those I believe misunderstand me. And perhaps I should not have taken you into my confidence that way, but I felt a bond between us that allowed me to vent my frustrations as I did. As you will learn son, the responsibility of leadership can be very lonely at times with no peer to converse with."

Lieutenant Kenzie felt very flattered by the older officer's sincerity of speaking his mind to him so profoundly. "Major Reno sir I can fully understand your position as second in command. And as you related there may be the possibility of a few officers holding forth petty jealousies because of your experience and the evident high esteem the troops have for you; but your gumption has obviously met with the full approval of General Terry sir, by the confidence he has placed in you by ordering you to lead this scout."

Reno's face lit up and the puffiness under his dark eyes seemed to melt away. "How very well stated. But that's right isn't it? The general chose me over Custer," the major's demeanor seemed to glow. In a low, yet pleased tone of voice, Major Reno went on. "My boy let me share a very personal thought with you."

Not knowing if he should or not Pat Kenzie went ahead and interjected a prompting. "Yes sir."

Major Reno looked to his left, to his right in a furtive manner as if to insure no one else was listening. "Mitch Bouyer has confided in me there are thousands of Sioux and Cheyenne massing as a single force for the first time in history. His scouts back him up on this and say it's the largest concentration of hostiles ever assembled. I believe this to be true. And I also believe we may run into the main body of the savages somewhere along the

Powder River where we are going to scout. Bouyer, he's half Sioux you know, he discounts my theory as he thinks they're nearer the Rosebud or the Little Big Horn. Anyway, the one thing we both heartily agree upon is there is going to be a tremendous clash between the army and the hostiles." Reno paused and in the faint moonlight Pat Kenzie, who had been listening intently, thought he saw a sparkling teardrop glistening in the corner of the major's eye. Then Major Reno placed his right hand on Kenzie's shoulder and in a soft voice, barely above a whisper said. "And my boy I want you by my side with your Gatling gun when that times comes. I want you there with me to share in the glory as we battle those savages."

In a voice that broke a little from the emotion of the moment, Lieutenant James Patrick Kenzie answered. "I will be honored to stand by you on the field of battle sir!" And he offered a formal salute.

Major Reno had at last, found a friend.

Chapter 30

Foot Hills of the Big Horn Mountains on Wild Goose Creek,
Wyoming Territory
3:00 p.m., Monday, June 12, 1876

A whispering hiss of boiling sap emanated from the Sibley camp stove as orange-blue fingers of flame attacked a fresh split log of green spruce an orderly had recently placed inside the barrel shaped wood burner. The hushing hiss of the burning tree sap was accompanied by a louder crackling and occasional muffled pop as the damp wood succumbed to the roaring fire eating at it. The stove was located near the rear of a large tent and the heavy canvas of the U. S. Army General Officer's tent was pushing to and fro slightly from a buffeting wind. This movement gave the white canvas an appearance the tent was breathing because of the steady rhythm of pulsations as the material snapped taunt then contracted from the wind hitting it. Although a chilling rain pattered a drumbeat on the outside of the spacious tent the Sibley camp stove functioned well at keeping the inside of the 25 foot long by 15 feet wide tent snugly warm as a robins nest. Every **few** seconds another sizzling hiss sounded as a droplet of rain water found its **way** past the stove pipe coupling going through the metal plate in the ceiling of the tent and fell on the hot stove.

This small symphony of camp life was not distracting to the four men sitting around a square table placed in the center of the tent between the two main ridgepoles holding up the structure. Nor was the bustling around **noise** a white-jacketed orderly was making as he prepared a new pot of coffee for the four officers that he would soon place on the hot stove to boil. All four officers were veteran campaigners and accustomed to the natural sights and sounds of their chosen profession. If anything, the fire, the rain, and the fussing orderly, were all pleasant sounds of home for the four uniformed men.

The thin, sinewy, compact build of Brigadier General George Crook made him appear shorter than his six feet, and even more so, dressed as **he** was in his favorite expedition attire of a baggy canvas suit. The sharp angular nosed commander of the Wyoming column fancied himself a great out-doorman and it was a small wonder he wasn't wearing his pith helmet, which many of his men joked that he slept with it on. The general's view of himself of being a vigorous woodsman didn't keep him from enjoying his

181

favorite card game while in the field. He was an avid Whist player and liked to think of himself of being a damn good player. Pulling thoughtfully at his left huge mutton-chop sideburn the general considered a bid. His short arched eyebrows over very close-set dark eyes were furrowed like chevrons that gave him an almost evil look as he studied the cards fanned apart in his large right hand. After a few seconds he closed the cards, then looking to his right, spoke in a gruff voice to the officer sitting there. "You bid two spades, is that right Anson?"

The well built forty-two year old cavalry officer from Thorntown, Indiana, who wore his black hair cut short and combed back, offered a dazzling smile that his large bushy mustache couldn't hide. In a twangy tone of voice and with deep-set brown eyes twinkling, Captain Anson Mills replied. "That's correct general----two spades." Glancing across the table to his partner; Major Alex Chambers, second in command of the combined infantry battalion, Mills gave the wavy brown haired officer a bemused quick wink.

This was meant to be intimidating gesture, which was not lost on General Crook's partner, the general's aide-de-camp, First Lieutenant Gregory Bourke who had declared one no trump just before Captain Mills' two spades bid.

General Crook eyed his squared faced, square chinned aide for a moment whose full black walrus mustache had twitched. The lieutenant stared back at his commander with a bland expression from his wide-set blue eyes with drooping eyelids that gave the young officer a drowsy look. Seeing no hint of encouragement from his partner General Crook rubbed his stubble of chin whiskers for a couple of more seconds then making up his mind the big eared general officer finally said. "Oh...very well then----four hearts."

To the general's left Major Chambers large drooping brown mustache seemed to sag even lower and his wide nostrils on his large nose flared a little from having been caught by surprise. The major's already scrunched eyes, that gave him a slight oriental look, narrowed even more as he stared at his card hand. Shaking his head back and forth he finally said. "That's too much for me, I pass."

Lieutenant Bourke likewise passed and Captain Mills fingered his contrasting gray curly goatee for a second before saying. "I cannot go any higher---I'll have to pass also."

Pleased that he had got the bid, General Crook's happy mood soon turned sour as his aide-de-camp laid down his cards face up to provide the dummy hand the general would use to play his card hand from. Studying the dummy hand General Crook looked up. "Only one Ace of Clubs? My God Greg what were you bidding no trump on?"

The other two officers smiled gleefully at the expense of the young lieutenant; anticipating a for-sure set.

John Gregory Bourke took no offense at his commander's harsh tone as he was used to the man's personality and knew full well the general's bark was worse than his bite. Bourke was also not intimidated by what General Crook had said. "If the general will look closely sir, you will note I have three protected Kings, including one in your trump."

"Humph, well we'll see, won't we?" And the general led his Nine of Hearts.

About three minutes later it got down to the last card and luckily, or skillfully as the case may be, General Crook using his aide-de-camps Ten of Clubs from the dummy hand beat Major Chambers' Nine of Clubs and the general successfully fulfilled the Whist game contract bid.

"Well done sir," Lieutenant Bourke got in his kudos first.

"Yes, excellent playing general," Major Chambers added quickly, somewhat annoyed the junior officer had beat him in praising the general.

The Hoosier cavalry captain had to settle for a grunted, "Good job general."

As it were, Captain Mills was the one General Crook rewarded with a smile from his rather ugly face that the wild growing mutton-chops couldn't cover. "Thank you Anson. I thought you and Alex had me set there for sure." Then looking over to his orderly who was sitting quietly on a folding campstool near the front flap, General Crook said, "Thurston, see to it if the coffee is ready, and if it is pour us all a cup."

The pockmarked face private jumped from his seat and moving quickly toward the stove said. "Yessir----I'll see to it right away sir, should be ready sure 'nough."

"And Thurston, after you serve the coffee go over to the other tent and you'll find a bottle of brandy in the bottom drawer of my field desk." General Crook was talking about an identical tent attached to the one they were in by a canvas tarpaulin that made sort of a porch or breezeway, which was used as his command post headquarters.

Stopping in mid-step the short statured private spun around saying. "Yessir, I'll take care of that jack-rabbit quick sir."

While the orderly striker fussed around with the large blue-black enameled camp coffee pot, General Crook sat back in his high back cushioned chair he carried with him on his baggage wagon, and said. "Let's relax for a moment gentlemen before playing another rubber. I think you'll enjoy a dram of this excellent brandy I have. Came all the way from Paris. A friend of mine sent it to me from New York."

In an effort to induce conversation Captain Mills said. "Even with this rain we're having its a lot better weather that what we've already been through."

Lieutenant Bourke picked up the thread by adding, "At least we are not suffering the blizzard conditions like we experienced on the Bozeman Road to reach Fort Kearny. Who would have ever suspected zero temperatures and that terrible gale-like wind during this time of the year?"

General Crook grunted, then said, "That is one item you can never out guess in these wilds my boy: Mother nature has her own way of doing things out here. The sun may be warm and shining one day and the next day you find yourself trudging through a foot of freshly fallen snow."

Major Chambers ran his right hand alongside his brown wavy hair that barely covered the top of his laid back small ears. This odd gesture of smoothing his hair back was a habit he used when he was about to embark upon a subject he wasn't really sure he should broach. "At least the foul weather kept the savages away from us for awhile as they couldn't find us; but considering they took pot shots at us three days ago I dare say any surprise factor we may have enjoyed in sneaking up on their village has gone by the wayside." The major paused and glanced at Captain Mills. "Anson tells me his scouting patrols are all being shadowed by bands of hostiles and my commanding officer Colonel Royall has advised me to double my pickets, especially around the horse herd as the sonsofbitches seem determined to steal some of our mounts."

After hearing the infantry officer's comments General Crook at first was a little peeved at the man for bringing up the unpleasant subject of marauding Indians. To some degree the general's initial reaction could be understood considering the fact the entire Wyoming column had been acting as it they were participating in a gala wilderness excursion and didn't want to be bothered by pesky hostiles. Since leaving Fort Fetterman the afternoon of May 29th, the thousand or so cavalrymen, infantrymen and civilian contract personnel, had inched their way along at a snails pace, having covered less than 160 miles in starts, stops, countermarches, and long delays in between. Poor weather conditions could be attributed for part of this laggardness: but mostly it was due to General Crook not seeming to be in any hurry to confront what his Crow scouts had reported to him were 3,000 hostile warriors waiting for the soldiers and just spoiling for a fight. So there had been much idle time, which didn't bother the rank and file any. Soldiers took advantage of the many hours spent in camp by writing letters, for those that could write, reading, for those that could read, washing their clothing in the cold, sparkling water of streams, playing various types of games, hunting and fishing, and of course trying to stay out of the way of *keep 'em busy* work details first sergeants were fond of creating. The privilege of an officer rank allowed a somewhat wider variety of pastimes of a leisurely fashion: for beside doing all of the same things the enlisted men did for enjoyment and entertainment, officers were also allowed to gather in the late afternoon to imbibe in a few before dinner drinks. Many of the evening meals were rather elegant affairs considering the place and circumstance of where they were being held. Wearing dress uniforms in the officers mess the commissioned leaders of the expedition would enjoy a finely laid table of well cooked food that was served by white jacketed attendants that could put to test some of the best restaurants in the cities along the frontier. These ordained gentlemen would chat amicably in good spirited, entertaining conversations long into the evenings.

These "roughing it" indulgences was encouraged by General Crook such as the leisurely lunch he enjoyed with his four officers this afternoon, which was followed by the general's favorite pastime, playing several games of Whist.

Fortunately for Major Chambers, two things softened General Crook's ire concerning being reminded about pesky Indian's. The first being Private Thurston bringing into the tent an almost full bottle of vintage brandy and the second was that the major's remark had rekindled an idea the general had been mulling over in his mind for the past few days. So after a few well poured glasses of brandy, instead of being upset by the infantry major's rather crude observation, General Crook warmed to the thought of sharing his battle plan with the three junior officers.

"You have a most colorful way of describing our dilemma of forcing the Indians to stand and fight Alex." General Crook smiled at Major Chambers. "However, I think you will find interesting, a plan I have developed to give the command better mobility to run down the red devils."

Seeing the general pause to take a healthy sip of his brandy and thinking he was expecting a response, Major Chambers dutifully asked. "And what plan may that be sir?"

Offering another thin smile General Crook replied. "I am going to reorganize the command to enable us to make a stabbing thrust directly against the hostiles. General Terry with Custer's command and Colonel

Gibbon appear to be in a stalemate situation at the present as far as I can determine. We are the only ones that have been in direct contact and have engaged the hostiles, so that tells me their main encampment is in close proximity to our tactical front. I think we can beat Custer to the punch this time and garner the honors that will be due for outsmarting these savages. What we will do is leave the wagon train at this location; strip ourselves of all miscellaneous gear and equipment that is not essential: mount two hundred of your infantry on mules who will accompany the detachments of the Second and Third Cavalry regiments for a fast moving thrust right at the heart of the red devils. We will move so fast that we'll catch the bastards napping and they won't know what has hit them until it's too late. What do you think about that Major?"

For a few seconds Major Chambers was too stunned to reply. Then finally finding his voice he all but blurted out. "Mount two hundred infantrymen on mules?" He paused but a second before continuing. "You are jesting with me aren't you sir? Pulling my leg for a bit of humor." The infantry officer had smiled when he said this: seriously thinking the general was making him the foil of an outlandish joke. But seeing the general's eyes narrow to bare slits with the dark pupils staring at him like simmering coals, Major Chambers felt a cold chill run up his back from the evil stare. He realized he'd made a mistake and a thought flashed through his mind: *He's serious, he really means to do this!* Major Chambers started to open his mouth to protest the insanity of the idea but General Crook cut him off.

"By God sir! If Hannibal made it across the Alps on elephants to attack Rome, then you better believe I can go to Rosebud Canyon on mules and horses!" To emphasize his declaration, General Crook slapped his large hand on the table which caused the gaily colored deck of cards to fly off the table in all directions except for the black Ace of Spades that floated down and landed face up in the center of the table.

Brigadier General George Crook

Chapter 31

Rosebud Creek Five Miles North of the Mouth of the Tongue River,
Montana Territory
6:45 p.m., Tuesday, June 13, 1876

"Crazy Horse! I say Crazy Horse, will you wait: I want to walk with you."

The fine looking Indian paused in his step and turned half way around in a graceful movement to see who was calling his name. Crazy Horse's stern looking features with its very light complexioned skin and dark, wide-set piercing eyes, softened to a more pleasant expression when he saw it was the Chief Medicine Man of the Northern Cheyenne, Charcoal Bear, who had hailed him. Crazy Horse greatly respected this wise old man who now approached him at a fast shuffling walk between the row of teepees. Standing still, Crazy Horse looked like a bronze statue of a Greek God; his clear-cut features that did not have high cheekbones like most Sioux, cracked along the jaw line as he offered a semblance of a smile. "Wise one-----you honor me by your request. I will be pleased to walk with you."

The slightly out of breath medicine man grunted in reply to the younger mans courtesy as he stepped up to the sandy haired man. "How I envy your youth," the stooped shouldered elder remarked. "There was a time when I could race with the elk on the hunt but now mister turtle gives me competition in swiftness."

The hatchet-faced, grizzled oldster was attired in full Cheyenne ceremonial dress. On his head he wore a bead-banded, full-feathered war bonnet that showed his one-time battle prowess. His fringed, deerskin shirt had a bear-teeth breastplate covering the front and the shirttail hung long over yellowish-white sheepskin pants that were tied at the upper feet with beaded leg bracelets. A wide bright red swath of cloth was wrapped around the old medicine man's waist as a sash.

Crazy Horse, on the other hand, was dressed in simple attire. His almost curly yellowish-red hair was hand brushed straight back and tied with a bit of blue cloth at the nap of his neck. The only mark showing his bravery as a warrior was a single eagle feather standing up straight in the back of his unbraided hair. He never wore more than one feather for Crazy Horse was among that small breed of warriors that never bragged about their combat exploits. He was mostly a silent man who let others do his bragging for him.

On this day however, he did wear one symbol that signified the esteem his people and other chiefs held for him. For Crazy Horse was one of the four Indian's of the entire Sioux Nation that was a "Shirt Wearer." This simple, unadorned buckskin vest was akin to the Medal of Honor in the Indian civilization, although it was never bestowed for any single feat of action, rather for an accumulation of deeds over a long period of time. It too was an emblem Crazy Horse seldom flaunted, but today was an important one and part of the responsibilities of being a shirt wearer was to preside over tribal spiritual events such as had been going on for the past twelve days. The rather short warrior, Crazy Horse, only stood five feet, eight inches; turned to Charcoal Bear and answered the medicine man's previous remark concerning age. "I find oh wise one while it is that my thirty-three winters are less than yours, that I too am finding the tortoise to be fleeter of foot than I once remembered."

Charcoal Bear chuckled at the admission. "I ponder sometimes that the great spirit may have erred in the way of our existence. By the time we have gained the wisdom to know how to properly use our bodies our youth has passed by and alas our bodies fail us. Then I witness our young bucks doing the same idiotic things that we did which wasted our limbs, and do you think they will listen to council? I fear not, because they have yet to gain the wisdom that comes with many winters. It would have been better had the great spirit allowed us to been born older and wiser then pass from this life with youthful enthusiasm."

Crazy Horse nodded his head. "Yes, I understand what you say. I find it difficult to try and convince my young braves not to do foolish things. They think they will live forever with the agility they now possess. When I warned them of the great thunder stick the white soldiers now have, which can do us great harm; they all laughed, saying our great numbers will overwhelm any such evil thing."

"I have heard of this thunder stick you speak of," Charcoal Bear interjected. "My heart tells me we must avoid this terrible weapon at all cost, even to demanding our warriors stay away from it."

Crazy Horse grunted. "Yes----if at all possible, but I fear it is out of our hands now. We know of the white soldiers to the north and to the east where the sun rises: and your Cheyenne scouts have reported a large band of them coming towards us from the south. Your heart is giving you sound council wise one, but my heart speaks to me that we are facing a tremendous battle whether we want it or not."

His remark effectively put a damper on the conversation for several seconds and the two walked along side by side in silence, each lost in their own thoughts. It was unusual for Crazy Horse to be as talkative as he had been because he was extremely closed mouthed. Many of his own tribesmen thought him to be down right odd in his self imposed silent manner and keeping to himself, almost like a hermit. But his respect for this Cheyenne Chief Medicine Man had made him expansive and he didn't mind speaking openly with him like he was doing.

Charcoal Bear must have sensed his companion's willingness to converse. After passing a yapping dog tethered between two lodges the medicine man asked, "You are going to view the climax of your Sun Dance I take it?"

"That is where I am going right now. Sitting Bull has been in a trance for quite awhile and his adopted brother Jumping Bull sent a messenger to me saying they are reviving him by dropping cold water on his face and if I want to be there to hear what the great spirit Waken' tanka has revealed to Sitting Bull then I should come at once."

"Then Sitting Bull is still in the dance circle near your holy forked cottonwood pole the virgin maidens selected?"

"I am sure that he is. It is the normal practice to place our medicine man on the ground near the dance pole after he has exhausted himself from dancing and staring at the sun to bring on the vision."

Charcoal Bear nodded his head. "I must say to you that while the Cheyenne do not perform such a profound ritual as your Sun Dance, I am most impressed by it as are all my people. It takes a very special man like Sitting Bull to order fifty pieces of flesh to be cut from his arms. I know how to withstand pain but I am not certain I could dance for hours like he has done with my blood flowing so freely. I believe I would surely faint too soon before realizing the fulfillment of my vows to Wakan' tanka."

"I think perhaps you are too harsh on yourself great wise one. Of course endurance is required to seek vision from the Great Mystery, but I think you have the fortitude if you were to make the commitment." Crazy Horse replied softly.

"Most kind of you to say that and I do accept the fact that great dedication is necessary. But I am thankful my people's ways are easier when evoking help from the great spirit than the rigors your people go through," Charcoal Bear responded. After a long pause the medicine man glanced over to his companion as they walked past a group of children teasing an elderly squaw. This disrespect to elders was allowed during the days of the Sun Dance. "It has come to my ears you had a vision as a young boy. That you saw a warrior riding a horse on the clouds that changed colors. This warrior only wore a single feather and the wind took all his clothing except for a waist skirt and there were no scalps on his belt. Yet he must have been very brave for he charged into battle amidst a thunderstorm with lightning striking like boom guns and arrows and bullets coming at him from all directions and the warrior disappeared into a mist leaving behind a red-back hawk gliding in the sky. I believe this to be a wonderful vision and it has many meanings. What did you make of it Crazy Horse?"

The Ogallala born warrior chief did not answer right away. He bowed his head in thought and continued his slow pace so the old man could keep up with him. After a minute or so his thinking took the bent that it would cause no harm to relate a better version of his childhood vision out of respect for the old medicine man. "My wise Cheyenne brother and friend, many people have confused my youthful encounter with the great spirit with other experiences and teachings I have related over the seasons. My father taught me to lead by example and not words. That is why I keep to myself and seldom have much to say. But for you I will tell of what came to me in that sweat lodge that day so many winters ago. A man on horseback came out of a lake and talked to me. He said it was not necessary for me to wear a war bonnet or to tie up my pony's tail when riding into battle when I got older. Then the shimmering golden image on horseback told me I need not paint my face and body with war paint to scare my enemies nor should I take scalps or brag about how many I have slain. What you related about riding into battle scantly clothed is fairly accurate because I interpreted the lack of adornment of beads and paint to include simple dress and I only wear a loincloth and belt for my dress as a warrior. And I never paint or adorn my pony. There were other things the golden warrior said to me but these are personal and I wish to keep it that way."

What the personal part of Crazy Horse's childhood vision contained had to do that no bullet or arrow would kill him as his death would come from strong men holding him while he was being stabbed.

Much to Crazy Horse's surprise Charcoal Bear said softly. "These old ears do not need to hear of how a man has seen the way he is to die."

Crazy Horse spun his head around. "How did you know this was part of my vision I keep private and don't talk about?"

The old man smiled a sad smile. "Contemplating death is always a very personal and private subject that should not be shared with others." And he said no more.

They continued on their way in silence.

The two men had already walked about a mile on their way to the large circle laid out that was guarded by older warriors. The huge Indian camp stretched for four miles from end to end and was a quarter mile wide. The Sun Dance circle was over 150 feet in diameter with small poles tied together by rawhide thongs making it into an arbor of sorts with the main feature being the center sacred pole the Sioux danced around. This circle was located on the flat bottomland a hundred yards away from Rosebud Creek. As Charcoal Bear and Crazy Horse emerged onto the tramped down grassy plain where young men were initiated into the ways of a warrior, flocks of people at the outer edge noticed them. A small group of holy men hovered around Sitting Bull who was now sitting upright and allowing his brother to wipe off his blood encrusted arms with a damp cloth. All of the many Indian chiefs, both Sioux and Cheyenne, formed a large ring around Sitting Bull a few yards from where he was being administered. They sat cross-legged on the ground watching the proceedings with submissive interest. In back of the chiefs stood a throng of onlookers, many of them Sun Dance participants who had seen Sitting Bull go into his trance after having danced and chanted for better than a dozen hours.

Having seen the approach of the two important Indian's, those on the outer fringe gave way forming a channel. Warriors among the group gave guttural warnings to open a path for Crazy Horse and Charcoal Bear to walk through and the two men strode purposefully to the center of the circle. The holy men around Sitting Bull also backed away as Crazy Horse walked up to the Sioux paraclete.

The 45-year-old recognized leader of the unified tribes smiled wanly when seeing his greatest warrior chief. "Crazy Horse my son and brother, please help me to rise so that I may speak to our people. I have the most wonderful news to tell that the great Wakan' tanka has shared with me."

Before reaching down for the big bodied Chief Medicine Man, Crazy Horse gave a slight bow of respect, saying. "It is a great honor to touch the flesh of such a worthy leader and great warrior oh mighty one."

Crazy Horse's remark about Sitting Bull being a great warrior was not just flattery. The raven-haired chieftain who parted his hair down the middle of his head and wore long braids had made his first coup on a Crow warrior during battle at age fourteen. For this he received his first white feather as a brave warrior. The next year fifteen year old Sitting Bull was awarded a ceremonial red feather indicating he had been wounded in combat. Over the ensuing 25 years the red and white feathers grew into a full war bonnet, which boasted a long trail of feathers reaching the ground. Despite his reputation for valor Sitting Bull's main hold on his people was his "good medicine." The five foot, ten inch tall Indian with a round face and high cheekbones, had an uncanny ability to predict victory and to know when to fight and when to withdraw. And his people came to believe the chiseled faced man with cold brown eyes and proboscis nose possessed divine powers that could communicate with Wakan' tanka, the Great Mystery or God who controlled all earthly events.

Getting shakily to his feet with the help of his brother and Crazy Horse, Sitting Bull stood stone still facing toward the west. He remained like this for over a minute while he regained his strength and composure. Although scantly dressed; clad only in a loincloth, his entire body and legs was painted with yellow, white and red colors. Although the paint was now streaked and dirty it gave the appearance he was fully clothed. Talking softly, barely above a whisper, Sitting Bull spoke to the two men supporting him. "Thank you for helping me my precious comrades. You may let go of me now so I may relate to our people the great vision."

"Are you sure my brother?" Jumping Bull asked. "You appear to me to still be very weak from your long ordeal."

Sitting Bull smiled. "I am filled with the strength of the Great Spirit my brother. Wakan' tanka will not let me fall."

After the two men released their grip Sitting Bull took several tentative steps forward and though he teetered somewhat he maintained his balance. Then raising both his hands upwards above waist level with fingers cupped and palms up, he began talking in a deep resonate voice. "My fellow chief's, my brave warriors and all of my children: Wakan' tanka has shown me a great vision. There are many soldiers coming that will attack our village...." Sitting Bull had to pause and hold out his right hand that he waved for silence to still the loud gasps and mutterings coming from the multitude after having heard what he had said. In a calm tone he continued, "You are not to fear and you must hear all that I have to say with open ears my children. These soldiers I speak of which is written on the clouds, were shown to me as falling headfirst from the sky into our village as were all of their horses. And they were all without ears and the voice said to me: I give you these because they would not listen and they dare to invade the sacred land of my people. As I looked closely I saw that all of these soldiers without ears were dead and other than their missing ears the bodies were all untouched which tells me we must not defile their bodies after we kill them. For the voice also told me this will be our greatest victory and the white man will run in shame from us and will be greatly afraid, as long as we do as the Great Spirit tells us. There will be sacrifices within the ranks of our brave warriors, also as I saw many upside down ponies going to the great hunting ground beyond the clouds with riders laying still on the ponies backs. But all of these warriors wore smiles and their ears were open hearing the wails and chants of their families helping them to the other life. So my children, we must prepare ourselves for this glorious happening."

When Sitting Bull stopped talking there was a long moment of silence. Then suddenly, as if on cue, a thousand warriors began yelling a war chant at the top of their lungs.

Chapter 32

Wild Goose Creek, Wyoming Territory
8:00 a.m., Wednesday, June 14, 1876

General George Crook, who just moments before had been concentrating on a dispatch he was preparing for General Alfred Terry outlining his forthcoming attack plan, looked up from his field desk with an expression of annoyance, after having been interrupted by his aide-de-camp. When he put down his nib point writing pen, his beefy hand brushed against the open bottle of ink almost tipping it over, but he managed to stave off the almost accident just in time by grabbing the squat inkwell at the top which dyed his fingertips a deep colored blue-black. This did not help his mood any and after glancing at his stained fingers he uttered an oath. "Well Horse Shit!" Reaching for a gun cleaning rag he wiped off his fingers and in a somewhat calmer tone of voice stared at Lieutenant Gregory Bourke with hooded eyes, and said. "I know I must have misunderstood what you just said Greg. Would you repeat that again slowly?"

Lieutenant Bourke was standing at stiff attention with his forage cap tucked under his left arm, staring straight ahead over the top of the general's head in the precise military manner of reporting to a superior officer. His brown, bushy mustache twitched minutely, and his drooping eyes blinked three times in quick succession before responding. "General Crook sir...er, I have been advised by Major Chambers to tell you sir that a---ah, female has been discovered in camp sir."

General Crook started to slam his hand down on the desk but had the presence of mind to remember the inkwell so instead drove his right fist into his left palm with a resounding slap. "By tarnation that's what you said the first time!" He shouted.

"Yes sir," Lieutenant Bourke dutifully responded to his commander's outburst.

"What in the Sam Hill is a woman doing with the expedition?" General Crook asked rhetorically, not expecting a response. Then slyly. "What is it, an Injun squaw one of the scouts snuck into camp?"

A little nervously Lieutenant Bourke said. "I'm afraid not sir. It's...I mean to say she's a white woman."

"A white woman? Well who in the hell found her and how did she get here, and what in the hell has she been doing?"

"Ah----from what I gather sir, she passed herself off as a man and the Wagon Master hired her at Fort Fetterman as a wagon driver." The lieutenant paused for a moment, then continued, "As the general knows sir they're breaking the infantry boys in on how to ride mules and from what I surmise she was ah...helping out when a frisky mule kicked her, knocking her out cold. When some of the boys loosened her, well actually what they thought to be his shirt to give him...her some air---that's when they found he...I mean the person...had breast."

"Breast?" General Crook said dumbly.

"Yes sir------female breast, sir." Lieutenant Bourke replied just as dumbly.

"I see," General Crook said after a ten second pause. "Well, where is this....ah person at right now?"

"She's standing by right outside sir. Major Chambers didn't know exactly what he was supposed to do with her and thought maybe you would want to talk to her sir," the aide-de-camp trailed off lamely.

"By *Jehashaphat* this is a downright calamity! What in the *sam hill* am I supposed to do with a woman?" The general's voice rose sharply again.

Lieutenant Bourke's right eyebrow lifted reflectively in contemplation at his general's remark of what he was supposed to do with a woman.

"Well *dangburnit* bring her on in here so I can figure this thing out!" The general finally decided.

His aide-de-camp offered a snappy "Yes sir," and spun on his heel to fetch the calamity the general described but was stopped by General Crook before reaching the office tent entrance flap. "Greg!"

Turning quickly around Lieutenant Bourke offered a questioning. "Yes sir?"

"Before you send her in here I want you to get the Wagon Master and Colonel Royal, and you may as well include Major Chambers. Oh, and Greg, make damn sure Strahorn, Wason and that Finerty fellow that was supposed to have went out with Custer and...what's that other fellows name from the New York Herald? Biggs or something? Anyway make sure they don't get wind of this. That's all I need is to have General Sheridan sending me a bunch of newspapers with headlines blazing that Crook is fighting the Indians with women in the ranks."

General Crook was referring to the five newspaper correspondents that accompanied his column with the blessing of the War Department: Robert Strahorn, who represented the Denver Rocky Mountain News, Omaha Republican, Cheyenne Sun and New York Times; Joe Wasson of the New

York Tribune and San Francisco Alta California; Thomas C. Macmillan, who wrote for the Chicago Inter-Ocean; John F. Finery of the Chicago Times and Reuben Briggs Davenport of the New York Herald. As much as General Crook enjoyed personal publicity showing him in a good light, much the same as Custer, the mutton-chopped expedition leader didn't have the flair or personality to be as controversial as Custer was. Or for that matter, the desire.

It took Lieutenant Bourke twenty minutes to round up the three principals General Crook ordered to be present and when they were all assembled he attempted to get right to the point. "Before I bring this......this female in here, I want to clear the air and make it perfectly understood the army is not going to take the responsibility for this thing to have happened. Mister Durant I'm laying the blame for this situation right at your feet because you are the one that hired this...this person. How in the devil did she manage to pass herself off to you as a man? That's what I'd like to know!"

Unperturbed, Jason Claymore Durant, the heavy-bodied, civilian contracted Wagon Master, shifted his chaw from one side of his mouth to the other, causing a small dribble of brown spittle to run from the corner of his mouth onto his unshaven chin. Wiping the tobacco stain off with the back of his gnarled hand the florid-faced, two hundred and fifty pound man said. 'Wait till you see her gen'ral...might jus answer that question fer ya without having to ponder 'bout it."

Lieutenant Colonel William B. Royall, the overall commander of the fifteen companies of cavalry, had to stifle a grin from the Wagon Master's impertinence and irreverent behavior.

General Crook's face reddened a little, but he just shook his head in disgust, saying. "Very well mister, bring her on in and we'll take a look at her."

Durant ambled over to the tent flap which he opened, and after letting fly a stream of tobacco juice, said in his deep, hoarse voice. "C'mon in here Clarence, the gen'ral wants to take a peek at ya."

A rather short person, not over five foot, six inches tall, dressed in filthy brown corduroy pants, a long dirty black dress coat, with a soiled gray flannel shirt and brown vest, stepped inside the tent and looked around with an unconcerned curiosity. Slim framed with a young-looking, weather-beaten, triangular shaped face, the wide-set, blue-eyed individual whose eyes laid in deep sockets sniffed a little from a projecting thin nose. The person stared at General Crook with a half way sneer on equally thin lips and stood in a relaxed posture.

197

Lieutenant Bourke was a little miffed at the person's attitude and snapped out. "Take your hat off in the presence of the general."

The short statured, round shouldered person glanced at the lieutenant with a bemused expression and said. "Awrite soldier boy," and removed the sweat stained, wide-brimmed, tan hat, slapping it hard on the right thigh which caused a cloud of trail dust to billow. Uncovered, the person revealed two large pointed ears laid back flat against the head and short-cropped straight black hair parted near the middle on the left side.

The four army officers appraised the flinty-faced person who stared back at them with narrowed eyes under thick, black, arched eyebrows. General Crook immediately saw that the small round chinned, ugly individual could be taken for a sour-faced young man. It also appeared that the youngster, who looked to be around twenty-four, has a taste for tobacco as one side of the narrow jaw line bulged like a chipmunk.

Clearing his throat, General Crook spoke. "Yes...humpph, humpph...Well it seems we have a little problem here...ah Miss, as it's come to our attention you are of the female gender..."

"That's what I heer tell," the person answered, interrupting in a high-pitched nasal sounding voice.

Looking over to the Wagon Master, the General asked. "You say she's been going by the name of Clarence?"

But before Clay Durant, as he preferred to be called, could answer, the woman spoke up. "Yep----that's rite. I signed on as Clarence Carney...took my dead brothers first name."

Shifting his glance back to the ugly creature General Crook said. "I see. What is your real name then?

"I was born as Martha Jane Canary but I mostly use Jane as a first name since I don't cotton too much to Martha."

"Jane huh?" General Crook mused. "More like Calamity Jane from the problems you're causing me and my command."

"Calamity Jane you say. Now I kinda like that. Sort of has a ring to it don't it now?" The woman smiled, showing small yellow teeth.

"Well Calamity Jane, whether it has a ring to it or not I guess that is something you will have to figure out. I'm placing you under arrest and you're going to have a twenty-four hour a day guard on you until Mister Durant can find a way to get you back to Fort Fetterman or anywhere else he may determine as long as it's away from this command." General Crook paused and looked to his two senior officers. "I know we cannot keep this from the troops so what I want done is get her dressed somehow, the closest to woman's attire as you can come up with, and keep her in one of the ambulance wagons. If any of those nosy correspondence's ask what's going on just tell them that Miss Canary here came looking for her brother. With us leaving early in the morning we might just get away with this without getting our necks axed." Then he turned back to the female. "And for you! You'll get what wages you got coming to you and you will be released without charges once a way is found to get you back to civilization. In the meantime, you keep your mouth shut. You understand that?"

"Yep bud, that I do," answered Calamity Jane.

Chapter 33

Yellowstone River, halfway between the Powder and Tongue Rivers,
Montana Territory
1:00 p.m., Thursday, June 15, 1876

Lieutenant William Hale "Bucky" Low rode easily on his big brown mare as did his riding companion, Captain Tom Custer. The two officers, along with six companies of the 7th Cavalry and two remaining Gatling guns, had left their base camp at 7:00 a.m. from the mouth of the Powder River. General George Custer was leading this combat patrol as ordered by General Terry, who remained at the camp location he had directed built, while waiting word from Major Reno.

The mission given General Custer was to check out the upper reaches of the Tongue River that was roughly forty miles from the Powder River base camp. But mostly the scout was formed with hopes of linking up with Reno's patrol of which no word had been heard since the major's departure on the 10th. Although the route of march was over extremely rough terrain wagons or slow moving infantry no longer encumbered the cavalry column.. Custer's command was now stripped for action and would only travel with mules carrying essential supplies. Just the same the cavalry was forced to take its time because of narrow trails being blazed through uncharted inhospitable land features. The slowness of traveling over the uneven ground gave the two officers, who had come to enjoy one another's company, the opportunity to talk.

"So tell me the truth Billy, were your surprised when my brother ordered you to come along on this scout?" Tom Custer asked with an easy smile.

"In a way I was, but with General Terry wanting to test my battery by sending out Pat Kensie with Major Reno it didn't come as too big of a surprise." Bucky Low answered.

"Yes, I suppose I can see how you'd feel that way," Tom Custer said easily, "but with all the controversy that's taken place regarding your Gatling's I thought perhaps the general's change of heart may have been unexpected."

"Oh it has!" Low answered quickly. "Actually General Custer never fails to amaze me and his more understanding attitude toward offensive employment of my guns have left me flabbergasted to say the least."

Tom Custer chuckled softly. "Brother George has never failed to amaze me either Bucky."

Taking a quick glance at the general's brother Bucky Low made an instant counter remark. "I didn't mean for my remark to sound disrespectful Captain Custer sir. What I intended to say was...."

With a short laugh Tom Custer interrupted. "Don't fret Bucky, it wasn't taken that way. I was just thinking about a personal annoyance I'm harboring because my good brother ordered all sabers to be packed in boxes and stored on the Far West. The general's logic of the Indian's generally scattering when charged by cavalry and our sabers not being of use has not convinced me this was a good move. And even though its become a practice lately that most officers do not carry their sabers into battle; my personal viewpoint holds, that with the fear the Sioux have of the Long Knife, if for no other reason, we should have taken advantage of that fear."

There ensued a long moment of silence while Bucky Low mulled over in his mind how he should respond to the general's brother on such a touchy subject that bordered on insubordination.

Tom Custer, sensing the younger officer's discomfort, laughed out loud and reached over from his mount to pat Low on his back in a camaraderie fashion. "I didn't mean to put you on the spot Bucky. Just because George and I are brothers doesn't mean I agree with every decision he makes and I'm quite certain the rest of the Officer's Corps shares similar thoughts." In an effort to put his riding companion at more ease Tom Custer decided to change the subject and said lightly. "Say---I noticed you changed the manner in which you're carrying your barrels. The way you have the two ponies in tandem are almost exactly the way medical personnel rig stretchers for long trek transport of causalities."

On a safer subject now Lieutenant Low answered without hesitation. "Yes sir. I found the side-by-side method with the leather sling to be less rigid in transporting the barrels but then I got to thinking about the narrow trails we sometimes have to traverse such as we're on now and there is no way two horses could ride side by side. You are right on the mark regarding the stretcher observation for that's the concept I borrowed. But I modified the configuration by making the distance between the horses shorter and continue to use the flexible leather and canvas sling as a pouch for the barrel system to nestle in. Seems to be working very well."

Turning in his saddle Tom Custer viewed the long line of mules and horses in trace behind him for a moment. "I'd say you've done a good job of it. Appears to me your ponies are doing a better effort at keeping up than those stubborn ass mules." Then turning his head to Lieutenant Low, Tom

Custer brought up another subject. "All your boys sober this morning after that rake set up his whiskey tent yesterday?"

Captain Custer was referring to a sutler by the name of James Coleman who had come up on the steamer Far West with several barrels of whiskey and can goods. Coleman and an assistant with the unlikely name of John Smith had put up a tent, partitioned it in half with crates of canned goods, then begun selling whiskey out of the barrels at one dollar a pint: officers on one side of the tent, enlisted on the other side.

This time Lieutenant Low laughed out loud. "What a mess that turned out to be. I couldn't believe General Terry allowed the men to purchase that rotgut; but then again that Coleman fellow is a registered government sponsored sutler so I reckon the general didn't have a choice. I ordered my two gun sergeants to keep their eyes on the men since my first sergeant is out with Major Reno. Some of the boys really got a snoot full and I imagine there's some terrible headaches riding with us today."

Grinning, Tom Custer said. "I have to admit I rather like the way my brother improvised for discipline problems since we could not very well bring a guardhouse with us on the campaign. Him having the provost detail toss the drunk and disorderly out on the open prairie to fight it out or sleep it off was a nice touch". Custer Paused for a moment to shake his head in mirth, remembering the hilarity at seeing the drunken antics and behavior that took place.

Thinking the void of silence was intended for him to respond, the first lieutenant responded. "It certainly was Captain Custer sir."

Custer glanced at his riding companion and said. "Well at least it gave the lads a chance to spend some of that pay that's been burning a hole in their pockets ever since we left Fort Lincoln. And by the way old man; even though we haven't shared a cup or two yet, I think we've become friendly enough that when by ourselves like this you can dispense with the sir and captain bit and address me as Tom."

* * * * *

While Captain Custer and Lieutenant Low were engaged in pleasant conversation, Major Marcus Reno's scouts had made a startling discovery, which the major had taken it upon himself to pursue even though it was stretching his orders considerably.

The major's original orders from General Terry had been simple and to the point: Follow the Powder River until reaching the spot where the river branched into Mizpah Creek. From that location head west to Pumpkin Creek. Proceed up the Pumpkin until reaching the Tongue River then follow this watershed tributary back up to the Yellowstone River. General Terry had estimated this 200-mile U shaped configured patrol route should take no more than twelve days. During this time the general would have the remainder of the 7th Cavalry move toward the confluence of the Yellowstone and Tongue to link up with Reno.

But as it turned out Major Reno had become disgruntled that few signs of hostiles had been found and none whatsoever of major tribal movements. So instead of heading back up north on the Tongue River he had Mitch Bouer lead the command west from the Tongue into the valley of the Rosebud. Having made the decision to disobey General Terry's orders Major Reno then ordered the head of his Arikara scouts to send several of them on ahead further into the valley to see if they could locate more definite signs of Sioux activity. It was here on June 14, the Arikaras found an abandoned Sioux camp near Rosebud Creek and with logic based upon experience it was determined the old village site had contained at least 360 lodges. With this many tepees having been lived in there was little doubt in Mitch Bouyer's mind they had discovered an encampment which had held 700 to 800 warriors.

Now at 1:00 p.m., after having followed the trail made by the Indians from their abandoned camp, Major Reno, Mitch Bouyer and Forked Horn, the chief scout of the Arikaras, stared grimly from their mounts at the evidence the patrol had been seeking.

Mitch Bouyer shook his head in a contemplative manner and eyed Major Reno before speaking. "Major----this trail is a good quarter mile wide if it's an inch. I'd say you're a standing on the main trail of the whole hostile band and that's a fact sure 'nough. Just look how this here ground is all tore up from lodge poles dragging on the travails they made up to haul their belongings. You could plant corn in those furrows and from what I'm a looking at you're talking better than five thousand injun's having passed by here...and that's down rite scary to think about."

Almost inanely Major Reno replied with a dreamlike quality in his tone of voice. "They're not going to the Yellowstone, they're heading south along the Rosebud."

Bouyer, who seldom smiled, managed a thin grin after hearing the obvious. "Yep--I suspect that's exactly what they're doing. I reckon they've got a mind to put the mountains between you soldier fellows and them. Old Sitting Bull sure ain't of the mind to be sitting still to wait for you, that's for dang sure."

The mountains Mitch Bouyer referred to were the low rolling hill range called the Rosebud Mountains, which in reality was not much of a mountain range to speak of at all.

Major Reno digested his borrowed scouts bit of wisdom then turned to the Arikara. "What do you make of this Forked Horn?"

The heavily-built, swarthy Indian grunted then offered an opinion. "I say we are less than two moons from finding more Sioux than your eyes would wish to see. Half Sioux, half white man Bouyer may be right saying his half blood brothers go to tall hills he calls mountains. But then maybe Sitting Bull and other chiefs may decide the valley of the Big Horn is better place to meet pony soldiers. Maybe they decide they have run far enough and will be waiting for you...huh?"

Mitch Bouyer took no offense at Forked Horn's reference to the Sioux blood flowing in his veins or the slur of being called a half-white man, which was the same of calling him a half-breed, which of course he was. Bouyer was an intelligent person, having been a protégé of the famous Jim Bridger, one of the best scouts ever produced in the west. Although Bouyer looked like an Indian, and spoke five different dialects, he basically lived as a Caucasian and held the respect of all army officers. He knew this was a sore spot with the full-blooded Indian scouts the army also hired and took Forked Horn's slur as piqued jealousy. He also knew how to get his own slight barb in by saying something to the major without calling Forked Horn by his name. "The leader of your Arikara scouts may have a point Major Reno. But regardless of what his fears may be it was my understanding that the reason of this patrol was to locate just what we have found. As it stands right now you're going to have to make the decision if we follow the trail or hightail it the forty or so miles up the Rosebud to the Yellowstone to find General Terry and tell him what's down here."

Forked Horn bristled a little at the cowardly implication implied by the half-breeds remark by making a couple of grunts.

Major Reno mulled over what decision he should make. Finally coming to a conclusion the major said, "What we'll do then is find a place to camp for the night that isn't all chewed up like this trail. At first light we'll follow the trail for a couple of more days to see where it leads us."

"That's fine with me," Bouyer answered cheerfully.

When Forked Horn did not offer a remark Major Reno prodded the Indian scout. "Well Forked Horn, what do you have to say about what I just said?"

The squat, flat-faced scout remained silent for several seconds then made a reply. "I think if we find the Sioux that the sun will not move very far in the sky before we are all killed. But you are the white chief and we will go on if you say to do so because me and my scouts are braver than your half Sioux white man thinks we are."

A cold shiver ran up Major Reno's spine from hearing the grim prediction and he licked his lips wishing he could take his flask out and take a drink from it. But the mood quickly passed for Major Reno, for all his faults, was no coward. So instead of thinking about his flask anymore he spoke in a low tone, yet steely sounding voice. "Then I say we will follow the trail."

* * * * *

What Major Reno had no way of knowing was that Mitch Boyer had made a poor estimate of the proximity of the Sioux and Cheyenne. For these massed tribes were better than sixty miles further south and were not even aware of the major or his cavalry patrol. However, these Indians were aware of other pony soldiers in the vicinity and were discussing what they should do about it.

Major Marcus Remo

Chapter 34

Near the lower end of Rosebud Creek, Montana Territory
9:45 a.m., Friday, June 16, 1876

Five Cheyenne warriors, Little Hawk, Yellow Eagle, Crooked Nose, Little Shield and White Bird, lay flat on their stomachs on top a wide flat rock shelf that stuck out from a large hill overlooking the wide valley. Their ponies were tethered behind them down slope in a narrow coulee; loaded heavily with field dressed buffalo meat they had hunted the day before. What they were all staring at in fascinated concentration had kept the five Cheyenne's mute for several minutes.

In a low guttural whisper Little Hawk broke the silence. "It is as if the whole earth is covered with blue soldiers. I have never seen so many white men before. I hope the Sun God has hidden us."

Crooked Nose was lying so close to Little Hawk that their legs touched, answered his companion. "When you and the others went out to kill a cow buffalo, while I tended our cooking fire, I saw two men ride up to that hill over there," he pointed a finger, "Both were leading a pony each and I thought they were Lakota's. They were in plain sight of me and surely must have seen me but gave no sign that they had. After they disappeared among the bluffs is when I waved for you to return."

"It is good that you did." Little Hawk replied in a low tone of voice. "We must return to our people and tell them of what we have seen."

It may have been fortunate for the five Cheyenne's that a heavy morning fog had obscured their presence because the two scouts from General Crook's command must not have seen Crooked Nose. But Crook was aware he was getting close to the hostiles he sought because he and his command had clearly heard the rattle of distant rifle fire made by the Cheyenne hunting party.

The Wyoming column had begun their march at 5:00 a.m. that morning with Crow and Shoshone scouts taking the lead. Behind the Indians followed fifteen companies of cavalry with a long mule train of packers in trace. Bringing up the rear was the mounted infantry battalion. The infantry had done better than expected when it came to General Crook's brainstorm of putting them on mules. Naturally the cavalrymen, Crow and Shoshone scouts had a good time of it watching the 175 infantrymen learn how to mount and ride 175 cantankerous mules. They roared with laughter seeing the walking soldiers being tossed around like rag dolls as they learned how to saddle and ride their stubborn, ornery mounts. But this morning not one infantryman was thrown when he got upon his mule. Morale and spirits was high within the entire command. Like most armies the great mass of soldiers were young men who were light-hearted, and possessed the careless courage of those without previous battlefield experience. The same could be said of the young Sioux and Cheyenne warrior, many who were barely into their teens.

Near midnight the five Cheyenne's of Little Hawk's hunting party found the new campsite of the combined tribes. While the five Indians had hunted the primary chiefs had made the decision to move from their old campsite. This move was about twenty miles northwest up a small creek that flowed into the Little Bighorn River that offered better grass for the huge herd of horses to graze. Here, Little Hawk and the others reported their discovery.

In a pouring rain the once sleeping Indian camp became a turmoil of activity. Several older chiefs tried to restore order and begged the younger warriors to use common sense and not to rush off to do battle with the white soldiers. But other chiefs, including Crazy Horse, knew there was no stopping the Sioux-Cheyenne war machine that was already in motion. As squaws and maidens began to dismantle teepees and packing essentials onto hasty made traipse, to move out of harms way further west to the Little Bighorn, warriors prepared for the fight they intended to give the white soldiers.

Chapter 35

Rosebud Creek, Montana Territory
10:45 p.m., Saturday, June 17, 1876

General George Crook stared grimly at the long trench his privates were digging on the bank of Rosebud Creek near several large bushes of wild roses that flourished by being so close to the waters edge. The sickly sweet fragrance of the bright red roses lent a funeral parlor atmosphere for the solemn soldiers going about their grisly work. The cloying aroma predominating the still cool air was appropriate; for the richness of the smell gave an authenticity to what was taking place.

Thirty-two stiff forms wrapped in army blankets laid in a long row behind the large pile of dirt the laboring soldiers were adding to as they put the final touches on the four foot deep hole. Once finished, this mass grave would be the final resting place for those non-commissioned officers and privates killed by the Sioux and Cheyenne that day.

Several small bon fires lit the surrounding area to give those men working sufficient light to perform the task assigned to them. The leaping flames from the fires produced an upward shower of twinkling yellow-orange embers which cast eerie shadows across the faces of onlookers as well as those with shovels and picks in their hands. The flickering shadows created a foreboding, almost ghastly appearance on the features of the soldiers and civilians that was somehow haunting. The crackling of the fire along with the crunching ring of shovel and pick in the soft, rocky soil, was the most prominent sounds heard except for a distant low chant and an occasional mummer of an order from sergeants supervising the burial detail. Everybody else was silent.

The far away whispering chant came from a small group of Shoshone scouts who were going through the mourning ritual for one of their comrades killed during the six-hour battle with the Sioux and Cheyenne. These Shoshones were further upstream and would continue their wailing dirge until first light when they would then bury their fallen comrade in a deep hole already dug by them.

The final shaping of the long trench next to the rose bushes went on for another fifteen minutes and then one-by-one the sweaty, bare-chested, grimy soldiers climbed out of the ditch and stood on the berm looking down at their handiwork. Those with shovels continued to hold on to the digging tools in their dirty hands because they knew their job wasn't over yet.

Colonel William B. Royall, overall commander of the two cavalry units, came up to stand beside General Crook. For a long minute the flinty-eyed, mustached, colonel remained silent and if Crook noticed his presence the general gave no indication. With an audible sigh the colonel at last spoke. "General Crook sir, they are ready."

Crook slowly turned his head toward his unit commander and stared at him for a few seconds as if noting the man's presence for the first time and wanting to make sure who it was addressing him. In a tired, sad voice General Crook said, "Do we have a site location drawn on one of our maps?"

"Yes sir we do. I did that personally sir, plus Captain Mills drew an excellent field survey drawing of the area sir." Colonel Royall answered.

"How about the chaplain; is he prepared to render services?" The general then asked.

"He's standing by sir."

"Very good." General Crook took a deep breath and in a much stronger tone of voice that had a vehement quality about it, continued speaking. "Bill---I want stones packed with mud to cover each man, and when they fill it in I want the dirt tamped down as tight as it can be done. And I want a huge fire made over the entire area and assign men to keep it going till daylight. When we leave for Goose Creek tomorrow I want you to march the entire column over the grave...I don't want them sonsabitches knowing where we buried our dead and digging them up so they can desecrate the bodies!"

Moved by the general's concern Colonel Royall saluted when he said. "Yes sir, I'll see to every detail personally sir."

General Crook nodded his head in acceptance of his officer's remark and offered a perfunctory return salute.

Colonel Royall started to depart to delegate the general's wishes when a question he'd forgot to ask came back to mind, "Oh, pardon me sir. What about the disposition of the thirteen Sioux dead we gathered off the battlefield?"

Without hesitation the six foot, broad shouldered, sinewy general officer answered, "Let the sonsabitches lay where you got them and let the damn animals and birds have at them!"

After the long trench was covered with earth the overnight bivouac settled down to obtain what rest could be gotten before moving back to the Goose Creek base camp. General Crook had decided on this move so the 26 seriously wounded officers and troopers could get better medical attention.

He also said a lack of rations and ammunition was a factor contributing to his decision to withdraw.

New York Herald correspondent Reuben Davenport took advantage of the bright lit fire being tended by soldiers over the mass grave to jot down a few notes in his dispatch log which he would use to broaden a news article he would write later concerning the battle just fought: *"The Sioux allowed Crook possession of the battlefield but in every sense of the word Crook was soundly defeated. He's claiming a victory but I look at a beaten army. Men downcast, without pride. If wrong then why retreat from battlefield. Crook found his hostiles he was looking for so why isn't he now going to give chase and go after them. From what I viewed it was one blunder compounded by blunder after blunder, all Crook's fault. Hostiles charged over the rolling prairie right up to the camp. Crook so surprised he gave conflicting orders which when carried out was done so with timidity for the most part. Soldiers so confused they shot at their own government scouts one of which may have been killed by our own troops. Troop F, 3rd Cavalry led by Sgt David Marshall surrounded, ran out of ammunition. Brave fight, used their carbines as clubs but all killed save one Pvt Towns who is badly wounded and tortured by hostiles till rescued by another troop. Towns said one very young trooper tried to surrender: handed his carbine to Indian who took it and beat the lad to death with it. Capt Henry shot in face through both cheeks, will try to interview him. Crazy Horse, Sitting Bull most likely led attack. Troopers report seeing Crazy Horse. They seem to respect him oddly enough. Heard one officer call him an Indian Napoleon. Is this rubbish or does he fit the image? Check on this more."*

Davenport's last entry in his journal for the night was a short note to remind him the Rosebud Battle had been fought on the hundred and first anniversary of America's Bunker Hill Battle. He thought about making a comparison.

* * * * *

Feeling they had won a major victory over the blue leg soldiers Sioux and Cheyenne warriors returned to their village in triumph. While they were fighting the village had been moved and now was close to the Little Bighorn River about five miles east from the old location.

For those families who received wounded men they spent their time tending the wounds. Other families went about mourning their dead warriors.

Only one Cheyenne warrior, Black Sun was killed, but the Sioux had 25 dead. More than three-dozen warriors from both nations were wounded, some seriously, and not all of them were expected to live.

The Cheyenne's quickly called the great battle, Where the Girl Saved Her Brother, because of an unusual episode that took place on the battlefield. A young Cheyenne woman named Buffalo-Calf-Robe Woman, wife of Black Coyote, who had went with her husband to the battle, saw her brother Chief Comes-in-Sight thrown from his horse, which had been shot dead. Comes-in-Sight found himself amid a force of enemy soldiers who came at him with a vengeance. Suddenly, his sister seemed to have come out of nowhere, having broke through enemy lines on her mount: Comes-in-Sight leaps on the pony behind his sister who carried him to safety.

For the Lakota's, who were now accustomed to the name Sioux that their enemies had given them, they gained a new battle cry that day. During one tremendous fight of the long fought battle, white soldiers were about to get the upper hand: an unknown warrior shouted out to those around him. "Take courage! This is a good day to die!" The warriors then forced the soldiers to retreat, their spirits stimulated by such a brave ideal.

A fourteen-year-old boy named Iron Hawk experienced his first battle. Though admitting to having been scared almost witless the youngster had fought hard and gained the respect of his fellow Sioux who had seen him. Iron Hawk accepted his first red feather as a wounded warrior with much pride.

Most everyone, not in mourning or tending their wounded, stayed up the remainder of the night celebrating and hearing the many tales of deeds recounted by warriors. Those warriors who had not participated in the battle listened with eager ears of the sagas being told by those who had fought. To hide their disappointment of not being able to relate tales of valor of their own, the many warriors who had not joined the fight all agreed this was not the Sun Dance vision of Sitting Bull. With serious expressions they declared to just wait until that day came and they would prove themselves as worthy as their comrades.

The Cheyenne Chief Medicine Man sought out Crazy Horse.

"Brave Warrior Chief and respected friend, I have but one question to ask you about today's battle. I know you do not like to tell of deeds you performed and what I have to ask has nothing to do with you personally."

Crazy Horse was standing near a large fire close to his lodge and had been staring up at the heavens when the older man approached him. He took no offense from the elder's remark and looked at Charcoal Bear fondly.

"You may ask me anything you want, O Wise One, and I will answer you with truth to the best of my ability."

"Thank you my son," the grizzled oldster replied. "Did the white eyes use their thunder stick today?"

Crazy Horse shook his head as he answered. "No wise one, I did not see any thunder sticks on the field of battle. These soldiers came from the south and they must not have the gun of evil. But we know the soldiers coming from the east have three such guns and I feel we will meet with them before too many moons."

"So today's battle was not the one Sitting Bull saw in his vision?" Charcoal Bear asked.

"It does not seem to have the elements the great Wakan' tanka told Sitting Bull and I can only surmise the vision has to do with the other soldiers who pull the thunder sticks with their ponies."

"I believe what you say is true Crazy Horse," the old man mused. "Yet, this terrible weapon has such great power. I am confused and do not understand what to make of it."

Crazy Horse was quiet for a moment before replying. "Our faith must lie with Wakan' tanka, it is written on the wind old friend."

Chapter 36

40 Miles North of Crook's Rosebud Battlefield, Montana Territory
3:30 p.m., Sunday, June 18, 1876

It could never be said that Major Marcus Reno was not a man or military officer of personal courage. His Civil War brevet promotions for bravery that saw him come from a lieutenant to full colonel is mute testimony showing the intestinal fortitude of the man's complex character make up. Sadly, Reno also had a "weak sister" side about him too that cropped up from time to time which caused him to be undependable as well as ineffectual. For the most part however he was able to mask the doubts he had about himself with a facade of authoritative, cold personality style of leadership.

For the past three days the unremitting responsibility of leading his detachment southward, without authority, deeper along the huge Indian trail had been eating away at him until he was now an indecisive nervous wreck. One thing that bothered him was the more he thought about the tremendous size of the gouged esplanade he was using to stalk the hostiles the more he thought about the amount of Indians it had taken to make such a swath. Reno truly felt his command might stumble upon the hostiles at any moment and since he was also convinced the trail represented movement of the entire Sioux Nation; he constantly asked himself what he was going to do with so many hostiles if he did come upon them.

There were other factors that plagued Major Reno's thinking as he rode slowly along the trace with his command strung out behind him with four of his eight Indian scouts out in front. He calculated his wing had covered more than 200 miles, which certainly made it a reasonable patrol already, plus having discovered a major route of hostile movement. He and his troops had traveled over some extremely rough country and was averaging better than 25 miles a day which was very good patrol marching by most military standards. But between the treacherous terrain and torturous time in the saddle, both men and horses were tired and spent. It was even worse on the pack mules and his most ardent ally, Lieutenant Kenzie was starting to grumble it was not a fair test for his Gatling gun, as the mules were not being given proper rest. Then there was the problem of rations getting low to the critical point and since he allowed no hunting with weapons for fear the hostiles would hear them he knew the men were grumbling about food also. Yes, a man could do a lot of thinking when he was by himself, mulling over what he was doing and having a lot of doubts.

Major Reno turned in his saddle to find his orderly. "Higgins! Oh, there you are. Take orders to the Command First Sergeant. We will halt for coffee to allow the animals to rest. And I want an immediate Officer's Call." Reno eyed his trumpeter for a moment to make sure the man was listening. "Officer's Call will not be sounded so you will inform the officers by word of mouth."

The trumpeter nodded his head in understanding while the young Striker gave a good salute, saying. "Yes sir, right away sir!"

In a matter of a few minutes his dozen or so officers, including Lieutenant Kenzie and the guide/scout Mitch Bouyer, surrounded Major Reno. While the enlisted soldiers went about the pleasant task of brewing themselves up some hot coffee their commander addressed his officer's in a halting tone of voice:

"Gentlemen I...ah... I have asked for you to assemble so I can...ah...inform you as to a...to a decision I have reached. My orders from General Terry were clear that in the event I---I mean to say we...found evidence of a hostile Indian trail, then it was my duty to report this intelligence to him as soon as practicable. I believe we have accomplished much more than was expected of us and I think it time we...ah...that we turn back to make the rest of the command aware of what we have discovered." Major Reno looked at Mitch Bouyer. "Mister Bouyer if you will see to it that the scouts out front are fetched we will wait here for them and as soon as they return we will then head north to the Yellowstone."

"I'll take care of that for you major," the half-breed scout answered.

"Very good sir. "Gentlemen that is all I have and if there are no questions you and your men get all the rest you can and prepare for a night march as I want to get back to the Yellowstone as quick as possible." Major Reno looked around him at the silent faces: there were no questions. "As you were gentlemen, get some coffee and see to your men."

After the officer's saluted their understanding and obediently turned to walk back to their men Mitch Bouyer got in step beside Pat Kenzie. Talking softly so the other officer's couldn't hear the Bouyer said. "The major may not be as stupid or cocky as I originally thought him to be. Now if that egomaniac Custer was leading us he would have forced marched us down the trail till we ran into the Sioux and Cheyenne and we would have all been kilt. It appears our boy has sense enough to know that discretion is many times the better part of valor. Sure can't fault him for that."

Pat Kenzie didn't know if Bouyer was being insulting or complimentary, but either way the young lieutenant didn't know how he should respond to the scout's remark so he kept his mouth shut.

Chapter 37

Confluence of the Tongue and Yellowstone Rivers,
Montana Territory
7:30 p.m., Monday, June 19, 1876

A soft rap on the canvas flap of General Alfred Terry's headquarters tent finally got his attention. The general was working on a dispatch he was going to send to General Sheridan in Chicago and at first he thought the slight sound he'd heard was the breeze causing the front flap to snap. It finally came to him someone was trying to knock at the tent door. His concentration of the report broken, he said in a somewhat gruff voice. "Yes, who is it?"

Captain William C. Hughes, General Terry's brother-in-law, stuck his head inside the tent entrance. "It's me general. A dispatch rider just rode in from Reno's command and I thought you'd want to know about it immediately."

"Oh, it's you Willie. By all means come on in. I didn't quite get all you said. Did you say there's word from Reno?"

The thin-faced officer, who was a member of his brother-in-law's staff, came closer and stood in front of the general's field desk. "Yes sir. I have the dispatch right here sir," he said, handing over a small leather pouch held shut with two straps. "Ah--sir. I asked the rider where he'd ridden from and he told me Major Reno will have reached the Yellowstone off the Rosebud sometime earlier in the day."

"The Rosebud!" General Terry said in a loud voice. "What in tarnation is he doing at the Rosebud?"

"I don't know sir," the slightly built officer answered lamely.

"Will by God I'm going to find out," and the general tore at the leather straps of the message pouch. As he took out the single sheet of paper General Terry noticed that his sister's husband was still standing a stiff attention. "Willie! For heavens sakes relax. There's nobody but the two of us here and I sure don't want to be getting any letters from Mildred how hard I'm treating you. Go ahead and pull up a camp stool there and have a seat while I read this thing."

Captain Hughes obeyed the general's request with a quick "Yessir."

General Terry scanned the report then shaking his head in a negative manner slammed the flat of his hand down on his desk making inkwell and nib pen jump. "He's found a big trail on the Rosebud where he's not supposed to be in the first place, and I'll be danged if he didn't follow it but only for a couple of days. What in tarnation is wrong with that man?" He voiced rhetorically. "Disobeys my orders then doesn't have sense enough to make up for it by deserting our first major sign of the hostiles. He says here he'll camp for the night on the Yellowstone and head this way in the morning. Now that makes a lot of sense too doesn't it?" General Terry paused and looked over to his brother-in-law in a speculative manner. Rubbing his chin a few seconds he spoke directly to the young captain, "Willie, Major Reno evidently doesn't have the common sense God gave a goose because the last thing on earth I want him to do now since he's found evidence of hostiles on the Rosebud, is to return here. I have an unsavory assignment I want you to do for me Willie. Go round up a four man detail of riders to be your escort and while you're doing that I'll be writing a message for Reno to stay put which I want you to deliver to him personal. You'll have to travel the better part of the night but that cannot be helped. When you find him I want you to tell that man to not only stay in place but don't even move one inch in this direction. Is that clear to you Willie?"

"Yes sir general, I understand perfectly. Should I get started right away sir?"

"Yes, but as you leave have my Adjutant come in. I also need to advise Custer to move on over to the Rosebud and link up with Reno. And have my orderly give Captain Marsh my compliments that I wish to see him. We'll move the remainder of the men from here up to the Rosebud on the Far West. Oh yes---don't you come back either. Once you find Reno you stay with him."

"Very well sir," Captain Hughes saluted his brother-in-law and hastily departed.

* * * * *

While General Terry was scribbling in his message pad to order Major Reno to halt his march toward the Tongue River, General Custer was sitting up his nights bivouac some twenty miles downstream on that very river. His scouts had found an old Indian campsite earlier in the day and Custer had spent much time investigating the area. There was no doubt the site was an old Sioux camp as determined from the various discarded items found left behind laying here and there on the ground where the lodges had been erected. After some consideration General Custer determined the location to have been a small village of around fifty tepees a Lakota tribe had used for winter quarters. One startling discovery was made when a skull and bones were found near the dead embers of what must have been a large fire. Sifting through the ashes troopers came up with a handful of burnt uniform buttons which caused Custer to immediately declare a cavalryman had been captured elsewhere and tortured to death at this camp. This roused the trooper's emotions to such a degree that they shot angry looks at their Crow scouts who quite naturally couldn't figure out why the white soldiers were upset with them. Just before finding the old Indian campsite the Negro scout/interpreter Isaiah Dorman had came upon a Sioux burial scaffold that was adorned with many decorative symbols. Dorman explained to Custer that the colorful emblems showed the dead Indian had been a very brave warrior during his lifetime. Although the U. S. Cavalry abhorred the mutilation and desecration hostile Indian's wrought upon slain white men, it never bothered the soldiers to perform similar deeds to Indian burial sites under the guise of gathering military intelligence. Without qualms, Custer ordered the burial scaffold dismantled and the body unwrapped for inspection. Isaiah Dorman removed the dead Lakota's ceremonial burial dress and found a wound on the upper right chest near the shoulder. Dorman noted the wound, which appeared to have been made from a bullet, still had a pinkish cast around it indicating the Indian had died recently. The dark faced, black haired interpreter attempted to explain to General Custer the significance of this fresh wound but Custer shrugged it off and ordered the body to be left on the ground naked. These two situations showed a major flaw in George Custer's reputation as a great Indian fighter. The discovery of the skull and bones of what were evidently the remains of a cavalryman had no tactical value to speak of, other than enraging the troops to a higher fighting spirit. Yet Custer wrote about the event at great length that night in his report book with much emotional prose. On the other hand he barely mentioned the finding of the dead Indian or the fact the man had recently died of wounds from being in a fight. Here was sound military intelligence, an important clue that hostiles were in the vicinity and had been in battle. His first thought should have been: "Did a soldier shoot him? When and where?" It may have given him an indication that General Crook's command had been in recent action. The fact that George Custer failed to grasp this shows that his reliability as a western field commander left a lot to be desired from his actual experience.

Chapter 38

Confluence of Rosebud Creek with the Yellowstone River,
Montana Territory
1215 p.m., Tuesday, June 20, 1876

Lieutenant's Bucky Low and Pat Kenzie were catching up on news from each other on what they'd been doing the past few days since they had been separated as their men went busily about the task of cleaning and oiling the three Gatling guns

Lieutenant Kenzie was emphasizing his recent adventure: "I tell you Bucky that dag-gone trail was bigger than the Baltimore to Washington Pike. I never have seen anything like it before in my life. Major Reno's scout Mitch Bouyer told me it had to have taken over two thousand Indians to have made a trail that big."

"You say you followed it for a couple of days. Why didn't Major Reno continue the chase and find out exactly where it led?" Lieutenant Low asked.

"Well I'll tell you," Pat Kenzie answered, "That's a question a lot of people are beginning to ask." The personable officer paused for a moment and looked around to see if anyone was within earshot. Satisfied the troops were too busy to overhear him Kenzie still lowered his voice when he went on talking. "Bucky, just between you and me I think the man lost his nerve."

"You're joshing me?" Bucky Low said in an incredulous tone of voice.

"No I'm not. When that old Crow whose head of his Indian scouts told the major there were more hostiles a short distance from us than he'd want to see; I think it really effected the man's thinking."

"That just doesn't sound right Pat. First you tell me how he wants your Gatling to be with him so you can share in the glory of standing beside him in battle and now you're saying he's got a yellow streak! That doesn't make sense at all."

Shaking his head back and forth Lieutenant Kenzie said. "It beats me but that's the way I see it. Why I wager we weren't more than a days ride from those blood thirsty savages when Major Reno stopped us and told us we were turning back..." The lieutenant abruptly quit talking as the sergeant in charge of Gun #2 strode purposefully up to them.

The medium built NCO stopped and with a formal salute, said. "Lieutenant Low sir. First Sergeant Steiner went to fetch the quartermaster on board the Far West that tied up a few minutes ago to see if the boat brought up any more fifty-caliber ammunition, so I came directly to you. My guns in good shape sir got it all cleaned up and oiled. Do you want us to reassemble it or leave it be as it is?"

Lieutenant Low countered the sergeant's question with one of his how. "I noticed when your men took the sections off the mules there was some rust forming on the cradle. Did the first sergeant say something to you about that Sergeant Evans?"

"Yes sir he did. Musta been from when we crossed that last little creek before meeting up with Major Reno's column is the only thing I can think of. But anyway, I made sure the rust is all gone and I had the boys put a heavy coat of gun oil on her."

"That's something you've got to watch closely Sergeant Evans. I know it was only the cradle but you've got to keep your eye on the entire gun because we cannot afford any malfunctions. Whose your oilier?"

"Private Hill sir," Sergeant Evans answered.

"You make sure Private Hill gives each man a quantity of oil and cleaning rags and then assign men to look after the different sections when they're broke down and we won't have that problem again. Now, to answer your question Sergeant, leave your gun disassembled and ready to move on a moments notice. You can go ahead and have your men set up their bivouac right here as I've been told we'll spend a night or so here. Tell Sergeant Gottlieb and Sergeant Heidenreich the same thing per my orders as soon as their crews get guns one and three cleaned and oiled."

"Yes sir...er, pardon me sir, did you say to set up camp right here next to General Custer's headquarters sir?" Sergeant Evans wanted to know.

"We're already here so this is where we'll stay until someone tells me I've got to move sergeant." Lieutenant Low answered.

"Yes sir." And the Gun Sergeant departed after a parting salute.

"God! I hate playing first sergeant," Bucky Low said in a low voice at the fading back of Sergeant Evans.

Lieutenant Kenzie chuckled. "Why's Gus trying to round us up some more ammunition for anyway?"

"With the way Major Reno accepted you into the fold, and Tom, I mean Captain Custer, advising me the general has pretty well decided to let us continue on with him on his next scout, I figured if we could garner additional ammunition it wouldn't do any harm to have it."

Smiling, Pat Kenzie said. "Tom huh? You and the general's brother must be getting along pretty well in my absence. But you are correct we may very well need some additional ammuni..."

The sound of loud raised voices coming from General Custer's headquarters tent stopped Lieutenant Kenzie in mid-sentence. Both young officers looked at each other, hardly believing their ears hearing the shouting voice of General Custer.

"And after flagrantly disobeying orders you cannot do better than say you thought it best to leave the Tongue River area?"

The raised voice of Major Reno tried to offer a defense. "I told you general it was a judgment call!"

"And a poor one at best if you ask me," Custer countered. "Your failure to follow up your find has now imperiled our plans by giving the hostiles an intimation of our presence. Think of the valuable time lost by your timidity! My God man all you had to do is send back a fast rider and we would have been following you in a heartbeat! And you're not even sure of the exact numbers or the final direction they took...."

Major Reno interrupted General Custer. "I explained to you we discovered five abandoned campsites which held between three hundred fifty to four hundred lodges. That gives a sound estimate of over a thousand warriors right there."

"Hog wash!" The general cut in. "Faint heart never won fair lady. Your disobedience of orders could be overlooked if you would have followed the trail until finding the hostiles. Then it would not be a guessing game on your part for you would have known the true size of the village and exactly what your regiment would be facing. But instead you come scurrying back with forsook determination which is a gross and inexcusable blunder!"

As Custer continued to deride Major Reno Lieutenant Kenzie said to Lieutenant Low. "Oh, oh---here comes General Terry."

General Terry looked madder than a wet hen. His brows were furrowed; mouth set in a grim line as he walked rapidly alone toward General Custer's tent. He had just debarked from the Far West and his intention was to get some answers from Major Reno. As he came nearer to the tent however he couldn't help but hear the triad going on inside. "Custer's got to him before I could," the general muttered under his breath."

General Terry paused outside the closed front tent flap to listen to what Custer was saying: "Damnit man! Few officers have ever had so fine an opportunity to make a successful and telling strike, and few have ever so completely failed to improve their opportunity. What General Terry should do is bring charges against you for Court-martial."

Standing outside the large white tent General Terry noticed his loud voiced cavalry commander had gained a sizeable audience of other officers and enlisted men who directed their faces to the headquarters tent in stunned silence. The general approved of what Custer had just said but knew it shouldn't have been done so publicly or noisily.

George Custer had just started voicing another comment when General Terry entered the tent. "Why you gave the order to countermarch I will never under..."

"At ease gentlemen,:" General Terry said, breaking in on Custer's discourse. Looking directly at Custer who was nose to nose with Major Reno General Terry continued talking. "That will be enough of that general. I too am disgruntled with Major Reno but what's done is done. Your voices have carried and I suspect half the camp now knows you two have been going at it. This is not the way for two line officers to settle their differences nor waste time over vain regrets." The general paused to give Major Reno a baleful stare. "Regardless of your duplicity Major it appears you have provided the most useful intelligence I have received so far regarding the size and location of the heathens. What must be done now is to talk sensibly and have you tell us in detail exactly what you have seen." Looking around the general eyed a camp chair and went to it. "Both of you sit down and let's get this thing ironed out."

Sometime later a badly shaken Major Marcus Reno left General Terry and Custer who continued to discuss a needed change in plans. Reno's vanity was severely wounded and he felt slandered. He didn't understand General Terry's unreasonable anger. To his way of thinking the only thing of a disagreeable nature he had done was to force the Department Commander to change his plans. *What was wrong with that? After all, did I or did I not bring back solid intelligence? Even Terry admitted that. And Custer? The man is mad, insane without a doubt! He had absolutely no call to treat me like I was some wet behind the ears second lieutenant, none whatsoever!*

The final straw to an already injured pride came when Major Reno entered the tent he shared with Captain Frederick Benteen. The good captain was sitting on a camp stool in front of a crude table with both arms propped on the table, his small square shaped reading spectacles low on his thin nose with a pipe in his mouth, reading a book. Glancing up and noting whom it was entering the tent, Fred Benteen managed a mischievous smile on his cherubic face. "Well, well----the return of the conquering hero. Are you walking stiff legged from that ass chewing you got old bean?"

Chapter 39

Aboard the Steamer Far West, Yellowstone River at Rosebud Creek,
Montana Territory
2:00 p.m., Wednesday, June 21, 1876

Brigadier General Alfred H. Terry had a cheerless look about him as he gazed at his several principal officers sitting at ease along a crude plank top conference table on the center lower deck of the river steamer Far West. Terry had decided to keep his final planning session small and other than General's George Custer and John Gibbon, the only other officer's in attendance were Major James Brisbane, commander of Gibbon's cavalry, and four members of Terry's staff. As a courtesy, General Terry also invited Captain Grant Marsh, skipper of the Far West, to sit in on the meeting. The seven officer's had joined General Terry and Captain Marsh for a noon day meal aboard the river boat but now it was time to get to work and with the dishes cleared except for coffee cups, General Terry addressed his subordinates in a low tone of voice:

"I will take the time to outline in some detail the strategy I have developed to bring about the capitulation, or if necessary the annihilation of this hostile band of Sioux. I think by now we all agree the hostile tribes are moving directly toward the valley of the Little Big Horn. From all indications they are in considerable force and it appears evident they have no intention of coming this way in an attempt to cross the Yellowstone. Therefore, I intend to abandoned this blocking position and reestablish one further south and to the west." General Terry paused for a moment to allow the soft murmur of voices to subside upon hearing his comment about moving southwest. He looked directly at Colonel John Gibbon as he once again resumed talking. "John, because your command is already half infantry I'm going to give you most of Jack's infantry as well."

Colonel Gibbon frowned sharply because he knew immediately General Terry had decided to let Custer have the honor of leading the attack against the Sioux and Cheyenne. Although disappointed he was not surprised since he felt General Terry relied too much on Custer. Dejected, he offered the Department Commander a dutiful, "Yes sir."

"What I have in mind for you John is to have you take your command to Fort Pease, and then travel down the Big Horn River until you reach the fork of the Little Big Horn. There you will sit up a blocking force using your infantry, Gatling guns and artillery. Major Brisbin's cavalry will be in position to assist you and to protect your flanks." Now Terry looked over to Custer. "In the meantime, while John is getting into position you Jack will be going down the Rosebud and will cross the divide to the Little Big Horn. You will move to the Wyoming Territory border, then swing back up on the west bank of the Little Big Horn and head north until you link up with John. If all goes as I envision you will have herded the hostiles right into the blocking force where they will either surrender or die to a man." General Terry paused for another short moment. Still looking at Custer, he asked a question. "I understand you have decided to take your Gatling gun battery with you. Is that correct?"

A smiling George Custer answered his commander with elation because he now knew his 7th Cavalry would be leading the attack. "Yes sir. I have determined that Lieutenant Low's battery will not impede my march. If by chance his Gatling's lag behind I will assign a troop to guard them and continue on the scout. However, with Low's improvised manner of hauling his weapons I do not foresee him slowing me down any."

"Very good," General Terry said. "But I don't want you pressing your march too rapidly even though you have the greater distance to travel. To tell the truth I hope you will run into General Crook and your two columns' can work north together. As it is I've had no word at all from General Crook but it's possible the two of you may link up although I'm not counting on it, nor will I order you to attempt to find him." The general turned to find his adjutant. "Ed, put up that map I had you and Major Brisbane work on last night." While Captain Smith fussed around placing a large drawing of the general area on an easel stand General Terry resumed talking. "I've given you a general outline of my intentions and now I want to go over the entire thing again in detail and point out the areas I expect both commands to scout as you proceed with your patrols. For instance George I want you to scout the upper reaches of Tullock's Creek to see if the Indian's may be there since the Crow's reported seeing a large pall of smoke in that area. You will note how Major Brisbane has placed pins on various points of the map and I will now discuss the purpose of this..."

The conference went on for three more hours as all phases of General Terry's plans were worked out on paper.

General Terry prepared to wrap up the meeting he had called. "We've completed a good days work gentlemen and I want to express my appreciation for all the expert input everyone has offered. This is especially true for you George and also you John. I realize the maps we have are not the most accurate and it was most gracious of you John to volunteer six of your most competent Crow scouts along with Mister Boyer to accompany George. Oh, and I should not forget George Herendeen who knows the Tullock's Creek area. With their familiarity of the general area I feel certain they will be an asset for the seventh."

Colonel John Gibbon nodded his head in acceptance of the minor bit of praise.

Terry continued talking: "Very well, let me sum up what we've accomplished and then I'll send you on your way to prepare your commands. Before I do that however, I want to mention Major Brisbane did an excellent job with our maps and my previous remark about the unknown factors of location and distance in no way reflects on his credible work. Now we know there has to be at least eight hundred to nine hundred hostile warriors somewhere near the head of the Rosebud or over on the Little Big Horn or the Big Horn itself. The region you will be traveling is rough and broken. You will run into deep ravines, high bluffs as well as rolling prairie and plains. This in itself means it will be extremely difficult for the two commands to act in concert. However, as long as the Montana column gets into position as outlined there should be no reason why the two commands cannot support one another." The general looked directly at Colonel Gibbon. "John, I've decided that I shall go with you instead of remaining idle on the Far West."

"It will be an honor to have you with us sir," Colonel Gibbon intoned.

"Ah--yes, thank you. Where was I now? Oh yes, since I mentioned the Far West." This time General Terry glanced at Captain Grant Marsh. "I want Captain Marsh to push his steamer up the Big Horn clear to the mouth of the Little Big Horn. I'm ordering a company of the Sixth Infantry to remain with Captain Marsh to act as his security."

Captain Marsh nodded his understanding. "Should not be a problem General Terry. With the high water we've had I see no reason why the Little Big Horn shouldn't be navigable. Might be able to push her up a little further on that stream if you so desire."

"Very good to hear that Captain Marsh. I may call upon you if the need arises to do just that. Now back to the matter at hand. While General Gibbon's column is making its trek west and then south, General Custer will follow the Rosebud and pickup the trail Major Reno discovered. I don't want you following this trail but go further south and swing back around to see if you pick it up again. Then you can follow it." General Terry paused and shared a glance with General Custer. Terry had noted that Custer was being remarkably quiet which was out of character for the man and Terry wondered if something was bothering him. He made a metal note to have a talk with him after the meeting broke up. "And that is about it gentlemen. I believe my strategy of a double attack in force will diminish any chance of a successful retreat by the Sioux. I further believe you two field commanders have the ability to take care of your individual commands against the savages in the event one of you come upon them before the other command can come to your assistance. Please know, as your commander, I have full confidence in the both of you as well as your commands. That is all I have to say. Are there any questions?" General Terry was surprised when Custer didn't offer a question or two or make any comment whatsoever. "No questions? Very well, this meeting is concluded."

While the other six officers picked up notes and other paper work they had on the conference table General Custer departed immediately, heading for the gangway to leave the Far West. General Terry had to walk fast to catch up with him and didn't reach him until Custer was off the steamer and heading towards his headquarters tent where he lived.

"Hold on a second Jack I want to walk with you." General Terry said in a loud voice.

Turning on his heels Custer waited for the general officer to walk up to him. "Yes sir." George answered with a questioning expression.

The two men walked at a leisurely pace toward Custer's quarters and command post. General Terry spoke. "Is something bothering you Jack? Perhaps something about my plan you don't like?"

George Custer turned a little and noted the concern on his commander's face. "No sir general: your plan sounds like a good one to me. We both know that once you face the enemy that most plans go by the wayside anyway but the pincer movement is right out of the books Napoleon and Clausewitz wrote. Your thoughts of a double envelopment are sound and should work fine. That is not my concern."

"Well what is your concern then?" Terry wanted to know.

Custer hesitated before answering then shaking his head a little he said. "I'm really not sure general. Just sort of a strange mood I cannot explain. My only disagreement with your assessment concerning the number of hostiles we will face is my belief there are nearer a thousand Sioux warriors, but that doesn't bother me as my regiment can whip any number of hostiles that dare stand and fight. The only other thing that crossed my mind that was not really to my liking is your order not to follow the Reno trail when I come across it. I am convinced that that trail will take me to Sitting Bull, Gall and

Crazy Horse."

"Well for heavens sakes man! If that's your only concern I rescind the order and say to you to use your own judgment and do what you think best if you strike the trail. As you pointed out orders are an outline. I am intelligent enough to be aware of the variables involved in any military venture of this nature and that orders will be followed to a loose degree so you can use your own discretion as circumstance dictate" General Terry paused for a moment outside Custer's tent. "You know Jack the more I think about it the more I'm inclined to give you freer rein. I'll give you a written set of orders in the morning that will further show you the confidence I have in you. After all, did I not intercede in your behalf to secure your services? That in itself should show the trust I have for you."

General Terry's remark perked up Custer and he was about to make a return conciliatory statement when Colonel John Gibbon hailed the two. "General Terry, General Custer. A moment of your time please." And the handsome officer came to them at a fast pace.

Custer invited both officers into his tent and offered them seats and brandy, which he carried with him but did not drink himself. Once everyone was comfortably settled, George Custer said, "Was there something specific you wanted to ask John?"

"Not ask Jack but to offer. When General Terry first gave you the attack scout I was more than disappointed because my column has been out here since February herding those savages and to tell you the truth my men have come to regard the hostiles as their peculiar property. I reckon I got to feel that way too and felt my boys should have had the honor in being in on the kill. But after I got to studying the general's plan the more it came to me why he made the decision he came up with." Colonel Gibbon paused to look at General Terry. "With the general's permission sir I'll say my piece but I don't want you to think I'm trying to second guess you."

"Go right ahead John. I understand why you and your boys would feel as you do. And I'll admit to being curious on what you may have to say so there's no problem on my part about second guessing." Terry offered a thin smile and lifted his cup of brandy as a gesture for Gibbon to continue talking.

"Thank you sir. I think General Terry gave you the primary mission George because your Seventh Cavalry is numerically stronger and with me fielding half infantry if I gave chase I'd have the weaker unit." Gibbon glanced at General Terry and saw him nod his head in approval. "So the more I pondered on this tactical strategy the more I became convinced that it will further benefit your thrust if I would loan you four troops of my Second

Cavalry to accompany you which would make your force even better."

General Terry slapped his leg with his hand. "Bully idea John. How about it Jack? Another battalion of cavalry at your disposal."

But Custer was shaking his head back and forth. "No sir, it's not tactically sound for it would weaken John's force too much and if he's successful in getting the blocking force into position as you outlined he's going to need all the cavalry he can lay his hands on. Besides, the Seventh can handle anything it meets!"

"Well, you may be correct," admitted Colonel Gibbon. "How about I give you a battery of my Gatling guns?"

"That's most kind of you as was your offer of your four troops, but my Lieutenant Low has developed a manner to accompany me without the need of pulling cumbersome limbers."

"Ah yes, that's right. I heard my battery commander mention that. Well, you cannot say I didn't try. Gentlemen, if you will excuse me I must get back to my command," and Colonel Gibbon stood up to leave.

General Terry also stood up. "I'll walk you back to the boat John."

With the two officers standing Custer also got up. He offered Colonel Gibbon his hand. "John, I really do appreciate your offer for assistance and I sincerely mean that."

The fine looking colonel smiled showing strong, white teeth. "Jack, you chase them to ground and by God the two of us together will chew them up!"

General Terry offered his hand to Custer and said. "I'll have Captain Smith get those orders to you I talked about sometime in the morning."

As soon as both men had departed General Custer looked around on the outside of his tent for his orderly. "John! John Burkman! Where in the sam hill you at boy?"

A rustling noise came from the side of the tent and John Burkman came tearing around the corner. "I'm right here General sir! Was piling up some wood back yonder thar sir."

Custer was surprised at the seemingly cheerful spirits of his part-time personal orderly because Burkman usually gave him a hard time when he yelled for him by being snippy. "John I want you to find Trumpeter Martini and have him sound Officer's Call."

"Right now general?" The reed thin orderly asked.

Custer's mood had returned to the previous melancholy feeling he'd experienced coming off the Far West and instead of being upset with his discordant man servant he answered softly with a great deal of restraint and patience. "Yes John, right now if you would please."

The wailing shrill notes from Trumpeter John Martini's polished brass horn brought the entire 7th Cavalry's subordinate officer's to General Custer's tent.

General George Custer outlined in general terms the operation plan devised by General Terry and the part the 7th Cavalry would be directly involved in. The large gathering of officers was most attentive as their commander continued with the detail requirements he was ordering for the next days scout. "I want each man issued one hundred rounds of carbine ammunition and at least twenty-four rounds of pistol ammunition. How they carry this load is up to them, either on their person or in saddlebags but I expect fifty round of carbine near their rifles at all times either mounted or afoot. And speaking of rifles brings up another point I want to emphasize. I shouldn't even have to bring this up but since I've noticed some rust on some of the weapons and a lot of dirty weapons I reckon I have better give you all a reminder to pass on to your men. A trooper's carbine and pistol are the primary tools of his trade whether he's in the cavalry or the infantry. They are the reason for his very existence: his claim and worthiness if you will for being alive. Without his weapon he is nothing with no meaning----an elk without legs, a grizzly without claws. But with his rifle he is somebody. Somebody to contend with, somebody to look up too. And while he has a functioning weapon and is alive, no enemy will ever take him for granted! So make sure your men clean and oil their carbines and pistols tonight as we cannot afford to have them malfunctioning during the heat of battle we are sure to find."

A low murmuring of approval sounded as most the officer's vented their pleasure at the poetic prose of what their commander had said.

General Custer had paused when hearing the "Well said", "Bully", "Here, here," and other voices of agreement that had issued; but without smiling or further acknowledgement at this praise he continued talking. "In addition to the ammunition the men will carry I want twelve of our strongest pack mules loaded with twenty-four thousand rounds of reserve ammunition. I want all sick, half-lame or used-up animals culled from the herd and left behind. Besides the mules that will carry our reserve ammunition we will require sufficient mules to pack fifteen days rations per man consisting of hardtack, coffee, sugar and bacon. Each trooper will carry a minimum of twelve pounds of oats for their mounts with orders to be careful in rationing the oats to their ponies, especially after a lengthy march, as I don't want the animals getting sick. I would suggest packing more forage if possible as the animals will surely need it before this scout is over."

This last remark brought forth the first raised voices of protest. Captain Miles Moylan was the first to make an objection. "General Custer sir. If I may make a comment. What you have ordered already will be stretching the capacity of our pack mules as it is. Your suggestion of toting additional forage may be the straw that breaks the camel's back!"

First Lieutenant Edward Godfrey quickly endorsed Captain Moylan's comment. "General Custer sir I must agree whole heartily with Captain Moylan. The mules we have are already badly used up from Major Reno's scout and they'll surely break down if forced to carry extra burdens such as additional forage."

Major Marcus Reno cast a sharp glance at the walrus mustached young commander of Company K who dared to blame him for the poor condition of the pack mules.

Reno need not to have concerned himself with the impertinence shown by the long-nosed, steely, blue-eyed young officer. George Custer quickly showed his displeasure by lashing out at both Moylan and Godfrey in an agitated, excited tone of voice. "Very well gentlemen, if that is your opinion you may carry what supplies you please. I caution all of you however, that may have a similar bent as these two officers, that you will be held responsible for your companies' welfare, including your mounts. The extra forage was a suggestion on my part, but bear this fact in mind: We will follow the hostile trail for at least fifteen days and it could be longer unless we catch up with them beforehand. I don't care how far it takes us from our base of supply we will find the hostiles without turning back! Keep in mind we may not see the supply steamer again until after engaging the hostiles." Custer paused to let his remarks sink in. Then, to punctuate his growing displeasure from hearing his subordinates question his judgment, he said. "Another suggestion I have to offer is that all of you had better figure out a way to carry along an extra supply of salt as we may very well have to live on horse meat before this scout is over with!" This last remark was almost shouted. Custer had to pause again, this time due to having got himself so riled. He took a couple of deep breaths, snorting air out of his nose like a horse. This settled him down and he continued with his briefing. "The last item of business I have to discuss is troop disposition. I have decided to break up the Wing and Battalion formations..." Custer was forced to stop talking again because of another flurry of murmurs that greeted his last remark. Satisfied he had gained their attention, he went on. "I will assign each company as we proceed as to your individual mission at a given time and each troop commander will report directly to me unless otherwise preordered by me to do differently. I want this clearly understood."

While Custer paused briefly to see if there was any dissention within the officer ranks on this momentous change in the tactical structure of the regiment, Captain Frederick Benteen nudged Major Marcus Reno standing next to him. Benteen whispered a cutting remark. "I say old bean, it appears you are now without a direct command. Could it be our great leader has made this grand change as a punishment to you for your disobedience of orders?"

Reno quickly offered a snarling reply. "The way I see it, since Custer is taking over Terry's job for our column, then that makes me the acting lieutenant colonel of the regiment. You can put that in your pipe and smoke it old bean!"

Custer ended his briefing. "This is all I have to say at this time. I shall be available at my tent or on the Far West if any of you have individual questions later on. I suggest that now you get back to your men and tell them to prepare to move out in the morning. Make sure their weapons are in good order and work on the supply items that I have talked about. You are dismissed gentlemen."

Custer turned and went into his tent leaving his unit commanders and other officers at a stunned attention. In groups of three and four the officers headed for their own campsites. There was much animated discussion from the various groups that centered on the command structure change and also the odd behavior Custer showed during his briefing. Most thought he acted like he was distressed or suffering a crankiness out of depression. Whatever the problem was his somber mood coupled with his lashing tongue had cast a veil of ominous gloom over most all of his officers.

George Armstrong Custer wasn't the only officer that seemed down in the dumps by thoughts of the coming campaign. General Terry's mood was grave and anxious and Colonel Gibbon likewise shared a gloomy demeanor by being extremely quiet. It appeared all three of the senior commanders felt the weight of unremitting responsibilities bearing down upon their shoulders with the knowledge their decisions could very well send a great number of men to a terrible death.

Battlefield command is always an extremely lonely position and while these three leaders were accustomed to seeing the results of orders that killed soldiers it was still an awesome liability to have to deal with for the preservation of one's mental sanity.

Everyone in the different commands went about easing individual thoughts of gloom in various ways. General Terry gave permission to tap a couple of kegs of whiskey that made the sutler on board the Far West happy. The sutler was busy anyway selling last minute items to both officer and enlisted men: snuff, tobacco, candles, flannel shirts, smoking pipes and navy straw hats were among the more popular purchases. Many decks of playing cards were also bought as a number of men figured a long night of poker to go along with their cups of whiskey were just the way to solve whatever doldrums they may have had. Others wrote long letters home or wrote wills or made hastily penciled instructions what should be done with personal effects in the event of their death.

The campfire talk that night centered on the next day's movement, as would be expected. Old time veterans told the younger troopers to expect hours of hard riding in the saddle because once Custer was on the scent there was no stopping him. One veteran campaigner who had not dealt with General Custer before was the first sergeant of the Gatling gun platoon. While having never served with Custer before Gus Steiner knew enough of the man's reputation as a terror on the campaign trail to offer some sage advice to his commanding officer.

"Lieutenant Low sir it's going to be tough for the men to get proper rest tonight due to the fact they've all got "ants in their pants" thinking about tomorrow. But if I was you sir I'd go ahead and order 'em to their bedrolls early even if they don't get much sleep. At least they won't be hung over in the morning from having boozed it up and more n'likely will get some rest in spite of themselves. With us tagging along on this venture with our guns I don't suspect we'll be getting much rest on the trail. We've never been on this long of a scout before and its a'going to take its toll on both men and animals, and that's a fact sir."

Lieutenant William Hale Low was a smart officer for he almost always took the advice from his Medal of Honor winner first sergeant. "See to that for me first sergeant if you will please."

Colonel John Gibbon

Chapter 40

Down the Rosebud Creek, Montana Territory
8:00 a.m., Thursday, June 22, 1876

The 7th Cavalry spent the early morning under a slate gray overcast sky with a raw northwest wind chilling the troopers as they went about their labor preparing for the forthcoming scout. Mules were loaded, equipment checked, ammunition and rations issued and first sergeant's fussing around their men like bantam rosters.

General George Armstrong Custer was knotting his ever-present, red scarf around his neck inside his tent which he was ready to vacate so it could be tore down and stowed on the Far West when Orderly John Burkman entered the tent unannounced. "General there's that Captain Smith fellow outside that says he's got some papers for you from General Terry."

Custer was too emotionally aroused with thoughts of the coming patrol to be annoyed at his overly familiar orderly and said simply. "Tell him to come in John."

Captain Edward W. Smith entered the tent and gave Custer a formal salute that Custer returned. "Good morning sir. Compliments of General Terry sir, your written orders for the campaign. Sir, General Terry requested I remain until you've read his instructions in case you may have questions I may be able to answer or to take back inquires to the general."

Custer took the pages of paper from the adjutant. "Very well sir. You may as well have a seat while I read the general's orders."

"Thank you sir," Captain Smith replied and found a canvas-covered campstool that he sat on.

General Custer likewise took a seat at his table and began reading the document which was hand written in the neat script of Captain Smith:

Camp at Mouth of Rosebud River, Montana Ter'y, June 22, 1876.
Lieut. Col Custer, 7th Cav'y.

Colonel:
The Brig. Gen'l Commanding directs that, as soon as your regiment can be made ready for the march, you will proceed up the Rosebud in pursuit of the Indians whose trail was discovered my Major Reno a few days since. It is, of course, impossible to give you any definite instructions in regard to this

movement, and were it not impossible to do so the Dept. Commander places too much confidence in your zeal, energy, and ability to wish to impose upon you precise orders, which might hamper your action when nearly in contact with the enemy. He will, however, indicate to you his own views of what your action should be, and he desires that you should conform to them unless you shall see sufficient reason for departing from them. He thinks that you should proceed up the Rosebud until you ascertain definitely the direction in which the trail above spoken of leads. Should it be found (as it appears almost certain that it will be found) to turn towards the Little Horn, he thinks that you should still proceed southward, perhaps as far as the headwaters of the Tongue, and then turn towards the Little Horn, feeling constantly, however, to your left, so as to preclude the possibility of the escape of the Indians to the South or Southeast by passing around your left flank. The column of Colonel Gibbon is now in motion for the mouth of the Big Horn. As soon as it reaches that point it will cross the Yellowstone and move up at least as far as the forks of the Big and Little Horns. Of course its future movements, must be controlled by circumstances as they arise, but it is hoped that the Indians, if upon the Little Horn, may be so nearly enclosed by the two columns that their escape will be impossible.

The Department Commander desires that on your way up the Rosebud you should thoroughly examine the upper part of Tullock's Creek, and that you should endeavor to send a scout through to Colonel Gibbon's column, with information of the result of your examination. The lower part of this creek will be examined by a detachment from Col. Gibbon's command. The supply steamer will be pushed up the Big Horn as far as the forks if the river is found to be navigable for that distance, and the Dept. Commander, who will accompany the column of Colonel Gibbon, desires you to report to him there not later than the time for which your troops are rationed, unless in the meantime you receive further orders.

Very respectfully
Your obedient servant
E. W. Smith
Captain 18th Infantry
Act'g Asst. Adj't General

George Custer took the time to reread the orders a second time and for the most part was extremely pleased with what he'd already read. He understood Adjutant Smith had used the old woodsman title for the Little Big

Horn by calling it the Little Horn but that was a trivial point and he would not question it for clarity. The minor irritation that General Terry once again emphasized by stating he should go past Major Reno's trail and continue south was offset by the extremely flattering words praising him of his zeal, energy and ability, plus the confidence Terry obviously had in him. Besides, the authority to use his own judgment as place and circumstance dictated gave him a free rein anyway, so he wasn't going to bicker with the general about Reno's trail. After reading the orders a second time Custer felt even better. "Captain Smith please be so kind as to tell General Terry that I fully understand his instructions and that I am most pleased with his orders. Please thank him for me and let him know that I have no questions from either you or what he has ordered."

Captain Smith departed General Custer's tent somewhat amazed and relieved for he was well aware of the man's hard-ass reputation and volatile personality when dealing with underlings.

Just before noon George Custer joined his brother's Tom and Bos on the flat expanse of ground the 7th Cavalry had staged for departure. General Custer was dressed in a full buckskin suit that was fringed. His red scarf showing brightly at his neck. He wore a light gray broad-brimmed hat to protect his sensitive face from the sun. Both his brothers, as well as his adjutant Lieutenant William Cooke and Captain Myles Keogh, all wore fringed buckskin jackets and their traditional blue army trousers with the yellow stripes running down both legs. After a few pleasant words were exchanged among the group of men General Custer mounted his horse Vic and trotted the stallion towards the head of the column where his flag bearer Sergeant Robert Hughes waited with Custer's personal standard. Sergeant Hughes had the swallow-tailed, red and blue banner with white crossed sabers unfurled and it was snapping wildly in the gusting wind. Custer had used this same banner since the Civil War and considered it an amulet that fostered his well-known "Custer's Luck."

General Alfred Terry had issued orders for a regimental parade as a gesture of giving the 7th Cavalry a proper send-off. Terry, along with Colonel Gibbon and Major Brisbane stood on a hastily constructed platform for use as a reviewing stage. Every trumpeter and bugler from Gibbon's column had massed along the outgoing trail to the Rosebud to play spirited music for the 7th Cavalry.

At a little past noon General Custer ordered Trumpeter Henry Voss to sound Forward and the long column of fours began moving slowly towards the reviewing stand with Custer in the lead. As he came abreast of General

Terry the Department Commander smiled, then said. "Jack--wheel Vic around to the side of the reviewing stand and join us here."

Custer gave the customary salute, saying. "Thank you sir." He motioned for Sergeant Hughes and Private Voss to follow him and after maneuvering Vic into position next to the platform spoke a loud order to his sergeant major, Sergeant Major William Sharrow. "Bill! Lead 'em out and I'll catch up later!"

The regimental sergeant major saluted, nodded his head in understanding, and then spurred his horse on down the trail.

As Major Marcus Reno did not have a letter company he could call his own he took it upon himself to follow directly behind General Custer's command staff group. The major wore the traditional army officer's field blouse and trousers and when he took General Terry's salute he almost knocked off his battered straw hat.

General Terry gave the embarrassed major a friendly smile, and then said. "Marcus, you help Jack find that trail of yours hear?"

Feeling better from the general's kind words Major Reno said, "Thank you sir, that I shall do."

Wing and battalion formations were normally prescribed on the basis of company commander seniority but there was some confusion when the regiment staged for departure. This was brought on due to General Custer breaking up the previous battalion and wing structure so as it turned out the various companies had formed for the pass in review in no particular order.

Just the same Captain Frederick Benteen jealously guarded his most senior captain status and insisted his Troop H be the first company to pass in review. Taking Benteen's salute along with Benteen's swallow-tailed guidon dipping in respect to the Department Commander, General Terry did as he had before by saying a couple of friendly words to the pudgy face troop commander. "You take care of yourself out there Fred. I don't want to be calling on your misses back at Fort Lincoln."

"No need to fret on that sir, taint a Injun alive going to take these curly locks." Benteen replied as he passed by.

Next came the Gray Horse Troop Company E, commanded by First Lieutenant Algernon Smith. The thirty-two troopers rode proud in their saddles knowing their uniqueness of all being mounted on strong grays. "Your men and horses look splendid Algy. You have a good scout." General Terry offered.

"Thank you sir," the black, short-cut haired officer with a striking black full mustache answered.

Terry turned to General Custer who was still mounted on Vic that put the two men on almost the same level. "Jack, they certainly look magnificent."

Offering a small grin Custer replied. "They're a good bunch of boys general. Outstanding morale."

Second Lieutenant Henry M. Harrington, as the only officer in C Troop because Captain Tom Custer, who on paper commanded the company was attached to his brother's staff, made the pass in review salute. Harrington had thick eye brows with striking brown eyes and a narrow pointed nose. The young officer got flustered when General Terry, with good natured humor chided him. "Now Hank, don't you let them boys of yours try and take advantage of you. You just listen to your first sergeant and you will do okay."

I Troop was led by Captain Myles Keogh who sported a Prussian officer-styled handlebar mustache and was immaculately attired in the standard officer's uniform. "You and your boys look mighty sharp Myles. Have a good hunt."

"Thank you sir," Captain Keogh said while saluting.

Then along came A Troop commanded by another Myles, Captain Myles Moylan, the outspoken officer with a flinty stare and large black walrus mustache. Moylan beat General Terry to the punch by speaking up as he saluted. "We're gonna teach 'em a lesson they'll never forget general!"

"You do that Myles and make sure you come back without an Indian haircut." Terry offered with a thin grin.

Captain Moylan snorted, saying "Not much chance for that to happen general."

Captain Thomas B. Weir was the fiery-tempered commanding officer of D Troop. He offered a precise military salute that General Terry returned. Keeping to his intention of offering a pleasant word for each of the troop commanders, Terry said. "Tommy, old salt, you keep a close eye on your greenhorns and have a good scout."

"They've shaped up pretty good general." Terry and Weir was referring to the large amount of new recruits Company D had absorbed within the past few months.

Following closely in trace of D Troop was G Troop with veteran cavalry Captain George D. Wallace in command.

"You and your boys look good George. I'll see you downstream in about two weeks." General Terry offered.

The string bean tall, smooth shaven, grim-faced officer did not say anything but nodded his head in acknowledgement as he saluted.

General Terry muttered softly to Custer. "George Wallace seems to be in a glum mood."

Custer replied in a serious tone of voice. "One of the most courageous men I've ever met sir. Always stews that his next combat will be his last yet he comes through in the pinch. It will take the first encounter with the enemy to get that dour expression off his face."

"Unusual man," Terry said, then quickly got his hand up to accept the salute given by First Lieutenant Edward S. Godfrey of K Troop who had just ordered his command an Eyes Right.

Close on the heels of Lieutenant Godfrey came Captain George Yates of F Troop with Lieutenant William Reilly leading the first platoon. "That's quite a mustache you got growing Georgie Yates. Did you grow that wild patch just for this campaign?" General Terry asked with a smile.

The old-line captain grinned, twisting his well-waxed, ten-inch long handlebar. "With this thing flappin' in the wind general I think me boys will always know where I'm at."

Young Lieutenant Reilly remembered to salute the Department Commander even if his commanding officer did not.

The column was now stretched out for a half-mile when Captain Thomas H. French's M Troop paid their respects to General Terry. "Tommy French how did you end up eating all this dust? I'm used to seeing you out ahead of everybody else." Terry joked.

The good-looking cavalry officer doffed his felt hat and made a sweeping motion with it in lieu of a salute although he did order Eyes Right and his guidon dipped. "I thought I was going to have to wrestle Jimmi Calhoun for this spot sir. But I'm sure General Custer will have me up front where I belong before this scout is over."

"Only if you pay me that five dollars you owe me on who would get the biggest elk," Custer exclaimed in a loud voice at the passing back of his friend.

The officer Captain French referred to when he rode by was First Lieutenant James Calhoun who commanded L Troop and was directly behind French. "Jimmy, Tommy said he had to wrestle with you to get ahead of your troop in the line." General Terry joshed with General Custer's brother-in-law.

"Don't believe a word he says sir, he pulled rank on me and that's how he ended up in front of me general." Lieutenant Calhoun said with a grin.

"Well, at least you're not the very last," Terry remarked.

"Near enough sir, but I don't envy Captain McDougall none."

Lieutenant Calhoun jerked his thumb over his shoulder toward the rear of the column where Captain Thomas M. McDougall's B Troop was riding security for the strung-out pack train of mules. Directly in front of the pack train and right behind L Troop was the Gatling gun platoon.

General Terry took Lieutenant William H. Low's salute, and then said. "Bucky Low, you've done an amazing job with your guns and I'm going to help you write a report to the Bureau of Ordinance when this is over."

"Thank you sir, that is most kind of you sir." Lieutenant Low answered; very flattered the general had called him by his nickname. He offered a second salute, as did Lieutenant Kenzie riding next to him who also gave a half bow to the general from his saddle.

As the first Gatling gun passed by with the barrel system slung in the new stretcher device with the use of two horses in tandem, General Terry nodded his head in appreciation while smiling at the same time at Lieutenant Kenzie's courtly bow. Right behind the leather and canvas sling the barrel was nestled in, came mules walking easily with the yokes on their backs carrying the remaining parts of the weapon.

General Terry glanced at Custer. "Look how he's got each wheel tied up on those yoke contraptions. Darn things looks like they'er going to fall off any second the way they sway but those mules don't even act like they'er hauling a load."

"It is amazing isn't it?" Custer said shaking his head back and forth. "Something that should have been looked into a long time ago, yet it took a dedicated first lieutenant to figure it out. And what we're seeing is just an experimental prototype that has been manufactured by hand from the guidance of that intelligent young man. Just think what could be accomplished if his idea is refined?"

"I agree Jack. I've read in a military journal where the marines have been toying around with a navy version of the Gatling which is a lot more compact than what we've got and have even went so far as to develop some type of tripod mounting for the weapon to rest on along with elevation and traverse adjusting wheels of some sort for firing. I believe it's called a Dahlgren or something similar to that."

"I continue to think it will take away the honor and glory of warfare as we know it general." George Custer remarked just before the first sergeant of B Troop rode by at the head of the pack train.

After returning B Troop's First Sergeant's salute, General Terry said. "Mac must be taking up the rear."

While the long string of laden mules began to slowly amble by General

Terry turned to Custer and spoke in a soft voice. "In answer to your last remark, perhaps so Jack, but the way I view it is anything that can help save the lives of our men by acting as a deterrent to long battlefield combat is worth the invention."

Custer shook his head again in a sad manner, not being able to grasp the thought of war without glory.

Terry changed the subject to get away from the destructive value of the Gatling gun. "What did your scouts do Jack, leave ahead of your regiment march by? The only one I noticed was Charlie Reynolds who was with your staff group."

"Yes sir they all took off before noon to wait for us up on the Rosebud. Counting the six Crows John loaned me along with Mitch Boyer and George Herendeen, my adjutant Cooke says we've got about twenty-five scouts." Custer paused for a moment, and then with a small smile said. "The Crow's call me Son-of-the-Morning-Star. I rather like that better than Yellow Hair and some of the other not so flattering names the Indians have for me. I'll say one thing, the Crow's are magnificent-looking men, and so much handsomer and more Indian-like than any I've ever seen. They call us Light Eyes and are really a very jolly and sportive group."

"Son-of-the-Morning-Star you say. I wonder what they call me?" General Terry smiled, not expecting Custer to answer. "Did you know Charlie Reynolds asked me twice to release him from his duties? Charlie's got this premonition he's going to be killed but I shamed him out of it I think."

"No, I did not know Charlie had talked to you about such a thing." Custer replied with one eyebrow raised. "He's a good man but his right hand is almost useless from felon and I'm sure that may have had something to do with such a request. Isaiah Dorman is treating him with some old nigger witchcraft remedy but it doesn't seem to be doing much good."

"Well, do you want me to go ahead and release him then?" General Terry asked.

"No, no---Charlie will be all right general. He's just suffering a case of the jitters along with his ailment I reckon." Custer shrugged.

The rear guard was in sight when Colonel John Gibbon was finally able to get a word in. "Jack your regiment is in splendid condition. Your boys sure are in high spirits and have presented a good appearance, and I am most impressed at the excellent quality of so many of your horses. Most of them look to be Kentucky breed. How did you manage to acquire such fine animals?"

George Custer took the compliment in stride and gave Colonel Gibbon a wide smile, showing his full set of strong teeth. "It's all in knowing how to wrangle a good deal with slippery civilian government contractor horse traders John. They'll try and slip in lame mounts on you all the time if you give them half a chance. Several of my boys hail from Ken'tuck and know a good mount when they see one."

"Well they sure enough have done a good job of it," offered Gibbon.

Instead of riding at the head of his security detail guarding the pack train Captain Thomas McDougall, Commander of B Troop, was with the rear guard. When he slowly rode by the reviewing stand the mutton-chop, whiskered officer who also wore a small bushy mustache gave a rather slovenly salute. He and his rear guard troops were already covered with a fine film of yellowish dust and with good-humored understanding of the man's predicament General Terry called out. "Tom I'll tell General Custer to stop early tonight so you and your boys can take a good bath in the Rosebud."

Offering a thin smile Captain McDougall replied. "We'll sure be needing it general."

"Well just remember you've got as an important job as anyone and I know you'll do it in proper style. You take care, hear Tom?" Terry called back.

"I sure will general and thank you sir." McDougall waved a limp hand.

George Custer stared at the retreating back of the last man in line for a long moment, then turned to General Terry. "Well sir, if you do not have any last minute instructions I think it time for me to say my goodbyes and join my regiment."

General Terry reached out his hand. "Jack you take care of yourself out there and I'll see you before too long. I have every confidence in you that you will do a bully job of it."

When General Terry released Custer's hand Custer saluted him. The other two officers, Colonel Gibbon and Major Brisbane both came over to shake Custer's hand and offer a parting word.

Custer smiled at the three officers then said, "I have lingered long enough gentlemen. With your permission general, by your leave and I shall be on my way."

"Permission granted Jack," General Terry said. "And good hunting."

The buckskin-clad commander of the 7th U. S. Cavalry gave a saluting wave of his right hand then nudged his horse Vic a little. Vic responded automatically to his master's order and high stepped out onto the path made by the prior passage of the horses and mules. Reining Vic to his right Custer spurred the mount gently and the large horse begun a trot. Custer's guidon bearer and trumpeter quickly followed their commander's trace.

Custer had not gone more than fifty feet when Colonel Gibbon's yelled after him." Now Custer, don't be greedy but wait for us!"

Turning in his saddle George Custer waved and replied. "No, I will not!"

The three officers on the makeshift reviewing stand all chuckled at this small bit of humor.

Riding back through the deserted campsite to the Far West, General Terry offered a comment to his two companions. "Custer is a happy now; off with a roving command of fifteen days to do as he sees fit with no interference from anyone, including me. I told him if he found the Indians not to do as Reno did, but if he thought he could whip them to do so."

Colonel Gibbon made a reply with a smirk on his face. "Sir that's like giving a newborn baby its mother's teat. I've never heard Custer admit there was anything he couldn't whip. But you are correct sir, Custer is in his element now and there will be no stopping him till he runs the hostiles to ground. You can mark my word on that."

* * * * *

General Custer called a halt for his regiment at a little past four p.m. after having only traveled some fourteen miles; Camp was set up near the base of a steep bluff, close to a nearby wood and the crystal clear cold water of the Rosebud. The primary reason for such a short days march was due to the problems and delays with the pack mules. For some unknown reason many of the mules had been loaded in a slip-shod manner and packs were continually falling off, which in itself was very upsetting to Custer. The rear guard of the pack train did not make it to camp until dusk, just a little before General Custer called an impromptu officers call.

It was near sunset by the time all of the 7th Cavalry officer's gathered at the outdoor command post of General Custer. In the twinkling light of a campfire the balding regimental commander addressed his officer's. "We did not achieve a good day's march today by any standard of proper scout procedure. We had packs falling from some mules before we even left the Yellowstone and the train was so spread out we can thank our lucky stars there were no hostiles about to take advantage of our sloppiness. It was the saddest burlesque of a military pack train I ever witnessed! This will not happen again! I am assigning Lieutenant Mathey to take charge of the pack train as for the physical responsibility of seeing they are properly loaded and he will report to me at the end of each day regarding the efficiency of the troopers doing the loading. If your troop has the responsibility of loading the mules and is found wanting, you will find me dealing directly with the troop commander. This sloppiness will stop and I trust you hear me good on this point." Custer paused to let that sink in, and then continued talking. "Gentlemen, my plan of attack is a simple one: we will find the enemy, and defeat them in a two prong assault. This is not a concern but what is has to do with is not letting them escape. We all know we're in enemy territory and the main emphasis of concern at this time must be to avoid at all cost of being detected. I am ordering that no trumpet calls be made except in the case of an emergency. Campfires should not be a problem as long as we control the number of fires in a sensible fashion. You troop commanders are directly responsible for your companies. The two things I shall decide are when we move out and when and where we camp. The rest is up to your discretion. All of you are veterans and know what is necessary without having me look over your shoulder. For the remainder of the scout you will have your stable guards call reveille on the men at three o'clock and the entire regiment will be ready to march two hours later. My intention is to do this patrol in easy stages of around twenty-five to thirty miles a day." Custer paused for a moment to collect his thoughts. Then remembering another subject he wished to broach, he said. "Now I want to explain why I did not take the offer of Colonel Gibbon to lend us a battalion of the Second Cavalry. It is my sincere judgment that the Seventh Cavalry Regiment is the best in the United States Army. We do not require one battalion or five battalions to show us how to do our job. As far as I'm concerned the only thing Brisbin's battalion would have done would have been to slow us down because we would have had to take the time to show them how a real cavalry regiment fights. There is gallantry in this regiment and there is more than enough talent standing right here with me this evening to whip any Indian tribe on the western plains. In simple terms gentlemen, we don't need the Second Cavalry or anyone else!" Custer had to stop talking due to the flurry of vociferousness huzzas his intended appeal to their esprit de corps had brought forth. Even with his pep talk having met with success Custer remained unmoved as if the whole thing had been a part of something expected of him to say on the eve of battle. When the officer's settled down the unsmiling Brevet General again spoke. "It is repugnant to me to have to end this council on a disparaging note but it has come to my attention that

245

several of my official actions have been criticized by some of the officers of the regiment to department headquarters. I do not understand this because I have always been willing to accept recommendations from the most junior second lieutenant of the regiment. Lieutenant Low there is a prime example. Now obviously Low is not some wet behind the ears second lieutenant fresh out of West Point, but he will tell you if asked how he came to me prior to leaving Fort Lincoln, and requested that I hear him out regarding some innovations he had made on his Gatling's. Did I or did I not take the time to listen to your proposal in a patient manner Lieutenant Low?"

Already embarrassed that General Custer had singled him out Billy Low offered a weak, "Yes sir you did."

"And Lieutenant Low didn't have to go behind my back to the Department Commander to get himself heard gentlemen. I will remind all of you that the Articles of War and Army Regulations both address referring criticisms of superior officers to higher authority without going through proper channels. If I obtain future knowledge of this happening again I will take the necessary steps to punish the officer who does so...."

Captain Frederick Benteen could no longer control his rising anger and interrupted Custer. "It seems to me general you are lashing the shoulders of all of us, to get at the few; now, as we are all present, would it not do to specify the officers whom you accuse?"

General Custer looked stunned after hearing Benteen's remark.

The long time line officer thought perhaps he had not made himself clear and spoke again. "General, will you be kind enough to inform us of the names of those officers who have so offended?"

Even in the dim firelight the other officers could see the blood rising in Custer's ruddy face. Stammering slightly, General Custer said. "Colonel Benteen, while I am not here to be chastised by you, I take pleasure in informing you, for your own gratification, that you are not among those officers whom I have alluded to."

"I'm mighty glad to hear that general." Captain Benteen responded.

Custer stared at Captain Benteen for a long moment, and then ended the meeting by saying. "General orders in event of an attack on our bivouac is each company will defend its immediate area and call for help by trumpet if required. Keep in mind any of you may feel free to bring me any criticisms or suggestions. We will chase the hostiles if we have to pursue them to the Nebraska agencies, and that is a promise gentlemen! That is all I have gentlemen, if there are no further questions, I bid you goodnight."

The officer's left the meeting feeling dumbfounded and amazed. The entire meeting was so un-Custer-like as they had never heard him talk that way before. No one could remember having heard him ever ask for advice and his dash and self-confident attitude seemed to have left him.

Captain George D. Wallace, who had a superstitious streak in his personality make-up, whispered to Lieutenant's Francis Gibson and Edward Godfrey, as the trio made their way to their troops. "I tell you fellows I do believe we are riding into a hornets nest sure as shooting. And I'll tell you another thing: with the way General Custer talked tonight I think he is riding to his last battle!"

Chapter 41

On Rosebud Creek 14 miles below Yellowstone River,
Montana Territory
4:00 a.m., Friday, June 23, 1876

The dim pinkish cast of a false dawn gave Lieutenant William Hale Low just enough light to clearly see the strong facial features of his first sergeant Gustavus Frederick Steiner. "First Sergeant as soon as the men finish loading the mules and horses I wish for you to accompany me as they eat breakfast for an informal inspection."

"Informal inspection sir? I'm not exactly sure what you've got in mind sir." First Sergeant Gus Steiner looked at his commander with a questioning expression.

"I know the men fairly well first sergeant but to be honest I'm not as close to them as you are in the physical sense and while I recognize all their faces there are some I have trouble putting a name to the face. This is the first time the platoon will see actual combat as a unit and I thought it best if I---ah-- said a word or two to the men and----well, sort to get to know them a little better I guess you could say." Billy Low trailed off a little lamely.

"I see," First Sergeant Steiner replied, then scratched his chin. "Well sir, I understand what you're getting at now, but are you sure you want to do that? I mean, it's sort of a old soldiers rule of thumb that you don't go and get too close to your men if ya know what I'm a'saying?"

A long moment of silence ensued which was punctuated by the happy chirping of a song sparrow holding reveille on its fellow birds. Then, in a low tone of voice Lieutenant Low said. "Because it may affect me if I see them die: is that what you mean first sergeant?"

"Yes sir, something like that." the first sergeant answered nodding his head. "But on the other hand I think it's a great idear for morale purposes sir."

"Well first sergeant I think I'm human enough that seeing anyone killed would bother me somewhat even though I do have the experience of having viewed violent death before: certainly not as much as you, but I understand your point. When I decided to go to West Point with the intent of making the army my profession I wasn't so naive not to know I was getting into the killing business. So while I appreciate you thinking kindly of my feelings Gus, it will not effect my ability to command the battery."

"Sir I did not mean to imply that I thought you were..." First Sergeant Steiner broke in.

Lieutenant Low interrupted what the first sergeant had intended to clarify by saying, "I know you weren't trying to be disparaging Gus. You mostly hit the nail on the head when you stated it would be good for morale, so go ahead and arrange my request with the gun sergeants and Lieutenant Kenzie and I will be by shortly."

"Yes sir Lieutenant Low." And the first sergeant gave his officer a respectful salute before taking off to arrange the "informal inspection."

A half-hour later Lieutenant Low and Lieutenant Kenzie strolled into the bivouac area of Gun #1 where First Sergeant Steiner and Sergeant Adolph Gotlieb were waiting expectantly.

The other nine men of the Gatling gun section looked up from their tin coffee cups with nosy interest seeing their gun sergeant talking to the two officers. They were more than surprised when the two officers and two senior sergeants walked among them as they sat on the ground around their campfire drinking a final cup of coffee before departing on the days march.

Sergeant Gotlieb made the various introductions: "Lieutenant you know Sergeant Charles Clarke who is my caisson sergeant."

"Don't get up sergeant, I just wanted to drop by and wish all you men the best on the coming fight we're sure to be in. Yes, I'm well acquainted with Charlie. You keeping that Irish temper of yours under the blanket Charlie?"

With a mischievous grin the grizzled, gray haired sergeant said. "That I am sor."

"And dis two men are Corporal's Jerry Suttmiller and Stacey Henry. Jerry, he drives the limber and our horse handler and Henry be our gunner," Gottlieb said in his broken English.

Lieutenant Low nodded his head at the two junior NCOs whom both said "Sir." by way of greeting.

"First Class Private William Krier be my loader sir." Gottlieb continued.

"I wager they call you Billy don't they Private Krier?" Lieutenant Low asked with a smile.

"Yes sir, that they do sir." The short, but good looking, dark-haired loader answered.

"Both dese fellows are ammunition carriers. Dis one here is Private Harold Stratton," Gotlieb said pointing a finger, "But ever body call him Holly. The other fellow is Private James O. Wade."

"Both you men have important jobs. Without your expert ability of having ready ammunition available your gun couldn't fire. Your nickname is

Holly huh?" Lieutenant Low said to the tall, ruddy-faced youngster. "How did that come about?"

The tall drink of water farm boy started to get up on his feet but Billy Low waved him back down. "Well sor its got ta do with my red face and me freckles that some time look sorta green, kinda like Christmas holly I reckon sor."

The next man was a rather short dark faced boy who was Gun #1's Ready man, Private Will Garvin. Lieutenant Low had a few words for him also: "You know Private Garvin, your job is very important too by making sure the loader has fresh clips at hand."

"Yes sir and I taint never failed him yet." The swarthy-faced lad answered.

"That is very good to hear. Keep up the good work."

"I aim to do that sir."

"Now dese last two fellows are the oilier and water boy. Private Thomas Tsarff be de oil man and our junior private is Joseph Renforth who is my water boy."

After meeting with the crew of Gun #1, Lieutenant's Low and Kenzie, along with First Sergeant Steiner walked over to the area staked out by the crew of Gun #2. Only this time the Gun Sergeant Donald F. Evans, after seeing what was going on at Gun #1's bivouac, had his crew standing in a loose rank around the campfire. Sergeant Evans saluted Lieutenant Low when he walked into the campsite. "Sir, I figured it might be easier if I sort of lined the boys up for you."

With a small smile Lieutenant Low said. "That was good of you sergeant but it really wasn't necessary as this is just an informal walk-through to wish you and your men the bully best and to see how you are faring."

"We're doing just fine sir and thank you for thinking about us." The medium built, close-set blue-eyed sergeant said. "You know my Caisson NCO Sergeant John Randall sir."

"Yes I do. How are you doing with packing your ammunition on mules instead of your caisson Sergeant Randal?"

"Taint no big problem sir," the short non-commissioned officer replied. "In some ways it's even better 'cause I don't have to worry 'bout gett'en that big sum-a-bitch in position fer unload'en. Jus bring up them mules and drop their loads on the ground."

"Yes, I can see where that would work better in this kind of terrain Sergeant."

"Shore does sir."

"Very good sergeant and keep up the good work."

"My horse handler here is Corporal Hazen Ward and this is Corporal Curtis Windsor our gunner."

Lieutenant Low nodded at the two corporals with a slight smile in acknowledgment of their dual "Sir's said at the same instant."

"First Class Private Michael Deaton is my loader sir and First Class Private Jimmy Dills is his Ready man."

"Yes, I remember seeing the both of you during our firing exercise when you was able to clear a jam. Did a bully job: made the battery look good." Lieutenant Low said.

"It's the bolts sir." Loader Deaton said. "Even with our newer model Gatling the feed system still jam the bolts sometimes."

"Yes, I know that continues to be a problem. At least they're easier to adjust the headspace and I understand Doctor Gatling is coming out with a lighter weight model with a much better feeding and bolt system."

"I'll be happy to see the new ones sir."

"So will I," smiled Lieutenant Low.

Stepping in front of the next man Lieutenant Low was introduced to the Water Man/Oilier by Sergeant Evans. "This is Private Roger Hill sir. Best damn oilier in the army."

"Good to hear that. Well its obvious Sergeant Evans thinks you are good at your job Hill. Keep up the good work."

"Thank you sir, and yes sir I will," the balding private answered with a blush creeping to his round face.

"This is Hill's Water Boy Private Noer. Pete here is one of our new recruits and he does a right smart job and is learning pretty fast."

"Keep up the good work Noer." Lieutenant Low offered.

The young, heavyset eighteen-year-old boy stammered a "Yes sir."

As Lieutenant Low stepped over to the next man Lieutenant Kenzie noticed the regiment was starting to form up. Leaning close to Low's ear Pat Kenzie whispered. "You better step it up Bucky the general is getting ready to take off."

Billy Low glanced to the far side of the creek where he saw all the activity going on.

Sergeant Frederick Heidenreich who was in charge of Gun #3 had also seen there was not much time left for what the lieutenant was trying to do. So while Lieutenant Low greeted the two ammunition carriers on Gun #2, Privates Ernie Qualls and Ricky Willis, Sergeant Heidenreich got his men lined up in two rows, four in front, five in back and instructed them to call out their names and position on the gun when the lieutenant came in front of them.

First Sergeant Steiner saw what Heidenreich had done and approved the sergeant's initiative with a half salute, half wave of the hand. Then getting beside Lieutenant Low he said in a firm voice. "We've got to get moving sir. Sergeant Heidenreich has got his boys in rank so just walk by them real quick like."

Lieutenant Low saw the wisdom of what Gun #3's sergeant had done and took no offense at Gus Steiner's terse observation. He still took his time by walking the ranks at an unhurried pace. The crew did exactly as they had been ordered when the lieutenant came in front of them: "Caisson Sergeant Kenneth Jackson sir." "Gunner Corporal Jesus E. Quintana sir!", "Horse handler and limber driver Corporal William Beck sir.", "First Class Private Jack Wells, sir...I'm the loader sir." "Private Earl Watts, Ready man sir." Private Yakey ah Wallace Yakey sir, I'm...I'm an ammunition man." "Ammunition Carrier Private Paul Craver, sir.", "The lieutenant knows me sir: Private Fred Thompson, Water Man and Oilier.", "Ah sir, I'm Richard Baum, that's Private Baum sir and I'm the Water Boy."

When all of the men had introduced themselves Lieutenant Low also took the time for a few words in a loud enough tone of voice that the entire platoon could hear him. "Men I apologies for not being able to spend more time with you this morning, but I wanted to come by and pay my personal respects for the bully job you are all doing and to thank you and say I'm mighty proud to be serving with all of you."

The troops beamed under Lieutenant Low's well-chosen words.

* * * * *

General George Custer halted his regiment close to five o'clock and issued orders to make camp. Custer was satisfied with the day's march of over 30 miles in twelve hours.

The campsite Custer selected was on the right bank of the Rosebud at the mouth of Beaver Creek. Although the two rippling streams converged at this location the water still tasted bad due to alkaline deposits. However, there was plentiful grass for the animals and the men made do with the water they had in their large canteens after finding out how bad coffee tasted using the brackish stream water.

Earlier in the day scouts found the large trail Major Reno had discovered on his aborted patrol. Upon seeing the huge trail that was over three hundred yards wide, General Custer turned to Lieutenant Charles Varnum, and said. "Charlie I swear by all that's holy this has got to be the biggest mistake Major Reno ever made in his life. Can you imagine not being willing to follow such a sure sign?"

Lieutenant Varnum replied in a neutral tone of voice after a moment's hesitation. "It does seem odd, doesn't it sir?"

The big trail was so mangled from hundreds of dragging lodge poles the Indians used for their travois to haul their belonging that it was difficult for the cavalry to follow along on it for fear of injuring the mules and horses legs. The regiment was forced to cross and re-cross the Rosebud a dozen times to keep alongside the twisting trace made by the hostiles. There was no thought on General Custer's part to head further south as suggested by General Terry. He knew the Indians were not too far ahead and he was going to find them.

There had been other evidence that the 7th Cavalry was now hot on the trail of their enemy. Several Indian campsites had been found and all the signs indicated the regiment was chasing a large number of hostiles that did not bother General Custer one bit as he could hardly wait to locate the main band. That night around his campfire, General Custer related a story to those with him, about the time during the recent war between the states how he had been the first army officer ever to ascend in a balloon to observe enemy troops. He ended his story by saying. "Oh how I would enjoy having such a magic carpet at my disposal right now. You cannot imagine how it is to soar high above the land where the eagles fly and look down on God's creation. And the marvelous reconnaissance that balloon offered: Not only could I see for miles but also detect enemy movement, size and structure and direction. Yes, it would be grand to see how far our enemy was from us and view the makeup of his camp."

The general's brother, Captain Tom Custer, whom had heard the balloon story a dozen times over the years, put sort of a damper on George's reminisces when he jokingly said. "Yes Armstrong, your flying about the skies in your old balloon could have told us where those Indian smoke signals were coming from today."

Curley – Custer's pet Crow scout
(Watched the battle from a distance)

Chapter 42

General George Custer adjusted the red scarf at his neck while looking up at the sky aboard his dependable horse Vic. There was just the hint of crispness in the early morning air but when the general lowered his head and spoke to his orderly John Burkman, his large white teeth gleamed in a wide grin. "It is going to be a bully day John. Clear skies, no ground mist and warm weather. Tis a good day to be alive!"

"Any day is a good day to be alive out in this God forsaken country!" The outspoken, thin orderly answered.

Shaking his head back and forth Custer glanced to his chief of scouts Lieutenant Charles Varnum who was astride his horse next to civilian scouts Charlie Reynolds and Mitch Bouyer. "The trouble with John is he cannot see beauty when it's staring him in the face. This is wonderful land and I can understand why the Indians love it so." Custer paused for a second then gave the morning orders to the three scouts. "Take all of the Crows with you and get well out in front before sending back any reports, unless of course you discover something significant beforehand. I will try to alleviate the large dust cloud we kicked up yesterday by staggering the regiment's march in several columns. That's it gentlemen, lets get crack'en!"

* * * * *

Some 25 miles distance from where General George Custer was giving orders to his troop commanders to begin the days march, Fast-As-The-Pony-Rides was making his own report to Crazy Horse at the huge Indian camping site on the Little Big Horn River.

"And you say Fast-As-The-Pony-Rides that you do not believe these are the same blue pony soldiers that we beat where the river stops flowing?" Crazy Horse asked.

"They cannot be my chief. The direction from which they travel is down the river of the rose flowers that feeds from the great yellow river above it." Fast-As-The-Pony-Rides said earnestly.

"Yet they are many of them, the same number of those we had our great victory." Crazy Horse mused out loud.

Thinking his leader was asking another question Fast-As-The-Pony-Rides offered an answer. "At least as many of those who turned their backs on our warriors and fled to the large water below us two moons away."

A hint of a smile crossed Crazy Horse's lips from having been told twice by his loyal scout of everything he had witnessed. "Then these must be the soldiers that will fall into our camp without ears as seen by Sitting Bull. I must go tell Sitting Bull and the other chiefs of this news you have brought but before I do I must ask one last question. Did you see any of these white soldiers pulling any of the thunder sticks you told about before?"

"No my chief, nor did I see any of the big boom guns or thunder sticks their horses pull," Fast-As-The-Pony-Rides said solemnly.

Crazy Horse thought about that for a moment in deep contemplation before voicing what was on his mind out loud. "Yet these must be the same pony soldiers that we know were coming from the direction where the sun rises. I wonder what they did with their thunder sticks?"

* * * * *

An hour after Custer's scouts had fanned out to the regiment's front the first report came back to the general written by Mitch Bouyer and carried by an old and very experienced Crow scout White-Man-Runs-Him.

After reading the penciled report General Custer handed it to his brother Tom to read. *"Have discovered fresh signs of Sioux. Three used camping grounds found, one of which less than one week old. Will continue scout. Bouyer."* "What do you think Bo?" Tom Custer asked, handing the report to Adjutant William W. Cooke whom also read it.

Ignoring his brothers question George Custer instead gave him a couple of terse orders. "Have Captain Keogh and your Lieutenant Harrington bring up I and C Troops and we will forge ahead a mile or so in front of the remainder of the regiment to look over these campsites. And pay my compliments to Major Reno and Captain Benteen that they shall divide the command and follow in two columns."

* * * * *

The leader of the six Crow scouts Half-Yellow-Face, who was known by his fellow Crow's as the warrior who carries the pipe, talked softly to his fellow scouts White Swan, Goes Ahead and White-Man-Runs-Him. "What is wrong with these light eyes? They make excuses for each sign we show them. Twice we have shown them smoke signals coming from the valley where the water runs they call Tullock's Creek and they laugh, saying it is but small clouds from the mist blowing from the hill-tops. Not only do they not listen but they do not see well either. Look at this," he used his toe as a pointer at the scattered buffalo bones and bits of hide strewn about the most recent Sioux campsite they had came across. "Can this be more than two days old? At each bend of the stream we now find traces of the Sioux. See how each blade of grass is eaten as far as the eye can see? I tell the fair-haired leader Son-of-the-Morning-Star that it would take a herd the size of the largest buffalo tribe ever seen to ruin the grass this way which means more Sioux warriors than we can count in a moon. And he tells me not to act like an old woman!"

"Yes, the light eyes do not heed our warnings on what surely awaits us," said White-Man-Runs-Him. "Earlier when I rode far ahead as the advance scout, I came face to face with a Sioux scout and we talked in sign language before turning and going our separate ways. The Sioux know we are here and what this scout told me in signs made a cold chill travel up my spine. He said for me to turn back and leave the white devils for they will all die and if I stay with them then I shall also die because the Sioux are waiting for them and are anxious to do battle and take their scalps."

The other scouts grunted a response upon hearing what White-Man-Runs-Him related. Then White Swan said, "Goes Ahead and I told the soldiers that this place where we stand was one large camp where great medicine was made." White Swan pointed at the still standing framework that circled the cleared area where Sitting Bull experienced his vision during the Sun Dance. "We did our best to tell the soldiers that this was but one camp, but they did not believe us. And when I showed them the drawings of dead men with Sioux all around them and told the light eyes the Sioux were not afraid, they scoffed at the idea of Indians standing and fighting. While the light eyes were scoffing at me the flag the soldier carriers for Son-of-the-Morning-Star blew down and when they put it back up it blew down again. I tell you comrades there is much strong medicine at this place and I am frightened by it. If their war flag cannot stand at this place; this tells me they will not stand for long when they find the Sioux."

* * * * *

At a little before eight o'clock in the early evening after scouting the huge trail for 30 miles, General Custer called a halt on the right bank of the

Rosebud to rest the men and animals and to allow everyone to fix something to eat. He sent a group of scouts on ahead with orders to find out exactly where the Sioux trail led as he was certain he was less than 30 miles from them.

As usual, Custer had picked a good campsite for the stand-down and while most troopers did not take the time to note the beautiful surroundings the area was lovely nonetheless. On the right flank of the regiment an extremely high cliff rose sharply which offered concealment of the bivouac from snoopy enemy scouts. It was a couple of hundred yards from under the lee of the high cliff to the smooth flowing water of the Rosebud. In between the camp and the fast moving creek was a large expanse of rich grassland that was studded with great masses of wild rose bushes that emitted a sweet smelling aroma. It was the many hundreds of rose bushes that grew wild along the stream that gave the creek its name. With a few lush trees intermixed among the grass and rosebushes, the entire setting was reminiscent of a well-tended park. Here, the horses and mules enjoyed their supper while the men of the 7th Cavalry went about making there's. Very few of the mules got the luxury of having their meddlesome packs removed from their backs because General Custer was contemplating a night march. Those mules that were unloaded carried the rations the troops needed for their meager meals.

As soon as the animals were taken care of, orders were issued it was all right to build cooking fires with the directive all fires would be extinguished at sunset. There was a sense of urgency in the air as the men went about frying up their bacon and boiling coffee.

M Troop top kick First Sergeant Timothy O'Hara made his way through his company bivouac, stopping briefly at each campfire to have a few words with his men. The old line sergeant knew a big battle was looming and like the good soldier he was he wanted to make damn sure his troops equipment was in tip-top shape and to also instill a morale boost to help the men's resolve in facing the horrendous prospect of combat.

"Billy me boys, I see yer feeding yer bellies with some fine bacon and hardtack. Tis a good soldiers meal it is." The big bull of a first sergeant said jovially.

Private's Billy Morris and Billy Slaper, better known by most as Billy One and Billy Two, looked up at their first sergeant with expressions of disbelief marked on their faces. The bolder of the two Billie's; Billy Morris, offered his sergeant a sarcastic rejoinder. "You have been in the cavalry too long first sergeant if you find this chow good eating. Now if we had some snap beans and corn on the cob, that would be real food."

First Sergeant O'Hara chuckled. "Ah that's right lad, you like your vegetables don't ye. Well boys, as soon as we show these heathens a measure of respect by giv'en 'em a sound beating, the sooner we'll be back to Fort Lincoln where you can eat all the vegetables yer bellies will take." The first sergeant paused and glanced at Corporal Wallace Benton. "Well corp are all yer boys in tip-top shape with clean weapons and ready to go?"

The short, bulky ruddy-faced corporal had been in the army long enough to know his first sergeant's walk through was a calculated ploy to prepare the men for battle. "That they are first sergeant but just the same I'll be hav'en the men a'look'en after their rifles again before the sun goes down. You can fairly-well say these boys are ready to kick some ass!"

The twinkling blue-green eyes of Timothy O'Hara crinkled to a minute wink to his junior NCO as he said. "Tis good to hear that Corporal Benton. Mind you now to have yer fire out before dark. Don't want the heathens to know we're a'sitt'en on their back porch do we lads?"

Billy Slaper understood the meaning of the sergeant's last remark and asked a quick question. "First Sergeant sir, are we really that close to the hostiles?"

With a wide grin First Sergeant O'Hara shook his head back and forth. "How many times do I have to tell you Billy Two that you don't have to call me sor? I shore must remind you of yer Pap lad. But to put an answer to yer question lad, from the word that comes a'float'en down from his honor's headquarters, I'd say we're not more than twenty-five miles from catch'en up with the heathens. With the good rid'en we've been do'en, that be not more than a days march before we be catch'en them."

Billy Two gulped, and said "Thank you si...er first sergeant."

Placing his right finger alongside his nose in a humorous salute the big Irish first sergeant smiled. "Keep on yer toes lads," and he left the trio, heading to the next campfire a few yards distance.

Four men were huddled around the small fire on their haunches eating bacon and hardtack when First Sergeant O'Hara walked up. The pleasant aroma of boiling coffee wafted upward to tingle the nostrils of the senior non-commissioned officer. "Now that's some good smelling java you got go'en thar First Class McCullough."

The senior private of M Troop, First Class Private John G. McCullough, glanced up from eating his bacon and seeing who it was that had addressed him gave a wide grin. "You're welcome to try a cup first sergeant, if ya got the mind to." The tall, lanky Texan with reddish blond hair offered.

"Well now, if ya got an extra tin I jus mite take half-a-cup." First Sergeant O'Hara replied.

A tin cup was quickly found and a portion of coffee strained into it and handed to the first sergeant. Testing the hot black liquid that was very bitter First Sergeant O'Hara stifled a grimace and said. "Now that's a pretty good brew. Did you boil this up Devil?"

The first sergeant was referring to Private Luther Higgins whom everyone, including General Custer called Devil. "Naw first sergeant Calvin fixed it up fer us... It was his turn," he added as an after thought.

Hunkering down with the four men First Sergeant O'Hara said. "So who taught you how to make coffee Private Switzer, your blessed mama?"

The round-faced private who was trying to grow a mustache looked sheepishly at his first sergeant. "No first sergeant, it was Fritz Neely there and Mac that showed me how."

The first sergeant glanced at Private Neely for a second and nodded his head. Then taking the time to force the remainder of the wicked potion down a few long moments of quiet ensued. After finishing the coffee First Sergeant O'Hara tossed the dregs into the campfire what made a small hiss for a second, then got to his feet. "Well, I better be gett'en along: got ta see how the other lads are a'do'en before nightfall. I want you to all make sure yer rifles are cleaned and see to it yer fires out as soon as ya get done eating. Try to grab a nap as I think the gen'erel has it in mind to do a night march." He looked directly at John McCullough for a second, and then said. "Mac, I've known you since the war and I can't think of a better man I'd rather have by my side in a tough fight. You take care of these boys here and show 'em the way of a stout heart. I know they'll listen to you so you tell them good that when the time comes they've got to stand by you and fight like the men I know they are."

For once in his life the slim, blue-eyed Texan was humbled by the outpouring of words he'd just heard and he truly felt the first sergeant was being sincere. He also felt a surge of pride and showed it when he answered. "You can best believe first sergeant those Indjun's will think they've got a tiger by the tail when they tangle with us'en's."

Elsewhere, other first sergeants were going about similar visits with their men, including pigeon-chested First Sergeant Gustavus Steiner who admonished his Gatling gun crews to mentally practice their parts in fast assembly of the three guns.

At nine o'clock three Crow scouts returned and with Mitch Bouyer and Isaiah Dorman acting as interpreters, reported to General George Custer what they had found.

"Hairy Moccasins says the Sioux have crossed the divide and must be sitting up somewhere up on the Little Big Horn," the dark-faced Isaiah Dorman who was married to an Indian woman said.

Staring directly at the black, crinkly-haired interpreter Custer asked, "Were they able to locate the enemy camp?"

Mitch Bouyer spoke up to answer the question. "That was the first thing we asked them general and while they didn't actually see the camp they swear they saw the hazy glow of campfires reflecting off clouds in the distance."

"How far away?" Custer wanted to know.

"They found a spot they call the Crow's Nest that's about twenty, maybe twenty-five miles from here, and from what Isaiah and I gather from listening to them the hostile camp can't be no more than five or ten miles from there," the half-breed Bouyer answered.

General Custer mulled that bit of information over in his brain for a while then made his decision. Turning to Lieutenant Charles A. Varnum, whom he had appointed to be in charge of the Indian scouts, Custer said, "Lieutenant Varnum I want you to take Charlie Reynolds, Mitch Bouyer here along with four Crow scouts and five or six of your best Rees to this place called the Crow's Nest and set up an observation post. You will send back a report to me as soon as you can outline whether you've been able to spot the enemy camp. If your scouts claim they can see the glow of campfires off the clouds then surely you should be able to view smoke rising at dawn. Get your scouts together and leave immediately lieutenant."

With a quick salute and "Yes sir," Lieutenant Varnum, Mitch Bouyer and the three Crow scouts departed.

Custer looked around in the dark and finally mumbled, "Where's my trumpeter?"

Regimental Sergeant Major William Sharrow spoke up. "I'll fetch him for you sir."

"I don't need to see him sergeant major; just tell Voss to pay my compliments to the troop commanders that I wish to see them. And if you can find Trumpeter Martini, tell him to help out Voss"

"Very well sir," Sergeant Major Sharrow replied, and went on his way to find his general's chief trumpeter.

It took the sleepy eyed Trumpeter John Martini and Trumpeter Henry Voss 20 minutes to pass the word to the dozen troop commanders. Although not specifically told to do so Private Henry Voss, when advising Captain

Frederick Benteen as to the summons, seeing Major Marcus Reno, told the major he was probably expected to attend too.

A silvery three-quarter moon cast just enough light for the assembled officers to see the face of their commander as he spoke to them. After explaining what the Crow scouts had reported and how he'd sent out another large contingent of scouts under the command of Lieutenant Varnum, General Custer then outlined his hastily devised plan: "Lieutenant Godfrey, I need to detach your Lieutenant Hare temporarily for duty to be in charge of the remaining scouts. With Lieutenant Varnum gone I need a qualified officer to supervise the rest of our scouts and Hare meets the requirements. I am aware that leaves K Company with just you as the only officer but it cannot be helped but I'm sure you understand."

"Yes sir I do," replied Lieutenant Godfrey, who added, "I've got a good first sergeant and two other sergeants and will make do without problems sir."

"Ah yes, very good lieutenant." Custer paused for a moment then with emphasis to show the seriousness of what he was saying, said, "Gentlemen, we are about to embark upon the fight of our lives! We will probably be outnumbered six to one but I have the confidence we will acquit ourselves as the professional soldiers that we are and soundly beat our enemy." The general had to stop for a moment as the prior hush of his officers suddenly sounded with murmuring whispers after hearing their commander admit for the first time they would be facing a huge amount of hostile Indians. "Okay gentlemen, as you were please." When total silence resumed Custer went on. "We will conduct a night march which will commence at eleven o'clock which gives you just a little over an hour to prepare your men. We will follow the trail the hostiles left and with luck we should be at the summit of the divide leading to the Little Big Horn sometime before daybreak. At this location I intend to conceal our presence while scouts reconnoiter our front in preparation for a surprise attack on the hostile village at dawn the next day. In the morning, after we have hidden ourselves, I will summon you again for the actual phase of attack. Return to your commands and prepare to move out."

As the troop commanders moved away to make ready to depart, Major Reno stayed behind to ask a question directed to General Custer. "What are your orders for me general?"

Using Reno's Civil War brevet rank Custer answered the major without hesitation. "Colonel Reno, consider yourself attached to my headquarters for the present but when the time comes I will have a special duty for you to perform."

Lieutenant W. W. Cooke
Custer's Canadian Adjutant

Chapter 43

The Little Big Horn River, Montana Territory
Morning, Sunday, June 25, 1876

As with most military operational plans; even the good ones such as the one developed by General Custer late last night, they sometimes have the tendency to go awry in the actual execution. This is primarily caused due to the unpredictability of an enemy. And this was the situation General Custer was confronted with shortly after daylight on this bright, sunny morning that showed signs of being a very hot day. Custer's original desire and plan to attack the enemy camp at dawn the next day was shattered when Lieutenant Varnum sent back a message that not only had the enemy camp been spotted but the Sioux was aware of the presence of the regiment as well. Further information came to General Custer around Ten o'clock that it appeared the hostile encampment was beginning to break up and the Sioux were scattering. What Custer did not know was this movement of Indians, as viewed by Lieutenant Varnum and the other scouts, was a small tribe of hostiles actually joining the huge camp of Sioux and Cheyenne on the Little Big Horn. All Custer could think of was the enemy was getting away. General Custer called a hasty meeting of several officers to change his plans because he was not going to allow the hostiles to disband and melt into the countryside as they fled from the 7th Cavalry.

Standing in front of his officer's, dressed in a gray flannel shirt, buckskin coat, blue trousers, and his scuffed long boots and regular army cavalry hat over his close-cropped hair, General George Armstrong Custer addressed his officer's with a simple order. "We are going to attack now! They will not escape from my regiment!"

General Custer's change of plans to commence the attack at this time instead of in the morning included dividing his regiment into separate battalions again. Captain Fred Benteen, whose H Troop had been leading the column, was given the command of D and K Troops led by Captain Tom Weir and First Lieutenant Ed Godfrey, respectively. The senior captain of the 7th Cavalry, Benteen was ordered to take his battalion of 125 men to the left at an angle until reaching the bottom of the valley.

General Custer then summoned Major Reno.

While on his way to meet with General Custer Major Reno passed Captain Benteen who was commencing his march at a forty-five degree angle down the long sloping grade that led to the Valley of the Little Big Horn. Reno offered his former tent mate a casual wave of his hand, and then asked. "Where's he sending you off to Fred?"

Shaking his white, curly haired, round head, Benteen replied with a tone of disgust in his voice. "On a damn wild goose chase if you ask me! He wants me to check out those bluffs ore yonder," pointing a hand to a distant ridgeline. "Looks like I've got a couple of canyon's to get through and if I don't find anything I'm supposed to check out the next ridge. Damn waste of time and energy, that's what it is!"

"Well you know how this regiment operates: ours is not to know the reason why." Major Reno said with distain. "You watch your step and take care of yourself and good luck." Reno gave a final wave and trotted on after the orderly who had been sent to fetch him.

General Custer didn't waste any time giving Major Reno his orders. "Colonel Reno I am putting you in charge of A, G, and M Troops. Your battalion will stay with me for the time being on my left flank until I give you further orders."

"Very well general," Major Reno said softly. Then in a louder voice, asked. "May I have permission to take along one of the Gatling guns?"

The request rather startled General Custer because he had all but forgotten he had authorized the platoon of Gatling's to accompany him. He remarked dumbfounded. "Where are they at?"

"Back toward the rear of the column sir in front of the pack train." Major Reno replied.

"With Captain McDougall?" Custer was still acting strange.

"Yes sir," Reno cocked an eyebrow at the seemingly stupid question.

"So they're holding up okay on the march I take it," Custer mused rhetorically.

"Well yes sir they are, or at least keeping up with the pack train." Major Reno answered, wondering why in the hell the man was acting so inane.

After a short pause General Custer looked Major Reno in the eye, and said. "I do not see any reason why not if that is what you desire Colonel. Permission granted."

Major Reno saluted, saying "Thank you sir," and rode back along the column to inform Captain's Moylan, Wallace and French, they were now a part of his battalion. And to tell Lieutenant William Hale Low that he required the services of Lieutenant Kenzie and the Gatling gun crew that had been with him on his scout patrol.

* * * * *

It was Twelve O'clock noon when the 7th Cavalry rode across the divide from the Rosebud as they prepared to go down into the valley of the Little Big Horn.

* * * * *

The command rode at an easy trot in a southwesterly direction from the Crows Nest, where General Custer claimed he couldn't see anything because of a haze. They traveled over grassy rolling hills with abundant sagebrush for ten miles when scouts out in front of the regiment reported back to General Custer of a new discovery about a miles distance.

"Just one tepee standing alone?" George Custer asked with a raised eyebrow.

Lonesome Charlie Reynolds rubbed his sore hand when he answered Custer. "Yeah but it's a significant find gen'rl. Its planted right smack in the middle of what was a big encampment and it's only a day or so old. I betcha the Indjun's ain't no more than a dozen miles up stream from thar."

"And it's a burial tepee for a chief or great warrior?" Custer asked.

"Yep, it shore 'enough is. Painted up real fancy with a lot of gifts to take along to the other world. A Sioux warrior for sure, and from the looks of the body I'd say he got himself shot up pretty bad somewhere. The wounds that kilt him are fresh, taint no doubt he's been in a recent fight."

Custer thought about that bit of information for a moment before speculating on a couple of theories. "Could have been from some of Gibbon's troops, maybe even Crook or perhaps a fight with another tribe."

Charlie Reynolds spit a bit of juicy tobacco on his right hand and began massaging the brown mess on his wrist. "I don't suspect it was no Injun that shot him but that don't really make no difference anyway. The main point I'm a'try'en to get over to you is with all the stuff we found laying around: even cooking pots still over cold fire beds, the Injuns left in a hurry and you got to think about what that means. Taint no doubt they know we're here and from the looks of things they may be high-tailing it."

Concern showed on General Custer's ruddy face. "Well----let's go take a look at this lone tepee and find where it leads us."

* * * * *

"There go your Indians, running like devils," shouted civilian interpreter for the Ree scouts Fred Girard as he waved his hat to attract the attention of General Custer.

General Custer spurred his big horse Vic and rode up to the 70 yards from the lone tepee to where Girard was sitting on his mount atop the summit of the knoll. Further down towards the river valley to his right Custer could clearly see tiny figures off in the distance he estimated to be about four miles away riding at a slow canter along side a forked stream that led to the Little Big Horn River. "By God that's got to be the rear guard for the village!" He exclaimed. "Sure as shooting they're running away."

Lieutenant Cooke, Custer's adjutant, who had rode up behind the general, stared at the distant band of about 50 Indians moving slowly on the right bank of the small stream. "They don't seem to be in a big hurry do they sir?"

His adjutant's observation made Custer take a harder look. "They'er playing games with us, that's what they're doing. Daring us to come after them while the main village makes its escape." Custer turned to Fred Girard. "Get your Ree's to chase after them so we can find out where the main camp is at. Its got to be further up the river but I can't tell because of that bluff blocking the view."

Girard waved a hand in understanding and hailed one of General Custer's favorite scouts Bloody Knife. Shouting to the gray temple older Indian Girard yelled. "Bloody Knife----take your Arikaras and pursue your fleeing enemy."

The long time scout for the white soldiers who had received a medal from President Grant gave a hand sign he would comply and hastened to gather the Ree scouts who were busy rummaging through the deserted Sioux camp ground.

In less than five minutes Bloody Knife and the other Ree scouts, along with Mitch Bouyer and his Crows and Frank Girard were staring up at George Custer who had rode down from the knoll to see why the scouts were not mounting their ponies to follow after the Sioux.

"What are you telling me Girard that they won't go after the Sioux?" Custer blurted out in a loud voice after hearing his Ree's refusal to track the hostiles.

"They say there's too many Sioux general and there's no sense for them getting themselves killed for nothing." The tall bearded interpreter said.

"Getting killed for nothing? Why they're nothing but a bunch of cowards. You tell them that and say that I also said if any man of you is not brave of heart I will take away his weapons, and make a woman of him."

"They're not likely go'en to cotton hearing that general." Girard warned.

"You go ahead and tell them like I said it to you." Custer insisted.

It may have been a matter of translation or perhaps the Ree's didn't fully understand the insult being handed to them by General Custer; but whatever it was, none of the white men were prepared for the resulting response: The large group of Ree scouts all began laughing and slapping at their legs in mirth.

Young Hawk, who was dressed in a blue cavalry jacket, stopped laughing long enough to say something to Fred Girard who in turn translated the remark to General Custer. "Young Hawk says if you were to take away the weapons of your white soldiers that are lesser warriors than the Corn Indians, it would take you a long, long time. But they are ready to do battle if you are as long as you lead them."

Mitch Bouyer translated what Young Hawk had said to the six Crow scouts. Before General Custer could respond to the Ree's remark Half-Yellow-Face, the leader of the Crow's spoke up. "Son-of-the-Morning-Star is like a feather borne on the wind and must go fly after these Sioux, but he must be told there are more of them than there are bullets in the belts of his white soldiers."

When Bouyer related what Half-Yellow-Face had said to Custer, the general's red weathered face blanched a chalky white, but the old Crow who carried the pipe was right when he said Custer had to go after the Sioux. Before Custer turned in his saddle to find his adjutant he said to Bouyer and Girard. "You tell your scouts my soldiers will show them who is brave. We will lead them against the Sioux if they have the heart to go with us."

* * * * *

The Adjutant of the 7th Cavalry, Lieutenant William W. Cooke halted his horse so quickly that the animal's front legs stiffened when it skidded to a stop which caused it to almost set on its haunches and raised a billowing cloud of dust. Cooke's fast gallop from General Custer left him breathless and he went through a minor choking, coughing fit to clear the dust from his lungs before he could report to Major Reno with orders. In his British sounding Canadian accent Lieutenant Cooke finally managed to deliver the orders General Custer had instructed him to give to Major Reno. "Very sorry for that sir. I lost my composure there for a moment. The warmth of the sun is stirring the dust considerably, say what! Compliments from General

Custer sir. The Indians are about two and a half miles ahead on yon river," he gestured toward the Little Big Horn River twisting in the valley below. "They are on the jump and you are to follow them as fast as you can and charge them wherever you find them and we will support you."

Major Reno's handsome face was covered with sweat-streaked dirt and he took a red patterned bandana from around his neck and wiped his eyes. Squinting at the anxious regimental adjutant Reno said. "I take it when you say on the jump you mean the hostiles are in retreat or fleeing."

In an arrogant tone of voice Cooke answered sharply. "Precisely!"

Ignoring the lack of "sir" from the prissy adjutant who was too close to Custer for his own good, Major Reno just nodded his head, then asked for another clarification. "And when my battalion catches up with the hostiles I am to charge them with the sure knowledge I may depend upon backup support from General Custer. Is that correct lieutenant?" Reno's last four words were said in a harsh, biting tone that took some of the wind out of Cooke's sails.

"Why, why yes sir," the adjutant stammered a little, "You will be supported by the whole outfit."

Reno wasn't quite done yet however. "What about Captain Benteen? Are you considering him as a part of the whole outfit?"

This question stumped Lieutenant Cooke. "I…I really don't quite know sir. I assume the general is thinking along the line that Captain Benteen's battalion cannot be far behind and will surely come double quick when he hears your action."

"I see," Major Reno said with hooded eyes. "Very well lieutenant, tell General Custer I understand this verbal order and will comply posthaste."

"Yes sir, very good sir," and Lieutenant Cooke gave a decent salute, spurred his pony and was off in another cloud of dust.

* * * * *

General George Custer stood stiffly in his saddle with legs straight which raised his bottom off the fine tooled, well-worn polished leather. He leaned forward slightly across Vic's long manned head to better see from his perch high near the top of the tall ridgeline overlooking the Valley of the Little Big Horn below him. The late afternoon bright sun reflected off the lens of his field glasses as he scanned the movement of Major Reno's battalion. With the binoculars at his eyes he offered his brother Tom Custer a jovial remark. "Now there's a sight to see! A well-trained squadron of cavalry crossing a ford with flankers out and scouts leading the way. You can say what you want about Reno but when it comes to maneuvering troops the man knows how to conduct an advance. Absolutely magnificent!"

Smiling, Tom Custer said, "Let me take a peek Bo."

Just as George handed his field glasses to his brother Lieutenant Varnum came riding up. Offering the general a casual salute the 7th Cavalry's chief of scouts said. "General Custer sir, I've been working along the top of the bluffs there," indicating with a jutting chin the ridgeline above, "and I've seen what I think is the main camp of the Sioux further up river. From what I have viewed I would say it's a large force of hostiles because it sure as hell is one big village. Damn thing must stretch for a mile or better."

"How far up river Lieutenant?" General Custer asked.

"I'd say not more than three miles sir." Lieutenant Varnum answered.

"Three miles," Custer mused to himself out loud, then was silent for nearly a minute as he stared below at Major Reno's battalion progression across the river. He glanced at the several officers and enlisted men of his staff group that surrounded him before speaking again. "My intention was to follow Major Reno across the river and hit the enemy camp right behind him but with them being this close I believe it would be prudent for me to head further north along the bluffs and make a flank attack. I'll have to think on this some more but in the meantime Lieutenant Varnum you may rejoin your scouts down with Major Reno."

Varnum gave a better salute this time, saying "Yes sir, very good sir," and nudged his mount down the slope where the last of the three troops were crossing the river that was twisted at the fording point in the shape of a horseshoe. The lieutenant took his hat off half way down his descent and waving it over his head shouted to the men below. "Thirty days furlough to the man who gets the first scalp!"

* * * * *

Due to thirsty horses that took advantage of the fairly deep, cold water of the Little Big Horn while crossing the river, Major Reno's three companies became entangled with one another upon reaching the little grassy peninsula formed by the horseshoe twisting of the river. A narrow land channel offered an exit from the inside of the horseshoe and the major ordered his troops to reform out on the large expanse of the valley bottom among a clump of Cottonwood trees. This reorganization of the three cavalry companies caused several minutes delay as Reno halted his column until satisfied

271

everything was back to normal as far as unit integrity was concerned.

While Major Reno was having his troop commanders align their companies Lieutenant James Patrick Kenzie was having problems of his own.

"My God Sergeant Gottlieb you've got to get those mules moving faster. Half of them are still in the river!"

The former German army officer shook his head back and forth in a helpless gesture. "Ach mein Lieutenant Kenzie, vhat am I to do, I cannot make the men carry the dumiasels!" Sergeant Adolph Gottlieb paused; suddenly realizing his tone of voice had been disrespectful which was completely out of character for him. He also knew his young lieutenant had no idea he had just called the stubborn mules dumb asses, so he tried another tact. "I think the mules be scared of the water sir. I'll drag them out with the horses if I have too. They should be better on the prairie land there." He gestured casually toward the wide expanse of grass and sagebrush where the three cavalry troops were now in formation and beginning a slow trot forward.

"Major Reno is commencing his attack sergeant! Do something! We've got to support him!" Lieutenant Kenzie said, his voice boarding on hysteria.

It was quarter to three when Reno's men saw their first large contingent of hostile Indians. The major had formed his 133 officers and men in columns of fours, three companies on line abreast. His 16 scouts were loosely scattered in front of the battalion with the major right behind them in the lead of his men. Goes Ahead, one of the Crow scouts waved his army cavalry hat over his head and yelled back to the trotting soldiers. "The Sioux are coming to meet us!"

Major Reno was near Goes Ahead when the Indian turned on his pony and shouted but didn't understand what the scout had said, even though a distant dust cloud gave the indication of many horses moving. Then civilian scout George Herendeen, who was riding a little to the left of Goes Ahead moved in his saddle and yelled over his shoulder to no one in particular "Hold on boys! The Sioux are coming!"

Major Reno tried to see through the swarming cloud of dust the hostiles had made, not knowing it was a tactic they were using by moving their pony herd further up stream and purposefully kicking up as much dust as they could for a screen. Although he was only able to actually see but a few Indians his mind told him there was obviously many more coming in his direction and after only a half miles march he quickly changed the formation of his battalion. He formed Captain Myles Moylan's Troop A and Captain

Tom French's Troop M in a straight line and placed Troop G, commanded by Captain George Wallace behind the other companies as a reserve force. The ground the battalion was now crossing over was a sandy mush caused by the Sioux ponies having eaten the grass down to a nub, leaving patches of wild sage on the flat surface which was badly rutted by the hooves of the horses that had grazed there. It was rough ground for cavalry to cross, but once the march resumed the line kept in good order with Major Reno riding about 25 yards out and centered in front of his battalion like a good cavalry officer was supposed to do.

Raising his hand for attention Major Reno turned his horse around to face his battalion and shouted as loud as his voice would allow. "At a gallop----forward!"

Reno's trumpeter riding close by took up the call.

Some of the men began to cheer and holler which for some strange reason annoyed Major Reno.

* * * * *

General George Custer in the meantime had turned his five companies to the north and was riding them along the ridgeline above the bluffs overlooking the Little Big Horn Valley. From time to time Custer would ride Vic to the edge of the bluff to check his bearings and to see if he could get a better view of the hostile village. He happened to be peering down into the valley when Major Reno started his charge. General Custer could barely make out the southern fringe of the enemies camp and it appeared Reno was chasing the hostiles who were not contesting his advance. A smile was on Custer's face when he turned from the bluff and rode back to the long column strung out on the ridge. Custer, upon seeing his brother Tom and nephew Autie Reed, said, "We've got them this time, Reno's caught them napping." While riding along the bluff line to reach the front of the column he took off his hat and waved it over his head, yelling to his men. "Hurrah, boys, we've got them. All we've got to do now if finish them up and then go home to our station."

* * * * *

"Rider coming," yelled Jerry Suttmiller, limber driver and horse handler for Sergeant Gottlieb's Gun #1.

Lieutenant Kenzie saw the fast moving horse with a cavalryman mounted on it tearing up the valley at a fast gallop heading toward the ford. Turning to Sergeant Adolph Gottlieb, Kenzie said. "Sergeant send one of your men and fetch that rider. He should be able to tell us what's taking place up front."

Sergeant Gottlieb gave a quick "Yessir!" then yelled to the water boy who was a pretty good rider. "You there Renforth, go tell that soldier Lieutenant Kenzie wants to talk to him."

Joe Renforth spurred his horse and with a "Yes sergeant," the young trooper was away in a flash.

The members of the Gatling gun crew saw Renforth stop the cavalryman but instead of the man following Renforth back to Lieutenant Kenzie, after a short interval with the cavalryman man gesturing wildly with his arms, he took off to the ford and splashed across the river while Renforth galloped back.

In an excited tone of voice Private Renforth loudly reported his brief conversation to Lieutenant Kenzie with Sergeant Gottlieb listening in. "That was a Private McIlhargy sir and he's carrying an urgent message from Major Reno to General Custer and said he couldn't stop to talk with you. He says there's all kinds of hostiles to the majors front and they're starting a mass attack against the battalion and the major wants some help from General Custer."

The young water boy with premature balding showing on his high forehead had gushed out his report so fast that it was all but gibberish to both Lieutenant Kenzie and especially Sergeant Gottlieb who didn't have a full mastering of the English language anyway. Lieutenant Kenzie had understood enough of the boys out of breath report to know Reno was in trouble and needed help fast. "Now calm down Renforth. Did whomever you say that fellows name was tell you how many Indians there are and how far away is Major Reno?"

"Sir, all he said was it's a strong force of Indians about a mile ahead," the premature balding young private said.

Turning to Sergeant Gottlieb Lieutenant Kenzie calmly gave an order. "Sergeant, get the gun off the animals and assemble it as quick as it can be put together."

"Yes sir! Okay you boys listen up to me. Unpack das mule's unt horses and put das gun together jackrabbit quick, unt I don't vant no back talk or sass. Now get crack'en!" As soon as he gave the order Sergeant Gottlieb dismounted so he could supervise the assembly.

While the nine men of the gun crew frantically went about the business of getting the component parts of their Gatling gun off the pack mules and out of the stretcher sling affair between the two horses, Sergeant Gottlieb has a question for his lieutenant after hearing the scattering sound of musketry beginning further up the valley.

"Ve are far away from the battle sir. How vell we get our gun up thar to help Major Reno?"

"I already thought of that sergeant. Use the poles we used for the sling as a limber between the two horses. Tie one end of each pole to the gun trail and use both horses to pull it."

Skeptical of the idea, Sergeant Gottlieb then asked. "Vhat if the poles break lieutenant?"

"Then we'll tie ropes to the damn thing and drag it sergeant!" Lieutenant Kenzie answered with conviction.

In the Blackfoot and Uncpapas village, which was nearest to Major Reno's charging soldiers, there was complete turmoil and confusion that soon spread to the other camp circles along the twisting Little Big Horn River.

Red Feather, brother-in-law to Crazy Horse, became aware of the shouting and turmoil and came out of his tepee just in time to see a young warrior come tearing through the camp yelling, "Get away as fast as you can, don't wait for anything, the white men are charging!"

Old men took up the yell as women and children began dashing around in preparation for flight. "Soldiers are here! Soldiers are here! Young warriors go out and fight them!"

Chief Red Horse did not have time to consult with any of the other many chief's, but clearly understanding the great peril, mounted his pony and began to restore order among his Miniconjou's. "Warriors! Take up arms and protect your women and children!"

Within a short time the aimless running around and shouting turned into war cries and determination as hundreds of Sioux and Cheyenne warriors mounted their ponies to meet the threat. Hundreds more on foot ran toward a hidden gully near a stand of tall timber to the south of their encampment. Individual Indians started brush fires all across the line of approach of the on rushing soldiers that created great bellowing clouds of dense smoke.

As the Indians emerged through the covering smoke to engage the white men the sounds of firing carbines began to rattle which inflicted the first casualties of the forthcoming battle and set afire several tepees and wounding a half dozen Indians.

* * * * *

Many of Major Reno's troopers had seen their comrades up on the bluffs and wondered what in the hell they were doing up there instead of down in the valley with them. When they saw General Custer waving his hat they all thought it was meant for them, that he was saluting them as they forged ahead and many of them started yelling in appreciation of the gesture. Evidently not understanding the morale boost created among his fast riding troopers, Major Marcus Reno shouted over his shoulder. "You can damn well stop that noise! No need to get excited as you'll have quite enough work to do."

The major's asinine remark soon bore predictive fruit as off in the distance he viewed more hostile Indians coming towards him than he'd ever seen before. Right then some terrible fear of panic gripped Major Reno and he knew he was leading his battalion into a trap. To his left 300 yards, he saw a ditch at least ten yards wide and fairly deep that was teeming with hostiles and to his front mounted Indians were coming out of the smoke and dust. He skidded his big Kentucky breed horse to a halt and raised his right hand over his head, palm up, and fingers splayed. The troops seeing their commander jerking to a halt likewise reined in their mounts in a cloud of dust. Captain's Moylan and French immediately trotted up to Major Reno. Reno greeted the two officers wide eyed but calmly said. "Order your troops to dismount, we are facing a trap and we will set up a skirmish line and fight on foot." Glancing at Captain French, he then said, "Send word back to Captain Wallace and have him join us on line."

It was Lieutenant Benjamin Hodgson who Captain French sent to inform the G Troop commander to dismount his men and prepare to fight on foot.

Captain George D. Wallace, who was no great fan of Reno anyway, sneered, then gave an uncalled for disparaging remark. "What's the matter, that yellow streak of his showing again? We've got the sonsabitches on the run with hardly no opposition, what the hell's the matter with the man?"

Lieutenant Charles DeRudio, who was up front, had an entirely different slant on Major Reno's decision to dismount, and told the major his feelings in a terse comment. "Good for you sir, if we would have went another five hundred yards we'd all been massacred."

Offering a thin smile at Lieutenant DeRudio's compliment, Major Reno began issuing orders. "M Troop to the left along where those prairie dog burrows are at. G Troop to hold the middle and A Troop on the right flank toward that copse of trees leading down to the river. We will try to advance on foot and push the hostiles back to their camp."

* * * * *

Lieutenant Pat Kenzie was not experiencing one of his better days of command. Three times the long poles pulling the assembled Gatling gun had snapped and he was now reduced to reinforcing the broken poles with sapling trees tied around the poles with rope. His prior retort of dragging the Gatling if need be was almost coming true. And the pack mules' carrying the guns .50-caliber ammunition was lagging behind at a painfully slow pace. Luckily, due to the military soldiery smarts of Sergeant Gottlieb, Caisson Sergeant Charlie Clarke carried four clips of ready ammunition as did First Class Private Bill Krier, the guns loader.

* * * * *

First Sergeant Timothy O'Hara gave a warning to his M troopers. "Act lively now lads and direct some of your fire to those heathens trying to get around in back of us."

Private William C. "Billy Two" Slaper was terrified at all the lead flying around him, but his first sergeant's calm demeanor had a settling effect and he pushed back his fear and shifted his position in back of the burrow he was using as a breastwork and took deliberate aim at a Sioux that was not more than 75 yards away. When he fired his carbine the all but naked Indian was violently thrown back as if someone had pushed him, and fell to the ground dead. Slaper immediately took another copper cartridge from his belt and inserted it into the open breach of his single shot carbine.

Private William "Billy One" Morris paused in his firing long enough to offer an encouraging word as his pal loaded his weapon. "That's one redskin that won't be tak'en no more scalps Billy boy!"

His bunkmate's words further settled Billy Two down but he still remarked in a nervous voice. "There's too many of 'em Billy and I'm running low on bullets."

Captain French, who was trooping the line heedless of the increasing volume of gunfire pouring into his position, overheard the two Billie's exchange and offered a quick word. "You boys are doing a bully job. I'll see to it you will get more ammunition."

Private John "Mac" McCullough, hearing his commander make this comment hollered out from behind his prairie dog mound. "While you're at

277

it get some for us too! The horse handlers back there in the trees ain't do'en any shoot'en Cap'tin."

Captain French took the insolent demand in stride and strode quickly back to where Major Reno was at near the middle of the defensive line. "Major Reno sir. My men are getting low on ammunition and some of the carbines are jamming because the extractors are overheating. I sent a couple of my men to our horse handlers to get what bullets they can offer and to rifle the other saddle bags but at our rate of fire we're using them up pretty fast."

Major Reno chewed his upper lip for a moment in concentration before saying anything. "I sent back that cook, Private Mitchell with another message telling Custer we require help. I don't know what's happened to Custer. Varnum said he saw him up on the bluffs with the gray horse troop, but that was twenty minutes ago." Reno paused and stared at Captain French with a pleading look in his eyes. "Well, Tom, what do you think of this?"

Captain French did not waste words in giving his opinion. "We're out numbered and out-gunned so what I think is we had better get out of here."

"I agree Tom," Reno answered. "Have your men pull back to that stand of timber by the river there and I'll inform the others to do the same."

If anything, the Indians were growing bolder and their fire was increasing and becoming more accurate as Captain French made his way back to his company. He called for his first sergeant. "First Sergeant O'Hara! Tell the other officers to move the men back to that clump of trees by the rivers edge."

The first sergeant said calmly, "Very good sor." and took four steps when he was shot dead along with Private Luther "Devil" Higgins whose blood splattered all over Private Calvin Switzer who began shouting hysterically. Mac McCullough grabbed Switzer by his shirt and shook him. "God damn you! Stop that screeching rite now you hear me!" And he shoved Switzer on the ground as Captain French yelled out. "Sergeant Ryan! You are now the acting first sergeant...get these men moving to those trees over there!"

Sergeant John Ryan yelled, "Yes sir," and immediately began to pull men from the skirmish line and point them to the grove of trees.

Billy Slapper was aghast from having seen his first sergeant killed right in front of his eyes. "Oh my gosh Billy! Look at all that blood oozing outta his head. I really liked First Sergeant O'Hara and now he's laying there dead."

Billy One was too scared to be overly sympathetic. "He was a okay fellow sure nough, but like you said, he's dead now and their ain't much we can do about it is there now?"

Billy Two had tears brimming in his eyes and said in a soft voice. "No, I don't suppose there is."

Several of the hundred or so Sioux that had infiltrated around the left flank from the ditch punctuated Billy Two's sad rejoinder with a smattering of rifle fire that splattered the young trooper with loose burrow dirt making him cringe down behind the mound clutching his carbine so tight his fingers were white.

Mac McCullough did not need to be told twice to move back and he quickly got in Private Switzer's face. "Calvin---get yer ass moving rite now." Then the tall slim Texan looked to Private Fritz Neely and the two Billie's. "C'mon boys its time to hightail it outta here."

Private Neely pointed to the limp body of Luther Higgins. "What about Devil," he said almost tearfully.

With the hard logic of a professional soldier First Class Private McCullough gave a harsh reply. "He ain't go'en nowhere Fritz, but you are so get a mov'en!"

* * * * *

General Custer was conferring with scout Mitch Bouyer about a big ravine that appeared to lead down to the river when his adjutant Lieutenant Cooke interrupted the conversation. "Begging the general's pardon sir but a dispatch rider from Major Reno has just arrived and I felt you would want to know about it posthaste, sir."

"That is quite all right Willie. Is it written or oral?" Custer asked.

"Written sir," and Lieutenant Cooke handed over a torn page from a officer's dispatch book.

Custer scanned the hastily scribbled note quickly which read: *Forced to dismount Bn and fight on foot due to overwhelming number of enemy. Running low on ammunition! Require your support NOW!   Reno.* The general turned to Lieutenant Cooke. "Where's the orderly that brought this?"

"He's right here sir," Cooke replied lifting his huge beard and using it as a pointer. "A Private Mitchell sir. You there Mitchell, come forward the general wants a word with you."

The overweight, sallow-faced private nudged his horse, which was obviously worn out as it stepped slowly with its head down. "Trooper Mitchell sir," the private offered, along with a sloppy salute.

Giving the middle-aged man a baleful glare, General Custer said.

"What's the situation down there Mitchell?"

The long time private was not awed to be in the presence of Custer answered the question in the manner of which he saw the situation. "A rite tidy mess for shore if you ask me. More fuck'en Injuns than I ever care to see again and they shore ain't scaret none. Had to ride rite through 'em I did and damn lucky to be heah with my hair on." And as an afterthought added, "Sir."

"Are you telling me Major Reno's command is surrounded?" General Custer asked.

"Shore did seem that way to me gen'ral. 'Bout six of 'em chased me on my way heah and I was so damn scaret Matilda was go'en to fall down I liked to crap my britches, but she got me heah." The bearded trooper patted his panting mares bent neck.

General Custer eyed the vulgar soldier for a long second, and then said. "See to your mount trooper and consider yourself attached to C Troop." Immediately dismissing the man from his thoughts the general spoke to his brother Captain Tom Custer. "Tom, fetch that Sergeant Kanipe of yours and have him carry an oral order to Captain McDougall to bring the pack train straight across country as fast as he can. It appears Major Reno will be needing ammunition forthwith so tell him if any of the packs come loose, to cut them away and hurry on with the remainder."

"I'll take care of it right away general." Captain Custer saluted his brother and went to find Sergeant Kanipe.

Then, thinking out loud General Custer said to no one in particular. "The best way I can help Reno is by relieving the pressure from the hostiles he's under by attacking the enemy camp from the flank." He glanced at Mitch Bouyer. "Mister Bouyer, we were discussing this ravine before the intrusion. You were telling me it goes all the way down to the river. In your opinion would this be a good spot to hit the enemy camp from?"

"Well sir, it's a pretty large Coulee and even though it narrows in spots I don't think you'd have any trouble getting your command down it. From what I remember from being in this area before is you'll find it widens out to a good ford with a big stretch of sandy area where the river has changed its course."

General Custer was quiet for a long moment, and then turned to Lieutenant Algernon Smith, whose Gray Horse Troop E he had been riding with. "Lieutenant Smith, proceed with your Troop down the ravine."

* * * * *

Lonesome Charlie Reynolds handed the half pint flask back to Lieutenant Charles Varnum after having taken a healthy slug of the raw whiskey. "That sorta hits the spot about right now lieutenant and I thank-ye."

The din of 500 boisterous, yelling Indians and their constant rattle of gunfire, coupled with the return carbine fire from Major Reno's battalion, made it difficult for the soft spoken, low voice of the 32 year old legendary scout to be heard. But Lieutenant Varnum took his pocket flask with a smile and turning to Fred Girard, said. "You want another snort Fred?"

The Ree interpreter wiped his mouth with the back of his hand, and then answered. "Don't mind if I do lieutenant. I got me a flask tucked away that we can all share later."

Custer's military chief of scouts handed the flask over, saying. "With the way those sonofabitches are closing in on this timber we may not have a later to share another drink."

Lonesome Charlie Reynolds adjusted one of his three Bowie knives he carried on his gun belt, which was digging into his groin, and he drawled. "Yes, I'd say old Georgie boy has got us in a fine fix this time." His eyes crinkled with a grin on his handsome face.

Just then a heavy volley of shots tore into the trees and underbrush near the area where Doctor Henry Porter was administering what aid he could to a soldier with a stomach wound in a little clump of bushes. The zing of the bullets made Varnum and Girard to lay flat on their bellies since the threesome was just a few feet from where the assistant chief surgeon was working.

But Charlie Reynolds, who was clad in his picturesque fringed buckskins from head to foot, and wearing his wide brimmed sombrero, stood up and cranked off a few rounds with his Winchester. He yelled a warning to Doctor Porter. "Doc! You best find another spot, the bastards got you zeroed in."

The civilian doctor looked up from the dying trooper to say something in return when another volley of hostile fire ripped through the trees and several bullets hit Lonesome Charlie in the upper chest and face. Reynolds dropped instantly and Doctor Porter, Lieutenant Varnum and Fred Girard all scrambled to the prostrate body.

The slightly open, staring blue eyes was all Doctor Porter needed to tell him that General Custer's favorite scout and good friend was dead. Just the same he bent an ear to the bloody chest to see if he could detect a heartbeat. Both Girard and Varnum knew he would not find one. Before the doctor lifted his head Lieutenant Varnum said. "There'll be hell to pay for this: Charlie was almost like a brother to the general."

Doctor Porter raised his head and looked soberly at the two men. "He'll be sorely missed by everyone, especially Captain Marsh, who was even closer to him than General Custer...."

Lieutenant Varnum interrupted anything else the doctor may have wanted to say with an exclamation. "What the hells going on? Did any of you hear a bugle call? Look behind us there at all those mounted troopers. Good God! They're moving out!"

Fred Girard looked nervous. "I ain't heard no trumpet but they're sure as shoot'en pulling out and that's the truth."

Lieutenant Varnum said one word. "Bastard!" And he took off running to the tree where his horse was tied and was mounted before either Fred Girard or Doctor Porter could react.

"Sweet Jesus Doc, we've got to get the hell outta here ourselves!" Girard yelled.

"You go on," the 26 year old, balding, walrus-mustached doctor replied, adding, "I can not leave that fellow alone while he is still alive."

"Suit yourself Doc but I sure as hell ain't go'en to get left heah alone. I wish you luck." Fred Girard left without another word.

* * * * *

Sergeant Adolph Gottlieb, who was riding next to Lieutenant Kenzie as the two senior men helped the crew of Gun #1 practically drag the cumbersome Gatling over the rutted ground with ropes, looked to his front in amazement. Not more than 200 yards distance a mob of blue coated cavalrymen were tearing across the landscape, heading towards the river, while more troopers continued to emerge from a stand of timber further upstream. There seemed to be no order to the mad dash the strung out line of soldiers was making and it appeared to be a panicked rout. Glancing to his lieutenant, Sergeant Gottlieb said in an excited tone of voice. "Was ist los?"

Lieutenant Kenzie was used to his sergeant reverting to his native tongue occasionally, especially when upset, and he yelled at him. "Speak English Adolph! What did you say?"

Like a candle being lit it immediately came to Gottlieb he had blurted out his question in German. "Vhat is going on over their sir?" he pointed a quick finger to the thundering mass of soldiers spurring their horses at full gallop.

* * * * *

Crazy Horse shouted to his Oglalas. "You have them on the run brothers! Chase after them and get many coups as you kill them!"

Seeing this great war leader ride after the fleeing blue coats inspired the warriors of all the various tribes that had been fighting the white devils at the prairie dog village and small grove of trees. With loud whoops and screaming the large number of Indians raised their war clubs and advanced rapidly from the flank to get among the retreating soldiers where they began to knock troopers from their horses. Either by circumstance caused by terror-crazed cavalrymen, or by some unspoken design of battle hardened Indians, Reno's battalion was soon divided into small groups as the Indians closed in on those in the center and rear. There was little fighting on the part of the soldier's, as their entire focus was to stay mounted and get to the river that lay ahead. Fred Girard brought his pony out of the timber just in time to see the Indians running amok among the fleeing cavalrymen and he turned, going back into the stand of trees.

Girard may have made a wise decision because the Indians who felt victorious had but one singular intent; to bring death to these stupid white men who dared to invade their sanctuary. Many warriors used their new Winchester rifles they'd got at various Indian agencies, and when they rode next to a fleeing soldier, they placed their rifle across their body at a level with the trooper's stomachs and pulled the trigger. When the seriously wounded trooper was flung from his mount, the warrior brave would stop long enough to smash the man's face with his war club, sometimes taking a quick scalp, before remounting his pony and pursuing another soldier.

* * * * *

Lieutenant Kenzie realized at once what was taking place, now less than 150 yards away. "Christ Almighty! We can't set up here, we'll be firing right into our own men."

Dropping his rope Sergeant Gottlieb shouted, "I vell ride ahead and tell them to clear us a field of fire!"

Pat Kenzie yelled at Gottlieb in alarm. "Adolph! You are too important on the Gatling. Get someone else to do it."

It took the former German Army officer a couple of seconds to determine who was least valuable for the operation of the Gatling gun and he quickly decided on Corporal Jerry Suttmiller, the limber driver and horse handler and also Private Joe Renforth, the water boy. "I vell order Suttmiller and Renforth lieutenant sir."

Lieutenant Kenzie instantly saw the logic of the sergeant's decision and with a wave of his hand, said. "Do it quickly Adolph, Major Reno is in big trouble up there and he needs us."

* * * * *

Doctor Henry R. Porter's seriously wounded patient died shortly after Fred Girard had taken off. The doctor's military orderly, Private Buford Wishard, had disappeared early on during the defensive phase of the battle, and the doctor had found himself alone and unarmed. Hostile Indians had begun to beat the bush inside the timber looking for surviving soldiers and accompanying the warriors were many Indian women who wanted to put their special touch on any wounded cavalryman still alive and to strip and mutilate the dead. The doctor realized full well the extreme danger he was in and knew his only chance for survival laid in getting away from the small woods. He managed to find his horse without a problem but the powerful black animal was so frightened by the screaming of the Indians and the constant noise of rifle fire, that every time the doctor tried to mount the horse, it would buck and shy away. Doctor Porter knew he would never make it across the expanse of terrain the battalion had followed without his horse so he ended up walking the animal out of the grove of trees hoping the witless beast would let him get on its back out in the open. It did no good. The horse continued to buck and rear as Indians rushed past him not more than ten feet away. A few of the Indians actually laughed at the black-suited man wearing a black bow tie as they tore past, yet unaccountably none slowed down to do him harm or to even shoot at him. Leading his horse like a mad man right in the middle of the Indian attack Doctor Porter walked half way towards the river which was still a good half-mile away with bedlam going on all around him. Once again he paused to see if the animal would accept him. Man and horse did a circling dance, round and around as the surgeon tried to gain a seat. At his wits end Doctor Porter slapped the big horse on its snout as hard as he could and the stunned animal paused long enough for him to get one foot in the stirrup. Before Doctor Porter could swing his other leg over the saddle, the black charger dashed off like the hounds of hell was chasing it. With a great effort the physician finally managed to get astride his horse but that was about it. He had no control whatsoever over the animal who ran the gauntlet through amazed Indians with its low-lying rider hanging onto its mane.

* * * * *

Corporal Jerry Suttmiller and Private Joe Renforth found Lieutenant Varnum trying to rally the men near the bank of the Little Big Horn River. Suttmiller quickly explained the dilemma the Gatling gun crew was faced with in wanting to help the battalion. "You've got to clear the troops outta the way or we can't fire!"

Lieutenant Varnum immediately took it upon himself to order corporals and sergeants to set up their men in a defensive line at the edge of the river where some troopers were already plunging into the water from the high embankment and trying to scramble up the other side and up a tall hill.

Major Reno, who was covered with the blood and brain tissue of the Arikara scout Bloody Knife who was shot next to him in the woods, took offense at Varnum's action. He rode his mount over to the lieutenant, and said in a sharp voice. "Just what in the hell do you think you are doing? I am in command here, not you lieutenant!"

"Sir, these two men are from the Gatling gun and their lieutenant is prepared to give support but is afraid he'll hit our men." Varnum answered in astonishment at the officer's rebuke.

Major Reno had all but forgotten about the lagging Gatling gun but his mind cleared in a flash with Lieutenant Varnum's reminder. "You keep doing what you can and I will fetch some more officers to assist."

* * * * *

At a distance of not quiet a hundred yards Sergeant Gottlieb saw what was taking place ahead. "Mister Kenzie sir, the major's command is setting up a defensive perimeter and is out of harms way from our Gatling except for a few stragglers."

Lieutenant Kenzie noted the line of cavalrymen along the riverbank and although hostiles were pressing on them very close, he gave an instant order. "Head to the near flank of the battalion and employ the gun without further orders."

Sergeant Gottlieb actually smiled when he said. "Yes Mien Herr!" Then he turned to his men. "Action front left oblique one hundred meters. Engage gun as soon as we stop!"

Private Jim Wade turned in his saddle to loader First Class Private Bill

Krier. "What the hell is a hundred meters...I wish that sonsabitch would speak English!"

The salty loader and Civil War veteran Bill Krier shouted a terse answer. "It can't be damn fur 'cause we're on top of 'em rite now, or they're on top of us, depending on how you look at it."

* * * * *

Crazy Horse saw the group of mounted soldiers pulling the wheeled weapon, which appeared at first glance to be one of the pony soldiers' boom guns. But it didn't have the large hole in the front barrel like a boom gun had, which he had seen before while a prisoner at the white mans fort. It looked like it had a number of rifle barrels sticking out of the front of it and without ever having seen one before Crazy Horse knew this had to be the dreaded thunder stick Fast-as-the-Pony-Rides had told him about. Shouting to those warriors near him Crazy Horse yelled. "Kill those soldiers with the boom gun, do not let them reach the river!"

But it was too late.

* * * * *

The well-drilled and excellent trained Gatling gun crew went quickly to their stations as soon as the Gatling gun came to a halt. There was nothing to set up except to place a clip of .50 caliber bullets into the ammunition slot and Bill Krier had that done in an instant. Corporal Stacey Henry was all ready sitting on the gunners seat with one hand poised on the firing lever looking up expectantly at his spotter Sergeant Gottlieb who stood by the right wheel.

Somewhat annoyed Sergeant Gottlieb yelled. "Don't vate on me dumiasle they're right in front of you, FIRE!

Corporal Henry immediately began to slowly turn the crank of his weapon.

* * * * *

Sioux and Cheyenne warriors could hardly believe what happened to them. The front elements of the charging Indians were no more than a hundred feet from the soldiers when the thunder stick they'd all heard about commenced firing. Fifty warriors were knocked violently from their ponies in an instant; horses barely had time to make a snorting screech before they and their riders lay dead or seriously wounded in a mangled heap.

* * * * *

"Get some more funk'en clips up here rite now!" Screamed number two ammunition carrier Private Harold B. "Holly" Stratton.

Sergeant Charlie Clarke, the caisson NCO, who was unloading the pack mules carrying additional bullet filled clips, yelled back "Suttmiller will have 'em to ya in a second!"

As Waterman/Oilier Private Tom Tsarff poured a bucketful of water on the breach mechanism that raised a cloud of steam as it sizzled on the hot steel, Ready man Private Will Garvin handed over to Loader Private Krier, the last available clip. The Gattling gun stuttered to a stop as Corporal Henry got off a last shot and Krier quickly took out the empty clip, tossing it to the ground, and replacing it with the one just handed him by Garvin.

"There's still a bunch of fuck'en heathens out there," Corporal Henry said calmly, "What about more clips?"

Garvin turned his head to where Wade and Stratton was coming up with armloads of fresh clips, and said. "Keep cranking corporal, they's more on the way."

Lieutenant Kenzie was reduced to doing little more than yelling encouragement to his men who were operating the gun with the best efficiency he'd ever seen. He did have his revolver out and if for no other reason than wanting to join the fight "Killer Kid" Kenzie, would occasionally fire a few shot at the charging hoard.

Major Reno was likewise doing little more than cheering on his men and yelling at them not to pay attention to the Gatling but to keep firing at the hostiles with their rifles.

Private Billy Slapper spoke loudly to his bunkmate Billy Morris over the din of gunfire. "Not much to shoot at with the way that Gatling has cleared the field. Look at them Indjun's skedaddling!"

What Billy Two had observed was true enough. Over 150 Indians lay dead on the ground in front of where Major Reno's men laid in hastily scooped out firing pits at the top of the river embankment. Among the dead Indians were Black Face, Still Water and Bright Face, all three whom had seen the power of the Gatling gun in action before, but bravely faced its destructive power anyway.

Crazy Horse had little difficulty in convincing his fellow warriors to leave the thunder stick alone, and to fall back and fire at the soldiers from a distance.   Reluctantly, the Sioux and Cheyenne moved back out of the effective range of the terrible weapon that had wrought so much death among their friends. Chief Gall was so upset about the stalemate that he tore at his hair. But Crazy Horse knew there were other fish to fry and while many of his comrades snipped away at Reno's men, the fearsome warrior chief rode back towards the village.

Trumpeter John Martin (Martini)

Chapter 44

The Little Big Horn River, Montana Territory
Afternoon, Sunday, June 25, 1876

General George Custer gazed across the Little Big Horn River from a sand spit leading to a natural ford. His five companies of cavalry were strung all up and down the coulee from the ridge bluff above to the two companies down by the water. Custer had split his detachment again, this time into two wings. He and his staff went with Captain George Yate's F Troop, whom Custer had placed in command and Lieutenant Algernon Smith's E Troop. Veteran cavalry Captain Myles Keogh was in charge of the other three companies, which consisted of his own I Troop, along with C and L Troops. Having made their way along the gentle sloping ravine to the bottom the Gray Horse Troop and Captain Yates F Troop were staged at the bottom and spread along the river bank staring along with their commander at the biggest Indian village any of them had ever seen. Those troopers stuck along the sloping trail leading down to the river were apprehensive as they kept hearing noises of movement to their left as they faced ahead to the river.

Directly across from General Custer was a pony herd of at least 1000 animals grazing on a huge natural meadow. To his left, and what appeared to be the northern end of the hostile encampment, the valley floor was covered with teepees as far as the eye could see. Custer realized the village was even larger but a bend in the river concealed view of the rest of the Indian camp. The two company elements had made their descent without opposition, but that fortunate event was about to change as Custer noted hundreds of hostiles gathering in an open horseshoe area between the rows and circles of lodges. This open area where the Indians appeared to be mustering was not unlike a parade field, or so Custer thought. Shaking his head in wonderment, the balding, blond haired cavalry leader now understood what the leader of the Crow scouts, Half-Yellow-Face, was trying to tell him earlier when he said there were more Sioux than his men had bullets on their belts.

Seeing the cloud of dust in the Indian camp grow denser as more Sioux mounted ponies in preparation to meet his command, George Custer looked to his right and in a loud voice, said. "Sergeant Major Sharrow!"

"Yes sir, right here sir!" The tall regimental sergeant major bellowed and nudged his big horse closer to the general.

"Have my orderly-trumpeter report to me at once."

"Yes sir!" Sergeant Major Sharrow looked around quickly and spotted Trumpeter John Martini behind the generals Color Sergeant. "You their Martin," the sergeant major yelled, using the young Italian's Americanized last name. The trumpeter looked directly at his sergeant major. "Come here now!"

General Custer spoke slowly to his orderly to make sure he understood what he was telling him. "You find Captain Benteen lad and tell him to get here fast with the pack train as we need all the spare ammunition we can get. Do you understand me son?"

The olive faced young man nodded his head and gestured with his hand as he answered. "Yes general Custer sir...plez to find Capitana Bent'teen, tell hom to bring mules with bullets fast. Ah...we need them."

"Sir, let me write a note," Adjutant William Cooke said. "That may be too much for him to remember."

"Very well," Custer answered, "But make it fast and tell Benteen we've found a big village."

Cooke tore open his little notebook instead of the large field order folder and began a hasty scribble. When he was done writing he glanced at the scrawl to make sure it was readable: *Benteen. Come on. Big village. Be quick. Bring packs. W. W. Cooke. P.S. Bring packs.* Cooke shrugged his shoulders. It wasn't the best field message he ever wrote but at least it got the general's point across. Handing the small slip of paper to Trumpeter Martini, he said. "You tell Captain Benteen what you can remember, but make sure you also give him this. If possible, you report back to me after delivering the order. Now don't waste anytime... leave right now!"

Taking the note and folding it, placing it in his tunic pocket, the trumpeter said, "Yes sir," and attempted to give a good salute that he had been practicing. The salute still came off like an European style of military courtesy with palm of the hand out but Lieutenant Cooke was accustomed to this, having served in the Canadian army, and didn't give it a second thought, returning the salute with a brush of his hat.

Martini spurred his horse back up the coulee just as the Sioux and Cheyenne charged towards the new threat.

* * * * *

Doctor Henry Porter considered it a miracle he had reached Major Reno's battalion alive. His black stallion's powerful legs had flown over the ground at a frenzied pace and before reaching friendly lines the stalwart surgeon actually passed some of those who had left the timber before him. The retreat to the river had turned into a rout and it was every man for himself. If a man's horse got shot it was certain death for the thrown rider. One such incident was the black interpreter Isaiah Dorman, whom Doctor Porter passed by in a rush. Dorman was on one knee firing his hunting rifle behind his dead horse at the ten to fifteen dismounted Indians closing in on him. Doctor Porter's stampeding steed startled the hostiles for a moment that gave Dorman time to give a final greeting. "Goodbye Doctor Porter, it was nice knowing you."

Now in the new defensive position with the lines more or less stabilized, Doctor Porter found himself busier than he had ever experienced before in his career. The only other surgeon that had been with Reno's command was Doctor James De Wolf, who was killed trying to climb the bluff in back of the newly established river defensive line. So Doctor Porter had little choice than to deal with the more than 50 wounded, some of them with serious wounds and some of them obviously dying.

Among those with serious wounds was senior Private John G. "Mac" McCullough, who had made it to the river with a shattered, left leg due to the heroics of Private Calvin Switzer. The young private saw Mac's horse go down in front of him and though six mounted Sioux was hot on his tail, Switzer paused long enough to yell at the wounded senior private to grab hold a stirrup, and dragged Mac to safety. Now, however, Doctor Porter had some bad news to tell Mac. "Private, your leg is so mangled that there is nothing I can do to save it. Gangrene will most surely set in which will eventually kill you and I have to tell you, that is a most unpleasant death."

"I reckon I've seen what gangrene can do to a man Doc during the War of the Rebellion and I also reckon I know what the cure is. What you're try'en ta tell me is its got ta come off----rite?" Mac asked with a thin grin.

"Why yes, that is correct private." Doctor Porter was rather stunned at the soldiers understanding and acceptance at his diagnosis.

"What ya got to put me out Doc?" Mac wanted to know.

Doctor Porter gave Mac an honest answer. "The only thing I can offer you is a bottle of medical brandy."

The happy go lucky Texan squinted an eye at the surgeon. "A whole bottle?"

"Yes, I was able to salvage several half-quarts, and I'll give you a full measure."

This time the lanky old time private's face lit up in a wide grin. "Hell doc, for a full quart you can take off the other leg as well."

* * * * *

Trumpeter Martini rode swiftly atop the long bluff passing Major Reno's detachment in the valley below as he went, noting with mild interest the fighting going on but not grasping the defensive posture the cavalrymen were in. It was near three-thirty in the afternoon when the young Italian saw a rider approaching him. At first Martini thought it might be a hostile Indian since several had taken pot shots at him since he'd started out with the general's message. He halted his horse and unsheathed his carbine to defend himself, then noticed the shock of blond hair on the rider's uncovered head.

Boston Custer checked his horse as he neared the cavalryman and then recognized the man as one of his brother's trumpeters. "Where's the General?"

Martini turned in his saddle to point in the direction he had just ridden, saying "He be back there ready to fight the Sioux. Right behind that next ridge you find him"

"Thanks. Where are you going?" Boston Custer asked.

"I take message to Captain Bent'teen from the general. Have you by chance seen him?"

"Yes I have----he's only a few miles back of me down on the lower part of the valley"

"Where you come from?" The trumpeter asked.

"I was with the pack train and wanted to be in for the kill...and I best be going if I'm going to be with the general in time for it." The younger brother of George Custer waved his hand, spurred his horse, and was away in a cloud of dust.

* * * * *

"Should we set up the gun?" Shouted Sergeant Frederick Heidenreich, Gun Sergeant of Gun #3 to Lieutenant William Hale Low.

For the past twenty minutes the two gun section of the Gatling platoon had fought on foot near the top of the large swale while the two companies of cavalry extracted themselves inch by inch to get out of the ravine that had taken them to the river. When the Indians sprung their trap by having infiltrated alongside the soldiers, using other smaller coulees and cuts to conceal their position, a degree of bedlam had occurred among General Custer's troops. When the Sioux and Cheyenne opened fire from the flanks down upon the cavalrymen, a massive charge from the village took place simultaneously and screaming Indians started splashing their way across the river.

Lieutenant Low looked around quickly and saw that the cavalrymen were mounting their horses amid the roar of continued Indian rifle fire and screeching. "No. I don't think so, at least not here. We'll have to wait until they make a solid stand of some sort as we don't want to be left all by ourselves."

First Sergeant Steiner, who had suffered a slight grazing arrow wound to his upper right arm, agreed. "Let's get 'em mounted up sir and join those boys pulling out toward that ridge up yonder."

The ridge Gus Steiner was referring to was above the tableland that split into a Y with a wide depression deep ravine to the northwest and a large narrow coulee branching off to the other side. This ridge is where Captain Keogh had already established a defensive position.

"Gus," Lieutenant Low yelled, "The general's heading to the left with those two companies toward the wide cut. I'll take Sergeant Evans gun and go with him; you take Sergeant Heidenreich's gun and head for Captain Keogh."

With a wave of his hand First Sergeant Steiner gave his understanding of his commander's order.

Eagle eyed Captain Thomas B. Weir, Commander of D Troop, spotted Trumpeter Martini when the message carrier was still a mile off. The gangly captain who wore a thick black mustache called out behind him in a loud voice to Captain Benteen. "Rider coming in!"

Benteen spurred his big bay from a trot to a canter and rode up to Captain Weir. "Yes, I see him. He's wearing army blue, what do you make of it, a dispatch rider?"

Weir, who had no great fondness for Benteen, gave a small sneer when he gave a sarcastic reply. "From the way he's beating that poor damn pony I'd say as sure I squat to shit he's in one hell a hurry about something."

The bug-eyed senior captain glared at his junior officer with a quick glance but did not say anything about his rude, vulgar retort. Captain Benteen did keep his detachment of three troops moving toward the fast moving rider at a trot and it only took a little under three minutes for the out of breath Martini to skid to a dust raising halt in front of the battalion.

Martini knew who Captain Benteen was and prodded his mount to the side of the captain's big bay. Offering another unusual salute the trumpeter said. "Captaina Bent'teen, I have message from General Custer that I am to give to you."

"Very well, hand it over." The impatient captain glared at the trumpeter.

Martini fumbled at his tunic pocket to get at the note Adjutant Cooke had written while at the same time trying to offer an oral report. "General Custer, he say you come fast wit de packs and he tell me to tol you this." Before Captain Benteen could open his mouth to berate the not so smart trumpeter, Martini found the note and handed it over. "Here is note Lieutenant Cooke give to me."

After reading the short note Benteen handed it to Captain Weir with the comment. "You will note the great manner in which our regimental adjutant writes filed orders...didn't even date or time the damn thing."

When Weir handed back the note without comment, Captain Benteen then said in a disgusted tone of voice. "What the hell's wrong with Custer? This is the second time in an hour he's asked me to bring up the pack train. Doesn't he even remember whom in the hell it was he put in charge of the damn thing? Christ almighty! If I would have followed his orders to the letter I'd still be off up in the canyons on a wild goose chase. If it wasn't for that long rattle of gunfire we heard earlier which made me decide to turn back north, this idiot here never would have found us."

A little too smugly, Captain Weir said. "Perhaps General Custer knew you would come to the sound of musketry."

Not catching the sarcasm, Benteen offered. "Humph, perhaps but doubtful." Then looking at Martini he said. "Did you know your horse has been shot boy?"

Martini was dumbfounded at the question and stuttered, "N...No...No sir," and dismounted to find his pony bleeding from a wound in its neck.

While the trumpeter worked on his mounts bullet wound Lieutenant Edward Godfrey, Commander of K Troop, Lieutenant Luther Hare and Lieutenant Winfield Edgerly rode up to see what was going on and Benteen let them read the note also. Captain Benteen discussed the note after all three had read it. "Cooke's got it wrong somehow. A minute ago I bad mouthed Custer for not knowing whom in the hell was in charge of the pack train but after thinking it over he knows its McDougall. Now there's no way he wants us to turn around and fetch the pack train because he knows McDougall is bringing them up." He paused for a second a glanced at Martini who had got the blood flow stopped on his pony with a mud and grass bandage. "You there, trumpeter! What's taking place up front there with General Custer?"

"Oh the general, he getting ready to make beeg attack on Indian village when he sent me to you. The Indians, they skedaddling and the general, he going to go after them." As an after thought Martiti quickly added. "And

Major Reno, he all ready in beeg fight."

The orderlies answer further confused Captain Benteen as well as the other officers. Benteen voiced his thoughts out loud, which was more or less the same thoughts his other officers were mulling over. "Now that adds sauce to the turkey. If Custer has commenced an attack already, he couldn't use the packs if they were right in front of him. Something's haywire here somewhere. The only sense I can get out of all this, if Custer is engaged with a strong force of Sioux he's going to need every man he can get. This fellow also said Reno was engaged in a fight when he left Custer. That tells me Custer's split the command or there's something going on we don't know about. Hey orderly, yes you there...How far away do you figure the general is?"

Martini took a long time before answering and even went so far as using his fingers to make his calculations. "It took me maybe forty minutes to find you Captaina Bent'teen sir."

"Forty minutes huh? Well that could be anywhere from five to fifteen miles gentlemen. Lieutenant Hare, place this boy with your men and lets all get going at a half gallop." Captain Benteen moved his horse forward as he spoke.

* * * * *

The plains Indians were for the most part extremely ferocious combat fighters with no quarter asked, or expected, and certainly none given. They were a savage, bloodthirsty lot and unequaled in their style of warfare. The primary flaw when engaged in battle was a lack of a solid command structure. Sioux and Cheyenne warriors had their own warrior societies with chiefs and sub-chiefs in a loose, if not honorary positions of leadership. The main problem was these warriors relying on their individual bravery to defeat an enemy instead of any coordinated effort of attack. The idea of anyone leading them into combat did not mean that they would take orders from that person, but rather the warrior chief in question was showing his courage by being out in front. Sometimes though, an individual chief had so much respect, daring and charisma, that it gave him the opportunity to rally his comrades to greater feats of gallantry. This was the case of the great warrior chief Crazy Horse.

When Crazy Horse rode back from the Reno fight he had a comparatively small number of warriors riding with him. However, as he rode upstream past groups of confused Indians that milled around not knowing whether to stay and guard the village their women were dismantling or to go fight the white devils. Crazy Horse's repeated battle cry gave them the direction they needed. "Today is a good day to fight, today is a good day to die: cowards to the rear, brave hearts follow me-----hear me warriors: Today is a good day to fight and to die! Only brave hearts follow me...cowards fall back to the rear and stay with the women!"

By the time Crazy Horse splashed across the ford and up the long coulee heading east in pursuit of the withdrawing soldiers, he had nearly a thousand warriors crowding behind him.

Other Indians were on foot traversing up a dozen gullies or already out in the open near the soldiers sniping at them from behind sagebrush hillocks, drawing closer to Custer and his men with each passing minute.

* * * * *

Sergeant Adolph Gottlieb was beginning to get very upset at Major Reno's lack of understanding. The five or six hundred Indians his Gatling gun had chased away were now dismounted and creeping back towards the defensive position from both the front and north river bank. They would raise their heads for only a moment from concealment to take a shot at the soldiers. Hiding themselves again effectively they'd wait a few seconds and make a short dash and move nearer to the soldiers. Major Reno's only plan to thwart the renewed hostile assault was to move his men away from the river up the high hill to where the wounded had already been taken.

The former German army officer voiced his displeasure to his leader Lieutenant Pat Kenzie. "Vee cannot get our Gatling up that hill assembled! And even if vee dismantle it again I do not believe the animals would make it. Vhat is the matter with this major? He should protect our gun but he is pulling all his men away. This is wrong! I say to you sir, if we are left alone we will be killed one by one. My men are brave and vell stand and fight but it would be better to abandoned the gun than let them die for nothing."

Lieutenant Kenzie knew of his sergeant's previous life as an officer in the Imperial German Army and had great respect for his judgment. "You are correct sergeant and I shall go talk to him."

The talk turned out to be an argument and any fondness Major Reno may have held for Kenzie, whom he thought an ally, soon turned sour with his adamant, almost hysterical refusal to listen to common sense. "Our position at the river is untenable," Reno shrieked, "I am not going to loose the remainder of my command to protect your gun. If you cannot move it up the bluff then destroy it and deploy your men as infantry!"

"You wouldn't have a command at all if it wasn't for my Gatling," Kenzie shouted back. "I've already lost one man dead and the Indians are getting closer all the time. I'm telling you with proper support you don't have to worry about digging in up here, we can lick them down there!"

Major Reno's face was beet red and contorted in near rage. "How dare you talk to me like that-----I will have your commission at a court-martial! You will either do as I have ordered you...."

Major Reno's rebuke was interrupted by the not too far distant blare of a trumpet call sounding Coming In. "What was that?" Reno looked to his left that was south.

The major had no sooner asked his question when a cheer went up from the troopers manning the hastily scooped out rifle pits along the crest of the hill. A Troop commander, Captain Myles Moylan, who was standing a few yards from where Major Reno and Lieutenant Kenzie had been going at it, shouted out. "It's Benteen and his command!"

Major Reno forgot all about the argument he had been having with Lieutenant Kenzie and dashed down the hill to the rivers edge yelling, "Where's my horse?"

An excited and agitated Major Reno rode out to meet Captain Benteen.

Seeing his former tent mate tearing toward him Captain Benteen shook his head back and forth once, and then glanced at Lieutenant Ed Godfrey and Lieutenant Winfield Edgerly. "He's sure got a burr under his saddle about something. Reckon I best ride out to meet him." And he spurred his horse to a full gallop.

Benteen was still 40 yards away when Major Reno began shouting. "For God's sake, Benteen, halt your command and help me. I've lost half my men already and there's thousands of Indians all over the place."

The gap between the two officers quickly closed and Benteen was at Reno's side in a matter of seconds. In a calm voice Captain Benteen said, "Steady yourself old bean, I'm not going anywhere just yet. What's this about thousands of Indians and where's Custer?"

Major Marcus Reno started explaining to the white, curly-haired captain what his three companies had been through.

* * * * *

Captain Myles Keogh looked northwest across the deep ravine from a small hill or knoll above the ridge he was on and wondered to himself what in the hell was Custer doing over there on a bluff a mile away. Keogh had dismounted Captain Tom Custer's C Troop, now led by Lieutenant Henry Harrington, and placed them along the hill in a skirmish line while holding the other two companies behind the knoll in reserve. His position was beginning to be hard pressed by the hostile Indians coming up the coulee that was his southern flank and he couldn't figure out if Custer was waiting for him to make a move or what. The long time cavalry captain knew one thing for certain: that he could sure use Custer's help because the Sioux and Cheyenne were coming up the coulee like a thousand ants carrying grains of sand. Only these ants were armed with rifles, captured carbines, bows and arrows and revengeful hate. Realizing he could waste no more time in speculation on what General Custer was up to, Captain Keogh called for his orderly. "Tell Lieutenant Calhoun I want L Troop to get down in the coulee and get those Indians away from us."

The young private orderly saluted with a "Yessir," and went to find L Troops commander.

The Cheyenne war chief, Lame White Man, was more than aggravated at his warriors. He could not believe they had scattered like blowing leaves when the white soldiers had scrambled down into the gully and began shooting their toy rifles. Lame White Man faced the soldiers who were on foot from atop his horse and yelled to those fleeing past him. "You are acting like women! Come.... we can kill all of them! I will lead---follow me!" He nudged his pony toward the 40 or so dismounted cavalrymen who were desperately trying to clear out the coulee.

Other war chiefs took up Lame White Man's battle cry and the before display of timidity in the face of the despised soldiers shifted to a more courageous stance. However, only the braver ones remained on their ponies, exposing themselves to the enemy gunfire. Most of the Indians started back up the coulee by making short, pre-planned dashes; waiting for a couple of minutes, them moving forward again, firing their weapons or launching arrows as they went.

The weapon firing became intense in the coulee and both sides suffered many causalities. Naturally this had an effect on the Indians but there was so many more of them crowded in the wide, sloping upward gulch, than the 41 cavalrymen of L Troop that was soon down to around 19 effectives. When one Indian would fall or become wounded, another went past him to take his place. Such was the case with sixteen-year old Standing Bear, who was out to get his second feather as a Sioux warrior. The young Miniconjou was riding up the coulee to join the fight when a Lakota passed by him with blood pouring from his mouth that dripped in a steady flow on to his pony's shoulders. The seriously wounded Indian could barely talk but he managed to voice a message to the teenage warrior. "My name is Long Elk. When you take a white mans scalp, you tell him my name."

Standing Bear answered. "I will avenge you Long Elk and say to the pony soldier just before I kill him that his death is from your hands."

With bent head Long Elk raised a feeble hand in salute to the youngster's tribute.

Captain Keogh knew he was in serious trouble and knew he wasn't going to get any help from Custer who's two troops were now engaged in fighting for their own lives across the deep ravine. Looking around wildly the captain screamed out to no one in particular. "Where's that fucking Gatling gun battery?"

First Sergeant Gustavus Steiner looked up sharply from where he was helping Sergeant Heidenreich, Corporal Quintana and Private Wells lift the barrel assembly out of the stretcher sling between the tow horses. Glancing at Sergeant Heidenreich the first sergeant said. "I'll stay with you to get it on the cradle, then go see what he wants."

Heidenreich nodded his head in understanding.

Ready man, Private Earl Watts was holding upright one wheel as Oilier Private Fred Thompson held the other. The strong as an ox Caisson Sergeant, Sergeant Kenneth Jackson balanced the heavy axle in his hands all by himself while Water boy Private Richard Baum and Ammunition Carrier Private Paul Craver fitted the wheels to the axle.

Captain Keogh roared again. "Son of a bitch---where's that Gatling gun?"

Sergeant Heidenreich yelled to Private Craver who had got his wheel secured on the axle. "Craver, get your ass over here and relieve the first sergeant so he can go see what that loud mouth is screaming about."

First Sergeant Steiner offered Heidenreich a half smile when the sergeant winked at him and as soon as Private Craver took hold of the heavy Gatling barrel he took off rubbing his arm where the arrow had got him.

As soon as both wheels were attached to the axle Sergeant Jackson then drug the equally heavy gun trail with affixed seat to the axle and worked the base plate into place over the six holes in the axle to match the six holes in the steel plate. Ammunition Carrier Private Wallace Yakey was waiting with six bolts that he slammed through the holes and seated them with a whack of a small sledgehammer. Yakey then got down on the ground and began working large washers and nuts onto the protruding bolts from the underside.

With no lost motion, while Yakey was still tightening the nuts with a gun wrench Sergeant Jackson, along with Water boy Private Richard Baum fitted the weighted cradle with the drilled hole in its center onto the axle plate of the gun trail making sure the hole matched the one centered on the axle. As soon as the cradle was in place the four men gently but quickly lowered the barrel system of the Gatling gun down on the cradle, easing the shiny steel rod at the bottom through the holes in the cradle and axle. When the barrel was seated Yakey shoved bolt pins through the hole on the protruding steel rod and secured them with cotter couplings. The Gatling gun was assembled.

In a less agitated tone of voice but still carrying a bite of irritation, Captain Keogh was saying to First Sergeant Steiner. "You're telling me the Gatling cannot be depressed low enough to fire down into that coulee?"

"Can't be done captain," First Sergeant Steiner replied. "If we placed the gun up at the head of that rise where it comes out of the gully we could kill them as they made their way up out of it or if they tried climbing over the edge, but not down into the thing."

Keogh pulled downward on his huge mustache for a moment in a worrying gesture as he viewed General Custer's brother-in-law, Lieutenant James Calhoun, come out of the coulee with his second in command Lieutenant John J. Crittenden, and a handful of surviving troopers. Lieutenant Calhoun was bleeding from a shoulder wound and two uninjured troopers were helping Second Lieutenant Crittenden along as he held his stomach with both hands. Having been temporarily distracted seeing the remains of his shattered company, this emotion came to an instant stop when yelling Indians waving blankets, and shooting rifles rode out of the coulee and headed towards the horse handlers behind the knoll. "My God! They're trying to get the horses!" He shouted.

Gus Steiner swung his head around and saw the group of Indians rushing to the cavalry horses being held by five or six troopers. He knew the horse handlers didn't stand a chance and even before the hand-to-hand fighting began, he yelled in a loud voice to Captain Keogh. "Right where you're standing is where we're going to fight and die, so you better get the remainder of your companies set up in some kind of a defensive perimeter!"

Stunned by the ordering outburst of an enlisted man, who had already started running back to his Gatling gun, Captain Keogh faced the reality of Steiner's words like a splash of cold water hitting him in the face. As if awakened from a nightmare the captain screamed to his trumpeter. "Blow Assemble On Me quick! Do you hear me? Do it NOW!"

The dry mouthed private placed his trumpet to his lips and after a false, screeching start, paused for half a second then blared out the rapid toned melody.

* * * * *

Captain Frederick Benteen may have had a lousy personality when dealing with his fellow officers but the curly, gray haired, cherubic faced man with a lispy voice, sure as hell was an organizer with a steady hand and gutsy demeanor. Within a short time after his arrival at Major Reno's defensive outpost, Benteen, for all intent and purpose, was essentially in charge and running both his command and Reno's.

Major Reno continued to troop the line and had a word or two to say here and there, but for the most part he allowed Benteen to have a free hand to run things as he pleased. One of the first items Captain Benteen took care of was to solve the problem of Sergeant Gottlieb's Gatling gun when Major Reno and Lieutenant Kenzie renewed their bickering over the disposition of the heavy weapon. Benteen's solution was simple. He ordered the senior non-commissioned officers to round up 50 troopers, and with a dozen horses tied to the gun with rope, virtually had the Gatling gun dragged and manhandled up the steep slope after getting it down the steep embankment of the river and up the other side. A reasonably flat spot was found near the northern edge of the rocky hill and the Gatling gun was dug in and positioned with its trail higher than the barrel, which meant it could fire down onto the valley below. A loud cheer had erupted from the besieged cavalrymen from their skirmish line up and around the hill when Corporal Stacey Henry was ordered to test fire a clip of ammunition in the direction of the hostile village. A cheer went up from the line when several tepees began burning.

The test firing had so frightened those Indians sniping at the soldiers from below that many of them retreated back to their village. This bit of luck helped several white men who were still alive across the river in the timber Major Reno had made his hasty retreat from. Lieutenant DeRudio, Sergeant O'Neill, Fred Girard and William Jackson, made a dash for it on Girard's and William's horses after the Gatling gun scared warriors and squaws out of the woods who had been combing the area for wounded cavalrymen.

The test firing of the Gatling had also caused a perplexing situation. Corporal Henry had barely got the last shot off when a faint echoing response was heard. Many troopers thought it was just that, an echo resounding off the bluffs while others swore it was a volley of carbines being shot which was the distress signal calling for immediate assistance in the

United States Cavalry.

Sergeant Gottlieb, with the backing of Lieutenant Kenzie, settled most discussions about the strange event when Gottlieb said. "Das ist a Gatling gun firing rapid fire."

* * * * *

The sustained rate of fire Sergeant Gottlieb and other members of the Reno/Benteen defense had heard was not carbines firing in volley as a distress signal as some thought. Although there was much distress on the long grassy rolling ridge between the deep ravine and sloping coulee where Captain Keogh's three companies were being slaughtered, Gottlieb had been correct that the steady rhythm chug, chug, sound transmitting five miles from him was in fact Gun #3 in action.

By the time First Sergeant Steiner had ran the thirty yards to where Sergeant Heidenreich's ready and manned Gatling gun was positioned, Custer's brother-in-law, Lieutenant James Calhoun, and his few remaining men of L Troop, were all dead or dying atop the small hill they had ran to after getting out of the coulee. There had been little chance for Calhoun's cavalrymen to respond to the trumpet call Captain Myles Keogh ordered, and while some of them attempted to traverse the several hundred yards to Keogh's position, it was futile. Mounted Indians galloped among the terrified troopers, counting coup by bashing heads with war clubs. When a soldier went down, a warrior brave would reel his pony around, leap from his mount, jump on top of the wounded white man with an ear piercing yell and begin tearing at the cavalryman's scalp with a long knife that was sometimes not that sharp. Sioux and Cheyenne warriors would do these deeds heedless of the other soldiers but a few feet away fighting for their own lives. Private Elmer Babcock was able to use his revolver and kill four Indians who had dismounted to take scalps. However, in the close quarter melee of hand-to-hand combat, the swarming Indians had the advantage and Babcock and his friend Private Francis Hughes, went down together, back to back, under the fierce onslaught. Other troopers were reduced to using their jammed carbines as clubs but there was too many Indians and the few whacks these soldiers managed to get in came to late to save their lives. In the dim pall of rolling black smoke created by cavalry carbines and a variety of Indian rifles, the warrior Yellow Nose snatched L Companies guidon which was stuck in the ground and rode off with a triumphant yell, waving the dove-tailed miniature American flag high over his head.

Captain Keogh's two companies shared a similar fate. While attempting to heed the trumpet call to assemble on their commander, the once scattered troops of C and I Troops found themselves bunched together in a low bowl area down from the small ridge above where the hostiles had pressed them. This made it a lot easier for the marauding Indians to kill them.

Captain Myles Keogh watched his big reddish-brown horse Comanche tear across the battlefield in fleeing panic and for a brief moment wished he was on top his faithful mounts back. But he had too many other things to think about and this bit of minute musing vanished as quickly as it had occurred. With a brave heart he reloaded his empty Colt revolver while muttering a small prayer that God would allow him to take six savages with him as he departed this life.

When reaching the Gatling gun First Sergeant Steiner's first order startled Horse Handler/Driver Corporal William Beck for a moment. "You and Thompson get the horses and mules in a ring around the gun and shoot them!"

"Shoot them?" Corporal Beck questioned in astonishment.

"Beck we ain't got time to fuck around, you heered what I said: shoot the animals so we can use 'em for breastworks." Gus Steiner said in a deadly voice.

Sergeant Heidenreich knew exactly what his first sergeant was getting at and yelled an order to two of his men. "Craver, Yakey, get all the packs off the mules, dump the ammo on the ground and fill the packs with dirt and set them in places between the horses and mules."

Caisson Sergeant, Sergeant Kenneth Jackson also realized the seriousness of Steiner's order and went to help Beck and Fred Thompson lead the ten horses and nine mules in a circle around the Gatling gun.

One by one the animals were shot in the head with revolvers as soon as a spot was selected. Some of the younger members of the gun crew had tears in their eyes seeing the horses and mules fall down in a heap, their limbs shaking in gruesome death throes. Water boy Private Richard Baum asked a question to no particular person. "How are we going to get out of here, and get the gun out of here without the horses and mules?"

Sergeant Heidenreich took it upon himself to provide a ready answer. "Son, you're going to be damn lucky if you walk outta here with your hair still on."

The eighteen-year old boys face blanched a sickly white and he asked no more questions.

First Sergeant Steiner effectively got their minds off seeing the animals killed. "Get your carbines and pistols ready so you can defend the position. You are going to have to man the gun and fight at the same time so make no mistakes boys. When someone gets hit I don't want to see anybody trying to tend his wounds until I tell ya. And I expect everyone to pitch in and do all the jobs on the gun when needed."

Steiner barely got his comment out of his mouth when Gunner Corporal Jesus Quintana who was straddling the Gatling on its trail seat, spoke in a loud, yet calm tone of voice. "Here they come, make sure we got a bunch of full clips ready to go."

Several of Captain Keogh's troopers had broke out of the depression and was running toward the Gatling gun in a desperate attempt to find some kind of safe haven. It was to no avail as hundreds of vicious Indians rode them down and either shot them or clubbed them to death. Warriors who had not been fortunate enough to have killed the half dozen or so soldiers who had ran away like crazy men, now focused their attention to the small group of white eyes that half crouched around a strange looking gun with wheels behind a circle of dead horses. The victorious Indians were now worked up to a frenzy. With irrational screaming fifty Sioux and Cheyenne kicked their ponies to charge the white men at a mad dash while other Indians ran at them on foot.

Sergeant Heidenreich lightly tapped Corporal Quintana on his right shoulder and in a fatherly like, hushed tone, said. "Okay Junior, you can open fire on them any time you like."

Corporal Jesus E. Quintana smiled a rare smile when he started cranking the firing lever. It was the first time his sergeant had ever addressed him by his nickname.

* * * * *

During the same time Captain Keogh and Lieutenant Calhoun did their best to ward off the onslaught of determined Indians, General George A. Custer, along with Captain George Yates and Lieutenant Algernon Smith, commanders of F and E Troops, were plagued with their own problems.

With a gentle rising hill to his back General Custer and his small command of about 100 effectives, were being pushed up the hill step by step by charging Indians. F Troop held the right flank while E Troop held the left. A few survivors of C Troop and Custer's staff held the center.

Most of the nine hundred or better Indians had dismounted and were creeping up closer to Custer's troopers on foot. Those who fought the soldiers mounted indulged in the usual wild charges and were killed or forced to retreat under the hail of carbine fire. A few warriors, intoxicated by the excitement of battle, rushed in on individual soldiers and fought them hand to hand. Most of these Indians were killed outright without doing much damage.

An out of breath Lieutenant William Low ran up to General Custer who was calmly firing his revolver at mounted Indians trying to get around in back of the skirmish line, which was already bending at the flanks into a half circle. "General Custer sir, my men have finally got the gun put together but there's Indians all around them."

General Custer paused in his firing and stared at Lieutenant Low with blazing eyes. "Where's your Gatling at son?"

"Right there sir," Bucky Low pointed to his right, down into a shallow depression around fifteen yards away.

Without hesitation General Custer hollered out. "Tom! Get a few men and come with me to get that Gatling gun up here."

Captain Tom Custer, his handsome face smeared with oily gun smoke instantly stood up from his kneeling position where he'd been firing his carbine and yelled at those troopers near him. "You there, and you and you. Sergeant Hughes, Boston, and you there Myers, follow me."

General Custer had already strode forward from his front line shooting two pistols as he advanced toward the depression where the Gatling gun crew was fighting off groups of Indians sneaking up on them. Captain Custer and his six-man detail quickly followed the general along with Lieutenant Low.

Once Custer and the other men reached the besieged Gatling gun crew, Custer, noted most the guns horses lay dead. He shouted an order to Lieutenant Low. "Have your men tie ropes to either side of your gun and use two of your horses to help pull it up that hill there." He pointed an arm to the rise behind where his beleaguered cavalrymen were fighting for their very lives. "Get it moving Bucky and we'll watch out for you...and for God's sake, don't forget to bring along your ammunition!"

Horse Handler/Driver Corporal Hazen Ward and Ammunition Carrier Private Ricky Willis both lay dead, each having been shot in the back by hidden Indians.

Gun #2's Sergeant, Sergeant Donald Evan screamed at his remaining men. "You heard what the general said, get your asses cracking! Sergeant Randall, move your mules to that rise: Noer, Hill, help him! Windsor, Deaton, Dills, Qualls---snag those two horses there, tie ropes to the trail and move the gun out fast."

As the Gatling gun crew responded to their sergeant's orders the small band of cavalrymen led by General Custer fought off the advancing hostiles that were coming closer from all directions. When the Gatling gun started moving most of the gun crew joined in the defense of their weapon and along with the other soldiers began backing their way up towards the small hill shooting as they went.

Another one of Major Reno's tactical mistakes when ordering his men up hill under the bluff was they had no way to replenish their water. The Four o'clock afternoon sun beat heavily on thirsty wounded men and all canteens were dry. Private Billy Slaper could no longer stand watching his tent mate Private Billy Morris suffer from thirst. It was bad enough Billy One was in terrible pain from a gunshot wound just below his right shoulder with the bullet traveling down to break his elbow.

Billy Slaper stood up from where he had been kneeling next to his buddy. Looking around at the many cavalrymen standing guard at Doctor Porter's improvised field hospital, he offered a challenge. "Hey you guys I'm going down to the river to get our wounded fellows some water, whose got guts enough to go with me."

Private Frank Tolan of D Troop raised his hand. "I'm game." Then turning to several of troopers from Captain Tom French's company, said, "How about any of you fellows?"

Privates Bill Harris, Tom Steven and Charlie Welch all agreed to go.

The five troopers gathered as many canteens as they could carry and made there way down the steep slope to the river with Indians snipping at them from a distance the entire time. Billy Slaper received a grazing wound to his leg that stung like hell but did not incapacitate him. On the way back up with the filled canteens the group of water carriers passed by Major Reno, Captain Benteen and Captain Weir who were having a heated discussion.

"By God if you won't give me permission I shall take it on my own responsibility to make a personal survey where that firing is coming from." Captain Thomas Weir yelled at Major Reno.

Red in the face and flustered, Major Reno yelled right back. "Captain you are being insubordinate talking to me like that and one more word out of your mouth and I'll have charges brought against you."

"Charges be damned!" Captain Weir shouted. "It's a damn act of downright cowardice not to be going to General Custer's aid. Damnit man! Can't you here that firing----they are fighting for their lives over there and need our help."

Captain Benteen tried to put some oil on troubled waters to calm things down. "Jesus Christ Marcus, let him take his troop over in that direction to see what in the hell is going on if he's determined to do so!"

"I can not authorize it but since Weir is in your battalion I suppose you have the right to order a reconnaissance." Reno nicely sidestepped the issue.

Shaking his head in disgust Benteen lost his previous calm manner and said in a loud voice. "Why is it every fucking sonofabitch wants to lay his God damn lack of resolve on my door step?" Not expecting an answer from Reno who stared at him wide eyed in shock, Benteen looked at Captain Weir. "Very well hero, go run a reconnaissance if you have to but keep in mind if you get up to your neck in horseshit out there you're on your own."

"I'm going to take the Gatling gun with me." Weir stated.

Looking at him bug eyed Captain Benteen all but shouted. "And just how in the hell are you going to do that?"

"I'll figure out a way." And with that Captain Weir turned on his heel and went looking for Lieutenant Edgerly to have him mount D Troop while he talked with Lieutenant Kenzie.

* * * * *

Lieutenant Low and Sergeant Evans got the Gatling gun positioned near the bottom of the small rounded hill where General Custer's decimated few remaining men huddled in a loose circle. After having fought their way along with Custer and his men to the rise, their arrival was well timed because the "Suicide Boys" were preparing to charge.

Lakota herald chieftains had arrived on the scene of Custer's action and went among the warriors shouting for them to stand back and allow the "Suicide Boys" to make their assault. For a few minutes the battlefield was comparatively quiet while the young suicide warriors rode majestically up from the river, where they had been preparing themselves for their heroic moment.

These gaily painted youngsters had rode the three miles from the river at a very slow pace in accordance with the ritual rite which allowed them to take their time so their weeping, chanting mothers, grandmothers aunts and sisters could give them a proper send off. They passed over the trodden battlefield, glancing this way and that at a scene right out of the pages of hell.

The landscape from the river bottom all the way to Custer's little, round molded hill was dotted with bodies of 7th Cavalry personnel. Here and there, crumpled forms lay, grotesque and twisted from violent death. At a distance it almost had the appearance of the tracking spoor of a grizzly bear leaving its droppings in a sporadic manner as it lumbered along, that a trailblazer could have followed without problems straight to Custer's hill.

It was obvious that Sitting Bull's admonishment to not desecrate the dead white soldiers' bodies as told to him in his vision, had been completely ignored. Most of the corpses were naked, having been stripped of their clothing by ferocious, scavenging squaws who had followed after their men in the wake of their advance. What individual Sioux and Cheyenne warriors had not accomplished in the way of mutilation on the white men, their women did with bloodthirsty abandonment. Penises were cut off and stuffed in mouths. Thighs and legs slit open in gapping, horrible gashes with broken arrows crammed in the wounds. Wooden slivers were pounded into dead men's ears to make them listen better in the hereafter. Faces smashed beyond recognition and in a few instances human hearts ripped out of chest cavities and laying next to the corpse half eaten. Disemboweled remains spilled on the sun-browned grass and with all the dead, scalps had been taken.

The young "Suicide Boys" looked upon the carnage with dispassionate interest, their only thoughts being that they too would soon lend their bravery to the slaughter. Naturally they had no inkling of who lay near their ponies hooves as they moved by, only that the marble white bodies streaked with blood and gore was one less white man they would have to contend with.

But not all of the bodies were white. Ree scouts laid among the dead, as did a few half-breeds. Minton "Mitch" Bouyer's body was badly mutilated, killed after he had released the six Crow scouts, including Curly Head, the 17 year old favorite of Custer's who now sat on a ridge a few miles away watching the slaughter. Mark Kellogg, who could have written the biggest story of his newspaper career, lay butchered, with his head scalp gone as well as his bushy, mutton-chopped whiskers that an enterprising Indian had taken for a trophy after having face-scalped the reporter. During the running fight, Regimental Surgeon Doctor Lord was killed along the trail leading to Custer's hill as was Lieutenant Harrington and Lieutenant Porter.

Elder warriors some 100 yards from the soldier's position on the small hill halted the "Suicide Boys." Better than 150 teenage warriors had volunteered for the honor of charging headlong straight into the defensive position set up by the dismounted cavalrymen ringed around General Custer. This was an important event in the warrior societies and for those youngsters who survived the onslaught; they would be forever revered for their gallantry. The same reverence would also go to the families of those young bucks that did not make it out of the charge alive. Older warriors heeded the herald's orders and stepped back or rode back out of harms way to watch the heroic action of their teenage braves,

"What in the hell are they doing?" Gunner Corporal Curtis Windsor wanted to know as he adjusted himself behind the Gatling gun.

Loader, First Class Private Michael Deaton, who was in his third battle with savages, nodded his head gravely and said. "They call themselves the 'Suicide Boys'. See how they're all painted up? That's a big deal of honor with the Injuns, all that red, black and yellow; it means they ain't scared of dying. What they're going through now is a little ritual of getting a final blessing from the medicine men. See how the other ones that was attacking us are keeping back? It'd be an insult to the Suicide'rs to fight before they make their charge. Won't be long before they'll be coming a'call'en though, you can bet on that."

"Well I reckon I'll have a good field of fire." Windsor mused looking along his iron sight.

Ignoring his gunners comment Deaton yelled across the Gatling gun to the spotter Sergeant Donald Evans. "Hey sarge, you best have the lieutenant tell someone on the general's staff that right after the kids hit us they'll be swarms of Injuns com'en at 'em from all directions. Windsor can concentrate on the "Suicide Boys" and the cavalrymen should watch out for the others."

Sergeant Evans waved a hand in understanding. "You're right Deaton, I'll go tell the lieutenant." Then glancing at Corporal Windsor. "Curtis, you ain't go'en to need me to spot targets fer ya so jus open up on the bastards at fifty yards if I ain't back...you heah?"

"I gotcha sarge." Corporal Windsor answered with a nervous squeak.

The "Suicide Boys" commenced their charge while Lieutenant Hale explained to General Custer what his guns plans were. Custer hastily sent yelling orderlies to pass the word.

At first it was extremely difficult for the quick on the trigger cavalrymen not to let loose their carbines on the distant charging hoard of bloodthirsty, yelling Indians screaming at the top of their lungs; but sergeants bellowing at them to hold their fire stopped the smattering of gunfire that had started.

Veteran senior private Mike Deaton, who stood ready to insert a fresh clip of .50 caliber bullets into the Gatling gun, talked soothingly to the gunner. "Steady, steady now corporal, let em get a little closer...that's the boy corp, let em ride right into it...you're do'en good, keep your nerve...steady."

Sergeant Don Evans ran back to his spotters position on the gun in time to note the thundering herd of young warriors were well within mass killing range. With a touch of coincidence he yelled "FIRE!" at the same instant as First Class Private Mike Deaton did the same.

Hearing the loud orders to fire come at him from two directions startled Corporal Windsor for a second and he jerked the firing lever a little to fast which sent out a six round burst from his reflexive hand movement. Scared he may have jammed his weapon he slowly turned the crank again and was thankful when it responded with the explosions of bullets leaving the barrel. Windsor, settled down to his pattern of moving the firing lever with a smooth, slow rhythm, making the Gatling chatter with it unusual chug, chug sound as it spit out its leaded missiles of death.

The Gatling gun had an immediate impact on the charging young warriors and greatly assisted them in living up to their titles as "Suicide Boys," or as the case was, dying as "Suicide Boys." The front rank of two dozen Indians went down with stumbling horses that had had their legs shot off. When the stunned braves attempted to stand from having been thrown, they were either shot down or trampled by their comrades in back who soon found themselves being violently punched from their ponies too and hurled to the ground with horrible holes gouged in their half naked bodies. Pieces of painted flesh flew through the air along with parts of arms, legs and severed heads. The carnage was total.

As predicted by Private Deaton, the thousand warriors who had stood idle to allow the "Suicide Boys" show their bravery automatically renewed their attack when the young braves had begun their charge. They went ahead and committed themselves to battle without thought given to what was happening to the teenage warriors.

On the Gatling gun Corporal Windsor screamed for a reload. It had only taken five clips to insure the soon to be grieving families of over a hundred young braves would be immortalized for their courage while half a hundred families would have to contend with maimed sons and brothers. Windsor now had other targets to worry about as no one was going to go over the five-foot high pile of horses and Indians that lay thirty yards from his gun in a line fifty feet across. Yelling at Sergeant Evans, Windsor said. "We've got to move the gun left or right I can't shoot through that shit in front of me."

Sergeant Evans, as the gun spotter had a wide range of targets to choose from and accustomed to making snap judgments, ordered. "Action right, seventy-five yards, fire at will!"

With Windsor remaining in his steel seat, Ammunition Carrier Private Ernie Qualls, and Water Boy Private Peter Noer, who had taken dead Private

Willis's place, moved the gun trail to their left until Sergeant Evans yelled. "That's good enough. Commence FIRE!"

Corporal Windsor moved the crank located on the right of the Gatling gun, which cut a swath through a circling group of warriors who just happened to be riding past when Windsor renewed his firing.

However, the numerical superiority of the Sioux and Cheyenne showed itself and one by one a cavalryman near Custer would fall over in a heap, either seriously wounded or dead. The Gatling gun crew likewise sustained additional causalities. Caisson Sergeant John Randall fell dead with a bullet in the back of his head while he loaded fresh clips. When Water Boy Private Peter Noer scrambled over to the fallen sergeant to see if he could help him, he too was shot dead from a fusillade of rifle bullets. Sergeant Evans was wounded seriously in the upper right shoulder and Lieutenant Low took his place as spotter, his left arm hanging limp with a bullet in it.

Water Man/Oilier Private Roger Hill yelled a concern in Lieutenant Low's ear. "We're outta water and the guns overheating."

"How about our canteens?" Lieutenant Low yelled back to make him heard over the din of battle.

"I've already used all our canteen water lieutenant!" Hill responded.

Lieutenant Low was quiet for a moment, and then asked. "You got oil left?"

"Yessir, plenty of oil." Private Hill said, nodding his head.

"Take a water bucket, fill it three-quarters with oil and get as many men as you can to piss in it." The lieutenant said grimly.

"Piss in it sir?" Hill asked wide-eyed.

"Damnit, you heard me Hill. Unless you can come up with some water somewhere else, PISS IN IT!"

Private Hill went to fetch a water bucket and was the first to unbutton the front of his uniform trousers. He didn't need any encouragement to urinate since he was about ready to piss his pants anyway.

It wasn't too long before the overpowering pungent, caustic aroma of evaporating urine and burning oil penetrated the nostrils of all those near the Gatling gun. The odor mixed with the acrid smell of burnt black gunpowder which was making the eyes water of both friends and foe alike as the battle raged. Private Roger Hill didn't seem to mind the sour smell though as he shook his head back and forth in wonderment when he said to Lieutenant Low. "It seems to be doing the trick sir."

Lieutenant Low likewise shook his head briefly when he glanced at Private Hill with uplifted nose, and said. "Yes, so it seems."

The Indians were becoming confused with the steady rattle of the Gatling gun and Chief Gall rallied a group of warrior by saying. "We must kill that beast or we will all die. Come at it from behind."

The fine looking Sioux Hunkpapa chief's tactic almost worked. General Custer saw immediately what the Indians had in mind when they begun riding up the reverse slope of the small hill in a charging mass. He moved rapidly among his few remaining men shouting encouragement. "Come on boys, we've got to stop them from reaching the Gatling gun."

Hearing the volley of gunshots coming from behind him Lieutenant Low looked over his shoulder to see a mass of mounted Indians tearing through the cavalrymen's line and riding over the rise coming at him. He got a glimpse of General Custer, standing, firing two pistols at the charging Indians. Low screamed at the top of his lungs. "ACTION REAR IMMEDIATE!"

This time, Corporal Windsor did not stop cranking his firing lever as his gun swung around to meet the new threat. The sweeping gunfire of the Gatling tore into the rushing hostiles and they were thrown from their ponies by the dozens as if a giant hand had swatted them. Then the weapon steadied and more Indians tasted the viciousness of a machine gun.

But Lieutenant Low, seeing how effective the traversing fire had worked, shouted out a command. "Keep moving the gun trail from side to side in short movements."

Chief Gall's remaining warriors were cut down like wheat being scythed in a field.

Crazy Horse had seen enough. "The thunder stick is a terrible, terrible bad medicine. We have killed most of the white devils as Sitting Bull said we would. Let us not see all our brave warriors die. We have won a great victory, we must see to our women and children now and leave these few with their thunder stick." He spat on the ground and turned his pony away from the small hill. Others soon began to follow him.

* * * * *

Captain Thomas B. Weir, with his second in command of D Troop, Lieutenant Winfield Edgerly sitting next to him, stared across the rolling grassy area to his front. He had got his bearings on where Custer's action was taking place from a high point about three miles to his rear. Now what he was seeing confused him greatly. To his immediate front, not more than a half-mile away he viewed a large band of hostiles riding around a small group of men on a flat ridge with what appeared to be a Gatling gun with dead animals all around it. Then, across the ridge past what looked to be a deep ravine, there was another small band of men clustered on top a small hill. There was a black bulk there too, which may have been a Gatling gun also. The odd thing he noticed about the small hill across the ravine was a long column of Indians walking and riding away from it. His immediate concern was the ridge where soldiers were obviously engaged. Turning to Lieutenant Edgerly, Captain Weir said. "We better get over there where it seems fighting is still going on. Is the Gatling gun still with us?"

"Its been bounced around pretty badly by pulling it along with that makeshift whiffletree we got the four horses tied to, but its still behind us." Lieutenant Edgerly stated.

"Well we may need it so keep that detail of men to help it along. Let's get on over there now!" Captain Weir nudged his big bay. Looking over his shoulder Captain Weir yelled at his trumpeter. "Trumpeter---blow Charge to let them know we're coming."

* * * * *

Corporal Jesus Quintana rested his head against the dead carcass of a mule as he yelled encouragement to First Sergeant Steiner through gritted teeth. "Take as many of the bastards with you as you can first soldier!"

Gus Steiner had been doing a good job of doing just that since he'd taken over the gunners seat after Quintana received gunshots to both legs, right at the kneecaps. There was no doubt in the first sergeant's mind that if Junior Quintana, through some unforeseen miracle, happened to live through this days combat, that the outstanding gunner of Mexican decent would loose both his legs. At the present time however, he did not ponder on that possibility, because it looked as if they were all going to die in a few minutes anyway.

Four members of Gun #3 were already dead and it didn't look promising for the other six Gatling gun crewmembers that along with First Sergeant Steiner were all suffering from wounds of one kind or another. While Quintana was the most seriously wounded, Sergeant Heidenreich and Private Earl Watts were close seconds. Heidenreich remained at his spotter's position with two bullets in his upper torso and Watts continued to carry clips to Loader Private Jack Wells even though his left arm was hanging by a shred.

The ring of dead animals had been the only reason they had lived as long as they had but from the massing of the Indians for another charge at them, it did not appear they would stay alive very much longer.

First Sergeant Gus Steiner glanced down at Corporal Quintana while Jack Wells slammed a new clip into the feed holder slot. In answer to the corporal's previous remark, Steiner offered a rueful smile, and then said. "This batch I'm a'gonna kill is just for you Junior!" And he slowly turned the crank while Quintana grinned and grimaced at the same time.

The not-too-far away blasting sound of Charge being bellowed by a trumpeter could not have came as more of a surprise to the seven men huddled together behind their dead animals than if General Custer had suddenly appeared and offered thirty day furloughs.

* * * * *

Lieutenant Colonel George Armstrong Custer wasn't feeling much like a general anymore. For the first time in his 36 years, six months and 21 days of life he felt the disillusionment of terror stab at his heart. Unfortunately, the panic of terror he was experiencing wasn't the only reason he felt prickly ripples of pain stabbing at him. A bullet lodged deep in his chest and a gunshot wound to his right temple from the Indians last charge was the primary reason that was causing his once bright blue eyes to cloud with a milky film. The hot afternoon Montana sun beat down upon him as he with great effort raised his hand to shade his eyes. His fingers brushed the only physical scar he had ever bore: a small white mark on his forehead caused from a skittish heifer his step-sister Ann Reed put him on that tossed him against a fence post when he was a lad of five. Although he didn't know it, his brother Thomas lay dead a few feet from him, as did his other brother Boston. Further away his nephew who was named after him, Harry Armstrong "Autie" Reed, laid in a crumpled heap dead at 18, his head bashed by a Sioux war club. Nor did he have any way to know his brother-in-law Lieutenant James "Jimmi" Calhoun lay dead a mile away in a small depression. George wanted to say something but it was so difficult to make words come out of his mouth and he couldn't understand why this was. He also didn't understand whom it was that was hovering over him and talking gently to him, nor did he understand the words the figure was saying that grew dimmer in his vision with each passing second.

Lieutenant William Low bent close to General Custer trying to comfort the dying man. Bending close to whisper in the fallen commander's ear, he said. "Sir it was you standing up and leading your men against that final horrendous charge that saved me and my men. That is something I shall never forget"

It must be Libbie George Custer rationalized to himself. Libbie, my dear buttercup. With a great effort he opened his mouth and with his last breath of life, said in a hoarse voice. "Libbie." It was 4:30 p.m. on a sunny afternoon at the Little Big Horn battlefield.

Chapter 45

Fort Abraham Lincoln, Dakota Territory
4:30 p.m., Sunday, June 25, 1876

Even though she had not felt like doing it Elizabeth Custer had went ahead anyway and welcomed a group of officer's wives into her home for tea, cookies and conversation, which was a traditional courtesy for a general's wife to do on a Sunday afternoon, when their men were deployed on a campaign.

The small parlor was crowded with chatting women that made it all the warmer inside the quarters, even with all the windows open. Libbie was moving around to the various huddled groups, smiling, saying a word or two, with a plate of cookies in her hand that her sister-in-law Margaret Custer Calhoun had baked. Her head was aching from a coming migraine and when the big Regulator wall clock started chiming the half-hour past four o'clock she put a hand to her temple.

Suddenly there was a muted scream followed by the clatter of a broken dish. All the ladies looked around and craned their necks to see what had happened. Elizabeth "Libbie" Custer lay sprawled on the floor.

"She's fainted," screamed Mrs. Madeleine McIntosh, wife of Lieutenant Donald McIntosh, who now lay dead on the Custer battlefield with a good portion of Custer's 7th Cavalry.

With a haughty sniff, a hand held fan going a mile a minute back and forth across her rather ugly face, short, pudgy Heather Benteen said. "It must be from the heat."

President Ulysses S. Grant

Epilogue

White House, Washington, D. C.
1:00 p.m., Thursday, August 19, 1876

President of the United States of America Ulysses S. Grant paced back and forth in his office while billowing great puffs of blue-white cigar smoke upward which hung like a halo over his head. With his agitated manner coupled with a bulldog scowl, Grant's aides were being extremely careful not to invoke his wraith in their direction.

The president mumbled words under his breath that was barely decipherable. "Now that boy Private Slaper and his comrades that went to get water under fire for the wounded I can understand that and the same goes for that old horse McCullough that lost his leg, as well as that Tex Mex fellow that lost both legs, but I'll be damn if I'll ever agree with this other hog-wash." Grant came to a halt in front of his old friend Lieutenant General Philip H. Sheridan. Taking the huge cigar out of his mouth and using it as a pointer he jabbed it at his long time friend and blurted out. "And just who in the hell is this young whippier-snapper anyway, this...this captain, that Terry endorsed his asinine recommendation?"

General Sheridan speaking softly replied. "Captain William Hale Low sir. He was in command of the Gatling gun battery with Custer. Only he and a handful of his men were left alive on the battlefield and were rescued by Captain Weir's company right before the hostiles renewed their assault. Damn lucky if you ask me that Weir or any of them made it back to the Reno-Benteen defense."

Grant snorted. "That's another damn story I want you to get to the bottom of. Custer was a stupid sonofabitch loosing five entire companies to a man like he did, but I tell you there's something fishy that happened out there and I want to know about it. So this Captain Low was in charge of the Gatling's huh? I don't recall seeing his name on any damn list for anything, what made him recommend Custer?"

"Congress bestowed a meritorious promotion on Low after General Terry wrote the lad up for the medal and I can only surmise you haven't got around to signing his commission as yet which is probably why you don't recall seeing his name." As an afterthought, General Sheridan added. "But he's brevetted until you do so..." With a minute pause he went on. "And concerning his reason for the ah...other thing, the boy swears Custer personally led the stand which allowed the Gatling gun to break the attack long enough for the remaining crew to reach Weir."

"I'll be a damned dyed-in-the-wool Democrat if that boy gets the medal after all this hullabaloo he's caused." President Grant shouted, jamming the cigar back in his mouth.

In a soothing tone of voice General Sheridan said. "With all the recommendations that have flooded the War Department for congressional approval since the...ah battle. I believe they agree with you Mister President regarding the medal and more than likely is the reason they gave Low his captaincy instead."

With another snort Grant spoke with his cigar bobbing. "Humph.... that's an order I should rescind too."

"That may prove to be extremely embarrassing Mister President," Senator Heister Clymer voiced. "Especially since the lad almost lost an arm."

Snapping his head around Grant focused his eyes on the tall senator from New York, whom he didn't like but had to put up with. "Yes I suppose it would be, but it sure as hell not going to be anymore embarrassing than what you've already got in store for me." Then added in a softer tone of voice. "I wasn't aware he had been wounded."

"He's doing nicely, but I always thought you were fond of Libbie Custer Mister President." Senator Clymer said with a raised eyebrow.

Instead of answering the senator's inquiry directly Grant softened his tone of voice and said to him. "Is she here yet?"

"Yes Mister President, she's in the garden where you had all the rose bushes planted." The senator replied.

The president emitted a low sigh. "Yes, you're right, I have always liked her. Courageous and loyal woman, a regular camp follower and a pretty little thing: met her several times during the late war. Well, I don't suppose its her fault she married such an ass, and not trying to talk ill of the dead." President Grant paused for a moment, emitted another sigh, and then said "Let's go get this over with, where's that damn piece of paper I'm supposed to sign?"

A short time later, with his outward mood completely changed, President Grant greeted Elizabeth Custer warmly. "How good to see you again my dear, even under these trying circumstances of such a solemn occasion."

Libbie was appropriately dressed from head to foot in dark black, including a half veil of mourning across her lower face. Offering her hand with a little curtsey, Libbie replied, "Mister President my Bo would be so very proud and my deepest and sincerest thanks go to you. May I introduce to you the general's father, stepmother and sisters? I believe you have met my father and mother before, Judge and Mrs. Bacon, but they too would like to pay their respects to you sir."

Grant was at his most gracious best as he met the family of the late George Armstrong Custer.

Then the Marine Band struck up Garry Owen the 7th Cavalry's battle song. It was the cue for President Grant to commence the ceremony.

When the last note of Garry Owen faded, President Grant, standing in front of Libbie Custer and her family and in-laws, turned his head, and then said "Adjutant----read the citation."

A full colonel from the Adjutant General's Corps began speaking in a deep, resonate voice. "War Department Orders of One August Eighteen Seventy-Five, as approved and directed by the Congress of the United States of America. The President of the United States Ulysses S. Grant takes pride in awarding the Medal of Honor posthumously to Lieutenant Colonel George A. Custer, U. S. Seventh Cavalry, Commanding, Brevet Major General of United States volunteers, for the following: Citation: On June twenty-five, Eighteen Seventy-Five, Brevet Major General Custer found himself and his command surrounded by a much larger force of hostile Indians. Disregarding his own safety General Custer stood in the face of continued hostile attacks to direct the fire and encourage the men of his command. When a vital position of his command's defense came under a direct assault from the rear, General Custer instantly recognized the seriousness of the situation and rushed to the breech and held the enemy off until reinforcements strengthened the gap. Overwhelming hoards of hostile Indians overran General Custer's portion of this gallant defense and he gave his life for his country. Eyewitness accounts credit General George A. Custer's valiant stand against a determined enemy as the reason they broke contact and retreated. His gallant actions were in keeping with the highest traditions of the U. S. Army and U. S. Cavalry. Signed under my hand this nineteenth of August, Eighteen Seventy-Five, Ulysses S. Grant, President of the United States of America."

A complete hush was evident as Grant's military aide-de-camp opened a velvet lined, leather oblong box and took out a red, white and blue-ribboned Medal of Honor with its five-pointed star and handed it to the President. Grant lifted the medal so Libbie Custer could get a good look at it, and then showed it to those in attendance both left and right. He then handed the medal back to his aide-de-camp who replaced it in the blue-black box and leaving the hinged lid opened gave it back to President Grant. In a humble tone of voice President Grant spoke to Libbie Custer. "My dear Mrs. Custer, this is but a small token of the esteem the people of the United States hold for your dearly departed loved one. Please accept this with my personal gratitude in memory of a fine officer, soldier and warrior."

Libbie took the blue-black case, gazed at the ribboned medal for a moment, then closed the lid; holding it reverently to her breast with both hands. Sparkling tears brimmed in her haunting, beautiful eyes. In a small, choking voice, she said. "Thank you so much Mister President. I know the people will never forget my husband."

U. S. Army Medal of Honor 1876

About the Author

Donald F. Myers was born and raised in Indianapolis, Indiana. In 1952 at age seventeen he enlisted in the U. S. Marine Corps. He retired from the Corps on 30 April 1973. Myers is Indiana's most decorated living Marine veteran. A recipient of two Silver Star medals for conspicuous gallantry, two Bronze Star medals for heroic achievement, five Purple Heart medals for combat wounds, Navy/Marine Corps Commendation medal for heroic achievement, Vietnam Cross of Gallantry with palm, and Vietnam Medal of Military Merit are among his 32 awards.

A graduate of Arsenal Technical High School of Indianapolis, Myers also attended East Carolina College and successfully completed the College Proficiency Examination Program through the University of the State of New York.

The U. S. Department of Veterans Affairs (VA) employed Myers after he was medically retired from the Corps. In 1990, he retired from the VA as a senior counselor. Myers also spent over 20 years with the Indiana Guard Reserve retiring from that military organization as a full colonel.

He has authored six books. A father of two sons and three daughters Myers resides with his wife Dorothy in Franklin Township, a suburb on the southeast side of Indianapolis.

LaVergne, TN USA
12 April 2010
178944LV00003B/13/P